THE SEER

FATED BOOK 3   LEGENDS OF PERN COEN

HANNAH E. CAREY

Published December 1st, 2023

Cover Design by Serenity Star Designs

Map by Lisette Marshall

Formatting by Serenity Star Press, LLC

To my own Bran of Blaidd, who has seen me through the fire, and to all who are left to find beauty from the ashes.

CONTENTS

Character List

Aengus: healer, servant of Fianna
Alannah: shapeshifter, servant of Fianna
Arwel: advisor to Seren
Awyr *(OW-air)***:** Seren's wolf
Blaidd *(BLY-th)***:** Wolf Spirit
Bran: shapeshifter, husband of Seren
Cadfael *(KAD-file)***:** husband of Esyllt, father of Seren and Eamon, former Ri of Blaidd, deceased
Ceinwen: Village Elder of Sionnach
Cian *(KEE-an)***:** healer, son of Sioned, cousin of Seren and Eamon
Cryfder *(CRUV-dair)***:** Seren's wolf
Domhnall *(DO-nahl)***:** son of Ri Muireann, advisor to Seren
Eamon *(EH-man)***:** son of Cadfael and Esyllt, deceased
Emer *(EE-mur)***:** warrior of Blaidd, friend of Seren, wife of Lewella
Esyllt *(EH-sisht)***:** wife of Cadfael, mother of Seren and Eamon, former Banrion of Blaidd

Felim: healer of Dearg

Fianna: Stag Spirit, Dark Spirit of Pern Coen

Fionn: brother of Cadfael

Gruffudd *(GRI-fidh)*: father of Bran, stablehand at Castle Clogwyn

Gwendolen *(GWEN-da-lin)*: Village Elder of Glas

Laoise *(LEE-sha)*: advisor to Seren

Lewella: warrior of Blaidd, friend of Seren, wife of Emer

Mair: healer at Castle Clogwyn, temporary advisor to Seren

Seachnall *(SHAKH-nal)*: warrior of Blaidd, friend of Eamon

Seren *(SEH-rehn)*: seer, Ri of Blaidd, wife of Bran, daughter of Cadfael and Esyllt

Sioned *(SHO-nehd)*: sister of Esyllt, mother of Cian

Tudwal: warrior of Blaidd

The Island Out of the Sea

The roar of Arth, the Bear Spirit, shook the earth and pushed the mountains up out of the water,
The powerful wings of Seabhac, the Hawk Spirit, created the wind that smoothed the jagged peaks,
Tyll the Owl Spirit flew over the land, pulling the trees out of the earth with his strong talons,
The hooves of Ceffyl, the Horse Spirit, pounded the valleys into being,
While the paws of Blaidd, the Wolf Spirit, dug the rivers and lakes,
Upon the completion of their work, the island of Pern Coen was created,
Gifted to the five clans to honor and care for.
But three Spirits remained, their offerings denied by the rest of those who resided in the Greater Spirit Realm,
Cigfran, the Raven Spirit, wished to bring death,
Fianna, the Stag Spirit, wished to allow decay,

Pysgod, the Fish Spirit, wished to allow for destruction,

And all wished for complete control over those who called the island home.

The Five Spirits were left to band together, diminishing the power of the Three.

Shunned by the Greater Spirits and their power reduced, the Three Spirits are forced to roam the Realm of the Mortals,

Sowing their darkness wherever they can and seeking to possess the souls of those who willingly give them.

CHAPTER 1

THE DARK ROAD
Aengus

THE HOUSE WAS ON *fire, the smoke making it impossible to breathe. How ironic that it was fire that would spell our doom.*

There was no time to waste. I had to get us out of here, but I could feel my steps slowing, my heart aching as I watched the home I had built crumble around me. Alannah's hacking cough brought me back to my senses.

"We have to keep moving!" I yelled back at her, tugging her along behind me as we dodged growing flames and crumbling wood.

We fought on, bursting through the back door only to discover that our troubles were just beginning. Men and women awaited us, brandishing torches, swords, pitchforks, and anything else they could get their hands on to use as a weapon. These were people I had once looked to as neighbors and as friends, but they were not friends any longer.

They screamed at us, hurling all manner of hateful accusations. The worst of their words were thrown at Alannah, the vileness of them making my blood boil. Just torching my home wasn't enough for them; they meant to kill us as well and make an example of Alannah. All because of what she had been born with. All because of what they didn't understand. In my haste to get us out alive, I hadn't thought to grab a weapon. I'd only though of keeping us from burning alive.

"You're not going anywhere!" a man, the villager baker I knew well, growled.

He lunged toward us, pitchfork raised, and I pushed Alannah behind me. I had no weapons, but I would not just give her over to them. I braced myself for impact, our attacker just inches away when a blur of smoke and sparks flashed in front of us. The man let out a scream that made the hair on the back of my neck raise as one of Fianna's shadow creatures latched onto his arm with a fearsome growl. More cries of alarm came from the villagers as more of the creatures sprang from the darkness, the air filled with the screams of the villagers and the creatures' eldritch screeches. The man who'd sought to run a pitchfork through my chest was clutching his badly wounded arm, the creature now biting into his leg. Blood streaked his skin, his face deathly pale. His arm was almost severed to the bone, his face twisted in agony—

I awoke from the nightmare soaked in a cold sweat, scrambling to throw the thin blanket off me. Pinching the bridge of my nose, I sat up in the creaky bed, taking in deep breaths that I hoped would calm my racing heart. The worst part was that the nightmare was no fabricated conjuring from my sleeping mind. It was a memory. All of it had been real, every last detail of it.

Letting out a shuddering breath, my gaze drifted to Alannah's shadowed form. She slept on beside me, her breathing deep and even and her features smoothed from the stress that so often marred them. It was still strange to me, in a way, how much she had come to mean to me in a matter of months. There had always been something about her that had caught my eye, but it was when I had begun to see her resilient spirit despite how cruelly life had treated her that my feelings had truly grown. And perhaps most of all, she believed in me and in the future laid before me. At times when I doubted that I could take the place Fianna was creating for me, Alannah was there to drive those weak-minded thoughts away.

I had never dreamed of a life as Ri of Blaidd. A few months ago, I would have never believed that a man like me could achieve such a thing. But Alannah had known differently. It was she who had encouraged me to take the blood that ran through my veins, blood that had been hidden from me almost my whole life, and turn it into something greater. And not just for myself, but for the clan. Our people deserved a strong Ri, one who did not have the weaknesses of Cadfael and his line. It was Fionn's blood that deserved to sit in the Great Hall of Clogwyn, presiding over the land. It was time for a new line of Ris to be ruling the Clan of Blaidd.

I readjusted my pillow with a sigh, staring up into the darkness. With my current unsettled thoughts, I knew I wouldn't be able to get back to sleep. Instead of tossing and turning, risking disturbing Alannah's rest, I swung my legs over the side of the bed and got to my feet. I fumbled a bit in the darkness, trying to be as quiet as possible as I grabbed a shirt to throw on with my sleeping pants and picked up a small dagger.

My steps slowed as I walked around the bed. A pair of glowing ember eyes stared back at me. As much as I wanted to ignore it, there was still a slight quiver in my stomach at the sight of the shadow creature. Its other three companions were asleep on the floor, but the one who had woken followed my every move as I walked to the door, leaving me with a prickle of unease in the middle of my back. I still didn't entirely trust the creatures, even with the bond I had forged to their maker, the Stag Spirit, Fianna.

When I opened the door, the shadow creature started to get to its feet. I spoke to it in Old Pernish, keeping my voice low and commanding it to stay. I half held my breath as it froze, cocking its head. I was still learning the ancient language required to communicate with the creatures. They still listened to Alannah better than they ever listened to me. To my relief, however, the creature lay back down, resting its head on its front legs. It watched me still, but stayed put.

I let out a quiet breath and then stepped out into the night. The coolness in the air made me glad I'd thrown on a shirt. Summer was still here on the island of Pern Coen, but the nights in the mountains were starting to cool, a subtle reminder that eventually the season would change as autumn took its hold over the land. For me, the steady march of seasons had begun to feel like a noose slowly tightening. There might be little sign of it now, but winter was coming. If nothing changed, the people would be left to suffer once again. This growing season had been as poor as the last and hunting was scarce, with much of the land still lying in ruin. The current Ri, Seren, had done nothing to heal the land, furthering the people's suffering. Though we shared a mother, a truth revealed to me by Fianna months ago, Seren had not chosen her allegiances wisely. She couldn't heal the land, not without Fianna's power, and she was too blinded by her loyalty to the Wolf Spirit to seek it out.

With a slight shake of my head, I forced myself to push the thoughts of Seren aside and left the hut behind, letting the light of the moon and the millions of brilliant stars guide me out of the clearing and into the forest. This had become a habit of mine when sleep evaded me, wandering the forest at night, searching for wild plants. My healer's blood still called to me, my years of honing my craft something I could not easily put away. So long as I stayed fairly close to the cottage, I felt safe enough during my midnight wanderings.

We were isolated here in the Coed mountains, the herder's hut we had found when we'd fled from Beag long forgotten by the rest of the world. It was a crude building, one I didn't particularly want to be in once winter came. As a precaution, I'd started trying to fortify the hut, but I questioned its ability to withstand the cold, harsh winter ahead. *One day it will all be a memory,* I reminded myself as I began scouring the brush that covered the forest floor. For now, we were biding our time at Fianna's instruction, but one day soon, Alannah and I would call Castle Clogwyn home. Seren would be stripped of the title that should have never been given to her and I would lead our people forward into prosperity. Fianna had promised.

I'd had my doubts about the Stag Spirit, raised on the stories of the destructive nature of the Dark Spirits and how they'd wanted to do Pern Coen harm. But over the last few years, I had witnessed firsthand the destruction done to Blaidd at the hands of the Wolf Spirit's supposed chosen Ris and had seen that same Spirit do nothing to stop it. More than that, I had discovered how much Cadfael had sought to ruin my own life. How he had forced my true parents to cast me aside, denied me knowing my blood kin, and I was certain he had played a role in my half-sibling denying my existence. I might question Fianna's methods at times, but the Wolf Spirit had no moral high ground. Not after it had allowed a man like Cadfael to keep the title of Ri, despite his long list of shortcomings, and not after it had sat back and done nothing while the clan had fallen further into ruin.

And then there is what Fianna has done for us, I thought, crouching down to collect a bit of goldenseal, the moonlight drifting down through the breaks in the trees guiding my hands. Despite my nightmares, I knew that if Fianna hadn't woken us when the fire had started and sent its creatures to aid us that night, the villagers would have killed me and Alannah both.

And it was those same creatures that had guided us to the abandoned hut in the Coed and continued to keep us safe from prying, unwelcome eyes, regularly protecting the hut and the forest around it. We owed Fianna our lives. I knew there was no denying that, despite my moments of weakness.

As I straightened, goldenseal in hand, I tried to ignore the niggling doubt that always flooded me when my thoughts drifted in my weaker moments. Those moments had cost me since I had made my blood oath to Fianna. The last time I had disobeyed it, not even a month ago, I had been left in crippling pain for three days. My heart was still conflicted over what I had done, but perhaps it truly had been foolish. Not even Alannah had understood what had driven me to do it. But with the gift that had been granted to me by the Spirits, healing was more than a skill; it was the very essence of my being. It called to me, compelled me in a way that I often couldn't fully put into words.

When I'd seen how close to death Bran had been, I hadn't been able to walk away. Instead, I'd gone against Fianna's commands. In the end, I'd done the bare minimum when I'd found him half-dead on the forest floor, hoping that perhaps by only keeping his soul from slipping from this realm to the next and leaving him with the supplies to try and heal himself, my actions would go unnoticed. But Fianna had been quick to remind me that it missed nothing. I'd paid for what I'd done and, in the end, had no idea if Bran had even lived after all. I doubted it, truth be told. The odds certainly hadn't been in his favor.

I rubbed the inside of my wrist as I ambled through the forest back toward the cottage. Even now, it was almost as if I could still feel the excruciating pain that had begun there before overtaking the rest of my body. The small mark on the inside of my wrist, resembling a scarred burn in the shape of antlers, gave off a soft, orange glow despite the darkness of night. A visible reminder of what I had sold my soul to: to Fianna, but also to a new future.

The dark outline of the hut came into view again as I stepped out from under the shadowy boughs of an ancient poplar tree. I squared my shoulders as I made my way back to the hut. My ever-anxious soul at least felt a bit more soothed after my walk in the woods. My whole life, I'd been drawn to aiding others, and this would be the greatest service yet. Fianna would cleanse Blaidd with its fires in order create its new order and then the clan would have peace. I had to see this through, no matter how dark the road might get.

CHAPTER 2

SHATTERED HEART

Seren

IT FELT AS IF I had aged ten years in just three months, and the burdens I bore continued to multiply. I rested a hand on the bark of a blackened tree trunk, desperately searching the dead tree for any signs of life, but as always, there were none. All around me were more trees in varying states of decay. The ground beneath my feet was nothing but dirt, now turned to a light mud from the rain the night before. No grass grew here; no animals called this now dead forest home. It was no more alive now than it had been over a year ago when it had first been brought to ruin by Fianna's fires.

My stomach twisted as I stepped back from the tree. A bitter taste filled my mouth and I fought to keep my shoulders from slumping. I didn't know how to fix this, and yet that was not even the worst of it. There was an entire clan relying on me to lead them, to care for them, and every day that passed in which I could not heal the scars on our land left by Fianna's darkness, they suffered. Winter would soon be knocking on our door, after a poor season of growing and large swaths of the land still left with deadened earth. I was doing everything I could to try and ease my people's struggles, including entertaining the idea of entering into trade with one of the kingdoms on the mainland, but I knew I was running out of time.

"Seren, Emer says we must keep moving."

Domhnall's call caused me to start. I turned, finding him standing between a broken, rotted out tree just a few feet behind me. He watched me expectantly and I could read the worry in his features: the stiffness in his neck, his strained smile, and the way he lightly tapped one foot. At times, his concern had felt stifling, but I could understand it. I hadn't been entirely myself these last few months. Not with Bran's abandonment, my continued failures to heal the land, and the rumors and fears that perhaps a servant of Fianna still lived, one who might very well be the man I had called husband. I understood the worry over my well-being, but surely no one could expect that these circumstances wouldn't change something deep within me? My world had been shattered, thrown off its axis, and I feared never being able to right it again.

The thoughts of Bran's abandonment made the knot in my belly twist itself further and I set my jaw, determined to push those painful memories aside. I had already wasted too many tears on him. Bran had made his choice and, in the end, it had not been me, or our people. Squaring my shoulders, I joined Domhnall, turning my back on the ruined forest. I'd foolishly hoped to find answers here, but I should have known I would have found nothing but continued reminders of all the ways I'd failed since taking the title of Ri.

"Even with the state of the roads with all this rain," Domhnall said, the two of us coming to walk side by side, "Emer believes we'll be back at Clogwyn by tomorrow night."

I nodded, not feeling nearly as encouraged by the news as I perhaps should have been. Part of me had been glad to venture north and get away from the castle, even if what had prompted the journey had been villagers struggling with their crops and herds. All that waited for me at the ancient keep was more troubles. I had a council who was split between supporting me and hating me. Not to mention a war band that, while kept in line by my warrior chief, was still full of those who would much rather someone else have the title of Ri of Blaidd. I had no shortage of detractors and in truth, it was only the vow I had made to the Wolf Spirit that had kept me going these last few weeks. Had I not made such promise to fight for my place as Ri and my people, I would have been sorely tempted to step aside.

Domhnall and I walked in silence for a while longer, soon reaching a break in the decay. A sharp line had been drawn through the forest. On one side, there was nothing but decay, and on the other, the trees and grass were bathed in brilliant green. As we stepped out of what was left of the ruined forest, Domhnall placed a hand on my arm, gently pulling me to a stop. I angled myself toward him, arching a brow in question as he lightly placed his hands on my upper arms, closing the distance between us.

"I know how this has all worn on you," he said, looking down and holding my gaze. "But we will find him. And when we do, he will pay."

I waited for the anger that had come and burned my belly at every mention of Bran over the last few months, but it was strangely absent. This time, I was only racked with regret and a desire for an end to all of this. I'd so hoped we would have found it in the village of Dearg. So much so that I'd defied the demands of my warrior chief, Lewella, and ridden north with the warriors to investigate the claims of strange happenings and a possible wolf shifter near the village.

To all our disappointment, the claims had come to nothing. Our trip to Dearg had been yet another dead end to add to the steadily growing tally. And what we had found in Dearg yesterday, heartbreaking as it was, hadn't been the worst I'd seen. Just three months ago, an entire village, Beag, had been wiped out by a raging fire. No one had survived to bear witness to the events, but we all knew Fianna was responsible. Seeing the destruction that had been wrought there had lit a burning anger in me. So many lives had been lost; some of whom I had known. Even now, the thought of Aengus made my throat thicken. What horrific death had he, and the rest of the villagers, met at the hands of Fianna?

"I worry how much time we have left," I said, my gaze flitting to what could still be seen of the ruined forest behind us. "How much time Blaidd has left."

Domhnall gave my arms a light squeeze, pulling my focus back to him. "I know."

As I stared up at him, it was hard to ignore the glimmer of desire in his eyes. Our relationship hadn't been without its struggles, but I had relied heavily on him since Bran had abandoned me. More so than a Ri would normally rely on their chief advisor—not that my circumstances were anything close to normal. No one had questioned when he'd made the decision to join me in my impulsive venture to Dearg. Not even I had questioned it.

I'd grown used to him acting as my shadow of sorts over the last few months. But being that close with him, spending that much time in his presence, had brought my attention to something I desperately wanted to ignore. An inkling that Domhnall's feelings for me had never really faded. That even now, he still wanted more. But I could not give him what he yearned for. I couldn't give that to anyone. Bran had shattered my heart into a million pieces and I feared there was no way to repair it.

Letting out a deep breath, I stepped away from him. "We shouldn't delay. I don't want to risk being away from Clogwyn longer than necessary." Who knew what those who despised me had gotten up to in my absence.

Domhnall released his hold on my arm, taking my hand again. "I'm here for you, Seren. I will always be ready to help you shoulder your burdens."

I pressed my lips together, giving him a nod, not trusting myself to speak. I couldn't give him what he wanted, wasn't ready to risk my heart again, no matter how heavy my burdens became. Bran and I had had such grand plans, idealistically thinking we would fix Blaidd and that peace would reign once more. But in the end, Bran had betrayed me and I had done nothing to ease my people's suffering.

Gently, I tugged my hand away from Domhnall's before continuing on deeper into the forest, heading toward our camp. The sun was bringing more heat to the day as it continued its slow climb in the sky and I swatted at a few bugs as I walked. High summer had begun to fade on the island, though autumn had not settled in to reign just yet. It would be another long, hot day of riding ahead, though at least we would be traveling along the banks of the Weindio River.

When we reached the camp, there was little evidence of it left. Emer was calling instructions to the small swarm of warriors as horses were tacked and the last remnants of our camp were packed away. I felt a slight twinge of guilt in running off and leaving others to do the work of breaking down our camp. Emer finished her conversation with a warrior and strode over to us when she saw us. My friend was dressed in the dark blues and rich brows of the warriors of Blaidd, her sword hanging at her hip and her dark brown hair pulled back into practical braids.

"We're almost ready to move out," she said. "I've had Ceol saddled for you, Ri Seren."

"Thank you," I replied, somewhat hating the formal tone we were forced to adopt in the presence of the warriors.

Emer had been a close friend for most of my life and even though I should have, I hadn't counted on this subtle change in the dynamic of our relationship. We weren't only friends anymore; now we were also warrior and Ri.

"Gwynt was giving us a little bit of trouble," Emer said, turning to Domhnall. "Perhaps best if you see to him."

Domhnall gave a slight grimace. His hotheaded stallion was known for being flighty and difficult to handle, despite the horse's strength and speed. Domhnall nodded and walked off, but not before giving my hand a light squeeze and flashing me an encouraging smile. Emer frowned as she watched his retreating back, crossing her arms.

"I know you still don't like him," I said with a sigh as soon as he was out of earshot.

"I don't like the fickleness of his temperament," Emer replied, "but I also want you to be happy. If the two of you have some sort of feelings for one another..."

"I'm not ready for anything like that again." I swallowed hard, hating how my throat thickened at the subtle mention of my ruined marriage. "But I won't deny that I have appreciated his support these last few months."

"I won't begrudge you that. Just know that I'm watching him like a hawk."

A hint of a smile tugged at my lips. "And I won't begrudge *you* that. I know we need to get moving. I don't like being away from the castle for long and I know Lewella will be ready to have you back."

Emer smiled at the mention of her wife and I hated the slight twinge of envy I felt in my chest. Both Lewella and Emer were good friends and had been nothing but supportive of me. I was happy for them, truly I was, but at the same time, the darker emotions that had surfaced within me in the wake of Bran's abandonment hadn't been so easily put aside.

Shrugging off my unhappy thoughts, I followed Emer over to where Ceol stood, tacked and being held by a warrior of Blaidd. I took my dun stallion from the warrior, murmuring my thanks before throwing the reins over the horse's neck and swinging up into the saddle. My people couldn't afford for me to give up now. Though my visions had been clouded more often than not since my father's death, the Spirits had spoken to me in whispers with cryptic symbols, warning me that Fianna was on the move and that it desperately sought the blood of the line of Blaidd, blood that I suspected could very well be my own. My defeat of the Stag Spirit months ago had been as premature as my father's. Fianna still had one servant yet and every piece of evidence I had pointed to that servant being the man I'd regrettably given my heart to. It didn't matter how much it hurt, I had to find him and break Fianna's hold on this land.

CHAPTER 3

TRAPPED

Bran

A LITTLE OVER TWO months ago, I'd thought I'd never get the chance to return home. I should have died. No one lived after being attacked by three shadow creatures, not even if they managed to get away before the creatures slaughtered them. But I had survived, and that had been thanks to one man.

I didn't know how Aengus had found me or what he'd been doing in the Coed Mountains, but even in my half-dead state, I'd recognized him. He'd pulled the poison from my body and left me the supplies to heal myself. Though I was no healer and my wounds hadn't healed cleanly in many places, I had managed to keep myself from slipping away into death.

In hindsight, I should have perhaps been more prepared for the creatures the night I'd set out to ambush Alannah after tracking her down, but I had been cocky, along with impatient to be done with my task and return home to Castle Clogwyn. I'd learned my lesson. I wouldn't make the mistake of trying to be the lone hero again. The next time I faced Alannah and the creatures, I'd have the full force of the war band of Blaidd with me.

How Alannah had cheated death when Lorcan had been destroyed, I didn't know, but I knew I had seen her with my own eyes. It had taken me a full month to track her down, but I had seen her alive and I had seen her with the creatures. How much more proof could I need that Fianna did still have one last remaining servant? And there were no doubts in my mind that she would have been motivated to frame me as one of Fianna's own, though what her exact purposes were, I still wasn't sure.

But whatever her dark plans were, Alannah was the one Seren needed to be warned of. Alannah was the way I was going to clear my name. Those last thoughts made me push myself harder as I raced through the forest in my wolf form, heading south. I could travel far faster as a wolf than I could as a human and with any luck, I would reach the castle by midday tomorrow.

I leapt down a jagged incline, forced to slow my pace as the forest floor became littered with more and more rocks and stones. As I picked my way across them, I flicked my ears back and forth, listening for any unusual noise. I needed to make it back to Clogwyn with all haste; I didn't have time to be delayed by hunters or travelers. At first, I heard only the wind whistling through the trees and the occasional small forest creature, but then I picked up the faint murmur of water.

I was close to the Weindio, having followed the great river south, and the deer trail I'd been following had apparently brought me closer still. I still had many more miles to travel before I stopped for the night, but the day was hot, leaving me overly warm. I made a slight change in my direction of travel, tracking east toward the river. The underbrush was still rocky, forcing me to slow to a trot. Deeper in the forest, I heard the crash of another, larger creature blundering through the trees. A quick sniff of the air told me it was a deer. My stomach grumbled with hunger, knowing that prey was nearby, but I ignored it and pressed on. I could hunt later, after I'd covered more ground.

A few moments later, another scent soon drifted on the wind, but this one gave me more pause. Horses were nearby, and humans along with them. I adjusted my course again in an effort to avoid them. I backtracked deeper into the forest before finally reaching the banks of the river. The smell of the horses and humans had become fainter, almost completely gone, as I ambled across the rocky river to the water's edge.

Sunlight glimmered and gleamed in a dappled pattern on the water as it shone down through the breaks in the trees. Thick forest covered the edges of both sides of this stretch of the Weindio, offering me ample cover if I needed it. I crouched down to lap up the cold mountain water, trying not to think of one of the last times I had been by the banks of this very same river. Seren and I had been fleeing for our lives that night and it was that night, by the light of the fire, that I'd been struck with how much I had still cared for her, even after years apart.

I hadn't wanted to leave her three months ago. I certainly hadn't meant to be gone almost the entirety of the summer, and I hoped that once I was able to give her my explanation, she'd understand why I'd done what I'd done. She'd already had so much trouble from those who doubted her; the accusations aimed at me had only made her life all the more difficult. My intention had been to handle things for her, to relieve her of one burden. I'd only intended to be gone a couple of weeks at most, but there had been factors outside of my control—like almost getting mauled to death by shadow creatures.

Once I'd drunk my fill, I backed away from the riverbank, turning to head back into the forest. My muscles ached from how hard I'd been pushing myself, but there was no time to rest. I'd already been gone too long. And Spirits knew Alannah and Fianna wouldn't be taking any rest from plotting their sinister schemes.

In hindsight, I blamed my next misfortune on my tiredness. Regardless, I wasn't paying close enough attention. I hadn't gone far when my back right paw was suddenly caught in a thin rope cord. The snare tightened before I could yank myself free, trapping me in place. I growled, glowering at the offending trap as I tried to pull free. Laid by some villager, no doubt. Not that I couldn't entirely blame them for doing so. These were hard times; many were struggling to feed themselves and their families. A trap like this one could have caught smaller game, such as a rabbit or squirrel, but instead, it had caught me. I tried to use my teeth to free myself, but it was no use. I was trapped.

CHAPTER 4

THINGS TO ANSWER FOR

Seren

I'D WANDERED OFF FROM the others again. It was the third time today since we'd ridden out and I knew Emer was starting to get frustrated with my longing to be on my own, even if she hid it well. But I'd needed time to think. We'd taken a short break at midday and a vision had come to me, brief but concerning. I'd seen Fianna's shadow creatures and again I had heard the Wolf Spirit whispering to me of the blood of the line of Blaidd.

Quite frankly, I was getting tired of the Spirits not elaborating on what they meant by that. I assumed they referred to me, but they gave no clear answers. I'd heard them speak of such things before my father had died, and in my pursuit of discerning such warnings then, I'd come to the conclusion it had meant no one else but me. My father was dead, as was my brother. My uncle and his children had perished as well. As far as the blood of the line of Blaidd was concerned, I was the last of it.

I'll have to keep fighting for clarity. There's no other choice, I thought, shaking myself out of my thoughts as the riverbank we were traversing grew rockier, making it harder for Ceol to navigate. I scratched the stallion's neck, slowing him to help him keep his footing. The others weren't far, a little behind me on the other side of the river. I'd promised Emer that I'd rejoin them at the fork in the river, where our party would leave the banks of the Weindio behind and take the main road back south to the castle.

Suddenly, I felt Ceol tense beneath me, the stallion raising his head as a loud, growling yelp echoed from nearby. I tensed as the noise came again. It sounded like the cry of a wounded animal, but I was still cautious. I reined Ceol to a halt and slid off his back, my pulse quickening as I armed myself with my longbow and quiver, the cry coming again. The noise didn't sound like a creature of darkness, but if it indeed was, I held a weapon that could defeat it. Rhonwen's bow had traveled with me wherever I went since I had used it to kill Lorcan and right now, I was particularly glad to have it with me.

At my cue, Ceol obediently walked along beside me, the two of us navigating the rocky riverbank as we followed the noise. The stallion was on alert, his nostrils flaring as he took in the smells on the wind. It didn't take us long to stumble across the snarling creature and when we did, I froze, feeling as if I had been punched in the chest. A large grey wolf was trapped in a snare, desperately trying to free itself, its agitation and frustration evident as it snapped at the cord with its gleaming white fangs. But I knew as I stared at the creature that this was no ordinary wolf.

I should have turned and walked away. I should have left him there. After all, he had left me. But I couldn't, my gaze locked on the wolf as it turned from an animal into a man. The transformation itself didn't startle me, not with as many times as I'd seen it, but seeing Bran as a man once more left my chest aching.

He didn't appear to have noticed me and, now in his human form, he pulled his foot free of the snare. Once released, he scrambled to his feet, only to half fall to one knee when his right ankle didn't support him. He cursed loudly before taking a few more halting steps. My throat constricted, my heart pounding as my shock morphed into anger. How easily he had left me and betrayed me. How easily he had thrown the love I'd felt for him back in my face. I *should* leave him here to suffer. If I had any sense, I'd swing back up onto Ceol and ride off in the opposite direction, but as I watched him half stumble across the rocks in obvious pain, I found that I couldn't. I let out my own muttered oath. Damn that man and making me care for him.

"Found yourself in a bit of trouble, have you?" I called.

He started, spinning around and managing to barely keep himself from falling over in the process.

"Seren." My name fell from his lips as little more than a gasp and he stared at me, wide-eyed. He leaned against a nearby boulder for balance.

Despite the quiver in my stomach, I instructed Ceol to stand and closed the distance between Bran and me. My thoughts raced as Bran stared intently at me, his brown eyes never leaving me. I'd envisioned this moment so many times these last few months. What I would say to him, how I would defend myself against whatever pathetic excuses he gave. I'd always thought my anger would be all-consuming and while I did feel a burning anger rushing through me, it wasn't the only emotion. Hurt, too, welled up inside, leaving my throat tight and my knuckles white where I gripped the bow.

Bran winced slightly when I reached him. "Seren, I—"

I slapped him hard across the face before he could finish, three months' of anger apparently impossible to contain when faced when the one person who'd hurt me more deeply than anyone else ever had. "That's for leaving me."

He rubbed his cheek, working his jaw and dropping his gaze. "I suppose I deserved that."

"I should leave you here after what you did," I said, hating how my voice wavered as I stalked back over to Ceol, tying Rhonwen's bow to my saddle for safekeeping. I would have expected Bran to have been more aggressive, but Fianna was a cunning master and the last thing we needed was for the bow to fall into its hands. "But you have things to answer for. At Castle Clogwyn."

I strode back over before he could flee, grabbing him by the arms and fighting to wrench his hands around in front of him so that I could tie his wrists. He was considered a traitor now— at the very least, untrustworthy. Lewella would expect him to be brought back to the castle for questioning. This was the moment we'd been waiting for, for months now. This was the key to defeating Fianna's hold in this realm—and still, treating my husband like a prisoner left my throat thick, my chest tight, and my hands shaking.

"Seren, wait! What are you doing?" Bran said, making a seemingly strange effort not to hurt me as he fought to get away from me. "I understand you might be upset but I—"

I let out a bitter laugh, his injured ankle making it possible for me to get the upper hand on him and pin his arms. "You think I *might* be upset? After you ran off in the dead of night leaving behind nothing but your handfasting bracelet and a poorly worded note?"

"I didn't mean to hurt you," he said, grunting as he tried to wrench his wrists free of my grip, but I was already winding a piece of rope around them. "That wasn't my intent."

Why was it an apology from him hurt worst of all? I shook my head, snugging the rope in place. This wasn't time to be fooled by his pretty words. I would leave it to Lewella to determine the truth once and for all, but right now, the odds were not in his favor. A few months ago, I would have believed I could discern such a truth. But not anymore. My visions had been clouded, likely by what little bit of power Fianna could wield in the Spirit Realm, and with the way the Stag Spirit's power had been increasing, I didn't trust myself not to be missing something vital.

"Whether or not hurting me was your intent, that's exactly what you did," I said, keeping a firm hold of him as I pushed him toward Ceol. There was still the issue of getting him on the stallion, but I would figure that out, one way or another.

He was breathing heavily, his ankle clearly paining him with each halting step he took. Yet he still had the strength to dig his heels in and jerk to a stop when we reached my horse.

"Seren, please," he said. "I need to speak with you. You need to listen to me. Alannah is alive. I've seen her with my own eyes."

"Alannah?" I scoffed. "That's the excuse you're going to go with?"

"It's not an excuse," he retorted, his set jaw showing the first hints of his anger. "I didn't mean to be gone as long as I was. It wasn't by choice. Alannah *is* alive and she's as tied to Fianna now as she ever was. Its shadow creatures still roam Blaidd, and they answer to her. They're the reason I was delayed."

I swallowed hard, torn between my duty to protect my people and wanting to believe his wild story. It would be convenient for him to blame his fellow shifter, a woman who by all accounts had died four months ago. And yet as I stood there, the both of us breathing hard with emotion as we stared one another down, I was uncomfortably aware that the man in front of me was not the same one who had left Castle Clogwyn three months ago.

He was leaner, a bit paler, with heavy bags under his eyes, as if perhaps he hadn't been well for some time. There was a scar, one that hadn't been there before, above his right brow, thin but jagged. I could see the glimpse of another peeking out from the top of his shirt near his right shoulder. Was it possible that he could be telling the truth? *Or he could be lying*, I told myself. *Again.*

"Save your story for Lewella," I finally told him, "and mount up."

"You don't believe me?"

The hurt in his tone made my chest start aching all over again but I steeled myself to it, squaring my jaw.

"What reason have you given me to believe you, Bran?" I snapped. "You ran off in the dead of night, not telling anyone where you were going or why. Knowing that there were doubts and concerns over what loyalty you had to Blaidd and its Ri. Then you show up again in the middle of the forest, accusing a woman who by all accounts is dead."

"We never found her body. You know that as well as I do. And I told you, I left because I was trying to help you."

"Trying to help me?" I jerked my head back, my tone incredulous. "Trying to help me by casting more doubt on yourself and painting yourself in the worst possible light?"

"My plan was to handle things on my own and then return. I didn't plan to be gone for months," he said, his shoulders bunched and his jaw ticking. "There were the fires again. The people were afraid and angry. I knew someone had framed me, I knew someone was causing trouble in Blaidd again, and I knew I wouldn't be of any use or help to you until I cleared my name. I just ran into more trouble than I expected."

"You should have discussed it with me. You should have told me." My voice cracked and moisture stung my eyes, as if I were feeling the hurt of his abandonment all over again. "We were supposed to do this together. How am I supposed to trust you and believe you when it's clear that you don't trust me?"

"I never said I don't trust you." His nostrils flared, but I saw the flicker of pain that flashed in his brown eyes.

"You didn't have to." I looked away from him, unable to meet his gaze as my voice grew harsher. "You are returning with me to Castle Clogwyn, whether you wish to or not. Mount up before you force me to do something I don't wish to."

A tense silence fell between us and I could feel the intensity of Bran's gaze even as I continued to look away, staring hard at Ceol's tawny shoulder. Finally, Bran gave a grunt and shuffled closer to the horse. With his hands bound, I was forced to help steady him, but between the two us and with the help of a large boulder, we got him up in the saddle. I hated being forced to be so close to him, forced to deal with the feelings and memories that came from touching him, but I had little choice in the matter.

We were far enough away from the fork in the river that I also had no choice but to ride with him. I fought to ignore the familiar sensations that coursed through me as I mounted, reaching around him to take up the stallion's reins. By hunching slightly, Bran made it easier for me to see around him, but the movement also brought us in closer contact with one another, filling me with more reminders of what we'd once been. Friends and lovers, husband and wife... until he'd shattered it all. I cleared my throat and urged Ceol into a trot. I couldn't afford to let myself think of such things right now.

"Are you traveling on your own?" Bran asked as I guided Ceol along the banks of the river again.

My stomach clenched. I didn't want to have these conversations with him. I wanted to hand him off to Emer and be done with it. Whatever had been between us might have been a game for him all along, but for me it had been real, and every moment in his presence made every aching hurt I'd felt over the last three months return with a vengeance.

"I do not owe you answers," I answered, working to keep my voice detached and cold. "You forfeited that three months ago."

He stiffened, his muscles tightening, but fell silent. I focused solely on directing my horse, refusing to allow room for anything else in my thoughts. I would get Bran to the others and let Emer assume responsibility for him. Once we returned to the castle, I'd have my answers and perhaps I could move on from him for good. If I had indeed just captured Fianna's last remaining servant, I could end my people's suffering and Blaidd could finally be free.

28

CHAPTER 5

THE TROUBLE OF GOOD INTENTIONS

Bran

I'D SPENT THE LAST three months envisioning my reunion with Seren. It was those dreams that had gotten me through the excruciating weeks of not knowing whether I would live or die. The reality, however, was nothing like I had hoped. I could still feel the sting of Seren's slap and even now I couldn't forget the cold fury in her green eyes.

At first, I'd been angry at her reaction, but when I'd seen the hurt in her features and heard it in her voice, I'd been left with the uncomfortable realization that maybe some of the anger she held toward me *was* deserved. I hadn't left in the best of ways, despite my belief that the decision to do so had been for her.

We'd ridden in silence for the last few miles. I'd given up trying to draw Seren into conversation. She'd have none of it.

There was something distinctly different about my wife after my time away. An icy bitterness in the way she spoke. A hardness to her expression and the way she carried herself. Things that I couldn't recall seeing before that reminded me too much of her father. What all had I missed these last few months? And worst of all, had I perhaps played a part in it?

Nearby shouts drew me out of my thoughts as we reached the split in the river. A handful of horses and riders stood by the water's edge, some of the animals drinking out of the cool waters of the Weindio while others stood quietly, waiting for their riders' next command. I spied Emer, along with a few other warriors I knew from my brief time in the war band. Cian was among the party as well, but it was the sight of the man riding up with Emer who made me stiffen. I didn't trust Domhnall. I never had and judging by the loathsome expression he fixed me with, I had no reason to start.

"What in the blazes happened?" Emer asked, she and Domhnall bringing their horses to a halt.

"I found him," Seren replied, "by the river. Caught in a snare. He's injured; Cian will need to see to it."

"So the traitor returns." Domhnall gave me a cold smirk as his stallion shifted underneath him and I clenched my jaw. Just how many lies and half-truths had he been telling Seren in my absence?

"Owen, Enid," Domhnall called. "Come get the shifter. We can't risk having him so close to Ri Seren."

"I believe," Emer said, her tone curt as she fixed Domhnall with a stony expression, "that the last I checked, *I* am the one in charge of the warriors here."

Domhnall at least had the decency to flush, flipping the end of his stallion's reins in agitation. "I don't think it wise to delay having him in the custody of warriors. It's a miracle he hasn't killed Ri Seren already."

"He came willingly," Seren said, showing the first hint of softness I'd seen since she'd found me. "Though I think it best if there are warriors watching him for now."

Emer nodded, calling one of the warriors, Owen, forward before instructing him to remove me from Ceol and take me on his mount. No one made any comment or showed any inclination to unbind my hands as Owen forced me off Seren's stallion. It seemed I was still to be treated like a prisoner. Never mind that by all rights I was Seren's husband, the Tiarna of Blaidd.

"Seren," I said as Owen shoved me toward his horse. "There's been a mistake. You're a seer; you should know that I haven't—"

"I am not all knowing. I do not know where you have been or who you have been with," she said, her voice gone cold again. "I have a clan to consider here, one that cannot afford for me to make impulsive or unwise decisions. When we reach Castle Clogwyn, Pennathe Lewella will hear whatever tale you wish to tell. Until then, there are risks I cannot afford to take."

I was roughly forced onto Owen's horse, hating every moment of it. This wasn't how this was supposed to go. I was supposed to return to the castle, show my wife just how fiercely I'd missed her the last three months, and use what I'd learned to help her defeat Fianna for good. I wasn't a traitor. I would never betray her thus, and it hurt that she believed such a thing.

At Emer's call, the small band moved out. The horses picked up a quick trot, moving away from the river in order to begin following the main road south. I couldn't tear my gaze away from Seren, even as she rode to the head of the column with Domhnall at her side. Whatever in the blazes had happened at Clogwyn in my absence, I wasn't going to sit back and allow myself to be branded a traitor.

We rode hard over the next few hours, until dusk began to settle and the decision was made to make camp in a large meadow just off the main road. I lost track of Seren as the camp began to take shape, Owen and his fellow warriors hauling me off his horse while Emer strode over to us.

"Ri Seren wants Cian to see to his injuries," she said. "I will see him there. Owen, you will join me."

A small sliver of hope filled me. Emer had been a friend, her and Lewella both. Surely, they couldn't treat me entirely unfairly. *Of course, you would have also said the same for your wife three months ago.* The niggling voice of doubt that drifted through my thoughts left my chest tight as Owen shoved me forward, the two of us following Emer into the half-constructed camp. All around us, tents were going up with speed and efficiency, horses were being picketed for the night, and fires were being built. I looked for Seren again but didn't catch any sign of her before being pushed into one of the canvas tents.

Cian awaited me inside, pulling all manner of healing supplies out of leather bags. He turned when we entered. I offered a hopeful smile but he didn't return it, his mouth pulled down and his eyes slightly narrowed.

"Ri Seren wishes his injuries addressed," Emer said, motioning to me.

"I will see to him," Cian replied. "The two of you may wait outside."

Emer pursed her lips, casting me a sidelong glance before looking back at Cian. "You're sure?"

"I can handle him," Cian said, inclining his head at the foot I was doing my best not to put weight on. "He's not in any condition to cause trouble."

"We'll be right outside." Emer gave a slow nod, slipping out of the tent with Owen following behind her.

I let out a quiet sight of relief when the tent flap swung shut behind them. Finally, perhaps someone would believe me instead of treating me like a traitor.

"I'm only doing this for her," Cian said, his tone flat as he jerkily pulled a few more things out of his bags.

Then again, maybe not. I wasn't able to stop a scowl from crossing my face, my frustration and anger mounting. "I would never hurt her. You know that."

Cian let out a short, bitter laugh. "You've already hurt her. If it wasn't your intention to do so, maybe you should have thought about that before you ran off in the night and abandoned her."

"I didn't abandon her." My muscles tightened as my temper rose.

"I'm not here to listen to your excuses." Cian turned back around, holding up a hand. "I'm only here to make sure you get back to Castle Clogwyn in one piece. Sit down."

I wanted to argue with him, but I didn't think he would listen right now. Muttering under my breath, I sank down onto a pile of furs, the movement only made more awkward by my still bound hands.

Cian had to cut my leather boot to get it off, thanks to the swelling in my ankle, and while I understood the necessity, it still only added to my annoyance. As he pulled off my wool sock and began to poke and prod at me, I gritted my teeth, trying to distract myself from the pain. Was this how it was always going to be? Forever unfairly judged by the mark on my back? I had thought I had earned the trust of the likes of Cian and Emer. I thought I had earned Seren's trust. Apparently, I had never been so wrong.

When Cian gave a particularly painful tug at my ankle, I was forced to bite the inside of my cheek in order to hold back a grunt of pain.

"Not broken," Cian said, finally releasing his hold on me. "But a considerable sprain."

He pulled out a long cloth bandage and I resisted the urge to rub my throbbing ankle in an attempt to get some relief. A sprain would be nothing for Cian to heal with his gift, at least. He crouched down in front of me again, taking a firm hold of my ankle once more. A brief pain flashed up my leg, but then it was followed by warm heat. Once he was finished, the swelling was almost completely gone and I was relieved to find that only a hint of discomfort remained.

"You'll need to stay off of it for a day or so," Cian said as he began to wrap my ankle. "The bandage will support it, but you need to give the ankle time to fully heal. And someone is going to have to find you another pair of boots."

I grimaced at the ruined boot a few inches away. It had, of course, been one of my favorite pairs.

"Thank you," I said once he tied off the bandage.

"As I said," Cian replied, rocking back on his heels, "I did it for her."

"I love her." I held his gaze, knowing my tone was on the edge of pleading but not entirely caring. I needed *someone* to listen to me. Alannah was out there, with Fianna and its creatures. There wasn't time to spare. "It was never my intention to hurt her, but what I learned when I was away was... alarming. I have to speak with her. This cannot be ignored."

"Whatever you have to say, you can save for Lewella." Cian straightened, getting to his feet. "I assure you that she will be thoroughly questioning you once we reach the castle."

"There isn't time for that. This threat is real, and it's dangerous."

"Whatever you have to share can wait for the warrior chief of Blaidd. We'll be at Castle Clogwyn by nightfall tomorrow. I think you've done enough damage as far as Seren is concerned."

"Damn it, Cian! Why are you all acting like this?"

"Three months, Bran. For three months, I watched her suffer." Cian clenched one hand into a fist, his jaw tight as he glowered at me. "I watched them try and tear her down, thwart her at every turn, use the mess you made as reason to undermine her, all while she was grieving you. You left, with no warning and no promise of return, and everyone else was left to pick up the pieces."

"I did leave a promise of return. I left her my handfasting bracelet. She should have known I was going to come back."

"*That* was supposed to be your promise of return?" Cian raised his brows, his tone bordering on mocking. "Then let me tell you it was a poor one. I saw the ridiculous note you wrote her. Whether you meant to return, whether you intended to hurt her or not, is irrelevant. You abandoned her, Bran. You cut her out and made a decision, a huge one at that, without her. I don't blame her for being angry and I don't blame anyone for not trusting you."

My teeth were clenched so tightly, my jaw ached and I breathed out hard through my nose. I wanted to keep defending myself, but even though I hated to admit it, his words pierced me like arrows. I'd been so determined when I'd left, but in all fairness, I'd also been afraid. That was why I'd left in the dead of night. I'd been afraid that I wasn't the man to be Tiarna of Blaidd, that my past and my gifting were costing Seren too much. So I'd set out to solve the problem on my own, to spare her any involvement. But perhaps, in my fear, I hadn't made the wisest of decisions.

"I admit my choices were poor, but that doesn't mean I've aligned myself with Fianna again," I said, practically willing Cian to believe me as I stared him down. "Seren's a seer. She can travel into the Spirit Realm. She would know if I was tied to Fianna."

"Seren's visions have been clouded. She is not seeing things as clearly as she once was."

"I would *never* betray her in such a way. Not after what she sacrificed for me." I pulled back the sleeve of my shirt, thrusting my wrist in front of his face. "There is no mark. See it with your own eyes. Fianna does not own me; not anymore."

He briefly glanced at my wrist before looking beyond me for an overlong moment as tense silence passed between us.

"Then my suggestion to you would be that you prove that," he quietly said, "and understand the mess you left behind."

He turned on his heel before I could respond, crossing the small space inside the tent. Going to fetch Emer, no doubt, but before he did, I had one last burning question. "Why is Domhnall here?"

Cian's shoulders tensed slightly, though he kept his back to me. "He is Seren's chief advisor."

"And yet it is not normally customary for the Ri's chief advisor to be traveling with them, unless the journey they're undertaking has some sort of political importance."

"You left her." Cian glanced over his shoulder. "He watched her suffer, the same as the rest of us. I can't hold it against him for caring about her."

My stomach hardened and I swallowed hard, but before I could press him further, he ducked out of the tent. I didn't want to think the worst of Seren, that she had been unfaithful in any way, but I had little trust in Domhnall. Had he seen my absence as an opportunity and sought to take it?

Even worse were the memories of the conversation I'd had with him the night I'd left. I'd been worried at the time, afraid, and in hindsight, I could see where Domhnall had preyed on my worst fears. True, I was the one who had given in to them, but I was beginning to wonder if I'd allowed myself to be played. Domhnall was ambitious, to the point of being ruthless.

The tent flap flew open again, pulling me out of my dark thoughts as Emer and Owen entered. Owen pulled me to my feet at Emer's instructions and I was unceremoniously escorted out of the tent. The camp had fully taken shape now, the tents set up in a circle around a large fire, where food was being prepared. My stomach growled and my mouth watered at the tantalizing smells. Through the haze of smoke, I briefly spied Seren, with Domhnall beside her. It was enough to make my jaw twitch and cause me to immediately lose my appetite. Owen shoved me along and I was shown to a tiny tent with a pile of blankets serving as a bedroll. After seeing me inside, Emer sent Owen back up to take up a guard post at the tent's entrance.

"I would recommend you not try anything," Emer said. "Just like I'd advise you to remember that I am in the tent right beside you. Food will be brought to you later and a guard will be posted outside this tent at all times."

"Castle Clogwyn was my destination anyway." I gave a light shrug, trying to show a bravado I didn't entirely feel. "Any chance of you untying my hands?"

"None."

I couldn't hold in my frustrated sigh. So much for that. Emer left and I managed to ease myself down onto the blankets without too much awkwardness or pain in my ankle. Outside, I could hear the noises of the camp as warriors went about settling in for the night. My stomach grumbled again and I hoped the food Emer had promised would be here soon.

In the meantime, I guess I should be figuring a way out of this mess, I thought with a sigh. There was still Lewella. Even if she had her own personal issues with me, I had to hope that she would believe and recognize the depths of the threat I had to share with her. Fianna wouldn't be sated until it had control of the entire clan. I was as weary of fighting it as anyone, but now wasn't the time to let down our guard.

Closing my eyes, I tried to give in to the weariness that was overtaking me, only to find that all I could think of was Seren. It hurt me that she would turn against me in such a way, enough that a deep part of me wanted to latch on only to that anger, but Cian's words had also stayed with me, ringing in my thoughts. I'd made more of a mess of things than I'd intended. The problem was, I wasn't sure how to fix it.

The hushed and harried voices outside the tent were what woke me. I sat up slowly, my body on full alert. My damn hands were still bound, the cord starting to chafe. I silently cursed how much clumsier it made me. It was still dark outside and I didn't think I'd been asleep for long. I didn't feel like it, at least; I was still exhausted.

Outside, the voices continued to grow more agitated. I glowered down at my bound hands. They, more than my lack of weapon, were what made me feel most vulnerable. Seren had bound me in such a way that the cord would shift with me if I dared to change into my wolf form. I'd hardly be able to run off or mount a defense with my front legs tied.

The talking suddenly ceased and the tent flap flew open. I tensed, barely able to make out anything in the dark. Someone came to loom over me and for a split second, I foolishly hoped it was Seren. But the build was wrong. My visitor was too tall to be her.

"So you've decided to come slinking back and cause more trouble," Domhnall said.

"I didn't come back to cause trouble," I retorted, my jaw clenched. "I came back to warn my wife and the people of Blaidd."

"It's a convenient little story you've concocted, isn't it? So fascinating how you've decided to lay the blame at the feet of another one of Lorcan's little lackeys. A woman who, by all accounts, is dead."

"I know what I saw. I don't have to justify why I'm here to you."

"But don't you?" Even though I couldn't see more than his shadow, I could hear Domhnall's smirk. "Did you forget who the chief advisor of the council is? I'm afraid you will have much to justify to me, shifter."

"Why are you here, Domhnall?" I growled.

"I am here to make sure that you know that Seren may have a weakness as far as you are concerned, but I do not. I got rid of you once. I can get rid of you again."

My stomach dropped, my blood heating. Could it have been Domhnall all along who had framed me as Fianna's servant? I couldn't forget our last conversation, the one where he had encouraged me to clear my name however I could. Had it been nothing more than a ploy to run me out of Clogwyn? "Tell me, was that a confession?"

"It was a warning. One you'd be best to heed."

"Then let me pass on a warning of my own to you. Stay away from my wife."

"Your wife that you abandoned? If only you could grasp how much damage you did to her. She's needed someone reliable at her side these last few months, while you've been off doing Spirits-knows-what."

"I had no intention of staying away as long as I did," I snapped. "And the last I checked, she is still my wife."

"For now. She can be granted an annulment easily enough, considering the circumstances. This is Pern Coen, after all, not the mainland, and you abandoned her. It's well within her rights."

The sick feeling in the pit of my stomach grew, followed by a bitter taste in my mouth.

"I love my wife," I said, enunciating each word through clenched teeth. "And I will be damned if I let you, or anyone else, tear us apart."

"How unfortunate that your own actions might already have you halfway there."

I snarled, trying to bolt to my feet, only to stumble and fall, a stab of pain shooting through my ankle.

Domhnall gave a mocking laugh. "Still as unpredictable and temperamental as ever, aren't you, shifter? Remember what I said."

He ducked back out of the tent, leaving me alone with my anger and frustration. *He's a damn fool if he thinks I'm going to simply step aside,* I thought, taking in a few deep breaths, my heart pounding. I might have hurt Seren, perhaps more than I'd anticipated, but I would win her back. Domhnall didn't know what we had been through together, the relationship we'd forged. We'd been strong once. We could find our way back to that. And if Domhnall had been in any way involved in framing me, Spirits help him because I *would* get to the bottom of it.

I lay back on my makeshift bed, silently vowing that I would get Seren to believe me. I didn't care what sort of proof I had to get for her and the council. I would not let this go. Our lives depended on it.

CHAPTER 6

TRAITOR'S WELCOME
Seren

THE LAST FEW MILES of the ride back to Castle Clogwyn were perhaps some of the hardest I had ever ridden. The closer we drew to the granite keep, the more I was confronted with the decision that lay before me: What to do with Bran? My heart wanted to believe him, to trust him like I once had, but my head reminded me that I was now Ri of an entire clan. Whether he was my husband or not, he had disappeared in the dead of night, in a particularly incriminating way. As Ri, I couldn't forget the rumors that circled about his loyalty, even if they were rumors that I didn't want to believe. As Bran's wife, I wanted to cling to my belief in him, but as Ri, I needed to treat him with the skepticism that was owed with his outlandish claim of Alannah being alive. I'd been on the battlefield, the same as him. There had been nothing left of Lorcan and his followers.

"Lewella will be thorough in her questioning." Emer's voice drew me out of my troubled thoughts and I glanced over at her.

The two of us were riding side by side, had been for the last five miles, our horses trotting down the wide dirt road that led to the ancestral home of the Ris of Blaidd. The castle itself was a grey speck in the distance, growing larger with each step our mounts took.

I worried my lower lip, hesitating a moment before responding. "Do you believe him?"

"I don't see how anyone could have survived that battle or that fire," Emer replied. "If the battle hadn't killed her, even if she'd used her gifting to get away, her injuries would have."

I bit down harder on my lower lip, knowing she was right and hating the part of me that desperately wanted her to be wrong. Just seeing Bran had overwhelmed me with emotions, reminded me how much I had missed him. Knowing just how strong those feelings were had left me all the more out of sorts. Even worse, it had left me wondering if my father had been right all along. That perhaps I *was* too weak to be Ri.

"Do you believe him?" Emer asked, casting me a sidelong glance.

"I want to." I kept my voice low, not wanting any nearby warriors, or even Domhnall, to hear me. Emer, however, I trusted enough to confess the truth.

"You loved him," Emer said, her tone softening. "He was your husband, not to mention that he saved your life on more than one occasion. It's understandable. Just like it's equally understandable for you to treat him with suspicion. You're Ri now; there are risks you can't take."

I nodded, swallowing hard and reminding myself of the truth of her last words. If it was Bran who was the traitor, the last remaining servant of Fianna, I couldn't risk letting him wreak havoc across Blaidd. There had been fires. There had been rumors of shadow creatures and a wolf shifter, the land wasn't healed, and the Spirits were whispering again. Those were all things that could not be ignored.

I stole a quick glance at Bran, riding behind us with Cian. His hands were still bound and his head was down, his scruffy beard and slightly too long hair only further hiding his features from me. Each time I looked at him, it felt like a blade to the heart, as if someone were reopening the hurt that had festered inside me for months. I'd begun to wonder if I'd ever be free of that pain.

As if he knew I was staring at him, he looked up and I quickly averted my gaze, focusing between Ceol's ears once more. I couldn't afford to get drawn into his soft brown eyes again. Let him coax me into believing his lies. Blaidd couldn't afford it.

Squaring my shoulders, I took in a deep breath and let it out slowly. Clogwyn loomed before us now, its walls promising me the same comfort and safety I'd known since I was a child. I was home and I'd have answers soon enough. Lewella would ferret out the truth of wherever Bran had been and what he had been doing. A messenger had already been sent ahead to forewarn my warrior chief of his impending arrival.

The clop of hooves on my left drew my attention and I looked over as Domhnall trotted up on his chestnut stallion, Gwynt. I mustered up a smile as he slowed the horse to ride abreast with Emer and me. He'd been such a stalwart supporter of mine the last few months, more so than I had ever seen him be. I hoped, perhaps, it was a sign of his somewhat mercurial temperament starting to mature.

"Ready to be back home?" he asked, keeping his tone light as he met my smile with one of his own.

"I'm ready for a soft bed, my wolves, and Rhodri's cooking," I replied.

He let out a laugh, throwing back his head. "I can't blame you for any of those. I'm certainly ready to be done with roughing it." He paused, dropping his voice. "It might all be over soon, you know. The nasty business with the council and the rest of them. If you've managed to capture the traitor..."

His hinting should have brought relief, largely because he was right. If I managed to do away with the last of Fianna's servants, defeating the Stag Spirit once and for all like I had vowed to, it would solve a great number of my troubles. And yet, I couldn't help but feel slightly sick inside.

"We'll find out soon enough," I replied, hoping my internal misgivings didn't come across in my tone. "Once we hand him off to Lewella."

"You're doing the right thing, Seren," he said, briefly holding my gaze before once again focusing on guiding his horse down the road.

I wished his words offered me actual comfort. I hated how much I questioned if I was doing the right thing. By the time we reached the castle gates, I'd begun to sweat from the warmth of the morning, and Ceol's stride was starting to slow. We'd ridden hard the last few days and I knew the stallion would be ready for a few days' rest. I scratched his neck as the portcullis rose, willing myself not to risk even a glance at Bran. All eyes would be on me the moment we stepped into the courtyard. I couldn't afford to look weak, to give the council and the people another reason to doubt me.

Once the portcullis was lifted, our horses trotted through. Lewella already awaited us at the top of the castle steps with six warriors at her side. *This will be over with quickly,* I reminded myself as we brought out mounts to a halt. Lewella jogged down the steps, her warriors flanking her, and strode over to greet me as I swung out of the saddle.

"It's good to see you safely returned, Ri Seren," she said, giving me the respectful nod I was due as Ri.

"Thank you," I replied, handing Ceol off to a stablehand who came to take him. "Cian has the prisoner. He was injured when I found him."

Referring to Bran in such an impersonal way left a bitter taste in my mouth, but I couldn't afford to do otherwise right now. I needed to appear indifferent, no matter what I felt inside.

"We'll handle him," Lewella replied, pressing her lips together. "And I will have answers for you as soon as possible."

I nodded, not trusting myself to speak with the tightness in my throat. Domhnall came up beside me as Lewella walked over to Bran and Cian, both of whom had dismounted. I didn't dare look over at them, focusing intently on the massive wooden doors at the top of the castle steps, my gaze tracing the outline of the wolf's head seal that had been etched into the old oak. Domhnall placed a hand on my shoulder, giving it a squeeze, and I let out a low breath to try and steady myself, listening to the scuffle of Bran being taking into custody by the warriors. He, of course, had no intentions of going quietly.

"What is the meaning of this?" Bran snapped as the warriors took a firm hold of both of his arms. "Lewella, it's me! You know me!"

She ignored him, focusing on her warriors instead, but when I stole a quick glance at her, I noticed the signs that told me this was as difficult for her as it was for me: the tightness in her jaw, the slight wrinkle in her brow, and the way she continually looked always just beyond Bran.

"Take him to the dungeons," Lewella said, motioning toward the castle doors.

"The dungeons?" Bran fought even harder, almost managing to yank one arm free before another pair of warriors stepped up to subdue him. He was pushed forward again, passing by Domhnall and me despite his continual balking. "Seren, you cannot be serious! If you would just listen to me, I can explain. I'm not your enemy. I never have been. You know that!"

Every word felt like a knife to my heart and I clenched my jaw so tight, my teeth ground together. Domhnall's grip on my shoulder tightened and he narrowed his eyes at Bran, who again tried to yank away from the warriors.

"Give him to me." Lewella motioned off one of her warriors, coming up on Bran's right side and yanking him back.

"I'm not a traitor," Bran growled, his eyes flashing with anger as his gaze darted between Lewella and me.

"You cannot leave like a traitor and then expect a hero's welcome upon your return." The words came out before I could stop them, full of the harshness and hurt that swirled within me. I focused hard on Lewella, lest one look at Bran make my resolve crumble. "Take him away."

She did as I requested, though Bran fought her and her warriors every step. For a moment, I wondered if he would try and shift, despite the fact that his bonds would shift with him, but he remained a man as he was marched up the front steps. Soon, he was forced through the front doors and I released a shuddering breath as they slammed closed behind him.

"You can hardly be faulted for this," Domhnall murmured, rubbing my shoulder. "He has made his choices and he will have to live with them."

I nodded, swallowing against the lump in my throat. "It's been a long journey. I'd like to get a bit of rest if I can before we have to debrief with the council."

"Of course." He paused, lowering his head and holding my gaze. "If you need me, all you have to do is ask."

"I know. Thank you."

I stepped away, causing his hand to fall, and strode up to the steps. I didn't want his comfort right now. The one thing I truly wanted was the thing I couldn't have: Bran. As I stepped through the front doors, I couldn't rid my thoughts of the look of betrayal in Bran's eyes as he'd been hauled away. I didn't have a choice but to do what I did, and even though I knew that, I felt that betrayal deep in my bones. *He betrayed you first*, I reminded myself. *For all you know, he could have been betraying you all along.* I had to remember that. It was the only way I would make it through the coming days.

CHAPTER 7

THE WRONG ENEMY

Seren

I WAS KEPT BUSY from the moment I stepped foot back into Clogwyn, which kept my thoughts from dwelling on Bran. He was never far from them, though, despite my best efforts. Domhnall had been quick to call a council meeting and while we'd gathered few answers in Dearg, the news of Bran's capture was largely well received, especially by Laoise, one of my biggest detractors. The only council member who had shown any hint of misgiving had been the one temporary member of my council, Mair. She was more than a temporary advisor, she was also a friend, and I suspected she was all too aware of how heavily the most recent turn of events weighed on me.

Lewella had promised me a full report on Bran first thing in the morning. Come dawn, we would have our answers, one way or another. I only wished I didn't fear them as much as I did. With a sigh, I pushed open the door to my mother's chamber, holding it for her so that she could shuffle through. At my feet sat my two wolves, Awyr and Cryfder, the pair waiting patiently until I gave them permission to enter the chambers as well. I was seeing Mother back upstairs after the evening meal in the Great Hall, the illness that limited her mobility causing her to need a bit of extra aid this evening. I'd been happy to offer it, her company far more preferable to most of the rest of the castle right now. Dinner in the Great Hall had been a miserable affair. The rumors had already started flying about Bran, and some of them were particularly harsh.

"Do you need anything else?" I asked Mother as we crossed her common room, the wolves at our heels.

"No, not tonight," she replied. I let the two of us into her bedchamber and she wearily sank down onto the edge of her bed with an exhausted sigh. "Olwen will be up shortly, and she can help me get ready for the night."

I nodded, wishing I could shake the sense of unease and aching pain that had settled over me since finding Bran. By the way Mother studied me in the candlelight, I suspected I was failing miserably at hiding my inner turmoil from her.

"Is there anything that *you* need?" she asked.

I bit down on my lower lip, my throat tight. A few months ago, I never would have envisioned her even asking me such a question. For most of my life, there had been an unbridgeable chasm between us, but it had vanished in the wake of Father's death. If nothing else, the two of us had grown closer through the heartaches of the last few months.

"An easy answer for what to do and what to believe, I suppose," I said with a sigh. "But I don't think even you can do that."

"Lewella will get to the bottom of it," Mother replied, placing a hand on my arm and giving it a squeeze. "You will know soon enough, one way or another."

"And if he is a traitor?" My voice cracked, my gaze firmly on the flickering candles just behind Mother's bed.

"Then you will do what you must. As you have always done. But..."

"But?"

"I do not say this to defend him. I'm well aware of what he did and the undue burdens he placed on you. But is there a chance that he is telling the truth and this woman still lives?"

I shook my head. "I don't know. So many of the bodies were so badly burned, we couldn't fully identify them, but for someone to have survived that battle... I can't fathom it. And yet, part of me wants it to be true."

To say it aloud felt like an admission of guilt and my stomach twisted. Still, though I never would have dreamed it years ago, I trusted Mother to understand. She had married a difficult man herself, after all.

"You loved him," Mother said, her tone gentle. "That isn't something that is so easily forgotten. These next days will try you, Seren, but do not forget that you are strong enough to weather them."

I leaned down and hugged her, blinking back my tears.

"Thank you," I murmured as I eased back from her.

Once I was sure she was comfortable and settled until Olwen arrived, I saw myself out, the wolves obediently following me. The hallways of the castle's east wing were blessedly quiet as I walked them, making my way to the Ri's chambers. It was only myself and my family who inhabited this part of the keep and I was particularly grateful for that tonight. I couldn't take any more of the whispered gossip. My heart was too torn and my soul too weary.

I was a few feet from my chambers when I noticed a shadowy figure standing near them. I tensed, silently cursing the fact that I had no weapon on me, though at least I had the wolves. The two of them pressed closer to me, picking up on my tension as they too honed in on the dark figure. I took a deep breath, pressing forward. There were warriors within shouting distance. I wasn't completely alone and defenseless.

The torch light on the granite stone walls offered some light and as I drew closer to my visitor, my tension eased, though I couldn't say the same for my guilt. Bran's father, Gruffudd, was pacing in front of my chamber doors, his movements harried and his stricken expression making my chest clench.

"Ri Seren," he said, hurrying over to me as soon as he saw me.

"Gruffudd," I replied. "Is there something I can do for you?"

"I know what he did and I know how it looks." By the light of the torches, I made out the redness that rimmed his eyes and his splotchy complexion, my stomach churning at his obvious signs of stress. "But must he be confined to the dungeons?"

I couldn't meet his gaze. "I'm afraid for the safety of the clan, he must be."

"He could have warriors watching over him, confined to a room. It's killing him, being down there."

I drew in a ragged breath. "Gruffudd, I am sorry, but it must be this way. We don't know where he's been."

"He's spent more time in those dungeons than anyone should ever have to. Please..." There was a sheen in his eyes, his agitation and desperation growing with each passing moment. I wanted to give him what he wanted, but how could I put the whole castle at risk?

"I must do this," I said, "for tonight at least. I need you to understand that."

"It's not the only option." One of Gruffudd's hands clenched into a fist. "I saw him. I saw what it's doing to him being down there. I know my boy hasn't always made the best choices, but he swears he's innocent."

"I know he does," I replied, my throat thick. "I'm not getting any enjoyment from this, Gruffudd. I—"

"Then do something about it!"

His angry shout caused me to jerk my head back. In my twenty years of knowing Gruffudd, he had never once raised his voice at me. I'd only ever seen him this distraught and desperate once before, the night he lost Bran the first time. I couldn't blame him for any of it, and yet my own frustration was building. I was Ri. I had a clan to worry about. This was more than just my feelings, or Bran's.

"Is there some sort of problem here?"

Gruffudd and I both started at Domhnall's call and I glanced over my shoulder to see him striding down the hallway toward us. He fixed Gruffudd with a dark look as he came to stand beside me.

"No," I said, shaking my head.

"Bran has paid his penance within these walls, ten times over," Gruffudd said, his nostrils flaring. "I'm not asking you to set him free; I'm just asking for him to be treated with a bit of decency. You're better than this, Seren. You're better than your father."

"*Ri* Seren," Domhnall corrected, his eyes narrowing at Gruffudd, who drew back his shoulders and defiantly met Domhnall's gaze.

"I cannot change this, Gruffudd," I said, trying to soften my tone. "I cannot risk it. I am sorry for that, but doesn't change the way things are."

"You could change it," Gruffudd retorted. "If you wished to."

"I believe Ri Seren has made her decision on the matter clear," Domhnall said, standing a bit taller as he moved a step closer to me. "Your pleas have been heard. I suggest you bid her goodnight and carry on."

Gruffudd's gaze darted between the two of us and though his face was still flushed, he gave me a stiff nod before turning and striding off down the dark hallway. My chest ached as I watched him go. How had it come to all of this?

"You didn't have to be so harsh with him," I told Domhnall after Gruffudd disappeared from view.

"He should not have been questioning you so," Domhnall replied. "You are his Ri. You gave him your answer. He must respect it."

"Bran is his son."

"Bran is also a traitor."

"We don't know that yet." My voice came out ragged and harsh and I stepped away from him, purposefully keeping my back to him to stop him from seeing the moisture pricking my eyes. I fumbled with the door handle, desperate for the solitude of my chambers.

"Forgive me," Domhnall said, stepping closer and gently laying a hand on my back. "I know this hasn't been easy for you."

I let out a long, low breath, finally pushing the door open. "No, it hasn't been. Was there something you needed?"

"I just wanted to check on you. I know how difficult of a day it's been."

I turned slightly, angling myself toward him, meeting his gaze and reading the sincerity there. It had been a difficult day for all of us, truth be told. None of us were at our best right now.

"Thank you," I told him.

"May I come in?" he asked, inclining his head toward the half open door.

I hesitated, worrying my lower lip as I fidgeted with the door handle. I should have sent him away, but while a part of me longed for solitude, another part of me dreaded the long night ahead. I doubted sleep would come easily and perhaps company would ease some of my mounting fears. And so I nodded, stepping into my common room before motioning for him to follow me.

The wolves trotted over to lie down in front of the hearth when we entered, and Domhnall closed the door behind us. I settled on the large fur-covered bench near the window that looked out over the dark Dail mountains, now only inky black peaks set against the star-filled sky. My shoulders slumped as Domhnall walked over to join me. I tried to banish all thoughts of Bran, tried not to think of him alone and locked away in the dark, but it was impossible.

Domhnall faced me on the bench, his strong features cast in shadows from the candlelight, and his expression softened as he looked down at me. He was a handsome man, one I knew plenty of women would be willing to spend their time with, but while I could recognize his attractiveness, what I felt for him was not what I had felt for Bran. *What I still feel,* I thought, my stomach twisting into a knot. It had all come rushing back when I had seen him, the all-consuming love and trust we had once shared, and I didn't know how to rid myself of it.

"I can't imagine how difficult the last two days have been for you," Domhnall said, gently placing a hand on my arm.

I couldn't hold back a sigh, dropping my chin. "More difficult than I perhaps expected."

"I admire you and the way you've pressed on in spite of all of this."

"I don't have any other choice but to press on." I took a deep breath, letting my gaze travel to the window. "Not with the vow I made."

The truth of the vow I had sworn to the Wolf Spirit had come out to the council months ago, in the wake of Bran's disappearance. In a way, it had felt easier, having others know what I had sworn before the Spirits of the island. It still hurt deeply that Bran had repaid the debt I had entered into for him with treachery, but there was no changing that now. And I would have agreed to it even without him, even if it was just for my people.

Domhnall took my hand in his, his touch light as his thumb caressed the back of my palm. "It is a heavy burden you have had to bear. Seren, you know that I care for you. I haven't wanted to push you, but I..."

I met his gaze as he trailed off, an odd quiver settling in the pit of my stomach. We had been dancing around this for months now—his feelings for me. I'd foolishly hoped I could keep carefully avoiding it, but as I looked into his eyes and saw the desire there, I knew that at some point, I would have to face it. For now, I was still wed to Bran, though I had every right to end that union in the wake of his abandonment. The council had been pushing me to do so for months now, to renounce my husband in every way, shape, and form, but for whatever twisted reason, I hadn't been able to bring myself to follow through.

"I want to be here for you," Domhnall said, his free hand coming up to cup the side of my face. "In every way."

I felt as if I were on the edge of one of the jagged, rocky cliffs overlooking the Cefnfor Ocean, about to plunge into the icy waters below, frozen and unable to respond. He dropped his head, closing the distance between us. These last few months, he'd been my rock. He hadn't abandoned me when things had gotten difficult. I should have been wanting this, feeling the same desire he so clearly showed, but all I felt was dread.

His lips touched mine, only for me to find that I could not return his kiss. As his mouth moved over mine, all I could think of was Bran: Bran locked away in the dark, desperate for me to believe him. There was a wrongness to Domhnall's touch that left me sick inside and as his hand slid to the back of my neck, I jerked away from him.

"I can't," I said, a bitterness filling my mouth as the words stumbled out. "I just... I'm sorry; I can't. Not now. Not yet."

There was a flash of pain in his eyes, his jaw clenching before he let out a long breath and smoothed his features.

"You've had a shock," he said, offering me a strained smile. "No one expected him to dare show his face here again, after all. But I can be patient. I can wait until you're ready."

My heart twisted. The trouble was I didn't know if I would ever be ready.

"Thank you." An awkward tension crept into the air as I got to my feet. I couldn't do this with him. He was my chief advisor, one of my only allies. I couldn't muddle those waters with feelings I couldn't return. "I'm afraid I'm exhausted after the journey and all the events of today."

"Of course." He rose as well, catching my hand again and squeezing it lightly. "Goodnight, Seren. I'll see you in the morning."

"Goodnight."

I remained where I was for a brief moment, watching him leave the room, the wolves barely acknowledging his departure. As soon as the door closed behind him, I released a shaky breath, rubbing my aching chest. Why did what had just transpired between Domhnall and me feel like the worst sort of betrayal? Bran had abandoned me. I owed him nothing. Ours was a marriage in name only. And still, as I brought up a hand to touch my lips, my stomach clenched and bitterness filled my mouth once more. Bran, it seemed, was not so easily forgettable.

Shaking my head, I called to the wolves and crossed the common room to my bedchamber. I hadn't been lying when I'd said I was exhausted. I hadn't been sleeping well for months, my dreams tormented by memories and heartache, not to mention my ever-present, ever-increasing visions that warned of darkness and fire.

Once in my bedchamber, I changed into a pair of sleeping pants and a shirt and then readied for bed. Awyr and Cryfder were quick to take up into their customary spots on the large four-poster bed, curling up into little balls as they settled in for the night. I soon joined them, slipping under the covers and adjusting the pillows to get comfortable. I closed my eyes, desperate for sleep, but as I lay in the darkness, it did not come. I was plagued with thoughts of Bran locked away in the dungeons and Gruffudd's desperate pleas coming back to me.

In the deepest places of my heart, I didn't want to think of the man I'd loved as a traitor, but what other choice did I have? He'd disappeared without a trace, the fires were back, and the Spirits were continually giving me warnings. And now he wanted to blame a dead woman for his misfortunes. It was all too suspicious. I didn't want to condemn him, but the safety of the clan was at stake. Our people had already suffered enough; I could not allow it to continue. If defeating Fianna meant condemning my husband, I would have to do it.

I turned again, causing Awyr to grumble as I bumped into her. My gaze fell on the shadowy thin glass vial on the bedside table. Cian had started making me the sleeping draught shortly after Bran had abandoned me, but I didn't want the fuzzy-headed feeling it brought tonight. I closed my eyes again, determined to force myself to sleep, but it wasn't long before I had to accept that that was a futile effort.

Throwing back my blankets, I muttered a few choice words in Old Pernish and sat up, scrubbing a hand over my face. My gaze flitted to the door, my stomach quivering with the thought that came to me. *You'll just lay eyes on him,* I told myself, worrying my lower lip. *Long enough to remind yourself what he did to you.*

Before I could second-guess myself, I swung my legs over the side of the bed and got to my feet.

Cryfder lifted his head and Awyr blearily blinked open her eyes, but I told them to stay. No sense in disturbing their rest with my tumultuous emotions. I quickly re-dressed into my clothes from earlier, letting myself out of my bedchamber and back into the common room. In moments, I was striding down the dark, empty castle hallways, headed for the dungeons. Torches lit my way and with the late hour, not another soul was in sight, thank the Spirits. I didn't need rumors spreading about why I was wandering down to the dungeons in the middle of the night.

The warriors standing post at the entrance to the dungeons gave me questioning looks but let me pass. As I followed the dank, dark, winding steps that led into the bowels of Clogwyn, my stomach churned again. I knew what would await me in the rows of cells and the closer I got, the more I wasn't so sure I wanted to face it. Another warrior, Seachnall, met me at the bottom of the steps, his brow furrowed as he gave me a nod of respect.

"Is there something I can do for you, Ri Seren?" he asked.

"Yes," I answered, clearing my throat and lifting my chin in the hopes of hiding my nervousness from him. "I would like to see the shifter."

I hated referring to Bran that way, hated that I now had this image to upkeep and that every single word I spoke and action I took was potential fodder for those who were all too ready to twist everything into arrows to use against me, but it didn't change the reality of my situation.

Seachnall gave me a skeptical look, pursing his lips before motioning for me to follow him.

I followed him down the narrow walkway. The cells were mostly empty and I wanted to keep it that way. I'd even disbanded Father's hand-picked guards since becoming Ri, giving such duties to warriors instead. Unlike Father, I took no joys in extracting vendettas and vengeance against our people.

When we finally came to a stop in front of Bran's cell, I asked to enter it. Seachnall raised his brows but instructed the warriors standing at the door to let me pass. One of them unlocked the cell with a long metal key, the hinges creaking as the door was pulled open. I took a deep breath before following Seachnall inside.

Despite the torch he carried, it still took my eyes a few moments to adjust to the dimness of the space. Lewella hadn't shackled Bran to the wall, one of my father's favorite punishments, but his hands were still bound as he sat on the floor in a dark corner. He scrambled to his feet when he saw us, his movements uncoordinated and unsteady. His gaze was hard as he stared back at me and a stab of guilt left my chest tight. How much would he resent me after all of this?

"You may leave us," I told Seachnall, not looking away from Bran.

"You're certain that's safe, Ri Seren?" Seachnall asked, casting Bran a dirty look.

"I have no intentions of hurting my wife," Bran said, an edge to his voice.

Seachnall looked at me expectantly and I nodded. He sighed heavily, muttering under his breath and wrinkling his nose at Bran before putting the torch on the wall behind me. As more dim light filled the cell, I could see where the cord around Bran's wrists was starting to rub and irritate his skin and he bore a few more cuts and scrapes than I remembered, most likely from not going to the dungeons quietly. As Seachnall reached the cell door, my impulses won over again and I called for him to stop.

"Unbind him," I told Seachnall, motioning to Bran.

"Ri Seren, I hardly think that's safe," Seachnall scoffed, shaking his head. "This man is a known enemy of Blaidd."

"Suspected enemy," I said. "Pennathe Lewella will confirm that one way or another come morning. Unbind him. You may re-bind him when I leave."

With an ugly twist to his mouth, Seachnall marched back over to Bran. He unsheathed a small dagger, his movements stiff as he cut the cord around Bran's wrists. As soon as he was released, Bran flexed his hands, eying me warily. I couldn't meet his gaze, as Seachnall left the cell, the door clanging shut behind him.

"Have you finally decided to believe me?" Bran asked.

"Your innocence will be for Lewella to decide."

"Because Spirits forbid you involve yourself with it."

His caustic tone brought all my anger rushing back to me, my body flushing with heat. I curled my hands into fists, finally meeting his gaze. "You left me! What in the blazes was I supposed to think? That damn letter from Drystan had surfaced, the fires were starting again, and there were rumors of wolves and creatures near them. I'm not seeing clearly anymore, not like I once was. Not even during the Purge were my visions this clouded, leaving me with nothing but riddles and more questions than answers. Then you just up and disappear in the dead of night. Tell me, what was I supposed to think?"

"I was trying to clear my name!" His shoulders had bunched and a muscle in his jaw ticked. "I'll admit I didn't go about it in the best of ways, but how can you even think that I would give my soul back to Fianna after all of this?"

"I am Ri now, Bran. I have a clan, my people, to worry about. I can't afford to let my personal feelings color my decisions."

"Now you sound just like your father. Tell me, was that not the excuse he made for the Purge?"

I took in a sharp breath, a squeezing sensation leaving my ribcage uncomfortably tight. "That was a low blow and you know it," I snapped, my voice shaking. "I am *not* him."

"You're ignoring the danger right in front of you, just like he did. I am telling you that Alannah is out there. She has shadow creatures at her side and every intention of finishing what Lorcan started."

"And yet you bring me no proof that she's alive." Even as I spoke, I couldn't fully look him in the eye again, my doubt niggling at me and leaving my stomach tight.

"I saw her with my own damn eyes," he practically growled.

"That isn't proof."

He muttered a string of curses in old Pernish before ripping his shirt off and tossing it on the dungeon floor, his nostrils flaring. I blinked rapidly as I took him in. Though he'd lost little of his enticing physique in his time away, that wasn't what made my breath catch. Scars crisscrossed his chest on his left side, starting at the upper part of his abdomen and up to his shoulder. I swallowed hard as I stared at them, unconsciously rubbing the top of my right thigh. I knew those scars. I bore my own. The jagged white lines and puckered remains of punctures could only have come from a shadow creature.

"Is this enough proof for you?" Bran said, his eyes narrowed as he jerkily gestured to his chest.

I didn't know how to respond, left to simply stare wide-eyed while a tense silence fell between us, my doubts circling around me like hungry wolves. It was harder to discount his story while staring at the marks on his body and even with his abandonment, my heart ached when I thought of the pain he would have suffered.

"I'm not lying to you, Ren," he said, his voice low as he held my gaze. "She's alive. She's out there. And she has a whole host of those creatures at her beck and call. You need to ask yourself: Do you have time to be chasing the wrong enemy?"

I jerked my gaze away from him, my throat painfully tight, before calling for the warriors standing guard. Led by Seachnall, they burst into the cell, their hands on their weapons, ready to defend their Ri.

"You will take him to a room in the warrior's quarters," I told them. "He will remain there under guard until Pennathe Lewella comes to retrieve him."

"What?" Seachnall jerked his head back. "You cannot be serious."

"I believe your Ri just gave you an order," Bran said, cutting his eyes at the other man.

Seachnall's grip on the hilt of his blade tightened and he glowered at Bran.

"I am quite serious," I replied. "Must I repeat myself, Seachnall?"

"No, Ri Seren," Seachnall replied.

Bran retrieved his shirt and pulled it back on. Seachnall muttered instructions to the warriors as they took hold of Bran, re-binding his hands. Their excessive roughness made my spine stiffen and my own nostrils flare. There was no excuse for it.

"And you will not harm him, Seachnall, unless provoked," I said. "Is that clear?"

Seachnall's mouth turned down in displeasure. "Yes, Ri Seren."

Bran's gaze locked with mine as the warriors finished restraining him, his chin lifted and his jaw set. But it was the glimmer of hope in his eyes that was my undoing. I turned on my heel and left the cell, blinking back the tears that threatened to fall. I knew I couldn't afford to be seen as weak, but despite my best efforts, I still found myself swiping at a few rogue tears as I hastily climbed the staircase.

Once back in the tower, I took a few deep, steadying breaths, fighting to calm my racing heart. I had sworn to the Wolf Spirit I would protect my clan from any threat, even if that threat was my own husband. But what if he truly wasn't the real threat after all? Releasing a shuddering breath, I stepped out into the hallway, winding my way back through the castle to the Ri's chambers. Bran was right about one thing: I could not afford to be chasing the wrong enemy. Not with Fianna still on the loose.

CHAPTER 8

PUT INTO MOTION
Aengus

I PAUSED IN THE middle of the ladder to wipe the sweat from my brow. I'd spent the better part of the afternoon working on the hut's less than adequate thatching. One wouldn't know it with the heat today, but in a few months, the cold weather would arrive. There was a chance that Fianna could expect us to winter here and the last thing I wanted was to be unprepared.

Rolling my sore shoulders, I descended the rest of the way down the ladder, only to hear a low eldritch hiss behind me as my boots hit the grass. Two of the shadow creatures sat near the bottom of the ladder. Their long talons gave them an awkward stance and their ember eyes glowed as they looked at me, one of them cocking its head.

It is time, Fianna said. *Things have been put into motion. There can be no delay.*

The shadow creatures let out a hiss, smoke billowing from their nostrils as I gripped the edge of the ladder. I'd known this moment had been coming—I could not take my place as the rightful Ri of Blaidd without it—and still, I felt unready. A noise behind me drew my focus and I looked over my shoulder to see Alannah rounding the corner of the hut, the other two shadow creatures trailing behind her.

"You heard it as well?" I asked when she reached me.

She nodded, placing a hand on my arm. "It is time for us to leave this place. Time for Blaidd to see just how powerful you are. That you can save them when Seren cannot."

I released a shuddering breath before hiking my shoulders back up, one of the shadow creatures coming to rub against my leg like an overly friendly cat. It took everything in me not to shrink back from it.

"We will go to Sionnach first," Alannah said, "and let the creatures do their work."

I frowned. "Let them start a fire? We're supposed to be helping the people, Alannah. Not harming them."

I have told you that the old Blaidd must be reborn, Fianna said, an edge to its voice as a pinprick of pain tingled in my wrist. *Through fire and ash. The old must be scraped away and you must prove your worth.*

"You *will* help them," Alannah said, placing a hand on my arm and rubbing it in a soothing manner. "You will be there to heal them after the fire has run its course. They will see your power and that they can rely on you. Once they realize that and learn the truth of your bloodline, they will have no more use for Seren and her ilk."

My chin dipped as one of my hands curled inward. It felt deceptive, creating a crisis to somehow prove myself to the people of Blaidd, and yet as the pain in my arm grew, slowly starting to radiate up to my elbow, I was uncomfortably aware that I was already into this too deep. Fianna held my very soul in its hands.

"You'll help them, Aengus," Alannah said, tipping my chin up to hold my gaze. "You'll see. And this isn't forever, only long enough to cleanse the land and teach the people to trust you."

I swallowed hard, nodding as I fought to push away my doubts. It was a wonder Fianna still had any patience left with me with. *And you will take care of them,* I reminded myself. *You'll heal them.* The creatures would send the land up in flames, but I would make certain none of the villagers suffered. I had my gift, after all, the ability to heal with a single touch.

"Come." Alannah pressed a kiss to my lips before gently tugging on my arm. "We must prepare to leave. Fianna does not wish us to delay."

I let her tug me along behind her, the shadow creatures surrounding us as we walked back into the hut. There was a spring in the creatures' steps, their eyes taking on a stronger fiery glow, as if they were eager for what awaited them. I shoved aside the uncomfortable feeling in my gut as Alannah began to gather our things. I had to learn to conquer these doubts, to stay the course the way that she did. The future of Blaidd depended on it.

CHAPTER 9

GONE TOO LONG
Bran

I COULD BEGRUDGINGLY GIVE Lewella that she was thorough and left nothing to chance, a mark of a good warrior chief. Over the last hour and a half, she'd questioned me repeatedly about every single thing that had happened to me since I had left Castle Clogwyn three months ago. I hoped I'd given her good enough answers, but her stone-faced expression left me wondering if it was enough.

As Lewella jotted down a few more notes on the piece of parchment in front of her, I shifted in my decidedly uncomfortable chair. She was seated across from me at the dark-stained hornbeam table in the center of her study, the only noise in the otherwise still room the scratching of her ink-stained quill. Outside, the sun was rising, letting in strong rays of morning light and when I shifted in my seat again, my stomach growled. The bread and ale I'd been brought while in the tiny room I'd been confined to for a better part of the night hadn't done much to ease my pangs of hunger. Though at least I was out of the damned dungeons.

"And you believe Alannah had four creatures at her disposal?" Lewella asked, a heavy wrinkle still in her brow as she paused in her writing to glance up at me.

"At least," I answered. "She could have had more. It wasn't easy to get close to her hut."

Lewella gave a short nod, drumming her fingers on the table before she lifted her quill and began scribbling on the parchment once more. A knock drew the attention of both of us and Lewella got to her feet, striding over to the door. As it creaked open, I caught a glimpse of Seren standing outside, along with another warrior, and my chest tightened. I wasn't entirely certain where we stood with one another after last night, but I clung to the hope that she'd finally decided to believe me.

After carrying on a hushed conversation at the door, Lewella ushered Seren into the study. Even after all the ways we'd inevitably hurt one another last night, my heart still quickened at the sight of her. She'd changed—and I worried not for the better in many ways—but I'd seen a glimpse of the woman I'd once known before she raced of out my cell like Fianna itself was chasing her. She looked as haggard as she had last night, the dark circles under her eyes leaving me to suspect she probably hadn't slept any better than I had. As she and Lewella reached the table, I sat up a little straighter in my seat.

"I do believe him to be telling the truth," Lewella said, gesturing to me, "as unlikely as his story seems. I think it wise to be cautious. The matter of Alannah most certainly requires further investigation on the part of the war band, but I do not feel that Bran needs to be held as a prisoner."

I couldn't hold back my sigh of relief, some of the tension leaving my shoulders. "There can be no delay in sending warriors after Alannah," I said. "There's no end to the damage she can do with those creatures."

"Believe me," Lewella replied. "I do not intend to take more time than necessary to do so. But I also do not want to go into this without my warriors being fully prepared."

"Do you think it wise if Bran goes as well to hunt down Alannah?" Seren asked. She wouldn't look at me, a fact that left me admittedly frustrated, but I supposed at least she trusted me enough to suggest Lewella send me with the warriors.

"Yes," Lewella answered. "If the council protests, remind them that he is not going on his own and he's the best source we have for finding her."

Seren nodded, taking a deep breath before finally acknowledging me. "Quarters will be prepared for you in the warrior's wing. I know your father is anxious to see you; I will be certain to send him over once you're settled."

"In the warrior's wing? Not in the Ri's chambers?" I asked, unable to hide my grimace. Her pronouncement stung. I belonged in the Ri's chambers, with her.

Seren stiffened. "I am not going to condemn an innocent man, but neither am I going to so freely let one who abandoned me back into my bed."

I winced, guilt leaving a twinge in my chest along with causing my memories of last night's fight to return to me. Regardless of everything else, it was difficult to deny that I had hurt her. I could still clearly picture it, the anguish in her eyes as we'd thrown barbs at one another with our words. That was the trouble with knowing someone so intimately: You could hurt one another in ways no one else could. I'd broken her trust in me, whether I'd meant to or not. It would take time to win that back, even if a part of me still was loath to admit it.

Another knock came at the door and Lewella called for the visitor to enter. Mair slipped into the room, giving Seren a respectful nod before addressing her.

"Ri Seren," she said, "King Evander's ambassadors from Darnic have arrived."

Seren frowned. "They're certainly early. I'll be there at once. Can you see them to the Great Hall in the meantime?"

"Of course, Ri Seren." Mair gave another respectful nod before leaving, while I was left with my head spinning. What in the blazes were ambassadors from Darnic doing here? The Clan of Blaidd and our eastern neighbor, the Clan of Tyll, had more to do with the mainland country than the rest of the island, but that was in trade, and not much trade at that.

"I'll get someone to see to Bran and then I will meet you in the Great Hall," Lewella told Seren, jerking me out of my whirling thoughts.

"What has called King Evander's ambassador's here?" I asked, shaking my head.

Lewella averted her gaze, staring intently at one of the far windows while Seren ducked her chin, lightly clearing her throat, before looking back up.

"I am considering all options to make certain the people of Blaidd make it through this winter, especially if Fianna is not vanquished by then," Seren said.

"All options?" My brow furrowed. "What exactly does that mean?"

"It means what it says it means." Seren angled herself away from me, turning to Lewella. "I'll see you in the Great Hall."

Lewella gave her a respectful nod and Seren strode from the room, leaving me with an uncomfortable feeling in the pit of my stomach as the door swung shut behind her.

"What is—" I began, but Lewella held up a hand, cutting me off.

"I can't give you that information right now, Bran. Seren has not been left with easy choices since you left here. I will send a warrior to see you to quarters, as I'm afraid I must be going as well."

She didn't leave me any chance to press her further, departing the room as well. I slumped in my chair, rubbing my forehead. I had been away from Clogwyn for far too long, that was for certain.

CHAPTER 10

THE GRANDEST PRIZE

Seren

As if last night's confrontation with Bran in the dungeons hadn't thrown me off enough, seeing him this morning, along with our visitors from Darnic arriving early, was determined to unravel me. I took a few deep breaths as I reached the massive doors of the Great Hall, the wolf's head seal etched into the aged oak giving me some comfort. I was doing the best that I could for my people. That was the oath I had sworn as Ri and the vow I had made to the Wolf Spirit so many months ago; no one could expect more of me than that.

The warriors standing guard at the doors respectfully inclined their heads before letting me into the Great Hall. I squared my shoulders as I strode into the expansive hall, determined to push my unsettled feelings aside. If I wanted any sort of alliance with Darnic, it would be best not to display all of our weaknesses. As soon as I got through this meeting, I could contend with the disturbing truth that Lewella believed Bran's tale that Alannah was somehow still alive.

To my relief, Mair and Domhnall were already seated with our guests at the Ri's table at the front of the hall. There were three ambassadors total from Darnic, two men and one woman. They were dressed in the richly colored fabrics of their people, adorned with the distinct and uniquely dyed checkered cloth that was handcrafted by the mainlanders. They each acknowledged me with murmured greetings and nods of respect when I joined them at the table.

My father had continued his father's tradition of keeping a simple trade alliance with our neighbors across the channel, but I wanted to take things a step farther. Our people needed more than what that agreement currently offered. After another abysmal growing season, we needed Darnic to agree to supply us goods, not just coin, in return.

"I believe we are just waiting for a few more to join us," Domhnall said, smiling at our visitors.

I tried to ignore the uncomfortable tightness that settled in my chest when I looked at him, my thoughts unwillingly flitting to what had transpired between us last night. I couldn't give him what he wanted, but I also couldn't afford to alienate him. I needed allies—and any personal feelings aside, he was skilled at things such as political maneuverings. At least if he bore me any ill will after last night's tense kiss, he didn't show it.

"King Evander sends his regards, Ri Seren," one of the men from Darnic told me, giving me an easy smile. "He was very pleased to hear of your desire to strengthen the alliance between the Clan of Blaidd and Darnic."

"I am pleased that King Evander was willing to consider a slight alteration to our existing agreement," I replied.

The door to the hall opened and the last two of my advisors, Laoise and Arwel, strode in, followed shortly after by Lewella.

Of the three of them, I knew I would have Lewella on my side. Laoise, I didn't trust not to try and undermine me any way she could, though I hoped Domhnall would use his position as head advisor to keep her in check, and Arwel almost always sided with her these days. The three of them joined us at the table and Domhnall began to make introductions. Callum, Duncan, and Isla were Evander's chosen ambassadors, all advisors to the king in some form or fashion. Duncan and Isla looked to be close in age, in their fifties, if I had to guess, while Callum was much younger, probably not much older than I was.

"King Evander understands that you wish for more than just coin from the kingdom of Darnic," Duncan said.

"We are willing to compensate King Evander in return," I replied. "In things that he would find most beneficial. Blaidd has always honored its agreement with Darnic these last fifty years and I can assure King Evander that he has no reason to fear that that we will not continue to do so."

"Yes," Duncan leaned forward slightly, giving a slow nod. "I must say that is part of why King Evander was surprised to hear of your request. Why the sudden desire for a change? Being that your people have always wished to so staunchly safeguard your independence and self-reliance."

I forced myself to keep my expression neutral. At least some news of our troubles in Blaidd had likely traveled to the mainland, but I hesitated to reveal just how desperate we were. Evander had always seemed like a decent enough man, but I certainly didn't know him well enough to trust him, or his ambassadors, completely.

"Ri Seren has an eye on strengthening Blaidd's ties both on and off the island," Domhnall said smoothly. "In both goods and coin. After all, this world of ours is broadening by the day. Pern Coen will not always be able to stay as insulated and isolated as it currently is."

"There have been a number of rumors that have reached the king's court of late," Isla said. "Ones that include rumors of Ri Seren divorcing her husband."

I stiffened. Had the news of Bran's betrayal truly traveled so far? And if so, how? Domhnall, Arwel, Mair, and Lewella looked as surprised by Isla's words as I felt, but Laoise only noticeably shifted in her seat. I resisted the urge to scowl at her. I was beyond weary of her undermining me at every turn and I wished more than anything that I had the power to remove her from the council. But my hands were tied in that regard. Laoise had served on the council long enough that it would take more than just me to expel her from the council. Domhnall would have to agree as well and he was hesitant to do so, reminding me that we still hadn't even found a replacement for Mair, much less for Laoise.

"I must question why such a thing would be relevant to this conversation?" Arwel asked, slightly raising his brows. "We are here to discuss trade, are we not?"

"King Evander wishes to propose an alliance," Duncan said, motioning to Callum, who passed him a rolled piece of parchment. "One thing would hinge on his marriage to Ri Seren."

Outraged flooded me and my face grew hot. This was absolutely not the alliance I had proposed. Nothing in the offer we had sent to Evander had even hinted at marriage. I was sorely tempted to grab the roll of parchment and throw it on the ground to make certain Evander's ambassadors knew exactly what I thought of such a suggestion, but Domhnall took hold of it first. He placed the parchment on the table between us, carefully unrolling it as we both began to scan the document.

My irritation burned hotter and deeper with each word I read. Evander wanted me to wed him, creating a tie of blood between our people. In return, Blaidd would receive the goods I had requested, things such as food, clothing, and livestock, while Evander and his people would continue to benefit from the fish, wool, and granite stone we sent him. *And he would get what he seems to deem the grandest prize of all: me,* I thought as I skimmed to the last few lines of the document.

As soon as finished reading, Domhnall passed the document around the table. Mair looked uneasy but Lewella and Arwel skillfully hid their reactions, their years of experience on my father's council on full display. It took everything in me to wait until the parchment had passed to all the members at the table before I spoke up.

"I am afraid the answer to King Evander's request for a marriage alliance is no," I said, keeping my tone stern as I squarely met Duncan's gaze,

"But you are divorcing your husband, are you not?" Isla asked.

Their audacity was truly astounding and I clenched one of my hands into tight fists under the table. "I am very much still married to my husband."

"For how long?" Duncan pressed. "Word has reached Vara that the man has been branded a traitor."

"A marriage alliance is *not* on the table," I replied, clenching my jaw.

"But what of—"

"I believe," Domhnall said, raising his voice slightly. "that Ri Seren has been quite clear in expressing that she has no interest in entering into King Evander's offer. We have offered the king things in return for the agreement we proposed. Our smithies are skilled; their swords and spears are second to none. The horses in the Ri's stable are of good stock. Many of them can trace their bloodlines back to the prized horses of the Ris of Ceffyl."

Duncan and Isla's expressions were pinched and Collum shifted in his seat. King Evander had clearly expected to me to agree to his ridiculous proposal. I wished more than anything that I could just turn them away, but I couldn't. The land had been so ravaged by Fianna and so much of it still lay in ruin, I deeply feared many of our people would not survive the winter.

"You ask much of King Evander," Duncan said. "We have swords, spears, and horses aplenty in Darnic. It is only fair he gets something of equal value in return."

"Perhaps some of your wolves?" Collum said, making a flighty movement with his hands. "King Evander has heard much of the tamed creatures. We certainly have nothing of the sort in Darnic."

I bristled in my seat. That was little more than an insult. The wolves of Castle Clogwyn were not creatures to be auctioned off to the highest bidder. They were a part of the fabric of this castle, the fabric of our very clan. They were sacred to the Ris of Blaidd; they always had been.

"No," I said, firmly shaking my head. "That is not an option."

"Ri Seren, you must be willing to part with something," Duncan replied, making a noise of disbelief in the back of his throat. "That is how a negotiation works."

Domhnall lowered his voice, bringing his head closer to mine. "Seren, would it truly be such a hardship to part with one or two of the wolves? Perhaps some of the pups. There were three litters this spring, after all."

I jerked my head back, infuriated by his very suggestion. He hadn't grown up at Clogwyn, and I knew he wasn't particularly fond of the wolves, but surely he understood what they meant to the clan.

"No," I hissed. "The wolves are not bargaining chips."

"We need something. What we offered is clearly not enough."

My stomach twisted as my thoughts raced. I wasn't offering up the wolves any more than I was offering up myself, but he was right. We *did* need something. Evander clearly wanted something rare, something he couldn't get anywhere else.

"Longbows," I blurted out. "We will be willing to give Evander ten longbows alongside the swords, spears, and horses. I know for a fact that you do not have such a powerful weapon on the mainland."

Duncan and Isla's eyes lit with interest and I swallowed hard, not quite meeting the gaze of any of the others at the table. It was a rarity that our bows departed the island; they'd been prized weapons for generations. Bows were common enough in the other parts of the realm, but the longbow was unique to our people. Unique enough that it would hopefully tempt Evander. *And hopefully he never decides to try and use them against us,* I thought, my heart skipping a beat as my mouth went dry.

"I believe the king would be most intrigued by such an offer," Duncan said with a slow nod. "Though I would advise you to at least consider King Evander's offer of marriage, we are willing to take back to him the offer with the addition of the longbows."

"We will eagerly await King Evander's response," Domhnall said, placing a hand on my arm and giving me a reassuring squeeze.

Domhnall and Arwel stepped forward to make written record of the additional agreement of longbows for the Darnian ambassadors to take with them and I rolled my shoulders, my muscles so tight, they were starting to twitch. Domhnall, Arwel, and Lewella saw the ambassadors out, Lewella answering Duncan and Collum's questions about the use and the accuracy of our bows. As the hall doors closed behind them, I allowed myself to slump in my chair, rubbing my forehead, a dull headache beginning to throb in my temple.

"You foolish girl," Laoise snapped, her arms crossed as she glowered at me from the opposite side of the table. "You have a king of Darnic ready to wed you and you turn him away without even considering it."

"I wish for an alliance to help our people make it through the winter," I retorted. "I do not wish to bind them to Darnic for generations. Not to mention that I am already wed."

"A marriage you would be wise to rid yourself of," Laoise said, shoving her chair back before getting to her feet. "You cannot speak of wanting to rid this land of Fianna and then let one of its servants roam these very walls. And your principles will do you little good when your people are left to starve."

Turning on her heel, she stalked out of the hall, her leather boots clacking loudly on the smooth granite floor.

"To age her ten years so that I could force her to step down from her position," I muttered as the hall doors slammed shut behind her.

"I cannot quite believe them pushing for marriage so strongly," Mair said, pursing her lips. "Surely King Evander realizes that such choices are yours and yours alone. Especially as Ri."

"I have heard that marriage is often different in Darnic," I replied. "More politically motivated than it is here."

"Still, you would think they would have the decorum to respect that it is not the same in Pern Coen."

"One would think."

I leaned back in my chair and let out a deep breath. Outside of Domhnall, Mair was the other advisor on the council I truly trusted. And still, I had never intended to keep her in this position for as long as I had.

"I'm sorry I still have no replacement for you," I said, a feeling of heaviness settling in my chest.

"There's hardly been time to do so, what with the fires and the peoples' struggles."

"Still, I know our agreement was that this wouldn't be long-term. I know you'd rather be in the infirmary than here."

"I've still been able to mostly keep up my duties there." She paused, briefly ducking her chin. "Though I suppose I would be lying if I said I wasn't feeling the strain of trying to keep up all of my responsibilities."

"I promise I'll double my efforts to find a suitable permanent advisor."

"I know you're trying. And Spirits know you've your own burden of responsibilities."

"Ones that keep growing by the moment." I sighed heavily, fidgeting with the end of one of my braids.

"The longbows are a good offer. Evander should take it. I doubt he'll get such an offer from any of the other clans. And perhaps Fianna will be vanquished before winter and we won't find ourselves having to rely on Darnic's generosity."

"I hope that now perhaps we are a bit closer to that than we were," I said, my thoughts flitting back to Lewella and her belief in Bran's story.

I trusted Lewella's judgment; she wouldn't have believed Bran without cause. On top of that, I could not forget what I had seen in the dungeons. A slight tightness settled in my throat at the memory of Bran's scars. They added weight to his story. If it was as simple as finding and destroying Alannah... and yet at the same time, I rightly feared not even that would be so simple. Especially if she had a horde of shadow creatures at her disposal.

"Lewella was able to get information from Bran?" Mair asked.

I nodded, hating how the ache in my chest returned every time I heard his name. "A lead, at least."

"Thank the Spirits for that. Maybe this *will* all be over soon."

I mustered up a smile, despite the knots in my belly, pushing myself to cling to the hope that she showed. If Bran had the answers we needed, if he was the key to finding Alannah and *she* was the real key to destroying Fianna once and for all, peace could reign in Blaidd once more. And that, more than anything else, was worth fighting for.

CHAPTER 11

DIFFICULT THINGS

Bran

THE ROOM I HAD been assigned in the warriors' quarters was a spacious one—a good thing, as I found myself pacing the room while waiting for my father's arrival, trying to work off some of my fractious energy. It chafed at me, knowing that Seren had met with ambassadors from Darnic while I was stuck here. I was still Tiarna, as far as I knew. No, I was not the Ri, but I still should have been involved in such things.

But so much has changed, I thought, stopping in front of one of the room's windows and resting my forehead against the cool glass with a sigh. It hurt, how much Seren didn't trust me. I wanted to cling to that and ignore the role I'd played in that loss of trust, but deep down, I knew I couldn't. I hadn't necessarily made the best choices when I had left this place.

There was a knock on the door and I started slightly before crossing the room to open it. Father awaited me out in the hallway and I stepped back to let him in, some of my tension easing with his presence. He'd come to see me in the dungeons last night and while it had hurt him to see me locked away again, almost as much as it had pained me to find myself behind the steel bars of a cell once more, it had also been a relief to know that at least someone cared.

"Thank the Spirits you're out of that place," Father said before pulling me into a hug.

I returned his embrace, my throat tight as we eased away from one another. It had hurt to leave Seren, but it had hurt to leave Father too.

"She believed you?" Father asked.

I'd told him last night why I had left, along with what had delayed me, and he believed me, even if no one else had.

"Lewella did," I answered. "And that seemed enough for Seren."

"At least you're out of that wretched dungeon."

"I…" I trailed off, swallowing hard as I averted my gaze, focusing on the stone floor instead of him. The words were on the tip of my tongue, but I still struggled with them. But who else could I confess this to if not Father? "I almost feel as if I don't recognize her anymore."

Father rubbed his chin before letting out a long, low breath. "Difficult things and difficult times have a way of changing people. I can't tell you what to do, Bran—that's between the two of you—but I suspect you will have a long road of hurt to traverse."

"I didn't mean for all of this to happen like this. I did what I did for her. Why can't she understand that?"

Father gave me a long, stern look. "I'm not making excuses for her actions, but did you truly go about it all in the best way?"

I let out a frustrated sigh, dropping my chin as I rubbed the back of my neck, feeling my cheeks heat slightly. "Perhaps not."

"I'm not pleased with all of her actions since you've returned either, but by all accounts, you did abandon her. And the clan has not been kind to her in the wake of it. At some point, the two of you are going to have to sit down and solve what's between you."

I managed a nod, a thickness settling in my throat. How had this all become such a mess? And what hope did I have of fixing it?

"Deryn has given me a little extra time for the midday meal, considering the circumstances. Would you prefer to eat it in the Great Hall? Or I'm happy to make us something at the cottage."

I hesitated, my chest tightening. It was tempting to retreat to his small cottage just outside the castle walls, but I was going to have to face the people of Clogwyn, and their scorn, at some point.

"I suppose the Great Hall," I said. "I'll have to get it over with eventually. That is, so long as you don't have any objections."

"I will never be ashamed to be seen with my son," Father replied, his voice thick with emotion as he held my gaze.

I blinked rapidly, clearing my throat. No matter what I'd done, no matter how many mistakes I'd made, he'd never stopped loving me. He placed a hand on my shoulder, giving it a firm squeeze before the two of us left my quarters. Coward that I was, I was glad we saw only a few castle servants on our walk. It gave me time to prepare myself for the inevitable disdain and unkind whispers that were certain to spread the moment I stepped into the Great Hall. Weathering that inevitable storm should have been my focus, but as we walked, my thoughts kept unwillingly flitting back to Seren.

The way she had treated me days ago had been nothing like the woman I'd known. It had reminded me far too much of Cadfael, but I wasn't so blind that I didn't miss the subtle signs that the Seren I'd known was still there. She had let me out of the dungeons, for starters—something Cadfael would have never done. My quarters were a far cry better than what I'd been reduced to when Cadfael had been Ri, and someone had clearly arranged for Father to be able to spend time with me today. Those things had to count for something.

When we reached the Great Hall, the doors had been propped open and a steady stream of people wandered in and out of the massive room. The morning and midday meals at Castle Clogwyn were informal affairs, food laid out so that the castle inhabitants could come and eat when it best suited them. I squared my shoulders as I walked into the room at Father's side, ignoring the handful of disdainful looks that were sent my way, along with a few shocked gasps.

We got plates of food and found a few empty seats in a far corner of the hall. My jaw was clenched so tightly by the time I settled in my chair, it had begun to ache. I'd never really been accepted within the walls of Clogwyn since the Purge, but now things seemed far worse.

"I see the accusations around me being a traitor weren't exaggerated," I said, my mouth turned down as I dug into my roasted venison stew, hoping the food would help distract me.

Father pushed a few of his cooked peas around his plate. "People assumed the worst. It didn't look good, Bran, when you left. Especially in light of that supposed letter from Drystan."

"The letter that was false," I snapped, unable to bite my tongue despite knowing that Father didn't deserve to be on the receiving end of my temper.

"The fires have them spooked. And then the rumors of creatures being at the scene of the fires, some folks saying they saw what they thought was a wolf; I'm not defending them, but when people are frightened, they don't use their best sense."

I stiffly scooped up another spoonful of stew, causing some of it to splatter, before popping it in my mouth. As much as I wanted to dwell on my own hurt, another uncomfortable realization was settling over me, one that centered around just how cunning Fianna could be. We'd had no idea Alannah had survived, and yet she had. That was something I was certain the Stag Spirit had had some hand in. The fires, the rumors, the fear that had been sown; Fianna and its darkness were relentless. Who was to say it wasn't behind all of it? We'd thought it defeated, only to find out we had never been so wrong. *And now,* I thought, taking a sip of my ale and trying to wash the bitter taste out of my mouth, *it seems even more bent on splintering this clan into pieces.*

Father and I were halfway through our meal when a woman approached our table. At first, I stiffened out of habit, but when Father gave the woman a smile, I forced myself to relax my shoulders. I could tell by the woman's dress, in particular the horse head emblem stitched into her dark grey shirt, that she worked in the Ri's stables, like Father. They were roughly the same age, the newcomer perhaps a year or two younger.

"Haf, my son, Bran," Father said as the woman set down her own plate of food and took a seat on Father's other side. "Bran, this is Haf. She came up from Cnoc about two months ago to work in the stables."

Haf and I exchanged greetings and to my relief, she didn't seem to immediately view me as some sort of threat. Father and Haf made small talk about the comings and goings of the stables, including a few new horses that had recently come from a breeder in Seabhac, and as they spoke, I couldn't help but notice a sort of familiarity and closeness between them. Still, I couldn't begrudge my father happiness. He'd grieved my mother hard and then lost me more than once on top of it all. Ashamed of it as I was, I hadn't exactly been there for him, especially these last few months.

"Deryn made the comment that a few of the yearlings will be sent to Darnic if this agreement is made," Haf said, taking a swig of her ale. "Seems Ri Seren is requesting horses that specifically have the blood of the Ri of Ceffyl's stock in them."

"They'd inarguably be the most impressive," Father replied. "And a few of the yearlings are as good-minded as they are striking."

"Of course, I also heard that it might not be horses at all that King Evander wants." Haf half shrugged one shoulder. "There's been rumors that what he wants more than goods or horses is Ri Seren's hand in marriage."

I half-choked on my drink, barely managing to keep from spitting it all over the table.

Haf winced. "Spirits, my apologies. She's still married to you, isn't she?"

I wiped my face with my sleeve before rubbing my aching chest. "As far as I'm aware, at least."

"There's been no divorce or annulment," Father said, giving me a sympathetic look. "Not any official one, at least."

"Was just talk I heard," Haf said. "Might not be any truth to it."

I nodded, forcing myself to take another bite of my food. I knew how gossip ran rampant in a place like this. Haf was right—there might not be any truth to it—but I still felt sick to my stomach as I half-forced myself to finish my meal. My relationship with Seren was in shambles, there was no denying that, and while she hadn't pressed for any sort of separation—yet—she would be within her rights to. I couldn't imagine Seren agreeing to bind the clan to the mainland in such a way. It would be unheard of, but did I even really know my wife anymore?

I managed another bite of stew, only half listening to Father and Haf's conversation. Seren might not want to speak with me, but there were too many unsaid things between us. We needed to talk, to get to the bottom of this all. *I* needed that. I wasn't ready to lose her any more than I was ready to give this clan up to Fianna. Not without a fight.

CHAPTER 12

CAST ADRIFT

Seren

Something followed me, making the hair on the back of my neck rise as I ran through the dark, shadowy forest. Moonlight danced in front of me, creating an odd path through the misty trees. I didn't know where it was leading, but I knew I needed to get away from what was pursuing me.

A large crash made my heart jump and I pushed myself faster. Some large creature was careening through the underbrush behind me. My chest ached, my breath coming in short gasps as a twinge of pain began to build in my side, but I didn't stop. I couldn't.

The moonlit path suddenly diverted, leaving me scrambling to keep from running into a towering poplar tree. Tripping over a fallen branch, I lost my balance, slamming down onto my side. Before I could lurch back to my feet, a deep-throated growl reverberated in the air. I whirled around to see a wolf barreling toward me. The creature was a strange, tawny gold color, its eyes gleaming with flames as it leapt at me, fangs bared—

I gasped, my entire body trembling as I was thrust back into the Mortal Realm. My heart pounded as if the tawny wolf were still right in front of me, ready to attack. I squeezed my eyes shut, taking a few deep breaths to reorient myself. I was in the Ri's study inside Castle Clogwyn, not in some strange forest in the Spirit Realm. I was safe here.

Once my pulse had calmed back down to a respectable rate, I opened my eyes, only to see that in the course of coming out of my vision, I had knocked over my inkwell, spilling the black liquid all over the table. I cursed, hurriedly snatching up the pieces of parchment that had been laying in front of me and pushing them out of the way. In my hasty scramble, I bumped into Awyr, the black wolf grumbling from under the table. Cryfder, who was stretched out under a window a few feet away, momentarily lifted his head, cocking it to give me a quizzical look before resuming his slumbering.

Muttering a few choice words in Old Pernish, I worriedly glanced at the parchment I'd saved, relieved to see that I hadn't ruined the hours of work that had been spent crafting the agreement that would be sent with the Darian ambassadors when they departed tomorrow. I'd spent the last few hours after the evening meal holed up in the study going over it again and again, trying to make certain the best terms had been put forth to the king while also avoiding any loopholes that might bind Blaidd into an agreement I wasn't willing to enter. I sincerely hoped that when we heard back from Darnic, it would be with news that Evander had accepted our offer.

Of course, I thought, rubbing my forehead and letting out a heavy sigh. *Were that my only problem.* A shiver passed down my spine as I thought back to my vision. This wasn't the first time I had seen the tawny wolf, but it was the first time it had attacked me. Again, my visions left me confused. With the news of Alannah, I would have expected to be plagued by a hawk, not an oddly colored wolf.

A knock on the study door pulled me out of my thoughts and I shook my head, calling for whoever was on the other side to enter. The door creaked open, revealing one of the warriors who was standing guard until I retired to the Ri's chambers.

"Ri Seren," he said, giving me a respectful nod. "The shifter is demanding an audience with you."

So, I thought, unable to stop myself from stiffening, *we're back to this then. Refusing to even refer to him by name.* It had been a standard practice when my father had been Ri and I didn't care for it. I wasn't ready to invite Bran back into my bed and I still wasn't decided about where matters should stand on his place as Tiarna, but I had thought I had made it clear that Lewella had confirmed his innocence and that I believed him.

"You may tell *Bran*," I said, "that I will speak with him in the morning."

The warrior gave me a brief nod and ducked back out of the room. I couldn't hold back another sigh as the door closed behind him. Spirits, what I would give to have all these troubles solved. Stifling a yawn, I got to my feet, carefully setting the parchment safely away in a locked drawer.

"Cryfder, Awyr," I softly called, rousing the wolves from their sleep. "Come. It's time for bed."

They both got to their feet, Awyr giving a shake as she crawled out from under the table, and followed me out of the study. It was late and the day had been long; combined with the fatigue from my vision, I was ready for sleep.

On my way out, I told the warriors about the mess I'd made with the ink, asking them to have a servant see to it, before making my way across the castle toward the staircase that would lead me to the Ri's chambers. As I walked, barely paying attention to my surroundings, my thoughts were consumed with the vision, Evander's ridiculous proposal, the news of Alannah, and my fears that my people would be in for a winter of suffering.

"Ren."

I started at the all too familiar tone, bringing a hand to my chest as a shadowy figure emerged from a nearby alcove. I knew him before he even stepped under the torchlight; only one person had ever called me by that name.

Awyr pressed up against my legs as Bran came closer. The flickering light from the torches that lined the granite walls illuminated his undeniably handsome features; features that were somehow made even more alluring as the shadows danced across them. It was useless to pretend I wasn't still drawn to him, despite all that he had done.

Cryfder, unlike Awyr, was quick to abandon me. The grey wolf let out a joyous howl, half-slamming into Bran with his eagerness, his whole body wiggling in excitement. Cryfder had always held a special affinity for Bran and he too had grieved his absence the last few months. As I watched Cryfder's quick forgiveness of the man who had abandoned him, I couldn't help but feel a slight twinge of envy. If only I could manage to forgive and forget so easily.

Bran scratched Cryfder behind the ears, chuckling at the wolf's antics, the noise low and familiar, sending both a warmth and an ache to my chest. It felt like a cruel glimpse of the life I'd once had—the life I so desperately missed. Bran's voice, his love of the wolves, the playful light in his eyes as he interacted with Cryfder. The hurt part of me roared back to life like a wounded beast, even as I longed for Bran's presence in my life once again. I shook my head, breaking myself out of my stupor. I couldn't afford to let my emotions run down that path.

"What do you want?" I asked, pulling my shoulders back as I worked to strengthen myself against the charm he so clearly still possessed.

"I need to speak with you," he replied, looking up at me as Cryfder contentedly plopped down on his rump at Bran's feet.

"Tomorrow," I told him with a slight wave of my hand. "It's been a long day."

I went to step past him but he stopped me, a pleading look in his brown eyes as he blocked my path. "Seren, please. I know the day has been a trying one for you. It's been trying for me too, but there are questions I need answers to. Things I wish to put to rest instead of hanging over us for Spirits know how long."

I fidgeted with the clan ring on my right hand, letting out a long, low breath. I'd been avoiding this, this conversation of where we stood. I'd told myself it was because there were other, higher priorities that demanded my attention, but in truth, it was because I was afraid. What emotions, which I had worked so hard to put to rest, would be unearthed again if I trod down that path? But I couldn't put it off indefinitely. *Get it over with,* I told myself. *Get it over with tonight and then you can leave him to help Lewella track down Alannah and be done with it.*

"Alright," I said with a soft sigh. "But we'll discuss this in private. In the Ri's chambers."

He nodded, falling in step beside me as we continued on down the hall. Awyr stayed at my side while Cryfder happily walked along next to Bran, a spring in his step and his tail wagging.

"I think he's grown again," Bran said, inclining his head toward Cryfder as we neared the staircase.

"He certainly takes over more of the bed than he used to," I replied with a rueful shake of my head. "I haven't seen him so happy since..."

I trailed off upon reaching the bottom step, my throat tightening. I silently cursed, clearing my throat before hurrying up the steps. Bran followed behind me, stopping me at the top of them with a hand on my arm, his touch burning my skin even through the fabric of my shirt.

"What were you going to say?" he asked, his tone gentle.

"He missed you." I shrugged one shoulder. "The first two weeks you were gone, he moped. I could barely get him to eat. He didn't understand why you left either."

Bran winced. "I know it's a poor apology, but I swear, I didn't mean to be away for so long, Ren. Or to hurt you."

I pulled my arm away from him, letting out a shaky breath. "In private, please."

If my emotions were going to get the better of me, I didn't want it to be in front of the entire castle. Bran pressed his lips together before giving another subtle nod, the two of us taking off down the winding hallways of Clogwyn once more. The silence was thick as we made our way to the castle's east wing, reserved for the Ri of Blaidd and their family. It was difficult to ignore Bran's nearness, or the tumultuous mixture of feelings he brought up in me—both longing and resentment.

When we finally reached the Ri's chambers, I ushered him inside first before closing the door behind us. Awyr wandered off to curl up on one of the large woven rugs while Cryfder eagerly fetched a well-gnawed bone from where he'd stashed it in a corner. He trotted back over to Bran, dropping the bone at his feet before looking up at him expectantly. Bran shot me a questioning look and I motioned for him to carry on before taking a seat in a nearby fur-covered chair. The moment brought memories of happier times that twisted my chest, but I couldn't bring myself to deny Cryfder his bit of joy.

Bran's smile returned as he got down on the floor with the wolf, the two of them engaging in a brief game of Bran tossing the bone and Cryfder retrieving it before the wolf finally took his prize to go chew on it next to Awyr. Bran cleared his throat, getting up from his place on the floor and coming to take a seat on the bench across from me.

"I do not mean to tell you what to do," he said, leaning forward to rest his elbows on his knees. "But I heard the rumors regarding the King of Darnic. The implications of tying Blaidd to the mainland through something such as marriage—"

I held up a hand. "I have already told King Evander that whatever agreement we come to, marriage will not be a part of it. Blaidd is a part of Pern Coen, not Darnic. I will not have that change."

Bran nodded, a tense silence falling between us as he rubbed his thumbs together. "So... we are still married, then?"

I tightly gripped one arm of my chair. "Yes."

"And my place as Tiarna?"

I let out a deep breath, focusing on one of the flickering candles and not quite trusting myself to look at him. "By law, you are still Tiarna of Blaidd. But I warn you that the council does not trust you. Not yet."

"I will do everything I can to help Lewella bring in Alannah. Fianna still has a servant, but it is not me."

The mention of Fianna caused my thoughts to flit back to my earlier vision. My chest constricted at the memory of the wolf, its eyes blazing with fire and its fangs bared. It likely wasn't the wisest idea to be spilling to him what I had seen, but I was at a loss. And Bran had been out there, with her, and with Fianna; perhaps there was some insight he could share. Not so long ago, I'd trusted him in matters like this and now, I was desperate.

"I still see a tawny-colored wolf," I said, "and the Spirits still whisper of the line of Blaidd. And I do not believe that it is Alannah who they speak of."

"And you do not think it is yourself?"

"If it is, I do not understand what they are telling me."

Bran was quiet for a long moment, his chin resting in his hand as he drummed his fingers against the side of his leg. "You mentioned Aengus not so long ago."

"And you were right then in pointing out that Aengus has no ties to the Wolf Spirit's bloodline."

"I saw him. He's the only reason I survived the attack from the shadow creatures. I don't know what he was doing in the Coed, but he was there. If he hadn't found me, I would have died."

My breath hitched. I had assumed he had perished in the fire that had destroyed Beag, but it seemed that somehow, against all odds, he had survived. "I can't see Aengus throwing his lot in with the likes of Fianna."

"Neither can I, to tell you the truth. And if he had, why would he spare me?"

I massaged my temple. If I went to bed without a headache tonight, it would be nothing short of a miracle. "Alannah is the wisest place to start."

"Undoubtably." He paused, the silence once again thick. "Ren, I..."

He waited until I looked over at him before continuing, holding my gaze.

"I love you," he said. "I never stopped."

I tore my gaze away from him, blinking rapidly at the damned wetness in my eyes. Spirits, how long had I yearned to hear those words? And yet I resisted them, feared I couldn't trust them. I could discuss the clan's troubles and the threat of Fianna, but this—this felt like having all my wounds from the past three months ripped open again.

"I know I made mistakes," he continued, inching closer to the edge of the bench. "But we were always better together and—"

"There is no *we*," I said sharply. "There ceased being a *we* when you slunk off in the dead of night without even a word. I can't just pick things back up like nothing ever happened."

He flinched, dropping his gaze to stare hard at his tightly clenched hands. "Are you ready to give up then? On us?"

I took a deep breath before letting it out slowly, willing my voice to remain steady. "I fear that I cannot trust you. Not anymore."

The shadows didn't hide the hurt that flashed in his eyes and I stiffened my spine, steeling myself against it. There would be no pretending he had never left, no picking back up as if nothing had changed. My heart couldn't take it.

"Can you give me the chance to prove to you otherwise?" he asked quietly.

I gripped the arm of my chair even tighter, my knuckles going white. Could I? Did I even want to? *Do I still love him?* Those words haunted me, rolling around in my thoughts as a quiver settled in my belly.

"I can give you a chance," I finally said, "but I can make no promises."

He held my gaze as he got to his feet. "I'm going to fix this, Ren. All of it."

I didn't answer him, my heart twisting as he saw himself out. Cryfder let out a whine when the door closed behind him, and I slumped in my chair. I'd never felt so confused and adrift, like a boat tossed in a storm in the middle of the sea. Bran, Evander, Domhnall, Alannah, Fianna, the mysterious tawny wolf... where in the blazes did I even begin to solve my troubles? With a frustrated sigh, I got to my feet, rolling my tense shoulders a few times before beginning to put out the candles for the night. I needed rest, especially in the wake of my vision. My troubles could wait for morning, or so I hoped.

CHAPTER 13

ASHES AND EMBERS
Aengus

THE SMOKE BILLOWED IN the air over the tops of the trees, the acrid scent of it leaving me wrinkling my nose. Fianna's creatures were at work, purging the land of its weakness. I paced at the mouth of the cave, watching the sun rise as a hazy orange globe in the smoke-filled sky. Fianna had insisted that I stay behind, just a half mile out from the village, while Alannah took the creatures to do their work. I was too valuable, it seemed, to risk getting caught up in the chaos of Fianna's fire. I was almost ashamed to admit that I was happy for it.

My misgivings and doubts still plagued me, worries that what we were doing wasn't the right thing. I was eager for the fire to burn itself out so that I could get to the village and end any suffering. For now, however, I was left to wait and contend with my pathetic weakness.

When I reached the mouth of the cave again, I took a deep breath, still somewhat amazed that the thick smoke in the air had no effect on my lungs, despite its foul odor. Our blood oaths meant that Alannah and I were immune to any ill effects from the Stag Spirit's flames. The people of Sionnach, however, would not be so lucky. *But you will heal them,* I reminded myself, flexing one of my hands as I stared intently into the slowly lightening forest. I feared not having it in me to heal an entire village, not with the way my gift always taxed me, but Fianna had promised that I would be able to do so. I had to trust it.

I heard the eldritch hisses first, the noise still able to raise the hair on my skin, even though I'd been living with the creatures for months now. Two of the creatures bounded out from among the trees, smoke billowing from their nostrils as they growled and nipped at one another. Behind them came Alannah, covered by a dark grey cloak that obscured her features. The creatures continued their aggressive exuberance as they bolted into the cave, one of them half jumping on top of the other and sending the two of them flying into a ball of smoke.

"They are ready for you," Alannah said, throwing back the hood of her cloak as she stepped just inside the mouth of the cave.

"How much has burned?" I asked.

"Most of the village." She shrugged, flicking a bit of ash out of her hair. "There are many wounded, but none of them died."

I swallowed hard, trying to ignore the guilt that made my stomach clench.

"This is for the best, Aengus," she said, leaning up to kiss my cheek. "For the land and for the people. You will save them. You will make sure they don't perish."

I nodded, my tight throat leaving me unwilling to speak and betray my weakness to her.

She turned her attention to the shadow creatures, speaking to them in Old Pernish, commanding them to remain in the cave. They snarled and snapped in return, sparks spitting from their mouths as they expressed their displeasure, but remained where she instructed. She motioned for me to follow her, departing the cave. Squaring my shoulders, I trailed behind her as we made our way through the hazy forest.

The closer we got to the village, the stronger the smell of smoke became and I fought the nausea that rolled through my stomach at the first glimpse of burned homes and fields. I might save their lives, but their livelihoods were already ruined.

Do not question what you don't understand, little mortal. Fianna's voice brought with it a sting in my wrist and I winced, rubbing at the antler-shaped scar. *This land must be cleansed.*

Shaking out my stinging hand, I shoved my misgivings aside. I *had* to see this through. Alannah and I passed among the wreckage, making our way to the village square. Amidst the chaos from the aftermath of the fire, the villagers barely paid us any heed. There were cries of pain from the wounded, people scurrying about as they tried to discern the extent of the damage done to their homes, herds, and places of business. Charred ash drifted on the air, most of the buildings still hot and smoldering from the unnatural flames that had brought the village to ruin.

When we reached the square, what had once been green grass was now nothing but blackened and singed earth. Only the stones surrounding the edges of the square itself had been left unscathed. People were gathered together in huddles, clinging to loved ones and nursing their wounds. Their haggard faces and cries of sorrow made my chest clench. Alannah was unaffected by the scene, her face an expressionless mask as we walked among the broken villagers.

My gaze fell on a mother and child, the mother covered in so much soot that her skin was almost completely grey. The young girl she cradled in her arms was badly burned on her arms and neck, the skin blistered and red. I couldn't stop myself, altering my course and heading right for the bawling child. Alannah followed behind, her gaze calculating as she looked between me and the injured girl.

"I am a healer," I said as I reached the pair. "I would like to help."

The mother started when I spoke, letting out a hacking cough as she clutched the child tighter to her. She narrowed her eyes at me as she took me in, glancing briefly at Alannah, who stood just behind me.

"Never seen you around these parts before," the woman said. "Who in the blazes are you?"

"As I said, I'm a healer," I replied. "My companion and I were traveling north and saw the fire."

The girl let out another wail that tore at my heart and the mother blinked rapidly, moisture sheening in her eyes. "Can you help her?"

"I can."

She murmured something to her child and I crouched down next to the girl.

"Hello," I said, softening my tone in the hopes of putting the clearly frightened child at ease. "My name is Aengus. What's yours?"

"C-cora," she sniffled.

"It's very nice to meet you, Cora," I replied. "I'm a healer. I'd like to take a look at your burns and see if I can get them to stop hurting."

Cora looked up at her mother, who gave the girl a tight nod. Tentatively, Cora held out one of her burned arms. I took it carefully, knowing the immense pain she'd feel even at the slightest touch. Tears rolled down her sooty face, her sobbing starting all over again, as I placed my hands over the blistered skin.

I closed my eyes, calling on the power deep within me. I had done this countless times, using the power given to me to knit together the skin and bone of the ill and injured, but this time, there was a rush of power like I had never before felt. It erupted within me, seeming to stem from the mark on my wrist, filling me with strength as I began to heal Cora's battered arms. The Stag Spirit had not lied when it promised I would be sustained.

Under my touch, the blisters began to disappear, with new fresh skin growing in their wake. I was used to my healing gift taxing me, leaving me often forced to administer more than one treatment in order to keep from completely depleting myself. This time, however, I felt no such weakness. As I finished with Cora's burned arms, there was none of my usual fatigue. I took a deep breath and turned my attention to the burns on her neck, along with the damage to her lungs from the smoke.

By the time I was finished, aside from her burned clothes and sooty body, the child looked as if no fire had ever touched her and her crying had ceased. Her mother stared at me wide-eyed, shaking her head in disbelief as she looked between Cora and me. Out of the corner of me eye, I caught Alannah staring at me with a confident smile, one that warmed me from the inside.

"Who are you?" the mother asked, bringing a hand to her chest as she broke into another cough.

I hesitated for a brief moment, my weaknesses making me want to shy away from the truth.

You are what they need, Fianna said as a tingling came to my wrist. *Tell them. Tell them who it is who will save them.*

"I am the rightful Ri of Blaidd," I said, holding the woman's gaze. "I am the last of Fionn's blood kin. And I am here to keep my people from suffering."

Her brow wrinkled, her head jerking back at my proclamation.

"But, how..." A series of coughs cut her off and Cora worriedly clutched her mother's arm.

"I was forced by Ri Cadfael to hide, but I will not hide any longer. Not while Blaidd suffers." I straightened, placing a hand on the woman's arm as she fought to catch her breath. "Let me heal you."

The woman nodded, her body crumpling inward as she clutched at her chest. I took a firmer hold of her shoulder, closing my eyes once more as another rush of power flooded me. This was what I was meant to do. I was meant save my people from their suffering and I would not rest—not until Seren was deposed and I had the power to move Blaidd forward into Fianna's prosperity.

CHAPTER 14

THE STAG'S SHADOW

Seren

WHEN THE NEWS OF the fire reached Castle Clogwyn, I was in a meeting with the advisory council in the Ri's study. It felt like a bad dream, an overwhelming sense that these continual horrors were never going to stop. The village of Sionnach had been almost completely burned to the ground. A haggard villager stood at the head of the table in the Ri's study, twisting his hands as he recounted his tale.

"Nothing was spared?" I asked, my shoulders so tense that a sharp ache was forming in the middle of my back.

"No, Ri Seren," he answered, his voice catching. "We lost all of it. Everything. Our homes, our livestock, the harvest... nothing was spared. And nothing would put out the flames until they'd destroyed it all."

My throat thickened, my heart pounding in my chest. If these fires didn't stop, there would be nothing left of Blaidd.

"How many were wounded?" Arwel asked.

"Most of the village." The man paused, shifting his weight where he stood. "But there was... a healer was traveling north and saw the fire. He tended to the wounded. No one's hurt now, but the village is still in shambles."

I pursed my lips, tapping my fingers on my thigh under the table. It wasn't unheard of; plenty of healers choose to travel from place to place instead of choosing a village to call home. Still, how could a healer, even a gifted one, tend to an entire village in such a short time?

"Warriors will be sent north," I said, "to investigate the fire and to help the people of Sionnach rebuild. I will send healers as well, in case there is any need of them."

"Thank you, Ri Seren," the man replied with a respectful nod.

He was escorted out by the warriors who had seen him in and I tried to ignore the looks of unease that passed around the table as the door closed. For all that I had been determined to bring peace back to Blaidd, it was only falling further into ruin at every turn.

"I will be riding north personally," I said. "This fire is clearly the work of Fianna."

"Are you sure that is wise, Ri Seren?" Arwel asked. "This is a matter Pennathe Lewella should surely be able to handle. I would argue that you are needed here. The agreement with King Evander is not yet set in stone."

"I will not be my father and sit idly in Clogwyn while my people suffer," I replied, squaring my shoulders. "The Darnian ambassadors will not have even reached the shores of the mainland yet. There is time yet before we hear from King Evander again. I will be riding north. To see to my people and to flush out Fianna's servant."

"The role the shifter might have played in all of this should not go ignored," Laoise said with a haughty sniff.

I couldn't stop a scowl from playing across my face. "Bran was here the entire time. Tell me, how could he have been responsible for a fire in Sionnach?"

"Spirits only know what powers Fianna could have granted him," Laoise huffed.

"I will not condemn a man on baseless accusations," I said. "I will travel north, along with whatever warriors Pennathe Lewella chooses to send, and we will continue our hunt for Fianna's true servant."

Laoise muttered something under her breath but fell silent. I could tell by Arwel and Domhnall's downturned mouths that neither of them were entirely in agreement with my plan, but they did not argue against me. Soon the council meeting was concluded and we dispersed. Arwel and Laoise were to meet with the village elder of Gefell regarding the state of the current late summer harvest while Mair was needed back in the infirmary.

I was tempted to bring her with me to Sionnach, not only for her healing skills but for her support, but it would be wiser to have her stay behind. Someone needed to keep an eye on Laoise and Arwel's endless plotting against me. With any luck, the castle could spare Cian instead. I left the study, intending to find Lewella and discuss the journey in more detail before I began packing my things, but Domhnall caught up with me in the hallway.

"I understand that you perhaps wish to give the shifter the benefit of the doubt," he said, coming to walk alongside me. "But I would hate for us to miss something important because we were swayed by his potential falsehoods."

"Bran has been here the entire time," I said with an exasperated sigh. "Lewella has found him nothing but cooperative. Sionnach is at the other end of the border. Tell me, how is it that Bran could be in two places at once?"

"You know how powerful Fianna is. You know the power and control Lorcan was able to exert over its creatures. All we have to go on is one man's word."

I took hold of his arm, taking a quick glance around the hallway to make certain we were alone before pulling him into a nearby alcove.

"It's more than his word," I said, a slight twinge in my chest as I remembered the scars that had crisscrossed Bran's body. "I am not condemning him without proof."

"And what of Drystan's letter?"

"Drystan was no more a reliable source than my father was. You know that as well as I do."

"Seren..." He pinched the bridge of his nose. "What if he is working with this woman he speaks of? What if he is feeding her information as we speak?"

"Again, there has been no proof of that."

"At the very least, you should keep him under guard here at the castle when we travel to Sionnach. Lest he cause trouble here while we are away."

"We?" I arched a brow.

"I do not wish to lead like my predecessor either," he replied, lifting his chin. "If you are to go, then I will travel with you. Let the people see that their chief advisor is supportive of their Ri in tackling this threat head-on."

I gave a slow nod. Differences of opinion aside, it would be good to have him at my side, as I had so often had these last few months. And good for the people to see his dedication to them and their well-being.

"There will be no need to keep Bran under guard while I am away," I told him. "I intend for him to come with us."

"What?" Domhnall's mouth fell open before he snapped it shut.

"He was a tracker, Domhnall. A scout. And while he might not be in league with Alannah, he knows her. If there are any clues that have been left behind, he will find them."

"And what if he leads you into a trap?" he asked, his jaw tight. "What if he leads you right into Alannah's clutches?"

"I have full faith in Lewella's ability to plan for any and all potential trouble." I laid a hand on his arm before I continued. "I am asking you, as your Ri, to put your personal prejudices aside. We cannot defeat this evil by squabbling amongst ourselves."

He breathed out sharply through his nose, a tense silence passing between us.

"And I must ask you, as your chief advisor," he said, his voice low. "As Ri, are you willing to put your personal feelings aside if he is found guilty?"

"*If* he is found guilty." Because I knew he wasn't. I might not want him back in my bed, but I believed Bran's honesty. Whatever misguided senses had drawn him away from here, it hadn't been to give his soul back to Fianna.

"Then I suppose we will both do as we must." Domhnall gave a slow nod and I let go of his arm.

"I must speak with Lewella about the journey. I'll see you at the evening meal?"

"I'll come with you to speak to her. I have a few hours before I'm expected to meet with the village elder from Cnoc."

"Very well, then."

Motioning for him to follow me, I stepped out of the alcove, turning right to head to the west wing of the castle where the warrior's quarters were located. As we resumed our walk, I cast him a sidelong glance. Tension remained in his jaw and shoulders, leaving me to believe that he was still far from at ease when it came to Bran. I knew the resentment he harbored, how much he had believed my father's words about shifters during and after the Purge. But he was not wrong. We both would have to do what we must. Our clan depended on it.

CHAPTER 15

FOOL FOR HIM

Seren

WE'D RIDDEN HARD FROM Clogwyn, through stormy weather and torrential downpours. The wet, muddy roads had slowed our progress and a journey that should have taken two days looked like it would take closer to four. The third day of our travel had been by far the most miserable. We had ridden through an evening of particularly heavy storms and we were all drenched. I scratched Ceol's wet neck as I pulled the damp leather reins over his head, the horse looking as happy as I was to be stopped for the night. It had been a miserable day of travel, to say the least.

All around me, warriors were picketing horses and setting up camp for the night. I led Ceol over to the rest of the horses. Once I'd untacked him and rubbed him down, I got him something to eat. As I gave him one last scratch on the neck, my gaze turned to the slowly forming camp. There was still so much work to be done. Despite my growing weariness, I started toward the area where the tents were being erected, but Domhnall stopped me. I started slightly at his touch. I was so tired, I hadn't even noticed him walking up to me.

"Come, let's get you in front of the fire," he said. "You're soaked through."

I shook my head. "There's still much to do."

"The warriors have it handled." He lowered his voice, bringing his lips close to my ear. "You're Ri now, Seren. You are responsible to far more than just them. Come, before you catch a chill."

I hesitated, my gaze lingering on a group of warriors working together to tie down a section of tent canvas, before letting him guide me over to the fire. Two warriors were banking the flames, the wetness of the ground and the wood making the fire particularly smoky. Domhnall fetched furs for us to sit on, placing them on the damp ground in front of the fire, and I sank down onto one.

"Here," he murmured, placing a dry cloak over my shoulders.

I thanked him, already beginning to feel warmer in front of the flames. The day had been cool, a subtle reminder of the impending changing of seasons. Autumn wasn't far off and as always, it would make its presence known here, in the northern parts of the clan, before drifting south.

I glanced over at the warriors working on the tents again, my gaze inevitably falling to Bran. I'd spent days now trying to ignore him, to view him as no different than any other warrior joining me on this journey, but he'd still occupied my thoughts. I was relieved to at least see that while the warriors weren't exactly being friendly with him, they weren't treating him poorly either. I was all too aware of the unfair and oftentimes cruel treatment he'd received at Clogwyn and from the war band when my father had been Ri and I would not have that repeated. My warriors would not stoop so low, not while I was their Ri.

"Feeling warmer?" Domhnall asked as he settled down on the fur beside me.

I nodded, pulling the dry cloak a bit tighter around me. "Yes. Thank you."

"Good."

The rest of the warriors, led by a man named Tudwal, soon joined us around the fire. I'd wished that Lewella had been able to come with me, but she'd had too many responsibilities tying her up at the castle. I didn't even have Cian at my side for this venture, as he too hadn't been able to tear himself away from the castle infirmary, especially with the short-handedness Mair's presence on the council was causing. He'd sent another healer in his stead, but I still felt slightly adrift without at least one of my closest friends at my side.

As was usual when traveling, the meal was simple: roasted duck that had been caught earlier in the day along with a bit of nuts and dried fruits. As I ate, I tried to keep my gaze from straying to Bran, but I didn't succeed. He was seated across from me on the other side of the fire and even with the smoke slightly obscuring my vision, it was impossible not to notice how he kept stealing glances at me as well. There was still so much unsaid between us, but coward that I was, I wasn't ready to fully face it.

Darkness had fallen over the forest by the time we finished eating, the light of the blazing fire casting shadows all around us. Excusing myself for the night, I got to my feet, stifling a yawn. It took everything in me not to steal one last look at Bran before walking away. I was almost to my tent when I heard Domhnall softly calling my name. I half-turned to see that he had left the fire as well.

"What is it?" I asked.

"I just wished to speak with you, is all," he replied, flashing me a soft smile. "Before you retired for the night."

I raised a brow, slightly thrown off by the request and wishing we were closer to the fire so that he wasn't bathed in darkness. "Is there something wrong?"

"No, nothing is wrong." He took my hand, closing the space between us. "I know things haven't gotten any easier for you, and you have handled this all admirably, but... I want to be there for you. I want to help you carry this burden."

"Domhnall..." I sighed, forcing back a groan. "You have helped me bear all of this, as my advisor and as my friend."

His grip on my hand tightened. "I know others might see it as wrong of me in light of my current position on the council, but I want more than that. I've always wanted more."

"I cannot give you more."

"But could you try? I know it is not as if my presence is distasteful to you."

"I cannot, Domhnall. I'm sorry." I shook my head, pulling free of his grasp and turning to leave, trying to ignore the quiver in the pit of my stomach. I valued his friendship, but I could not give him what he wanted. I didn't know how to make that clearer than I already had. Giving myself to him would be as much of a lie as giving myself to Evander. I didn't love him, not in that way.

"Wait." He latched onto my arm, turning me back around. "Seren, I love you. I've been waiting for you to be ready to hear it, but I can't hold this back anymore."

My stomach churned. I'd thought—hoped, rather—that we'd put this behind us. That whatever he felt for me, he would set it aside knowing that I didn't feel the same. I was married, for Spirits' sake. There was no romantic future for us.

"Domhnall. I value your friendship; I always have. But I cannot return something that I do not feel."

He clutched my arm even tighter, to the point that it began to hurt, and I yanked myself free of him.

"It's him, isn't it?" he said, disgust in his voice. "It's that damn shifter."

"Bran has nothing to do with this."

"You were a fool for him before. Are you truly going to be a fool for him again? Did you not learn your lesson when he abandoned you? He's not worthy of you and he's not to be trusted!"

One of my hands clenched into a fist at my side, my nostrils flaring. "You are very close to overstepping your bounds with your Ri. I have told you I cannot give you what you want. This conversation is over and I do not wish to have it again."

I went to turn away but he jumped in front of me, blocking my path and grabbing onto my upper arms.

"How can you say that when you've never even given me a fair chance!" he snapped. "I've been here this entire time. I never once betrayed you or abandoned you. Have I not done everything for you these last few months? How can you know you feel nothing for me if you won't even try?"

"I do not have to justify this to you. Let me go." I yanked one arm free, my hand going to the hilt of my dagger as part of me wished I'd had enough sense to bring one of the wolves on this journey with me. I'd never seen Domhnall be this forceful, not with me at least, and there was something about this side of him that put me on edge. Even with my hand on my blade, he didn't let go of me and my pulse quickened, my stomach growing hard.

In the faint light of the moon, I could tell that his eyes were overbright and his forearms were strained. "If you would listen to me—"

"I believe she told you to let her go."

Bran's voice had a threatening chill to it as he appeared out of the darkness, coming to stand close enough at my back that I could feel the heat of his body. Domhnall's face twisted in anger, but he abruptly released his hold on me.

"One day you're going to slip up and make a fatal mistake, shifter," Domhnall snarled. "And I hope that I'm there to see it."

He stalked off, slipping away into the darkness in the direction of his own tent. A shiver passed down my spine and I stepped forward on slightly wobbly legs, biting my lip as I turned to face Bran.

"Thank you," I said. "I'm sorry he spoke to you in such a way. I will make certain he and everyone else know that treating you in such a manner will not be tolerated." The words felt stiff as I tried to keep the necessary distance between us, tried to pretend that we were nothing more than a Ri and a warrior.

"Has he done that before?" Bran asked, an edge still in his voice and his jaw tight. "Pushed himself on you like that?"

"Not like that, no." I fidgeted with the hilt of my dagger, not quite able to meet his gaze.

"I know you trust him, but be careful around him, Ren."

Not so long ago, I would have shrugged him off and reminded him that while Domhnall had a mercurial temperament, he was trustworthy, but tonight's interaction had shaken me as well. It had unnerved me, how forceful Domhnall had gotten and I was beginning to wonder if I had been the one who had been a fool to trust him.

I cleared my throat, shifting my weight where I stood. "Was there something you needed?"

"Was just walking to my tent and heard raised voices. I just wanted to make sure you were alright."

There was a twinge in my chest, a longing to believe that he did still care about me. The wounded part of me still shied away, but I'd be lying if I said that I didn't wish to believe him when he said he still loved me. In the end, however, the wounded part of my heart was what won.

"I'm fine, thank you," I said. "We've a long ride tomorrow. Goodnight, Bran."

"Sleep well, Ren." His voice was soft, tinged with a bit of longing that threatened to undo me.

I ignored it, turning on my heel and walking off to my tent. Spirits, these next few days would be long ones, being forced to be in such close proximity to him. It had been easier to avoid him, easier to forget what we'd once had, at Clogwyn. I'd get no such luxury here.

You've a job to do, I reminded myself as I ducked through the canvas flap of my tent. *A servant of a Dark Spirit to hunt down so that you can protect your people.* I couldn't afford to be distracted by any stubborn, lingering feelings for Bran. As I shed the two cloaks I'd been wearing and kicked off my boots, my gaze fell on Rhonwen's bow, carefully wrapped and propped up against my saddlebags in a corner. It was a silent reminder that I had a vow to keep, above all else.

CHAPTER 16

WOLF'S BLOOD

Bran

We reached Sionnach the following day, the sun beginning to set as we rode into the village. To my relief, Domhnall had kept his distance from Seren; or rather, she had kept her distance from him and he'd been wise enough not to push his luck. I hadn't cared for what I had witnessed last night. I wished more than anything that Seren had never made him her chief advisor, but it was too late for that now.

As we rode past the rubble and wreckage that had been left in the wake of the fire, Copar let out a sharp snort and I stroked the blood bay gelding's neck in reassurance. Lewella had insisted I travel in my human form for this journey, not wanting to alarm the villagers with the presence of a shifter with the rumors tying the fires to a rogue shapeshifter. Of course, the rumors *were* true; the people of Blaidd just wanted to hold the wrong shifter at fault.

The homes around us had been reduced to blackened soot and ash, with not an animal or human in sight. The shadows gave the village even more of a disconcerting air in the descending darkness. The scene, the smell, and the eerie silence brought back far too many unpleasant memories. I had witnessed too many scenes like this one for far too long. We had to find Alannah, and soon.

When we reached the village square, it was clear that it had not been spared, the ground scorched and burned. Only the large granite standing stones around it had withstood the flames. A lone trio of villagers, one of whom I assumed was the village elder, awaited us in the middle of the square, their expressions grim. Tudwal called for us to bring our horses to a halt and I was quick to swing off Copar, pushing my way through the rest of the warriors. If I was to hunt for any sign of Alannah, I needed to hear what the villagers had to say.

To my surprise, Seren called my name before motioning for me to join her, Tudwal, and Domhnall. When I reached them, I handed Copar off to one of the nearest warriors at Tudwal's instructions. Domhnall scowled at me, his posture rigid.

"Do you truly think it wise to involve the shifter in this conversation, Ri Seren?" he asked.

"Yes," she replied, her tone sharp. "Though you can consider your concern noted."

Domhnall huffed but Seren ignored him, squaring her shoulders before walking off toward the villagers. The three of us followed behind her and I was careful to try and keep Tudwal between me and Domhnall. I didn't want to be any closer to the petulant advisor than absolutely necessary.

When we reached the villagers, a woman who looked to be in her mid-forties gave Seren a respectful nod, though her expression remained chilly. Her two older male companions followed suit, but neither of them looked any happier to see us.

"I was deeply concerned to hear of the fire here, Elder Ceinwen," Seren said. "Please know that whatever you and the people of Sionnach need will be at your disposal. I have brought a healer from Castle Clogwyn with my party and he is able to remain here as long as you need him. Warriors will also remain behind to help you with rebuilding."

"Your healer is irrelevant," Ceinwen replied. "Though there is much rebuilding to be done. The people of Sionnach have lost everything and worse than that, they are left to fear that this may happen again."

Seren worked her jaw before taking a deep breath. I couldn't blame her for her frustration. We were hardly being met with a warm welcome, despite Seren personally coming to see how the people of Sionnach fared and offer them aid; it was far more than Cadfael would have ever done.

"Rest assured that I will do everything within my power to bring an end to this darkness and ease the people of Blaidd's suffering," Seren replied. "The healer that has come with us is skilled, I assure you of that. He can help ease the burden of your village healers after such a tragedy."

"Again, there is no need. We have no wounded left in Sionnach now."

Seren's face paled and my own stomach clenched.

"You lost them?" Seren asked, a slight break in her voice. "All of them?"

"No," Ceinwen answered, lifting her chin. "They have already been healed."

Seren's brow furrowed and Tudwal cocked his head. My own chest tightened as I tried to make sense of the elder's words. There was no gifted healer in Sionnach, as least as far as anyone at Clogwyn knew. And even if there was, even a gifted healer on their own surely couldn't have so quickly healed the wounds of an entire village after such a fire. I'd spent enough time with Aengus and Cian to know the limitations of such power.

"Healed by who?" I asked.

Domhnall gave me a dark look as Ceinwen turned her attention to me. "By a healer. One of the gifted. He was traveling this way with his companion and upon seeing the devastation, he gave the people of Sionnach his aid."

"And what was this man's name?" Domhnall asked.

"His name was Aengus." Ceinwen's gaze slowly drifted back to Seren, her expression growing hard. "And he is the rightful Ri of Blaidd."

I felt as if I had been punched in the gut. There were more men named Aengus than the one I had called friend, but it was far too similar to ignore in the present circumstances. But what would have he been doing here? And what in the blazes would cause him to make such outlandish claims.

"Whatever claims this man may have made," Seren said, a slight tremble in her hands as she fidgeted with the clan ring, "they cannot have been true."

"I know what I saw with my own eyes." Ceinwen folded her arms, drawing herself up. "And I know you are not the last of the blood of the line of Blaidd."

"You would be wise to watch your tongue in front of your Ri," Domhnall snapped.

"The Ri who continues to let my people suffer?" Ceinwen retorted.

Domhnall's face reddened, one of his hands curling into a fist as he opened his mouth, but Seren took a firm hold of his wrist, never breaking her gaze on Ceinwen.

"I am doing everything I can to end this and ease the people's suffering," Seren said. "And I swear to you that I will continue to do so. That is why we are here."

Tudwal cleared his throat. "What of this man's companion?"

"A woman." Ceinwen shrugged. "Traveling north with him."

"What did she look like?" I asked, a sinking feeling in the pit of my stomach.

"Tall, red hair," Ceinwen answered. "She didn't give a name, but they weren't here long. They had business to attend to elsewhere."

My gaze darted to Seren, the two of us sharing an uneasy glance as a coldness settled in my core. Alannah had been here, and she had brought Fianna's darkness with her. Had Aengus truly thrown his lot in with the likes of her? And why? It wasn't like him, not in the least. Lorcan had tried to recruit him to the Stag Spirit's side countless times, and Aengus had always firmly rebuffed him.

"My warriors will wish to check the area for any signs of Fianna's servants," Seren said. "We will remain here for at least a day, perhaps more, depending on what your people need. We'll camp outside the village. I don't want to impose on the people of Sionnach any more than we have to. When we do depart this place, my healer will remain here for at least seven days' time in case you have need of him."

Ceinwen gave a curt nod, her lips pinched. "Very well, Ri Seren."

We left Ceinwen and her companions behind, Seren motioning to me as we strode back over to the rest of the warriors, all of whom had waited patiently at the edge of the square.

"I wish for Bran to scout the area in his wolf form to see what he can find of Alannah," Seren told Tudwal.

"I can have warriors go with him," Tudwal replied.

Seren gave me a questioning look, raising her brows, but I shook my head.

"I'll do better on my own," I said. "I can cover more ground that way. Though I appreciate the offer."

"Very well," Tudwal replied.

"Seren, should you really be sending the shifter out all on his own?" Domhnall asked, a crease marring his brows as he grimaced.

"Yes," Seren said with a hint of exasperation. "Bran is a better scout than anyone else here and knows Alannah far better than the rest of us," She paused, focusing on me. "You will report back to Tudwal, who will bring you to me to share what you have found."

I nodded, a little flutter of relief coursing through me at the instructions and the task she'd laid before me. She had some faith left in me, at least. "Understood."

"I'll leave Tudwal to discern how best to send you out without alarming the villagers," Seren said. "I suppose let's get us all settled for now."

"Yes, Ri Seren," Tudwal replied, giving her a respectful nod.

He began calling instructions to the warriors and my heart began to thrum with anticipation. Alannah had been here and I was going to find whatever clues she'd left behind. She and Fianna would be destroyed if it was the last thing I did. I only hoped that Aengus' innocent life wouldn't be destroyed in the process.

Tudwal made me wait until nightfall before venturing into the forest to begin my hunt for any signs of Alannah. While Sionnach itself was in a valley, it was surrounded by the tall, craggy peaks of the Coed mountains, giving Alannah plenty of places to hide.

While I didn't think I would actually find her—she would be smarter than to stick around after a fire—I hoped that with the heightened senses of my wolf form, I could find some evidence that she'd been here. I picked up a trot as I scaled one of the mountainsides, following a stream north to see just where it would take me. Alannah was no stranger to surviving in the wild and she would have stuck close to water.

All around me, I heard the night noises of the forest. An owl hooted in a nearby tree and the summer insects were singing a chorus of song as I padded along a few feet from the banks of the stream. I kept my nose to the wind, searching for any hint of Alannah's scent. The rain had passed over the valley, which meant that any lingering trail that Alannah or Aengus had left in their wake would be easier for me to find.

Seren and Lewella might not doubt Alannah's involvement, but others did. If I could find proof tonight, it would strengthen my story and my innocence. The thought pressed me onward into the darkness, helping me push back the fatigue that still lingered from our long journey.

And yet what of Aengus? The thought brought with it a tightness in my belly. I wanted to think there had been a mistake, that Ceinwen hadn't been remembering correctly or had heard the healer's name wrong. Or perhaps that Aengus had passed through here but Ceinwen had been wrong about his companion. Aengus was a healer at his core. He wouldn't have been able to pass by a suffering village and not lend his aid. But the pieces of the story didn't add up. I didn't want to think the worst of my friend, of the man who had saved my life not so long ago, but doubt warred within me.

Shaking my head, I pushed off thoughts of Aengus before scaling a small rocky outcrop. Alannah needed to be my focus right now. I reached the top of the slippery moss-covered rocks and hadn't gone much farther when I caught the faint scent. It was hers—days old, from what I could tell, but it was still there. Quickening my pace, I let the scent guide me through the dark forest. I dodged more rocks and fallen limbs, scrambled over the half-rotting trunk of a fallen tree, until I finally came to a small cave burrowed into a mountainside.

The scent was strong enough to tell me that she had been in this place. But there was another scent too, one that made my stomach turn: Aengus'. I sniffed around the cave, holding on to a faint hope that I could find more than just Alannah's scent to prove my story to Tudwal and Seren. The Spirits rewarded my diligence. Just outside the mouth of the cave, I found what I needed. A hawk feather lay on the forest floor, half hidden by a pair of lush ferns. I recognized its tawny red and white color and even if I hadn't, the scent coming off it confirmed just who the feather belonged to.

I carefully picked it up in my mouth before turning and taking off in a lope. I needed to get it back to Seren at once. One step closer to finding Alannah and one step closer to fully proving my innocence.

CHAPTER 17

SECRETS AND LOYALTIES
Seren

MY THOUGHTS HAD TRAVELED down many roads I would not have wished them to since hearing Ceinwen's chilling words. I fidgeted with the clan ring, running my thumb over the wolf's head engraving and sapphire gemstone that was set into the ancient gold, as I paced in the darkness. I'd hidden from the others since Tudwal had sent Bran off, not wanting the warriors to see the fear that had taken hold of me with a viselike grip. They already thought me weak, saw me as nothing compared to my father. I did not need to give them more reasons to see me as a Ri not worth following.

For months now, the Spirits had been whispering of the blood of the line of Blaidd. I should have seen this; I should have known. I'd seen the similarities between Aengus and my brother, Eamon, when Bran and I had been fleeing for our lives from Lorcan, and Aengus had taken us in. And yet, how did it fit? And what was he? A cousin, a sibling...

I shook my head, letting out a shaky breath. There were secrets here, ones I would have to uncover. It was possible Aengus, or even Ceinwen, could be lying, but deep in my gut, I felt a truth I didn't want to believe. Months ago, I had pressed Sioned about the possibility of another blood relation, only for her to deny it. But even then, I had feared that I had been lied to. This time, I wouldn't allow anyone to put me off so easily. There was another out there who carried the blood of the line of Blaidd. Whatever secrets my family had been hiding, I would get to the bottom of them. And if Aengus had indeed turned to darkness, I would react accordingly. For what other choice did I have?

The knot in my belly twisted itself tighter and a burning settled in my throat. More than anything, I wanted Ceinwen to have been mistaken. I could barely stomach the thought of Aengus as my enemy. Tudwal called to me from outside the tent and I started slightly before bidding him to enter.

He ducked through the canvas flap with Bran on his heels. While the handful of candles in my tent gave some light to the space, the two of them were still cast in shadows. Bran had flecks of dirt on his sleeves and pant legs and his hair was tousled, but something about his rich brown eyes ensnared me before I quickly looked away, focusing instead on Tudwal.

"Ri Seren," Tudwal said, giving me a nod of respect that Bran mirrored. "The shifter believes elder Ceinwen was telling the truth."

A heaviness took root in my chest as Tudwal motioned Bran forward.

"I picked up Alannah's scent at a cave a little over a mile from here," Bran said, fishing something out of his pocket. "I found this as well, along with traces of Aengus' scent."

I took the red and white hawk feather he offered me, feeling a flood of Fianna's darkness as I did so. I could not catch Alannah's scent the way that Bran could in his wolf form, but the feather was hers; I was certain of it. *And it's proof,* I thought as I surveyed it by the light of the fire. *Proof that even the council will be hard pressed to deny.*

"Well done," I told Bran before turning back to Tudwal. "You may leave us."

Tudwal's brow furrowed, his gaze flitting between the two of us before he gave another low nod.

"As you wish," he said, taking his leave.

Once he was gone, I took a few steps back, stowing the feather safely away in one of my packs. The darkness that oozed off it made my stomach roil, leaving me not wanting to keep hold of it any longer than necessary. When I straightened, I was careful to keep distance between me and Bran.

I hadn't wanted to discuss Aengus in front of Tudwal, not with the potential danger such talk had the power to bring. While Tudwal had been nothing but respectful over the course of our journey, I couldn't be certain where his loyalties lay. I wasn't blind to my unpopularity and if Aengus and I did share the same blood, that in and of itself was a threat. Especially in light of how quickly Aengus had won over the people of Sionnach. I wasn't even certain I should trust Bran with such talk, but he was the only one here who knew Aengus as I did.

"What did you find of Aengus?" I asked.

"His scent, nothing more," Bran answered. "Though there were traces of Fianna's darkness in that place."

I forced myself to take a deep breath, even as my heart beat hard enough to leave a slight ache in my chest. "How deep did Aengus' loyalties to Lorcan run?"

"Aengus never had any loyalty to Lorcan," Bran said with a firm shake of his head. "He aided Lorcan with his gifting out of his sense of duty, nothing more. I know for a fact that on more than one occasion, Lorcan tried to pull Aengus into his band, but Aengus soundly rebuffed him every time. I knew him, Ren. I just don't see it."

"I do not wish to think such dark things of Aengus, but I cannot ignore tidings such as this. And men will do foolish things for love. Or what they mistakenly believe is such."

Bran clenched his jaw, working it for a moment before letting out a long, low breath. "I know the power she can wield, not to mention how relentless she can be when it comes to getting what she wants, and I understand his presence would be foolish to ignore, but he..." He trailed off, licking his lips and looking up to meet my gaze before continuing. "I would have died alone in those mountains after the creatures attacked me if it hadn't been for him. It doesn't make sense. Why would he have saved me if he was serving Fianna?"

The knot in my belly twisted itself a few more times. It *didn't* make sense. None of it did. Why was Aengus claiming himself to be the rightful Ri of Blaidd? Why would he have thrown his lot in with a being like Fianna? He wasn't a fool. He would know the cost of giving his soul to such a being.

"I don't know," I said with a heavy sigh. "But I'm afraid there is no choice but to find out. And if he has been ensnared by Alannah and Fianna..."

I trailed off, not needing to finish. Bran knew what I could not bring myself to say. Fianna's servants could not be allowed to roam this land unchecked. Blaidd had suffered enough and the Stag Spirit had gained far too much ground as it was. The darkness that had spread through the land like a poison had to be ended, even if that meant striking against a man who might very well be my blood kin.

I cleared my throat, trying to regain some semblance of control over my runaway emotions. "While we remain here, I wish you to discern as much as you can about Aengus and Alannah's whereabouts and where you think they may have gone."

"Understood," he replied.

"That is all," I said, slightly angling myself away from him as an awkward tension crept back into the air.

I didn't know how to be around him anymore. The easiness that had once flowed so freely between us was gone. And now, no matter how much I longed for his comfort, I still feared I would wake up one day and he would be gone.

He took a step toward me, hesitantly reaching out as if to place a hand on my arm before dropping it. Letting out a low sigh, he rubbed the back of his neck before slowly looking up and meeting my gaze. The pain and uncertainty I saw in those amber brown depths mirrored my own.

"I don't know what to say, Ren. I don't know how to fix this, even though I want to. More than anything."

"Maybe some things aren't meant to be fixed." The words slipped from my lips before I could stop them. The hurt I'd harbored and let eat me from the inside for months had festered, and now there was no way of stopping it.

He looked as if I had struck him, his sharp intake of breath so loud that it seemed to fill the space between us. "You don't mean that."

My throat tightened and I bit down so hard on my lower lip that I tasted the metallic tang of blood. "I don't know how to go back to what we once had after all of this."

The tension that filled the air was thick, full of unspoken hurts and pain. It took everything within me not to meet his gaze, not to go to him and let him wrap me in his arms while I soaked up his strength. To let him hold me as I grappled with realities I didn't want to face. But in the end, I stayed where I was, my feet fused to the ground like stone. Finally, he gave me a stiff nod before brushing past me and walking off.

When he reached the tent flap, however, he paused. His back was still to me as he spoke, but there was a firmness, a resolution, to his tone that was impossible to ignore. I might have lost the fire within me to fight for us, but he clearly had not. "I will respect your wishes and give you your space. I will hope that one day perhaps you can forgive me for my actions, but you should know one thing: I am not leaving."

My breath caught as he ducked out of the tent and I blinked rapidly, tears stinging my eyes. Though I fought to deny it, I questioned if, before this was all over, I *would* need him again as I once had. The news of Aengus had shaken me to my core and I deeply feared facing this darkness alone.

CHAPTER 18

CROOKED PATHS
Aengus

TO MY RELIEF, THE events in Sionnach eased some of my persistent misgivings over the path I had chosen. I had helped the people, saved many of them from a painful death. What had Seren done for them in their time of need? True, their homes, crops, and livestock suffered for now, but soon, when I was Ri, I would put an end to all of that and Blaidd would once again prosper. I had seen the desperation in their eyes and the relief and adoration on their faces when I had healed them. They were ready for a new ruler, a strong one who would realize that there would be no future without Fianna.

There was a lightness to my steps as I neared the entrance to the hut, laden down with the herbs I had gathered from the surrounding woods over the course of the beautiful late summer afternoon. A strong breeze and the shade of the still green trees had kept the temperatures comfortable and I wanted to be prepared for the next time I was sent to heal my people. I could do much with my gift with Fianna's added power, but it still felt wise to have some of the more natural remedies at hand.

One of the creatures was lounging outside, lifting its head and briefly pinning me with its ember eyes as I stepped through the door. I didn't flinch this time when the creature looked at me. I was slowly becoming more used to the strange creatures, just as Alannah had said I would. I eased the door shut behind me, balancing the basket full of wild herbs and plants on one arm, only to start slightly when I turned back around.

Alannah was bent over our bed, stuffing a canvas bag full of clothes. Two of the creatures sat at her feet, their eyes blazing and their bodies practically vibrating with energy. When I walked up behind her, she started, placing a hand on her chest as she whirled around to face me.

"Aengus," she said, offering a nervous smile. "I didn't think you would be back so soon."

I slowly set the basket down on the rickety table we used for meals, my heart starting to pound and my palms starting to sweat. I hated this part of me, these fears buried so deep inside of me, always waiting for the opportunity to surface. It had taken years to teach myself how to become confident with my craft, to learn how to put people at ease in what were often their lowest moments. I had yet, however, to be able to fully bring that confidence to other aspects of my life. And it was moments like this, moments where my thoughts raced with all sorts of worrisome possibilities, that I was reminded of that the most. Where was she going? And why had she said nothing of it to me?

"What is going on?" I asked.

She let out a soft sigh, flipping her braid over her shoulder. "I must leave here for a little while with the creatures. Fianna has commanded it."

"Alone, you mean?"

"There would be nothing for you to do." She caught my hand, giving it a squeeze. "It's just that the creatures are growing restless here. The last fire has them anxious for more and it makes them difficult to control. Fianna only wishes for me to take them out into the mountains, let them burn a bit of wilderness to soothe them. Then I'll be back. It will only be a couple of days."

I had no reason to doubt her. I knew how difficult the creatures were to control. Fire was in their blood and they lived for releasing it. And still, my chest tightened as I stared down at her. Something felt off. Something I couldn't name or express, but felt all the same. A tingling in my arm made my muscles tighten and out of the corner of my eye, I saw the antler-shaped scar take on a glowing sheen.

You let these foolish fears rule you far too much, Son of Blaidd, Fianna hissed. *It is time for you to put them aside.*

"I could come with you," I said, though I immediately regretted it as the tingling in my arm turned into a burning pain that left me clenching my teeth, my hand curling into a fist.

She shook her head. "Fianna needs you here. With the way things are escalating, there's too much of a risk of someone finding this place. It needs you to stay behind, with one of the creatures to guard you."

"Do they not all need to go with you?"

"It's the oldest that Fianna has commanded to stay behind, the one with the most control." She motioned to the two fractious creatures at our feet. "These young ones will travel with me and by the time I return, they'll be much more manageable."

I forced myself to nod. She was stalwart in her plan and the burning in my arm served as a reminder of Fianna's displeasure with my worries and lack of confidence.

"Very well," I said, unable to suppress a soft sigh of relief as the pain in my arm vanished. "I understand."

She placed a hand on the side of my face, caressing my cheek as she gave me a slow smile. "I won't be gone long, I swear. A few days to get them deeper into the mountains so that they don't cause harm to any of the villagers."

Her touch and the soothing tone of her voice eased something deep inside me in the way that only she could. There was something about her and the power that coursed through her that drew me in over and over again. A sort of addiction, in a way, that was impossible to shake. I could not do this without her. I had to trust her, just as we both had to trust Fianna.

"I will be anxiously awaiting your return," I told her before lowering my head and capturing her lips in a kiss.

She wrapped her arms around my neck, pulling me close in a way that had me suspecting that her departure might become slightly delayed, not that I would have any complaints. I had to trust this path we were following, no matter how winding and crooked it became. Fianna was right in demanding I learn to cast aside my doubts and fears. I could not rule Blaidd with such weakness. The end would be worth it. I had to believe that.

CHAPTER 19

FATAL WOUND

Seren

DESPITE ALL MY WARRIORS had done to try and help the people of Sionnach rebuild, they appeared more than happy to see our party depart for Castle Clogwyn. Whatever Aengus had done to enchant them all, he had done it thoroughly. Though in truth, I doubted I'd ever had their loyalty, not with the half-truths my father had spread about me and the tumultuous circumstances surrounding me taking the title of Ri. But one thing was for certain: I did not have their loyalty now. Those thoughts in particular plagued me as our horses galloped down the road leading south. I was anxious to get back to Clogwyn, to press my mother and Sioned about Aengus' claims, but even the fleetest horse could not make the journey in one day alone.

The sun was setting on the horizon, behind the distant peaks of the Dail mountains, and underneath me, I could feel Ceol's growing fatigue with every stride. We would not scale the Dail tonight, instead stopping in the nearby village of Traeth to rest before continuing on in the morning. I hoped our welcome in Traeth would be warmer than the one we'd had in Sionnach, but I wasn't holding my breath.

I smelled the smoke first before the village came into view, my stomach churning at the all too familiar acrid scent. Tudwal shouted for our company to stop, our horses sliding to halts, their heads lifted high in alarm as we got our first look at the glowing flames. The cries of the villagers rang out in the air and I looked on in horror as the fire licked its way from building to building. Darkness swirled in the air, so thick it felt as if it choked me as much as the smoke. Fianna was here and where there was fire, there were its creatures. *Which means Alannah as well,* I thought, my stomach hardening.

"Take the warriors and help the villagers put out the fire," I told Tudwal. "Bran will be coming with me."

"Ri, Seren," he replied, his tone deep with disapproval. "I do not think that wise for you to be—"

"Fianna's creatures are here," I said, "and they will not be allowed to leave this place alive. Not while I have the means to destroy them."

I didn't wait for him to answer, untying Rhonwen's bow, which was strapped to my saddle. The bow was the only thing that could kill the shadow creatures, and the finicky weapon could be choosy about who wielded it. So far, it had thankfully always responded to me. I located Bran, motioning him over to me. He maneuvered Copar through the group of warriors, Tudwal calling commands to them, trotting the gelding up to Ceol's side.

"Go ahead and shift," I told him. "And be on the lookout for her. We have creatures to hunt."

The two of us dismounted. We'd have an easier time on foot. The horses of the Ri's stable were trained to be bold and brave, but even the bravest of mounts struggled when it came to dealing with the creatures from the Spirit Realm.

I grabbed the quiver that matched Rhonwen's bow, turning back around in time to see Bran morph from the form of a man to that of a large grey wolf. At this point, the oddity was hardly alarming to me. I yelled for a warrior to see to our horses and then raced off into the smoke, Bran at my side.

While Bran couldn't kill the creatures in his wolf form, he could wound them—not to mention his skills at tracking. If anyone could find Alannah in this chaos, he could. My chest ached as we rushed past the burning buildings and panicked livestock. Once again, my people were losing everything. The smoke stung my eyes, making them water as I scanned the area for any sign of the creatures. A bark from Bran drew my focus and I looked over just in time to see him take off toward a burning barn.

My pulse quickened and I followed after him, yanking an arrow from my quiver. The barn was already half destroyed, the building creaking and groaning as the flames engulfing it climbed higher. It appeared that the occupants had gotten out, though my heart hurt for what had already been lost. Bran was a grey blur amidst the smoke, following something only he could see and smell, but as we raced around the back side of the house, I saw it too. A pair of glowing ember eyes stood out in the hazy air and an eldritch hiss that made the hair on the back of my neck rise reached my ears.

The creature sprung at Bran, its fangs bared. I nocked my arrow, loosing it at the creature. It feinted to the right, keeping me from making a killing blow, though my arrow still connected with its shoulder. It shrieked in rage, turning its attention to me. Bran was quick to distract it, snapping at its side and giving me the opportunity to nock another arrow. With the beast focused on Bran, I loosed again, this time striking true to its heart. The creature faltered, its choking, rageful cry making me want to cover my ears as it collapsed to the ground. *One less,* I thought. *Now to find the rest.*

As Bran trotted back over to my side and I couldn't stop the slight worry that filled me, I scanned him for any sign of injury, relieved to see none. The familiarity of this, of together fighting Fianna and its creatures, was enough to chase away my lingering bitterness toward him. There was no space for it in a moment like this one. Not when we were fighting for our lives. Another screech filled the air, my thoughts interrupted by two more creatures barreling toward us.

Bran launched himself at the first creature, drawing it away from me. It took everything in me to focus on the creature still left instead of worrying over him, but I had to trust that he could hold his own. My first arrow didn't land where I wished, grazing the creature's hindquarters as it maneuvered away with its unnatural speed. I had wounded it, caused black blood to drip from its smoky body, but it was far from defeated.

I dodged out of its way as it sprung at me, its bloody fangs narrowly missing my thigh. I nocked a second arrow. This one at least embedded itself in the lower part of the creature's ribcage. It limped heavily, its eyes still burning bright with rage as I nocked yet a third arrow. But before I could loose it, the creature darted off, stumbling into the burning barn.

My heart pounded as I glanced over at Bran, still tangling with the remaining creature. I had no desire to let the wounded creature get away, especially not when it was so close to death, but neither did I want to leave Bran on his own. Still, there were no signs of him being injured as he grappled with the remaining creature. If anything, the creature looked far worse for the wear than Bran did. He knew the shadow creatures well after his time serving Lorcan. They were formidable foes, but no stranger to him.

Ripping my gaze away, I made my decision in a split second, bolting off into the barn. I would kill the creature inside and then hurry back to finish off what Bran had started. The building groaned as I entered it and the thick smoke made me cough. One look at the charred, flaming walls told me I could not afford to linger in here long.

Half-blinded by smoke, I searched for the creature, trying to avoid popping embers. Soon, I spotted it, hidden behind what had been a stall. It still stood on unsteady legs, black blood dripping from its side, but it had lost none of its fury, shrieking and snapping at me as I drew near. Something creaked loudly above me but I ignored it, hastily nocking an arrow and loosing it. This time it hit true, catching the creature right in the center of its chest. Black blood spurted from the fatal wound and the creature fell to the ground in a heap of smoke and ash.

A creaking groan came from above again and I turned around, bolting for what remained of the door. I needed to move fast—not only for my own safety, but for Bran's as well. I'd taken only a few strides forward when the groaning above me turned into a heavy crash. There was a blow to the back of my head, a burning in my hand, and then it all went dark.

CHAPTER 20

TO HER DOOM
Bran

I DIDN'T THINK WHEN I saw the barn beginning to crumble. I just ran. Seren was in there. The building creaked and groaned all around me and the smoke stung my eyes as I stumbled through the burning building, searching for any sign of Seren. Sparks flew and fell through the air, the flames turning the wood into blackened, charred sticks. With the smoke, it was difficult to pick up Seren's distinct scent and my heart thrummed in my chest, fear gripping me at the thought that I might not find her. And Spirits help me if there were more creatures in here. I narrowly dodged a falling piece of wood, feeling the heat from the flames.

I saw her hair first, her sooty blond braid just visible behind a fallen beam. I quickened my pace, racing over to her. At first, I thought she was dead, but the shallow rise and fall of her chest soon assured me that she was only unconscious. A dead shadow creature, an arrow sticking out of its hide, lay a few feet from her, slowly disintegrating into a pile of ash.

Above us, there was an unnerving creaking groan. I needed to move quickly. I grabbed Seren by the back of her cloak, praying that the strong silver clasp at her neck would hold and not break. I began to drag her backward but stopped when my gaze fell on Rhonwen's bow. Seren must have dropped it when the beam hit her. I couldn't leave it here, not when it was the only way of defeating the creatures, but I'd be damned if I left Seren either.

Releasing my hold on Seren, I bounded over to the bow and picked it up with my teeth. The trouble was, I couldn't both carry it and drag her. There was hardly time to come up with a good choice, and I ended up slipping her arm through it before folding that same arm across her chest to try and hold the bow in place. Running back around behind her, I latched onto her cloak and resumed pulling.

With each step I took, my muscles quivered. The thick smoke made it almost impossible to see and the barn's groaning grew even louder. There were more loud crashes as wood continued to crumble around us, but I forced myself to press on. We weren't dying like this. Not if I had anything to say about it.

The first brush of cool air at my back gave me a much-needed burst of energy. I let out a growl, tugging even harder as I continued dragging Seren across the ground. A quick glance over my shoulder told me we had reached what remained of the barn's entrance. I dug into the last bit of strength I had and with a few more strong tugs, freed us from what had almost become our fiery prison.

I continued dragging Seren, even once we were free of the flames, wanting us as far away from the building as possible before it came down. *Just a few more steps,* I told myself, trying to ignore my panting as I half stumbled in the charred grass.

Two more strong tugs and I released my grip on her, just as the burning barn gave a loud rumble before crashing in on itself.

"Ri Seren!"

The shout made me start and I looked to my left to see Tudwal and another warrior running up. From what I could see, the fire had begun to slowly burn itself out and there were no more signs of Fianna's creatures. I shifted, though the transformation left me feeling weak and slightly lightheaded. It drained me each time I shifted and I'd already pushed my body close to its breaking point in getting Seren out of the burning building.

"She was unconscious when I found her," I told Tudwal as he crouched down beside me.

Tudwal felt for Seren's pulse, his expression grim. A hacking cough tore from my lungs, leaving me doubling over as my body protested the copious amounts of smoke I'd inhaled. Tudwal released Seren's wrist and I got my first good look at the burns covering her left hand. My stomach clenched. We'd left the healer who had traveled with us in Sionnach and we were still a full day's ride away from Castle Clogwyn.

"We'll get her to the village healer," Tudwal said, getting to his feet and motioning a warrior over. "The fire is getting under control and the creatures seem to have vanished."

"I'm coming with you," I replied, straightening as well.

Tudwal cast me a sidelong glance. "I suppose you could use a healer yourself."

I could only imagine what I looked like, covered in soot and ash, along with minor cuts and scrapes that I'd earned battling the shadow creatures. Bits of the creatures' poison had leeched into my body, some of my wounds having a distinct burning sensation, but I had survived worse. Tudwal took Rhonwen's bow before instructing a warrior to pick Seren up and carry her. Though I wanted to argue that I could carry her to wherever we were going, my growing lightheadedness made me all too aware that I wasn't in any shape to do so. Tudwal was right: I probably did need to be seen by a healer.

Trudging along behind the warrior carrying Seren, I worked to try and take deep breaths despite the ache in my lungs. Seren was a fighter. She'd survived a direct attack from a shadow creature; she would survive this. As we passed the charred-out husks of buildings, many of them still smoldering, my thoughts shifted to Alannah. If the creatures had disappeared, then Alannah was most likely gone as well. I doubted she would have mastered Lorcan's skill of commanding the capricious beings from afar in a few months' time. She would have been forced to go where they went to keep control of them. *At least there's a few less for her to command now,* I thought, my gaze flitting to Rhonwen's bow, which Tudwal carried with an appropriate amount of respect and care.

Our victory was a small one. I was reminded of that as we walked the ruined streets of Traeth. There wasn't much of the village that had been spared and all around me, I was met with desperate, frightened faces. After Lorcan and Cadfael had died, I'd hoped to never see such destruction again. It angered and disturbed me that there seemed no end to it. *And that creature came far too close to leading Seren to her doom,* I thought, my gaze once again falling on the unconscious form of my wife as another cough ripped from me. It gnawed at me, the things unsaid between us, how I had hurt her, just as it frightened me that she might be ready to give up on us. And yet at the same time, she'd trusted me enough to have me at her side as we'd faced Fianna's monsters. I wouldn't lose her. I couldn't. Not like this.

CHAPTER 21

CLOUDED VISION

Seren

I AWOKE TO A painful burning sensation in my left hand, a throbbing head, and an aching chest. It took my eyes a few moments to adjust to the dim darkness, the two candles on the other side of the room not offering much light. The room was both small and unfamiliar. I sat up halfway in the narrow bed, unable to suppress a groan.

There was movement to my right and a shadowed figure whirled around. It was Domhnall, which meant I wasn't among the enemy. I remembered the fire and running into the barn after the creature, but little else.

"You're awake," Domhnall said, walking over to my bedside.

There was something in his tone, a hint of displeasure, and in the set of his shoulders that left me with a niggle of unease. Something had shifted between us that night on the road, and not for the better.

"The fire? The warriors and the villagers? Rhonwen's bow?" I asked, pushing myself to sit up more despite the sharp, stinging pain in my hand. I glanced down at it, now covered in thick cream-colored bandages. Clearly, I had not come out of my fight with the shadow creature unscathed. Another mark on my body from this unending battle with Fianna, it seemed.

"The bow is in safekeeping and the fire is out," Domhnall answered. "The injuries the warriors sustained were largely minor. Only a few of them lost their lives. Tudwal has had any available warriors helping the villagers with the damages and seeing to their dead. I can say that the welcome we've received here has been far better than what we received in Sionnach."

He didn't bother to veil the disgust in his voice when he spoke of the far northern village. I wasn't exactly pleased with what had transpired in Sionnach, but I also found that I didn't care for his clear disdain. The villagers of Sionnach were still my people. I still owed them my protection and care as Ri, whether they cared for me or not. *And I have failed them,* I thought, worrying my lower lip. The only promise I'd kept to the people of Blaidd had been outlawing the hunting of shifters, but the people were still losing their lives and their homes to Fianna's darkness.

"Where exactly are we?" I asked, covering my mouth with my arm as I coughed and using my good hand to rub my aching chest.

"The village healer's home. He's been tending you since Tudwal had you brought here yesterday afternoon."

"A full day has passed?" I grimaced; Spirits only knew what I'd missed in my unconscious state.

"Not quite. It is not yet dawn."

"And Bran?" My chest tightened at my last memories I had of him battling one of Fianna's creatures. He could be dead now, for all I knew.

Domhnall's lip curled before he crossed his arms and looked away, staring intently at the room's one hide-covered window. "You were asking for him. Almost all night."

"He is my husband," I said, my voice hard even as I felt my cheeks flush slightly.

Domhnall's features twisted into a scowl. "So he is."

"I am asking you how he has fared."

Domhnall didn't answer at first, his eyes cold as he stiffly rolled his shoulders.

"I am asking you as your Ri, Domhnall," I said, narrowing my eyes.

"He's alive," he replied, his tone flat.

I slumped back against the pillows, letting out a breath of relief. Bran was still here, with me. No Spirit had escorted his soul from this realm to the next; not this time. Another cough erupted from my chest, making me wince. I'd clearly inhaled far too much smoke in the burning building.

"I should let the healer know you're awake," Domhnall said, his gaze still slightly averted.

A tense silence filled the air, almost as if he were waiting for me to say something, but I was weary. I didn't have the energy to deal with his petulance. Muttering under his breath, he turned and let himself out of the room. As soon as he was gone, I swung my legs over the side of the bed, unsteadily getting to my feet. I needed to see to my people.

At some point, my no doubt ruined clothes had been exchanged for a clean pair I'd brought with me in my saddlebags. I didn't see my boots anywhere, meaning I'd have to go on a hunt for them. Drawing a deep breath, I took a few steps, grumbling at how woefully unsteady I was. The throbbing headache I'd awoken with only increased with each step I took. I sighed in frustration. I didn't have time for this.

I'd only made it a few, uneven steps away from the bed when there came a knock at the door. I started so badly, I almost tumbled over, barely managing to grab onto the back of a chair to steady myself. In doing so, I hit my injured hand and the stinging, sharp pain made me hiss. I called for my visitor to enter, only to have my words cut off by another bout of coughing.

The door creaked open, revealing an older man, laden with a bag of what looked like healing supplies and carrying a basin of water. The healer, I presumed. He frowned as he stepped into the room, closing the door behind him.

"Ri Seren," he said. "I must insist you return to bed. I'm afraid you're not well enough to be up yet."

"I have things I must see to." I shrugged him off. "I must see to the villagers, and my warriors—"

"I do not mean to downplay your importance," the healer replied, speaking slowly as if choosing his words with care. "But Warrior Tudwal has had things well in hand. The people of Traeth are grateful for him and for your timely arrival. You have sustained considerable injury during the fighting. As a healer, I must insist that for now, you rest."

I closed my eyes, taking in a deep breath as I tried to stifle my mounting frustration. I loathed to admit it, but he was right. I *had* been injured, whether I liked it or not. With a heavy sigh, I shuffled back over to the bed.

"Please tell my advisor that I wish for him and Tudwal to speak with me as soon as possible, so that I can get a better assessment of the situation," I said, awkwardly crawling back into bed mindful of my injured hand. Spirits forbid I brush it against anything with the fiery pain that followed.

"I will make certain that message is passed on," the healer replied.

He pulled a chair over to my bedside, rummaging around in his bag before turning his attention to my bandaged hand. I hissed again as he unwrapped it, despite the care he took. The skin underneath was red and weeping, burns covering my hand and working their way up to my wrist. My stomach tightened. I could ride one-handed, but I'd hardly be able to fight, much less draw a bow. Spirits help me if we ran into any more of Fianna's creatures on the remainder of our journey back to Clogwyn.

"This will hurt," the healer said before passing me a flask of what I assumed was some sort of spirits.

Nodding grimly, I took it from him and took a large swallow. Over the years, I'd assisted Cian with tending to burns enough times to know it wasn't going to be pleasant. Pain radiated up my arm as the healer began to clean the burns and I ground my teeth, fighting to keep quiet despite the pain, but before too long, a few muttered curses in Old Pernish escaped my lips. My shoulders sagged in relief when he was finally finished. He applied a salve, the concoction blessedly soothing, before carefully wrapping my hand once more in soft linen bandages.

"You're very lucky those burns didn't travel farther," he said as he tied off the last of the cloth. "It's a good thing our Tiarna got to you when he did."

My brow furrowed slightly, my heart lurching at the mention of Bran. "How has he fared?"

"He was not unscathed, but he has healed quickly. His injuries were minor compared to yours." The healer started to get up but paused, clearing his throat. "It was valiant thing he did, pulling you and the bow from that barn. And it has not gone unnoticed by the people of Traeth."

He got up and gave me a respectful nod, gathering his things before seeing himself out. It appeared I had Bran to thank for my saving life, and for keeping Rhonwen's bow from perishing in Fianna's flames. Had I been too harsh on him since he'd returned? Even a village healer, it seemed, could see something honorable in him, even after the long months of him being painted as a traitor to the people of Blaidd. I had been nothing but unkind to him and in return, he had selflessly risked his life for me.

Using my good hand to fidget with the corner of one of the blankets, I swallowed against the thickness in my throat as Bran's haunting accusations from not so very long ago in the dark of the dungeons came back to me. I didn't want to be my father. I didn't want to let anger and bitterness poison me as it had done to him, but as I sat in the dimly lit room, it was harder to lie to myself about how little of my father's tendencies I truly possessed. I *had* let my bitterness fester since Bran's disappearance. And it had colored my actions, whether I wished to admit it or not.

I bit my lip and my chin dipped. Once again, Bran had saved my life at great peril to his own. What else did I want from him? Even if I still shied away at the thought of completely giving him my heart again, it wasn't fair to keep treating him so poorly and pushing him away. He had admitted to his mistakes and asked for my forgiveness. Was it truly fair to him to keep denying him that? How much had I let my hurt cloud my vision and keep me from seeing things clearly?

And was this not what I wanted? I thought, an uncomfortable feeling in the pit of my stomach. *The people of Blaidd learning to accept shifters. Learning to see them as people and not the monsters Father painted them as?* I'd done nothing but reinforce that narrative these last few months, pushed and goaded by the council to do so while my anger had left me willing to oblige. Shame made the back of my neck heat and I was glad I was alone in the little room as I wrestled with my guilt.

Bran had made a mistake, yes, but what servant of Fianna would have saved not only me, but the clan's only weapon against it? There was no reason for him to continue to be treated like the enemy. I needed to come to terms with my own hurt and stop lashing out at him instead. He deserved that much.

Chapter 22

A Trial of Trust

Bran

I WAS DESPERATE TO see Seren. Tudwal had given me news of how she fared, but it still wasn't the same as seeing her myself. I'd had half a mind to barge into the healer's home and demand that I be allowed to check on her, especially when I'd heard that Domhnall had already visited her twice now, but I was uncomfortably aware that even saving Seren's life hadn't been enough to banish the suspicion that the other warriors, even Tudwal, held for me.

It was early morning, the sun just breaking over the Dail, and like the rest of the warriors, I was readying myself for a day of helping the villagers tend to their dead and their ruined homes. The fire had spared nothing and reminders of the blaze were everywhere one looked: in blackened skeletons of buildings, soot-covered stone, and the haggard faces of the villagers.

I was seated around a fire with the other warriors, in front of the small circle of tents where we'd set up camp, within walking distance of the village square. As the others talked with one another over their breakfast, I'd been left to sit a little away from them, shoveling down the thick porridge we were having for breakfast. I'd earned myself some begrudging respect from the villagers for my efforts to save Seren, but my actions had done little to impress the warriors of Blaidd. Not that I was completely surprised. Most of them had been loyal to Cadfael and they didn't much care for Seren or shifters.

"Bran!"

When I heard Tudwal calling me, I hurriedly shoveled down the last few bites of my porridge. He pushed his way through the huddle of warriors, making his way over to me.

"Yes?" I replied.

"Ri Seren wishes to see you."

My heart leapt and I bolted to my feet. "She's improved, then?"

"The healer believes she will be ready to travel again in a few days," he answered.

I took my empty bowl back to the cook, then hurried to follow along behind Tudwal. As we left our camp to enter the village, making our way down the narrow streets to the healer's home, my palms started to sweat. I didn't know exactly where Seren and I stood with one another, or what my reception would be, but I was anxious to see her. I'd come too close to losing her in that burning barn.

The healer met us at the door, ushering us inside. His home was simple and carried the pungent scent of herbs, a smell I'd long ago begun to associate with Aengus. There was a twinge in my chest at the thought of my friend. There'd been no sign of him here, during or after the fire, and I'd allowed myself the small hope that maybe he hadn't gotten tangled up in Alannah and Fianna's tangled web of darkness after all.

"This way," the healer said, motioning for me to follow him.

I did so, Tudwal staying behind in the slightly cramped great room. It wasn't a far walk, no more than a few feet to the room in which Seren awaited me. The healer left me at the door and I took a deep breath before entering. She was sitting up in bed, the sunlight streaming in behind her and casting her in a soft golden glow. Her left hand was bandaged and my chest tightened at the sight of it. I'd never forget finding her in that barn, or the terrifying split second of fearing that she was dead.

She turned her head toward me, clearing her throat. "You have my thanks, for what you did. For me and for Rhonwen's bow."

For a moment, I stood in stunned silence, blinking rapidly. While I might have hoped for it, as cold and mistrustful as she'd been of me, her gratitude wasn't what I had been expecting.

"You don't have to thank me for that," I said, shaking my head. "I would never leave you to die, Ren."

She swallowed hard. "I know that things have been... difficult between us since you returned." She paused, smoothing the blankets that covered her and staring intently at them for a moment before looking back up at me. "I've reacted harshly, too harshly. The least I can do is offer you a chance."

My breath caught and I slowly took a few steps closer to her. I wanted nothing more than to wrap her in my arms and kiss her the way I had longed to for months, but she wasn't ready for that now. She was barely ready to attempt trusting me again. I flexed one of my hands, forcing my racing heart to calm. I had to take this slowly for her—for us.

"I recognize that I've broken your trust," I said, holding her gaze. "And I realize that I've done a poor job of showing it, but I never stopped loving you. I never will."

I paused, noticing the way she'd clenched the blankets tightly with her good hand, her shoulders tense. *Not too fast*, I reminded myself. *You can't be pushing her right now.*

"I understand you might not feel the same way after all that's happened," I softly finished. "I can respect that. All I'm asking for is a chance."

She brushed back a few loose strands of her hair, her forehead wrinkling before she gave a slow nod. "I can give you that."

Hope filled me, making my chest feel light. Once again, I was left pushing back the impulsive urge to take things further. But I'd just gotten her to consider trusting me again. I didn't need to go and ruin it. A knock at the door startled us both, breaking the precious moment of intimacy that had sprung between us. Seren called for her visitor to enter and I couldn't stop myself from tensing when Domhnall stepped into the room.

"I've spoken with the village elder," he said, brushing past me as if I weren't even there. "I just wished to report to you on what all was said."

"Thank you, Domhnall," Seren replied before her gaze briefly flitted back to me. "That will be all for now, Bran. Thank you."

The last thing I wanted to do was leave her, but I recognized her dismissal. I'd made progress, but there was still much trust to rebuild before I was once again able to stand at her side as her devoted Tiarna of Blaidd. I gave her a respectful nod, my gaze lingering on her, allowing myself a few moments to drink her in, before I turned and left. My steps were a bit lighter as I rejoined Tudwal in the healer's great room. Seren was willing to give me, give us, another chance and I would be damned if I ruined things this time.

CHAPTER 23

HEART'S YEARNING
Seren

I CONSENTED TO STAY in Traeth for another full day, but by the end of it, despite the healer's protests, I would not be dissuaded from leaving the following morning. I needed to return to Clogwyn. Lewella needed to know of what we had seen and what we had learned so that plans could be made. My burned hand was still in poor shape, but Cian would be at the castle and with his gift, he would be able to finish healing my hand, along with the damage to my lungs.

As I watched the warriors around me ready their horses, I cradled my bandaged hand against my chest. The rising sun was burning off the light mist that had settled on the ground the night before. There was no longer any trace of the encampment the warriors had called home for the past two days, though behind me, the scars of Fianna's fire could clearly be seen all over the village. I had promised Traeth's elder that I would send him more warriors once I reached the castle, but even I knew it wasn't enough. Nothing would be enough until the fires finally ceased.

The ride ahead through the Dail was going to be a far from pleasant one, my lungs still aching and my left hand mostly useless, but it had to be done. I wasn't moving with any manner of grace in my current state and when I'd arrived at what had been the encampment, Tudwal had sent a warrior to go tack Ceol and bring my stallion to me.

While I'd waited, I'd found myself looking for Bran among the haggard faces of the warriors, but I had yet to see him. It had surprised me, in a way, how much I had wanted to see him this morning, though I still wasn't certain I entirely trusted such longings just yet.

I fidgeted with the edge of my dark blue cloak, trying to rein in my runaway thoughts. Right now, my focus needed to be on my return to Clogwyn and my impending discussion with Lewella. *And Mother,* I thought, trying to ignore the uncomfortable feeling in the pit of my stomach. I needed to know how Aengus fit into all of this and if the rumors surrounding him were true, even if that meant a potentially uncomfortable conversation with my mother or aunt.

"Seren?"

I started, turning as Domhnall walked over to me with Ceol in tow, the stallion tacked and ready to begin our journey.

"Thank you," I said, taking my horse's reins with my good hand.

He frowned, looking down at my bandage. "Are you certain you're up to this?"

"I'll be fine. We need to get back to Clogwyn. There's no time to waste."

"But your hand—"

"Cian will see to it once we're back at the castle."

He let out a slow, frustrated breath. "I just worry about you."

"I'll manage. It's not as if I'm riding into the Dail on my own."

"I worry because I care." He took a few steps closer, dropping his voice. "I have tried being patient with you, but I have been wanting you for so long. Almost losing you in that fire...I love you. I *know* you can learn to love me in return."

My pulse quickened and my toes curled inside my boots. Why would he not let this go? "I have told you that I value your friendship. I need you to understand that what is between us cannot be anything more than that. Not now, not ever."

His face flushed. "It's that damned shifter. It's always him. He's who you wanted, never mind that I was the one holding vigil at your bedside. He abandoned you, Seren! How can you even consider taking him back after what—"

"I am well aware of what Bran did," I retorted. "What is between the two of us is none of your business or your concern. You are an advisor and a friend. I value you in both of those positions, but you *must* let this go."

"Mark my words," he said, his nostrils flaring. "You are going to regret this, clinging to him. I only hope you realize your fatal error before it's too late."

"You would be wise to remember who it is you are speaking to." Heat flushed my body as one of my hands curled into a fist, causing my nails to dig into my palms. "I am still Ri."

Turning on his heel, he stalked off, disappearing into the small mass of horses and warriors a few feet away. I kicked at a few loose stones with the toe of my boot, letting out an exasperated sigh. If he could not put this jealousy aside, I would have to seriously reconsider his position as chief advisor. *As if you have anyone else you truly trust who could take that position.* My stomach clenched at the thought and I fumbled with Ceol's reins, awkwardly tossing them over his head. The first thing I had to do was get back to Clogwyn.

I eyed the saddle, taking a moment to try and discern the best way to mount. It wouldn't be an easy task with only one hand. With my good hand, I gathered the reins, along with a bit of Ceol's mane, before attempting to lift a foot into the stirrup, but without my other hand to help balance me, I almost toppled over. In my scrambling to remain upright, my left hand banged against the saddle. I cursed as a fiery pain shot up my arm.

"Need a leg up?"

It shouldn't have, but hearing Bran's voice somehow managed to chase away much of my frustration, replacing it with a comforting warmth. I steadied myself before slowly turning around. He stood just a few feet away, holding Copar by the reins. The sturdy blood bay gelding stood calmly at Bran's side. It wasn't lost on me how Bran had taken to Copar over the course of his few months of living at Clogwyn, and I was glad for it. We never would have managed to escape Lorcan without the little bay horse.

"If you'd be willing," I said. "It would probably be wise."

Bran told Copar to stand, the gelding obediently remaining where he was as Bran walked over to me. Bran crouched down slightly and I bent one leg so that he could take hold of it. He softly counted to three and I gave a little jump as he boosted me up into the saddle. My injured hand still made some contact with the cantle, eliciting another wave of pain, but I was mounted.

"Thank you," I murmured, taking up Ceol's reins in my good hand. Like all of the horses in the Ri's stable, the stallion had been trained to predominantly be guided by his rider's seat and legs, something I was extra grateful for, considering my current predicament.

"You're welcome." Bran lightly placed a hand on my knee, his touch stirring up a wave of heat and sparks within me that I'd thought long gone.

"If you need anything," he said, holding my gaze, "you know where to find me."

I nodded, the subtle tightness in my throat enough to catch my words and trap them there. It seemed that I had opened a door by agreeing to give him another chance and now I wasn't certain I would ever be able to close it again. Bran dropped his hand, giving me a slight nod of respect before walking back over to Copar. I let myself linger for a moment, watching him mount up and admiring the grace with which he'd always moved, before ripping my gaze away from him, urging Ceol forward. I needed to find Tudwal, not be indulging myself with fanciful thoughts of Bran. We had a long journey ahead and I needed to stay focused on my people. And that meant staying focused on defeating Fianna.

Chapter 24

Hidden Blood

Seren

THE JOURNEY THROUGH THE mountains had been arduous and I was exhausted by the time we reached the castle, but there was no time to rest. Still, before I could hunt down Mother, I was corralled into a private room in the infirmary so that Cian could tend to my injuries. I sat by a small circular window overlooking the gardens, tapping my foot on the stone floor with impatience and gritting my teeth as Cian unwrapped my bandages.

"Spirits, Seren," Cian murmured as he examined my hand.

The skin was red and weeping, my hand itself swollen. It hurt like the blazes, truth be told. I'd done it no favors trekking over the Dail before it had healed.

"I had to return here as soon as I could," I said, shrugging one shoulder.

"I could have perhaps done this faster if I'd seen you immediately," he replied with a grimace. "But as it is, this will take a few treatments. And I might not be able to heal it cleanly; there might be some scarring."

"I can live with a bit of scarring." I already bore jagged scars on my right leg from the fangs of Fianna's creatures. Some things couldn't be helped and I refused to feel shame over the marks on my skin. They meant I was still alive in this realm, despite the Dark Spirit's ill attempts.

Cian pressed his lips together before he fully covered my hand with his own. I relaxed a bit in my seat, feeling the warm heat from his gifting as he began to heal the burned skin. My eyes briefly fluttered shut as the stinging pain in my hand was slowly replaced by a soothing sensation. Rain pattered on the window beside me, a steady noise in the otherwise quiet room. Before too long, Cian released his hold on me, getting to his feet and wiping at the slight sheen of sweat that sat on his brow.

"That's as much as I can do for now," he said. "I would continue to keep it wrapped just to be safe. I can give you another treatment first thing tomorrow morning."

I nodded, rotating my hand back and forth. The skin was still pink, but it looked realms better than it had and the pain had significantly lessened. "I will, thank you."

He lightly bandaged my hand and then saw me out, giving me a brief hug when we reached the door.

"I'm glad you're back, and mostly in one piece," he said as we eased apart.

"You and me both," I replied with a half-smile.

Leaving the infirmary behind, I made my way across the castle to the main staircase. My next order of business was to speak with Mother. I wanted what had been said of Aengus to be nothing more than rumors, but I knew I would be a fool to discount it. Especially after months of hearing the Spirits whisper to me of the blood of the line of Blaidd.

Mother's condition more often than not confined her to her chambers, and changes in weather, like today's heavy storms, always aggravated her joints. I would most likely find her in her chambers. The walk from the infirmary to the Ri's wing of the castle had given me the opportunity to think of what I would say, but I found that by the time I reached my destination, I was no more sure of myself than I'd been hours ago. I knocked on the door, my stomach quivering. Olwen, the castle servant who had long helped look after my Mother, answered, greeting me with a kind smile.

"Ri Seren," she said, giving me a nod of respect as she stepped back to let me in. "Mistress Esyllt will be glad to see you. I'll let her know you're here."

I made myself comfortable in the common room while Olwen walked into the bedroom. Outside, a rumble of thunder broke through the steady fall of rain on the windows and I twisted the clan ring on my finger, the gold metal cool against my skin.

When the door to the bedroom opened, I started ever so slightly and tried to settle the churning in my stomach. Mother shuffled out with Olwen, her steps stiff and short as she leaned heavily on her cane. I winced at her visible pain, wishing that I could have put this conversation off. I deeply wanted to, but it could not wait. This threat had grown far too large and if another in the clan had claim to the title of Ri, I needed to know.

"Thank you, Olwen," Mother said, easing down into a chair across from me.

"Olwen," I said, clearing my throat, "if I could have a private word with my mother?"

"Of course, Ri Seren." Olwen gave us both respectful nods before disappearing off through one of the servants' doors.

Mother raised her brows, slightly tilting her head. "What is this about, Seren?"

I hesitated, a bitter taste in my mouth as I desperately searched for words. The silence between us grew thick and a furrow began to settle in Mother's brow.

"When I was in Sionnach," I began slowly, "there was a rumor that was spreading. A rumor that centered around a man who claimed to be carrying the blood of the line of Blaidd."

"As you said," Mother replied, though she did not fully meet my gaze, "a rumor. Nothing more."

"Mother," I said, leaning forward in my seat, "I must know. Did Fionn have any children that I do not know? Was Father ever... unfaithful?"

Mother's face slowly took on a paler pallor, her hands clenched together in her lap. I waited, but she gave no answer.

"Mother, please. I must know. This man is very much alive and very much real. I cannot ignore him or his claims of kinship."

Silence stretched between us, only broken by the occasional roll of thunder outside, and the pain in Mother's expression was almost enough to make me give up demanding an answer from her. But I couldn't afford to let this go. These secrets had the power to upend everything I was fighting for.

Finally, Mother spoke, though her gaze did not move from her lap. "Fionn had another child. I know that because..." Her voice wavered as she continued, "I know that because the child was mine."

"Yours?" I jerked my head back, an odd ringing in my ears as I grappled with what she had revealed. I had expected many things, but not this. Father, with his arrogance and cruelty, had been the one I would have believed to be unfaithful, not Mother.

"Yes, mine." She took in a deep breath to steady herself, though I could see the whiteness in her knuckles as she continued to clutch her hands. "It was not your father who first captured my heart when I was nothing more than a servant in this place. It was his brother."

"Then why..." I shook my head, my thoughts feeling fuzzy. "Why did you marry Father?"

"Cadfael was a jealous man. I suppose you have already suspected that much by now. While I had fallen for Fionn, Cadfael had apparently fallen for me—or at least the idea of me. Some days, I've wondered if Cadfael saw it as some game, stealing me away from his brother. He wasn't used to being denied, in anything. Whatever it was to him, he was successful in his efforts. He convinced me to believe things that weren't true and by the time I figured that out, certain decisions had already been made. I was wed to the young new Ri of Blaidd and Fionn had gone off to the eastern coast to nurse his broken heart. Not that it was entirely that simple, of course, for I found out a few weeks before I was to marry your father that I was carrying Fionn's child."

"Did you tell Fionn of his child?"

"Cadfael forbade it." Her tone was flat as her mouth twisted into a sour expression. "Then he spun me the lie that he would let me keep the child, convince the clan it was our own, and when the time came for the title of Ri to be passed on, he would simply choose for it to go to one of his own children. But when the child was born, Cadfael went back on his word, forcing me to give up my son." She stopped short, dropping her quivering chin. "I am not proud of it. Every day, I wish I would have fought harder to keep him. Or at the very least, to have forced Cadfael's hand to have allowed my son to go live with his father. But I didn't, and no sooner had I named him than he was ripped away from me, sent to live with villagers in Cnoc to be raised without any knowledge of his true parentage."

My thoughts raced, my chest feeling as if a heavy stone had settled upon it. I had a half-brother. One I had never known even existed. One who I had quite possibly laid eyes on, not even knowing that we shared the same blood.

"What did you name him, Mother?" My voice was rough and thick, my mouth dry and my stomach clenching as I waited anxiously for her answer.

"Aengus. His name was Aengus."

My chest hitched, one simple name driving home the truth she had laid before me. There had been no lie, then, in Sionnach. Aengus carried the same blood I did—the blood of the line of Blaidd.

"You have seen him?" Mother asked, her voice cracking. "He lives?"

I hesitated. How did I tell her that yes, her son lived, but he might very well be the servant of a Dark Spirit? Or at the very least, cavorting with one. It had clearly broken her to lose him and I had no desire to add to her grief.

"Yes," I answered, ignoring the niggling feeling in my chest that came with skirting the truth. "He does live. And it appears he is at least aware of his connection to the Ri's line."

"Perhaps you could reach out to him. Now that Cadfael is no longer here to carry out his threats. I..." Mother released a shaky breath, a sheen of tears in her eyes. "I would very much like to see him."

My heart shattered for her. Why had Aengus gone and quite possibly thrown in his lot with a Dark Spirit? If that truth was confirmed, it would only cause Mother more pain. I should have told her the truth then, but like a coward, I shied away from it.

"Perhaps," I said with a strained smile, even as I wondered if I was really any that different than my father with my lies.

Eventually, I would have to tell her the truth. It would come out, one way or another, but not right now. A few moments later, I excused myself, leaving the room in a strange sort of fog. The truth was exactly what I had feared. I had a half-brother, a man I had once called friend, and now that same man might very well be the weapon Fianna used to plunge Blaidd into ruin.

CHAPTER 25

BURDENS TO BEAR

Bran

SOMETHING HAD BEEN BOTHERING Seren at dinner. Her shoulders had dragged low all evening and she'd barely picked at her food. The latter was particularly unusual for her. Seren loved eating—she always had—and I could attest that tonight's meal had been delicious, as always. She'd left the hall not long after she'd arrived and secluded herself in the Ri's chambers, giving me no chance to try and discover what had her so unsettled.

I'd been tempted to go to her, to press her to tell me what was wrong, but I was trying to be respectful of her wishes to take things slowly. For right now, the best thing to do would be to give her her space, even if everything within me screamed for me not to. *Though it shouldn't surprise you that you're not the one she turns to anymore,* I reminded myself as I slipped in through the partly cracked stable doors. I had greatly miscalculated in my impulsive decision to leave and try and battle Fianna on my own. I'd hurt her and broken her trust, but by the Spirits, I wouldn't make that mistake again.

Squaring my shoulders, I wandered down the dirt aisleway of the large stable, looking for Father. Lewella had kept me busy since our return from Sionnach, having me help her formulate a plan to flush out Alannah, which hadn't left me much time to spend with Father. I knew he was on night duty tonight with two other stablehands, seeing to the horses one last time after dinner. The stable itself was quiet. With the warmer temperatures, most of the horses were out for the night despite the rain, though some of the older ones had been brought inside to weather the storm.

As I passed by the rows of stalls, I listened to the soft noise of horses munching on hay. Only a few carefully placed lanterns lit the space, leaving most of the building cast in shadows, but it was peaceful, reminding me of my boyhood. I'd grown up in the stables of Clogwyn, worked in them myself for a few years before the Purge. Eventually, I found Father coming out of the stall of one of the older broodmares. He greeted me with a smile, brushing off his dirty hands after he closed the stall door behind him.

"That bored you had to come down to the stables in the rain, eh?" he said.

"Needed to clear my head," I replied, fidgeting with a latch on one of the empty stall doors.

"Well, this is a fine place for it. I've got two more horses to check on; you're welcome to come with me."

I nodded, falling in step with him and we walked on to the next stall, Father pushing a wooden cart full of sweet-smelling hay. This was a familiar chore for me, making certain the horses kept in the stable had water and plenty of hay before locking up for the night. There was something soothing about shadowing Father while he went through the methodical motions; it was a way to try and get my mind off my worries for Seren and my growing concerns about Fianna.

"Lewella has certainly been keeping you busy since you returned," Father said, gathering up a large armful of hay while I opened a stall door for him.

"Fianna is no easily vanquished foe," I replied as he stepped past me, carrying the hay in to the waiting horse. "Lewella knows that."

I wished I'd been able to spend more time with him since my return, but unlike her predecessor, Lewella valued both my skills and my intimate knowledge of Fianna and its servants. She had kept me at her side, pulling any information she could out of me and even going as far as to use me to help train a select few warriors in how to best defend and fight against a shifter. To Lewella, there were plenty of useful things I could teach the warriors of Blaidd.

"I can certainly say I will be ready to see the last of Fianna." Father tossed the hay to the horse before stepping back out of the stall. "Almost two years of being terrorized by that being is long enough."

I murmured an agreement, following him to another stall, the topic of conversation switching to more mundane things like the training of the spring foals and the stablehands' predictions of the coming winter. I was happy to be distracted by the subtle reminders of what my world had once been, before the Purge and before Fianna's darkness had covered this land. Soon, Father was done tending to the last of the horses and he bid me farewell. We went our separate ways, him heading for the back side of the stable to get to the cottages while I made my way back to the front of the building to return to the castle.

It was the whine of a wolf that stopped me in my tracks. I wasn't far from the entrance to the stable and in looking toward the source of the noise, I spotted Cryfder sitting outside one of the stalls with Awyr. While Awyr paid me little heed, Cryfder fixed me with a hopeful expression, his tail wagging and his ears pricked. My throat thickened for a moment. I'd missed him while I'd been away and I hadn't seen much of him since returning. I didn't like to think on it, but I had abandoned him too. It just turned out that he was far more forgiving than others. Perhaps more forgiving than I deserved.

I altered my course, walking over to the wolf and curiously glancing around for Seren. Wherever the two wolves were, she was certain to be somewhere nearby. I soon spied her in a darkened corner of the stall, stroking the neck of the old broodmare who was inside, out of the rain. Cryfder whined again, practically throwing himself against my legs and his tail began to loudly thump against the wooden stall door as I scratched him behind the ears. The noise drew Seren's attention, causing her look over at me. She was slightly obscured in the shadows, but there was a weariness in her stance that tugged at my heart.

"Ceol's dam, isn't she?" I said, inclining my head toward the mare.

"She is," Seren replied, not quite meeting my gaze. She continued rubbing the mare's neck.

A brief, slightly awkward silence passed between us. Cryfder plopped down at my feet, pressing his face against my knee, before Seren roughly cleared her throat.

"If anyone asks... I'd prefer not to be found. Not right now, at least."

I gave a slow nod, a wrinkle settling on my brow. It was harder for her to get a moment to herself now that she was Ri—I'd seen that before I'd left these walls months ago—but I still caught the unsteadiness in her voice. Whatever had driven her here, I suspected it was about more than just a lack of privacy.

"I won't tell a soul," I told her, stepping closer to the stall door. I paused, hesitating. I didn't want to pressure her, but I'd do anything to be able to comfort her right now. "Is something wrong?"

She began to shake her head, only to stop halfway and release a shuddering breath that was far too close to the hint of a choking sob for my liking. I unlocked the stall door without thinking, telling the wolves to stay where they were before letting myself inside.

As I crossed the stall, Seren remained where she was, but the closer I got to her, the more my worries grew. Her eyes were red-rimmed and there were tracks of dried tears on her cheeks. A haunted look lingered in her green eyes and she bit down hard on her lower lip as I came to stand in front of her.

"What is it, Ren?" I softly asked.

For a moment, I thought she wouldn't answer me, but whatever had shaken her was enough to make the walls she'd put up against me come crumbling down. For tonight, at least.

"I can't..." She broke off, visibly swallowing. "If it's true that he's gone and thrown his lot in with Fianna, I can't kill him. Especially now that..."

Her voice caught, her lower lip trembling, and my heart twisted. Something had upset her, had rattled her deeply, and I wanted nothing more than to fix it.

"Who?" I asked, careful to keep my tone gentle. "Aengus?"

She nodded miserably, staring down at the clan ring on her hand as she twisted it with her thumb.

"Believe me," I said. "I've struggled with that too. I'd be dead if it wasn't for him, many times over. I don't relish what everything seems to point to. But if he *has* sworn himself to Fianna, he has made his choice, full well knowing the outcomes. It doesn't make it easier, but he would have known the consequences of swearing such an oath, and it's possible that none of it is true, that he was in Sionnach by a mere matter of coincidence."

"It's more than that." She still wouldn't look at me, a tremble in her hands as she continued to fidget with the ring.

I frowned. "What do you mean?"

She didn't answer again and I forced myself to wait her out, not to push. There was clearly more to this than just the matter of Aengus, but I understood her pain. It mirrored my own. Aengus was a good man, a man who went out of his way to help others. I still held out hope that my fears were for nothing and Aengus was as innocent as I wished him to be, but I also had come to terms with the fact that I needed to prepare myself to accept the worst.

"He's..." She broke off again before drawing in a deep breath, slowly lifting her gaze to meet my own. "He's my brother."

She couldn't have stunned me more if she had tried. I was speechless, reeling from her unexpected confession. I recalled the claims that had been made in Sionnach, that Aengus was the rightful Ri of Blaidd, but I'd been willing to write them off as outrageous rumors, nothing more. Perhaps even something made up by Alannah to cause more trouble for Seren.

"Your—your brother?" I shook my head, stumbling over the word. Even though I knew she wouldn't lie about something like this, I still found I couldn't wrap my head around it. "Ren, what are you talking about?"

"I noticed the resemblance," she said slowly, continuing on as if she hadn't heard my response. "When we were in Beag. I thought I was being silly then. Eamon was dead and so were all of my cousins. But the Spirits have been whispering to me of the blood of the line of Blaidd, warning me of a danger surrounding it. The golden wolf, the rumors in Sionnach, it all fits. I asked Mother to tell me the truth. I thought perhaps it was my father who had been unfaithful."

She blinked rapidly and I took one her hands in my own, hoping to offer some comfort for whatever wrenching news she had to break. To my utter astonishment, she didn't pull away, only laced her fingers with mine, as if holding onto me was helping her, grounding her somehow.

"It wasn't him," she said. "Mother fell in love with Uncle Fionn first, before Father drove them apart, and it was Fionn's son Mother carried when she married my father. My half-brother that she's kept hidden for these last twenty-five years."

I couldn't stop my sharp intake of breath. My first thoughts would have been that Cadfael had fathered a bastard. *But it was Esyllt,* I thought, a heaviness settling in my stomach. *And if Aengus has Fionn's blood, he by all rights has a potential claim as Ri, especially in the wake of Cadfael's death.*

"I couldn't even tell her," Seren said, her posture slumping even more. "When she asked about her son, I couldn't even tell her what he might very well be, what he might have given his soul to. Like a damn coward."

"It's a lot to take in at once," I told her, squeezing her hand. "For you and your mother."

"I can't stomach it, Bran." She looked up at me with a pained stare. "I can't stomach killing my own kin. But what choice will I have if he has tied himself to Fianna? And yet how can I forget that he saved my life? And yours. He's my half-brother, for Spirit's sake. How can I be expected to destroy him?"

I wished more than anything I had answers to give her, but as I gazed down at her, my chest tight, I knew that I didn't. There would be no easy answers for a situation such as this one.

"We'll cross that road when we come to it," I told her. "We don't know for certain where Aengus' loyalties lie."

"But it doesn't look good."

"No," I replied, releasing a sigh. "It doesn't."

"I didn't want to become him," she said, a sheen of moisture building in her eyes. "I swore I wouldn't. And yet here I am, failing the people of Blaidd, letting Fianna run rampant, feeding my bitterness and throwing you in the dungeons, lying to Mother... And I fear that I am not so different from my father after all."

I pulled her into my arms, the sheer heartbreak she showed in her confession my undoing. For a split second, she tensed, but then pressed herself against me. I held her close, resting my chin on top of her head.

"You're not him," I said. "You're not ignoring Fianna. You're not condemning shifters to death. There is time yet to tell your mother the truth about Aengus. Once we even know what that truth is."

"But what if I become him?" she asked, the words barely above a whisper. "What if there's too much of him in me and I become a monster just like he was?"

"You won't," I said, holding her a little tighter.

"But I—"

"You won't, Ren. You won't because I know you. You might have skirted close to the edge of something, but there's a little darkness inside of us all. It's up to us to decide whether or not we wish to feed it."

She released a shuddering breath, pressing her face against my chest. A few trembles wracked her body and a bit of moisture began to soak into my shirt. I kept my arms around her, trying to offer her what I could, that I was here by her side. When her trembling ceased and her breathing calmed, I eased back from her. I cupped the side of her face, using my thumb to gently wipe at a few trailing tears.

"Do you remember what you told me once?" I asked her. "When I was struggling to come to terms with all I had done at Lorcan's command?"

She shook her head.

"You told me that I was a man who had made some poor choices, but that didn't mean I wasn't a good person." I paused, holding her gaze as her chest visibly hitched. "You're not your father, Ren. I may have made those accusations once out of anger, but you are not him. You have the power to make different choices than he did. You already have. And whatever the truth turns out to be with Aengus, I swear to you that I will be here to help you bear it. I won't repeat my mistakes and force you to bear such a burden all on your own."

Tentatively, she covered my hand on the side of her face with her own, the feeling of her skin touching mine sending warmth straight to my core. How I had missed this connection, this intimacy between us. Ever so slowly, she eased away before turning her head to brush the lightest of kisses across the inside of my palm.

"Thank you," she whispered.

A shiver of delight coursed through me, fanning the flicker of hope I'd been desperately holding onto. But almost as soon as her lips had touched my skin, she dropped my hand, quickly backing away and putting space between us.

"It's late," she said, ducking her chin. "I have an early morning tomorrow with the council. Goodnight, Bran."

I managed to mumble a goodnight in response before she hurried out of the stall. She called the wolves to her, striding off down the stable aisle and through the doors into the rainy darkness. I lingered where I was for a moment, my thoughts still reeling with all that had just passed between us. The dark web we'd found ourselves part of was growing more twisted by the moment, but as I listened to the rain pound on the roof, I could still feel the heat of her lips on my skin. There might be hope for us still and this time, I would be there for her, like I hadn't been before. No matter what other darkness and long-held secrets of the past reared their heads, nothing would drive me away from her again.

CHAPTER 26

PAINLESS DEATH

Aengus

THIS TIME, IT WAS not to be a fire that would strike at Seren's reign. Fianna had planned something different. I had thought the fires were the hardest things for my soul to bear, but this was somehow worse. I tried my best to ignore the feeling of dread that had settled deep within me as I dragged the small dead doe across the forest floor. The shadow creatures and Alannah trailed behind me, the creatures sniping and growling in annoyance at being held back from what they no doubt deemed their prize, but Alannah kept them in check.

She was unaffected by what had just happened, but I was haunted by how the doe had died. The creatures had flushed it out, cornered it in a dense thicket, leaving it no escape, and then, I had done as Fianna had commanded, despite my anguish and self-loathing. Not that the Stag Spirit had left me any choice with the brutal pain that had burned in my arm until I had done its bidding.

I had never killed before. I had only ever used my gifting to heal. Today, that had changed. I had walked up to the doe, placed a hand on its trembling neck, and instead of using the power within me to heal its life, I had snuffed it out instead. *It was a painless death*, I thought. *A quick one.* I had been repeating the same mantra to myself over and over again as we'd trudged through the forest in the growing darkness of dusk, but it had done little to soothe me.

It was not lost on me what I had done, but I had sworn an oath that I would not be able to go back from. And still, the dread lingered. I would need the life of others to sustain my own now. Without it, I would die. Forest creatures, Alannah had said. That would be how I would sustain myself. No different than hunting. At least, that was what I kept telling myself. *Painless deaths,* I reminded myself once again. The same creatures would get no such mercy at the hands of a hunter or a wild predator.

The forest around us soon thinned, making our going a bit easier, though my shoulders and back still ached from lugging the deer. It was a smaller creature, quite young, but still, dragging its dead body through the forest was no easy task. By the time I heard the faint rushing of water, I was beginning to pant. Our destination was almost in reach and that was enough to make my pick up my pace.

To my relief, it didn't take long for the trees and thick underbrush to begin to clear, being replaced by smooth stones and damp earth. The rushing grew louder and soon, the wide banks of the Weindio River were stretched before us. I came to an abrupt halt, half-dropping the doe. The creatures went to lunge at the dead body, but Alannah gave a sharp command in Old Pernish and they backed away, though I could swear I saw a sulkiness in their ember eyes.

"Quite a feat," Alannah said, coming up to caress my biceps with one hand, "carrying a creature that far."

I gave her a weak smile, knowing she was trying to distract me from what was to come next.

"It will probably take both of us." Her gaze dropped to the crumpled body of the doe as she pursed her lips. "To get it in."

I rolled my sore shoulders, pushing back the doubting thoughts that tried to fill me, even as the tingling pain in my wrist returned. I had to do this. This was the next step of unseating Seren, of ridding the clan of the Wolf Spirit's poisonous line.

Taking a deep breath, I bent down and grasped the dead animal's forelegs. Alannah came around to its haunches and between the two of us, we heaved it over the bank of the river and into the water. It briefly sunk before resurfacing again, the current carrying it toward the village of Glas. I couldn't seem to tear my gaze away from the macabre scene, my stomach clenching involuntarily. The dead body would poison the water, making it unsafe for the very people who relied on it. The damage the dead doe caused would reach the village far before Alannah and I would be able to. I hoped the people would not fall too ill before I was able to heal them.

"We should make camp before we've lost all light," Alannah said, drawing my attention back to her.

I nodded and turned to leave, but she stopped me with a hand on my arm. I looked over at her questioningly, half-wondering why she even stayed with me and my wretched weakness. If I couldn't stomach a simple task such as this one, how was I going to lead the people of Blaidd as Fianna's chosen?

"I know this is hard for you," she said, "but every passing day, we are getting closer. They're starting to see the truth, that you will make a far greater Ri than she will. It will be worth it in the end, just as Fianna has sworn."

Her words soothed some of the ache inside of me and as I stared into her eyes, I found myself envying the confidence she so easily wore. Alannah had never doubted our purpose.

"It is... hard for me," I replied, my chin dropping. "But I know you are right."

The people were speaking of me and what I had done to heal the villagers of Sionnach in their time of need. They were anxious for a new leader. Seren had taken the role of Ri on tumultuous footing and with her inability to control Fianna, the people were ready for change.

"Tonight, we celebrate," Alannah said, her tone firm as she took both my hands in hers. "We are one step closer to you taking your place at Castle Clogwyn. It won't be long now. I can feel it."

She tugged me closer, bringing her lips to mine, and I wrapped an arm around her waist, more than willing to let myself get lost in her kisses. I would have no other as my Banrion, for I would have never made it this far without her. We *were* one step closer. That was what I needed to remember, even in the midst of my darkest doubts.

CHAPTER 27

GLIMMERS OF GOLD
Seren

THE GOLD GLIMMER OF the clan ring shimmered below the clear water and I plunged a hand into the icy river. The ring had slipped from my hand and I knew that I must get it back. The urgency I felt from the Spirits was almost suffocating. Yet every time I tried to grasp the thick golden ring, it slipped through my fingers.

A curse of frustration escaped my lips and once more, I tried in vain to retrieve it, until a menacing growl erupted behind me, making me freeze. I barely had time to look over my shoulder before the golden wolf crashed into me, pushing me into the river.

The cold water shocked my system and pain filled my arm as the wolf bit into my shoulder. I fought it, trying to shove it off, but it only pushed me deeper and deeper under the water. My lungs burned, desperate for air—

I gasped when I came to and the presence of water surrounding me pushed me into even more of a panic. I scrambled out of the large metal basin, only to realize as I half-slipped on the wet granite floor that I was not being drowned in the middle of some river in the Spirit Realm, but had merely been taking a bath.

Releasing a shuddering breath, I grimaced at the mess I'd made in my blind panic. There was water all over the floor and one of the candles on the small table had been knocked into the basin. I was lucky it hadn't burned me on its way into the water. Shivering from more than just the cold, I hastily snatched up the blanket that had been laid out by one of the servants and wrapped it around myself. Thankfully it appeared to have stayed mostly dry. My gaze flitted to my right hand, the clan ring still firmly on my finger, just as it had been every day since my father had died.

"Ri Seren? Is everything alright?"

I was barely able to stifle a groan at the muffled voice that drifted in through the door. I couldn't do anything on my own. Even now, a warrior stood outside my bedchamber. I understood Lewella's concerns for my well-being after the incident in Traeth, but it was becoming exhausting, feeling as if I never had any privacy.

"Everything is fine," I called back before starting to dry myself off.

The vision had put a quick end to what I had hoped would be a relaxing bath. But clearly there would be no relaxing in the water tonight, not with the memories of the golden wolf drowning me. An ache settled in my chest as I wrung the water out of my wet hair. I feared that the golden wolf I had been seeing in the Spirit Realm was meant to represent Aengus. I had not yet confessed my suspicions, much less Aengus' lineage, to the rest of the castle, but I could not keep such secrets forever. The council would need to know the truth, as would the people, but I still fought to put it off as long as I could. A weakness, I knew, but one I couldn't seem to overcome. For now, only Lewella knew the truth of Mother's confession. Well, and Bran—not that I had exactly meant to tell him.

That night in the stable haunted me still, as did the wild impulse I'd had to press my lips to his skin. It had awoken something in me, desires I wanted to keep buried, and I'd done everything in my power to avoid him since. Not that my avoidance had done much to banish him from my thoughts.

"Ri Seren?"

The warrior's voice made me start and I almost dropped the now damp blanket. "Yes?" I replied.

"Pennathe Lewella is here, and she has a matter to discuss with you. She says it is urgent."

"I'll be right out."

My pulse picked up ten notches as I hurriedly grabbed my sleeping gown from the back of a chair. As I tied the front of it closed, my gaze briefly lingered on the faint scars on my left hand, the last reminders of the dark flames that had almost taken my life. It wasn't lost on me that the golden wolf I'd seen in the Spirit Realm had had every intention of killing me. There was no doubting the ending Fianna wished to bring about, as far as I was concerned. *But Fianna didn't kill me in Traeth,* I reminded myself. *Just like it didn't kill me at the Gwanwyn Festival.* In truth, it had been one too many brushes with death at the Stag Spirit's hand than I was comfortable with, but I could not give up now. The vow I had sworn to the Wolf Spirit to protect my people was one I would keep, no matter what.

Once I was dressed, I gathered up my robe, slipping it on and belting it around my waist before grabbing a soft pair of hide and fur slippers to ward off the cold of the stone floor. If Lewella felt like whatever this was couldn't wait, I knew better than to doubt her. There was little time to do anything with my hair and I settled with quickly running a comb through it and leaving it down. It was just Lewella, after all. I'd known her for years and we'd been friends long before we'd been Ri and warrior chief. If this matter was urgent, there was no time to waste.

Making sure my robe was secure, I let myself back out into the common room. The warrior who had been standing guard must have been dismissed by Lewella, for he was nowhere to be seen. Lewella stood in the middle of the common room, Bran beside her. I half-stumbled to a stop, my chest hitching at the sight of him. His hands were clasped behind his back, his expression solemn, but as our gazes locked, the flicker of desire I'd felt that night in the stable roared back to life.

Clearing my throat, I tore my gaze away from him, focusing on Lewella instead. "This matter is urgent?"

"I'm afraid so," Lewella answered. "I sent Bran out early yesterday to do a bit of scouting."

I worked to keep my expression neutral, despite the twinge in my chest. I hadn't even known he was gone. Of course, I *had* gone out of my way to avoid him after my clear mistake in letting my lips touch his skin. That moment had been too intoxicating, reminding me of everything we had lost. I had promised him a chance, but that didn't mean I needed to let my heart run off with me the first chance it got.

"He's brought back news I believe you will want to hear," Lewella continued, her grave words chasing away my lingering desire as fear began to slowly grip me. "And it is news I do not believe we can wait to act on. Villagers have gotten severely ill in Glas. Rumors are spreading that the people think that Fianna has something to do with it."

I frowned. "An illness? Not a fire?"

"So it appears," Lewella answered, "but it seems whatever it is has come on suddenly, and to more than one household."

"I picked up Alannah's scent in Glas," Bran said. "I fear that there might be some truth to the people's fears of Fianna."

"And yet no fire." This was a change, a considerable one, and one that left me extremely uneasy. Fire had always been Fianna's weapon, wielded by it and its servants. Why would that change now? "You truly think this is Fianna's work?"

"Yes," he answered, holding my gaze.

A chill traveled down my spine. If Fianna had changed its tactics, it would only make the task of destroying it all the more difficult. Damn the Dark Spirit for being such a cunning enemy.

"We'll prepare to leave in the morning." I said. "I want to get to the bottom of this at once. I wish for Cian to join us to learn more about this sickness, and I wish for Bran to come as well. If there is any chance of flushing Alannah out, we must take it."

"Yes, Ri Seren." Lewella gave a respectful nod. "I will make certain a group of warriors is ready to leave at first light."

They took their leave—there would be much to arrange before dawn—but Bran paused in the doorway, glancing back over his shoulder. His gaze lingered on me, a flare of desire in his brown eyes that I felt in my very core. It had been not so long ago that he would have been sharing these chambers with me as my husband. Was it possible that we could mend what had been broken between us?

This isn't the time for that, I chastised myself as he ducked through the door behind Lewella, the moment over almost as soon as it had begun. *Not with Fianna throwing another twist into this fight.* No, I had other matters I needed to focus on—matters that were far more pressing. I walked back into the bedchamber and began cleaning up the mess from my bath. The work offered some distraction from the deepening fear that had taken a firm hold of me. Fianna had changed its game, once again proving what a formidable foe it was. What was it going to take to be able to stop it?

CHAPTER 28

A HINT OF UNCANNY
Aengus

HAD IT NOT BEEN for Alannah, I surely would have gone mad over the three days we spent in the wilderness outside of Glas. She'd distracted me, reminded me of our purpose each time my thoughts had strayed. And yet despite her continued cajoling, by the time we finally left our cavern shelter, I couldn't help but feel a sense of relief. The suffering would end today. I would see to it.

We entered the village on foot, though this time Alannah chose to stay in her hawk form, not wanting to take a chance of being recognized. There had been whisperings of not only warriors of Blaidd in the area, but of Bran as well. The people of Glas would remember me and my features, but there was no reason to give them the chance to be able to remember Alannah's. We couldn't risk being discovered.

I kept the hood of my cloak drawn over my head, the driving rain of the day making me look less conspicuous. I'd been to

Glas a handful of times over the years to treat all manner of ailments. When I'd lived in Beag, I'd been the closest healer, outside of Glas' own; certainly the only healer with a gift. I had been well received then, but the uncertainty of how I would be received now left my stomach tight as I trudged down the muddy road that led into the heart of the village. At least I had seen to my newest needs before entering the village. My blood called for the lives of others now since that fateful day I had killed the doe, but I had been able to sate such needs with the life force of wild animals. Even if I felt the urge to take the lives of others, I should be able to resist it.

Alannah fluffed her wings, her feathers tickling my ear. She was perched on my shoulder and her nearness helped soothe some of my anxieties. As the houses around us grew denser, I squared my shoulders. Few of the villagers were out and about with the rain, but the ones who were gave me wary looks as I strode past them. No doubt I was an odd sight shrouded in my cloak and with a red-feathered hawk on my shoulder.

For all of their suspicious glances, none of the villagers stopped me, at least. The churning in my stomach continued to grow with each step I took. I knew exactly where I was headed, but Spirits only knew if I would be welcome. At one time, I had once been good friends with Felim, the village healer of Glas, but I hadn't seen the other man in months. Not since Beag had been destroyed and Alannah and I had fled into the mountains.

Felim's home was where I remembered it, near the center of the village, not far from the village square. The square was the heart of every village in Blaidd, where folk gathered to barter and sell, celebrate the seasons, and pay their respects to the Spirits. Today, however, the village square of Dearg was eerily empty. A silent reminder of the dismal state of the clan and how much my people desperately needed me to bring about change.

Which is why you must do this, I reminded myself as I walked up to Felim's front door. Like my own home in Beag, the healer's knot was etched into the center of the weathered oak. The pair of twisted, interlocking trees signaled to all who saw it that a healer resided here. It was an ancient custom, one that was still kept by many healers across the island. I had been one of them once. I knocked, silently cursing the damp sweat that was beginning to form on my palms, a sure sign my nerves were getting the better of me. Some days I truly wondered how in the blazes the Stag Spirit was going to use the likes of me.

It didn't take Felim long to answer and his eyes widened as he pulled open the door. He looked the same as I remembered him, short and broad with dark eyes and even darker hair. He wasn't much older than I was, ten years or so, and like me, he'd lived alone, though his solitude was not by choice. His wife had passed a few months after I'd first met him, an unfortunate accident where she'd been thrown from a horse and instantly killed.

"Well," Felim said, looking me up and down. "Folk have been swearing you were dead, but you look as alive as anything to me."

"Quite alive, thank you," I replied, mustering up a half-smile. He hadn't slammed the door on my face yet, thank the Spirits.

"Come in and get out of this infernal weather." Felim stepped back, motioning me to come in.

I allowed myself a quiet sigh of relief as I did so. As soon as Felim shut the door behind me, I pulled back the hood of my cloak, careful not to dislodge Alannah in the process. Felim's gaze fell on her, his brow wrinkling slightly.

"Interesting choice of pet," he said, raising a brow.

"I found it wounded in the forest," I replied. "I couldn't leave it."

"No, you wouldn't be able to." Felim's smile broadened and he gave a rueful shake of his head. "Always were a bleeding heart, weren't you? Come, dry off in front of the fire. Can I get you anything to drink?"

"No thank you," I replied, following him into the common room.

We settled in chairs across from one another, the steady drizzle outside lightly pattering on the thin hide windows that allowed a bit of light into the room. Felim's home, with its familiar scent of herbs and remedies, brought back memories of my old home in Beag, leaving a slight ache in my chest. I'd planned to build a future for myself there, but now it was nothing more than a pile of ash and rubble.

"If you don't mind me asking, how in the blazes are you alive?" Felim said, leaning back in his chair and crossing an ankle over his knee. "From what I've heard, there's nothing left of Beag after those creatures ran rampant."

"The only answer I can give you is that the Spirits spared me," I answered. "I was badly wounded, but I was able to get away into the forest and hide, as well as eventually heal myself." It wasn't a complete lie, at least, even if my palms sweated a little more with my well-rehearsed story.

"I would certainly say they spared you, my friend. I'm glad you're still in the realm of the living, I assure you that. I feared the worst when we heard the news of what befell Beag. What brings you this way?"

"Just passing through," I replied. "It's been... difficult, to find a place to settle since the incident in Beag."

"I can't imagine it would be easy to start over after such a loss. Though, I must say, your timing is as uncanny as it ever was."

"Oh?"

"I spent most of this morning dealing with a sick family down near the river. Fourth one since yesterday." He grimaced.

I forced my expression to stay neutral. I couldn't give us away. "I'm in no rush. I could stay a few days and help, if you wished."

"I wouldn't say no to the help, especially with your gift, but only if you were willing to do so."

"It's no trouble," I told him with a wave of my hand. "You know I'm always willing to lend aid."

"You're a good man, Aengus. You always have been."

My stomach lurched and the weakness in my knees made me glad I was seated. I was doing this for the right reasons. That was what mattered, wasn't it?

Felim shifted in his seat, drumming his fingers on his knee. "There are some rumors I've heard of late. Outlandish ones, truth be told."

"How outlandish?"

"There's been news from the north. People saying that a healer named Aengus healed the villagers in Sionnach after the latest fire there. I thought it was all talk at first, or they'd gotten the name wrong. I'd assumed you were dead, after all, but now that you're here... Well, there's rumors that you've been claiming to be the rightful Ri of Blaidd."

I could have sworn I saw a sparkle in Alannah's keen golden eyes and I meet Felim's gaze head on, just as a slight tingle settled in my wrist. *Tell him,* Fianna whispered. *It is time for you to own who you are.*

"That is no rumor," I said, the tingle in my wrist easing with each word I spoke. "There were things that were revealed to me when my mother passed not so long ago, things that have turned out to be true. My real father was Fionn of Blaidd, and I have as much of a right to that title as the woman who has claimed it for herself."

Felim took in a sharp breath, jerking his head back as he stared at me in bewilderment. "You're serious?"

"I wouldn't lie about this, Felim. And I think you've seen as well as anyone else how this clan has fared under Seren."

"Things have been bad in these parts, there's no denying that." Felim rubbed the back of his neck. "But... what in the blazes do you plan to do about it?"

"For now, I plan to help my people. I'm more than willing to stay for few days and tend to those who have taken ill. If you would be willing to give me a place to stay."

"Of course; think nothing of it. I would appreciate the help." His gaze flitted to Alannah. "I take it the bird is staying as well?"

"She's quite tame," I replied, stroking the top of Alannah's head, only to have her nuzzle into me in return. "She won't be a bother."

"I've got a spare room." Felim rested his hands on his knees before getting to his feet. "I'll show it to you."

I stood as well, following him out of the great room and down a narrow hallway, a sense of elation filling me. I had been wrong to doubt Fianna. Its plan was unfolding exactly as it had foretold it. I would heal my people and I would be one step closer to bringing Blaidd into its new future.

CHAPTER 29

GAMES OF DECEPTION

Aengus

AFTER SEEING TO THE four ill families that evening, we were up before dawn the following morning to tend to them again. The first three families had been lucky. I had been able to heal them all last night with my gift, but even with Fianna's power, I had been almost completely drained by the time we reached the last home, though I had at least managed to give the whole household of five short treatments. If Felim had noticed my newfound strength and stamina, he hadn't commented on it, and those I had healed had been too relieved to be free of their ailment to focus on anything else.

The desperation of the people of Glas was palpable, even without the sickness that had befallen them. Everywhere I looked, there were barely growing fields, gaunt faces, and sickly herds. The people suffered, all because Seren continued to cling to the Wolf Spirit's false promises.

My anger at her burned as Felim and I walked up to the door of the fourth family's home. On my shoulder, Alannah nuzzled against the side of my neck, as if she could feel my agitation. The touch of her cool beak and soft feathers eased some of the anger coursing through my blood and I took a deep breath just as the door was flung open. My focus needed to be on those who were still ill. I would deal with my half-sister later.

"You've returned." The family's oldest son, a boy of almost sixteen by the name of Liam, stood in the doorway with a broad smile despite his drooped shoulders and haggard expression. He'd been only minorly ill, unlike his parents and younger sisters, though that had meant it had been him who had been left to the task of caring for the rest of his family—a large responsibility for one so young.

"As we said we would," Felim replied, clasping the boy on the shoulder before we stepped into the small home.

Liam led us back to his parents' room and I was pleased to see the both of them sitting upright in bed, looking a good bit healthier than they had last night. The wife, Helyg, greeted us with a weak smile.

"You're looking like you're feeling a good bit better," I told them, setting my bag of healing supplies on the bedside table.

Alannah gracefully flew off my shoulder, perching on a chair that had been shoved in a corner. She had received a few suspicious looks here and there, but people were willing to overlook much when you held in your hands the power to save their lives.

"Thanks to you," Broc replied. "It's a lucky thing for Glas that you stopped through here to visit with Felim."

"I like to think the Spirits guided my steps," I said, pulling a few things out of my bag. "I'd like to have a look at the both of you first. Then I'll follow with another treatment before I go and see to your daughters."

Liam and Felim hung back in the doorway as I crouched down at the bedside. Helyg's constitution was the weakest in the family, and she had been gravely ill last night, but I was pleased that she felt much stronger today. As I moved on to Broc, I noticed Felim studying me with a curious expression as I worked to draw the poison from Broc's body.

"One more day of rest," I said, releasing my hold on Broc and feeling only a touch lightheaded as I backed away from the bed. "I believe it will be the same for the girls."

"Thank you," Helyg said, grasping my hand as tears shone in her eyes. "If you had not been here..."

"As I said," I replied, giving her a smile and gently squeezing her hand, "I believe the Spirits guided my steps. And..." I paused, searching for the right words, even as a familiar tingle began in my wrist. *Tell them,* Fianna hissed. *They must put their loyalty in you.*

I lightly cleared my throat, holding Helyg's gaze. "I will always do whatever I must for the people of Blaidd. For my people."

Broc's brow furrowed and Helyg quizzically cocked her head.

"I know these times have been hard," I said, blundering on and hoping I wasn't making a mess of things, "but do not think your suffering has gone unseen. Ri Seren is not the only one with a claim to the title of Ri. I am my father's son and it is Fionn's line that will be seated in Castle Clogwyn, not Cadfael's, if I have anything to say about it."

Helyg released a soft gasp while Broc pursed his lips. The silence that followed was tense, a twitching starting in my left eye. By the Spirits, if I had ruined it all with my stuttered, inelegant words...

"Spirits know you have done more for us than Ri Seren ever has," Broc finally said. "The clan needs strong leadership, the likes of which we haven't seen from Cadfael's daughter."

"I promise you that when I am Ri, your suffering will not go unheard. It is peace I want for Blaidd," I replied. "And peace that I *will* bring."

I left them to rest, Alannah resuming her perch on my shoulder as I gathered my bag and Liam led us to his sisters' room. As I'd hoped, the two girls had responded well to my light treatment the night before. This morning they were bright-eyed, hungry, and ready to get out of bed. I gave them another treatment before passing on instructions to Liam and their parents that the girls, too, needed one more day of rest. Soon, Felim and I departed, the sun now considerably higher in the sky than it had been when we first had arrived.

"I have a hunch," Felim said, pausing as we stepped onto the dirt road. "One that I'd like your thoughts on."

"Of course," I said with a slight nod.

He motioned for me to follow him and the two of us took off at a brisk walk. We didn't go far, diverting down a smaller, narrower path that cut through a few homes, past barely growing fields and pens full of goats that were far too thin, until finally reaching the banks of the Weindio. Felim grimaced as he looked out at the calmly flowing waters, the two of us coming to stand on the river's rocky bank.

"I've begun to wonder about the water," Felim said. "All of the ill families rely on this river, not just for their water source, but for fishing as well. It's the one thing they have in common. I got word early this morning that two of the village boys found a dead doe washed up on the riverbank not far from here. The animal could have poisoned the water, that could certainly make folk sick, but... there's something about that idea that doesn't add up."

"Oh?" I said, a sick feeling settling in the pit of my stomach as guilt gnawed at me.

"There was no mark on the doe. No clear way the animal would have died. The butcher apparently checked its body and found no signs of sickness or drowning inside it. Which leaves me to wonder one thing... has Fianna's darkness found its way here to Glas?"

The tingle in my arm began again and Alannah tugged at a strand of my hair, not particularly gently.

Tell him, Fianna hissed. *Tell him he is right.*

"I think you're not wrong," I replied, the pinpricks of pain fading. "And I think an even more important question is if Fianna's darkness *has* found its way here, what is Blaidd's current Ri going to do about it?"

Felim's grimace deepened. "Not much, I don't suspect. At least, not much of anything that will make a real difference."

"Do the villagers have another source of water?" I asked. "In light of all of this, it's probably wise for them to avoid the river right now."

"A stream," Felim answered. "On the other side of the village. I question if it could sustain an entire village, but there are a few villagers who have their own wells. It might be enough, for a little while at least."

"Better than more people falling ill." I inclined my head toward the water. "This could take out an entire village if unchecked."

"I'll speak to the village elder. Get her to start spreading the word."

"It doesn't hurt to be a bit too cautious in situations like this one."

Felim made a noise of agreement, the two of us turning and stepping down off the rocks, back onto the narrow path. We wound our way back through the trees, past homes, and finally to the main road. I rolled up my sleeves as we walked out onto it, running a hand through my hair. The day was growing warmer and a light sheen of sweat had broken out across my skin.

"Would you come speak with the village elder with me?" Felim asked. "It might be good if Gwendolen hears this from you as well."

"Certainly."

The connection would be a wise one to make. I would need support for this end game of ours. I could not just walk into Castle Clogwyn and claim myself as Ri of Blaidd. Let me prove to this Gwendolen how useful I could be. Seren wouldn't help our people, but I would. Felim headed west, back toward the village's center, and I followed along beside him. Once we reached the village square, the elder's home wasn't far. In fact, it was fairly close to Felim's own dwelling.

I had almost begun to relax, to think that this scheme of ours would go off as easily as we'd hoped, when the sight of a horse outside the elder's home left me feeling as if a stone had settled on my chest. The animal was finely bred, its coppery chestnut coat gleaming in the sun, but more than that, it bore the clan colors on its saddlecloth and the clan seal engraved into its leather tack, which meant the animal could only belong to a warrior of Blaidd.

Alannah stiffened on my shoulder, hissing through her beak, and my stomach clenched. Felim, oblivious to my mounting fears, went up and knocked on Gwendolen's front door. *Get ahold of yourself, mortal,* Fianna snapped, a flare of pain running up my arm. *You will stay for now, let the elder see your face, see who you are, then you will come up with a plausible excuse to leave this place. Now is not the time to confront Cadfael's whelp. Soon, but not yet.*

I swallowed hard. *As you wish.*

The door to the home opened just as I joined Felim on the front steps. A middle-aged woman with short brown hair and scrutinizing brown eyes greeted us.

"Felim," she said, her gaze flitting from him to me. "I wasn't expecting you."

"I'm afraid I have something urgent to speak with you about," he replied.

"It seems this is a morning for urgency." She stepped back, motioning for us to enter. "Come in."

I followed behind Felim, the nausea in my belly increasing as we stepped into a modestly sized entryway. We trailed along after Gwendolen, but as we neared the great room, I placed a hand on Felim's arm, slowing him slightly.

"I would appreciate you not mentioning my name," I said, keeping my voice low. "Not with a warrior of Blaidd lurking about."

He cast me a sidelong glance before giving me a slow nod and the two of us stepped into the room.

"Whatever you wish to discuss, Felim," Gwendolen said, motioning to a warrior who was seated in front of the stone hearth. "I suspect that Aran here will wish to hear it. He has ridden ahead of his party. It seems Ri Seren is on her way to Glas now that the rumors of Fianna's darkness visiting here have gotten out."

My heart pounded as the warrior turned his gaze to us. There was no mistaking what he was, not in his deep blue and gold attire and embroidered leather armor. His sword and dagger were strapped to his hip while a quiver was slung over his back. He studied us for a brief moment; to my relief, his expression showed no sign of recognition. Still, even being in the same room with him made my skin crawl.

"Two more families fell ill yesterday," Felim said. "That brings the total to four households. Their symptoms have been the same and with the dead doe found this morning, I believe the river is likely poisoned."

"So, not the work of Fianna then?" Aran asked, raising his brows. "Just the bad luck of a wounded animal falling into the river?"

"The doe died of no natural causes," Gwendolen snapped. "Do not make light of my people's suffering, Warrior Aran."

The warrior's cheeks ever so slightly flushed and he briefly ducked his chin as Gwendolen focused back on Felim.

"Those who have fallen ill?" she asked. "How have they fared?"

"Healed now," Felim answered. "But I fear others might not be so lucky if something is not done."

"I will make certain word is spread to the people, telling them to avoid the river." She paused, inclining her head toward me. "Who is your companion?"

"A friend," Felim replied. "Another healer. He was passing through and offered his aid. I would have not been able to heal the families so quickly without him."

Gwendolen made a humming noise, Aran once again glancing over at me with a slight frown.

"It sounds as if we are in your debt then...?" Gwendolen gestured to me, waiting for me to offer a name.

I hesitated, not certain if I should reveal my name to her or not with the warrior here. Curse it all, I was no good at these games of deception.

Lie, you fool, Fianna snapped. *You cannot tell her the truth with the Wolf Spirit's lackey sitting right there. Lie to her and then be on your way.*

"Cadoc," I said, relieved when I at least didn't stumble over the name. "I was happy to be of service."

"Do you intend to stay in Glas, Cadoc?" Gwendolen asked.

"I'm afraid I cannot," I answered. I hadn't the faintest idea where we were going, but Fianna had made it clear we wouldn't be remaining here.

"I wish you safe travels then, and thank you for your aid." Gwendolen turned to Felim. "I will make certain the villagers know they need to rely on the stream and their wells for now. Hopefully we won't have anyone else fall ill. If the two of you will excuse me, it appears I have a Ri to prepare for."

"Of course," Felim replied. "You know where to find me if you have need of me."

We took our leave, my heart pounding as I forced myself not to bolt from the house. Once outside, Felim and I struck out across the village square, which was beginning to teem with a bit of activity. A few villagers were engaged in some sort of barter involving scrawny-looking sheep and chickens. Others passed us by with carts pulled by weary-looking horses. Felim stayed quiet as we walked back to his home, but his pinched lips and wrinkled brow told me that his silence didn't mean he didn't have things he wished to say. The second we were back inside the confines of his home with the door closed firmly behind us, he let them loose.

"You're leaving?" he said, crossing his arms.

"You heard what was said as well as I did," I answered, widening my stance and mirroring his crossed arms with my own. "Seren is on her way here. I cannot stay here."

"So you promise Blaidd's people hope and then run out at the first sign of difficulty."

"That is not what I am doing," I retorted, my anger making my spine stiffen. "Believe me, I want nothing more than to confront her. But what good will I do the people of Blaidd if I end up locked away in a dungeon? Or worse."

"You really mean to do it? To challenge her?"

"I do," I said, holding his gaze. "When the moment is right, I will not hesitate. Things can't continue as they have and clearly, she has no handle on the situation."

Felim let out a long exhale, hanging his head and rubbing his temple. "People are going to talk, Aengus. You've already told some of them who you are."

"Let them talk. Let her hear that there is another who carries the same blood as her. It won't matter if she can't find me."

He gave a grim nod, gesturing behind him. "If you leave out the back, folk will be less likely to notice."

"Thank you," I told him, briefly clasping his shoulder. "I just need to gather my things."

I hurried back to the small room I'd been staying in, glad I didn't have much to pack. It took me no more than a few moments to stuff my extra clothing into my bag. I slung it over my shoulder, careful not to hit Alannah as I did so, and hurried back into the great room. Felim led the way to the back door. He opened it for me and I went to step through, but Felim stopped me with a hand on my arm.

"For what it's worth," he said. "I think you'd make a far better Ri than her."

I couldn't suppress my smile. Others were starting to believe in me, in the future I could bring. Perhaps I could do this after all. "Thank you, my friend."

I raced down the back steps, taking off into the woods. The tree coverage left me feeling less exposed and once I'd put some distance between myself and Felim's home, I slowed my pace. We would need to avoid the river, as Seren and her warriors would no doubt be drawn there, but there was plenty of wilderness to disappear into.

I was trying to plot the best way to retreat back into the mountains, when Alannah flew from my shoulder, dropping to the ground right in front of me as she shifted back into her human form. I skidded to a stop, barely keeping myself from slamming into her.

"We're not running just yet," she said.

"What are you talking about?" I shook my head. "Fianna said that now is not the time to confront her and quite frankly, I agree with it."

"We're not going to be confronting her." I went to keep walking but Alannah blocked me again. "We're not done here, Aengus. Not yet."

"I fail to see what we gain in staying." I went to step around her around again, only to have her roughly grab my arm and yank me to a stop. A burning sensation erupted in my wrist and I gritted my teeth.

"We cannot defeat Seren by force," Alannah snapped. "Not now. But there's still plenty of traps we can lay for her. Including in her inner circle. We wait here until Fianna says otherwise."

I nodded and the pain in my arm vanished.

"Come," she said, gently tugging on my arm as her features softened. "I know the perfect place to wait for the opportune moment."

I let her pull me along deeper into the thick trees and underbrush. I had to trust her and I had to trust Fianna. I only wished such a thing were easier to do.

CHAPTER 30

ON THE HUNT
Bran

WE WERE NOT MET with a warm welcome in Glas. Aran, the warrior Lewella had sent ahead of us to inform the village elder of our impending arrival, met us at the village outskirts. As we rode past the clusters of thatched-roofed homes and small farms to the village square, we were met with dark looks and muttered words, the tension in the air impossible to ignore.

Seren rode at the head of our column with Lewella, and it was clear that she was the object of the villagers' ire. One of them even went as far as to try and throw a bucket of rotted vegetables at her before a warrior intervened. It angered me that they treated her so poorly, even if part of me could understand what drove them to do so.

None of the grand dreams Seren and I had had for Blaidd had come to pass and now, autumn knocked on the clan's door. With failing fields that would yield no abundant harvest, dead forests devoid of any game, frightening fires, and now apparently mysterious illness as well, desperation was setting in. The people were looking for someone to blame and Seren, unfortunately, was far more tangible than a Dark Spirit.

When we reached the square, we found a middle-aged woman, two men, and an older boy awaiting us. I brought Copar to a halt and swung from his back. Lewella subtly beckoned me over and I handed my gelding off to a nearby warrior before joining her and Seren. Domhnall scowled as I came to stand at Seren's side. He'd been in a particularly foul mood since we'd left Clogwyn.

I'd heard rumor that he hadn't even wanted to come on this last-minute venture, that Seren had forced his hand, insisting that the people needed to see a united front between them since Domhnall's role was as her chief advisor; rumor had also spread that there had been nothing but constant bickering on the council of late. I hadn't had a chance to discern the truth of such rumors, and Seren had been intent on avoiding me since that fateful night in the stables. In some ways, things were better between us since the fire in Traeth. Our brief interactions weren't as full of the bitterness as they had once been. But I wanted more; I wanted her. Even now, I could still feel the phantom touch of her lips on my skin.

"Ri Seren," the older woman said, drawing me out of my wayward thoughts. She inclined her head respectfully to Seren and the men and boy beside her followed suit.

"Elder Gwendolen," Seren replied. "News has reached Castle Clogwyn of ills befalling the people of Glas. I came as soon as I heard and I have brought healers with me, as well as warriors."

"I'm afraid much of our most pressing troubles have already been largely solved," Gwendolen replied. "But come. We can discuss this more privately."

My thoughts raced as Gwendolen motioned for us to follow her. It was just like in Sionnach. Had Aengus somehow beaten us here? But what was his game? Fianna took life; it didn't restore it. There was something we were missing here, something important. Something we needed to uncover sooner rather than later.

The warriors remained in the square at Lewella's instruction while Seren, Lewella, Domhnall, and myself crossed the square with Gwendolen and her companions. Upon reaching the elder's home, we were escorted into a great room. I came to stand to the right of Seren, moving quickly enough to cut Domhnall off from doing the same. He muttered an oath but I ignored him, clasping my hands behind my back and focusing on Gwendolen.

"As I said, Ri Seren," Gwendolen said, making a dismissive gesture with her hand, "much of our immediate troubles have already been solved. I am afraid your healers are irrelevant. Our village healer, Felim"—she paused, motioning to the darker-haired man standing on her left—"has assured me that those who were ill are almost once again in perfect health. And we found the source of the sickness. Though I will say that requires further investigation."

"And the what is the source of this sickness?" Seren asked.

"A dead doe, found on the banks of the Weindio by Ellis and a few of his friends." She paused, inclining her head toward the boy. "Felim suspects it poisoned the water."

"Do you still have this creature?" Lewella asked. "My warriors and I will wish to look at it."

"In a way," Gwendolen answered, this time gesturing to the man beside the boy. "Our butcher, Dilwyn, has searched the creature for any signs of illness, as we could find no visible wounds."

"I do not doubt Dilwyn's skill," Lewella replied, "but I still wish to take a look as well."

Gwendolen glanced over at the butcher, who gave a slight nod. "If that is what you wish," she said, turning her attention back to Lewella. "Dilwyn can take you to it when you are ready."

"Thank you," Lewella replied.

"If the river is tainted, how do you plan to solve the need of another water source?" Seren asked.

"There is a stream that runs near the village, one that comes from Ioliare and doesn't feed into the Weindio," Gwendolen answered. "A few of the herders have wells as well. It's no long-term solution, but it can be made manageable for the immediate future."

"And those who were ill were all healed?" Seren's gaze flitted to Felim. "That seems quite a feat. You have a gifting, I assume?"

Felim briefly ducked his chin. "I do not, no. But I had a friend who was passing through who possesses such a thing."

My pulse quickened and Lewella stood a little taller, ever so slightly narrowing her eyes at the healer.

"Quite lucky timing," Lewella said. "Perhaps you would be willing to share the name of this friend."

"Cadoc," Felim answered.

It wasn't the name I was expecting. *But do not forget that Alannah was here,* I reminded myself. *If he's tied up with her, who knows what treachery and tricks she'd try and sow.* A name could be easily lied about.

"I assume you met this traveling healer?" Seren asked Gwendolen.

"I did," Gwendolen replied, lifting her chin. "The people of Glas owe him for his aid. He certainly did more for them than their own Ri."

"A Ri who rode out from Clogwyn at the first word of there being trouble in Glas," Seren said, a light flush tinging her cheeks.

"And what shall you do for them, Ri Seren?" Gwendolen's eyes grew hard, her expression bordering on mocking. "Summer may still reign now, but it will fade, and what little has been sustaining the people with it. What will you do when your peoples' bellies cry for food as the winter snows set in and there is none to be found after yet another year of poor harvest. When they seek food in the forest, only to find it empty and bare because even the wild creatures cannot survive. What hope is there for the people of Blaidd in you selling us off to the mainlanders in exchange for a bit of coin?"

"You will be wise to watch your tongue," Seren retorted. "I am well aware of the troubles that haunt Blaidd and I am doing everything that I can to put an end to them. You think that I do not know that winter will soon knock on our door? And I have entered into no agreement with Darnic, much less sold my clan to its king. I will not lie and say that I did not reach out to him, for I did, but I did not do so out of greed. I did so to help my people."

Gwendolen pressed her lips into a thin line, jutting out her chin, but stayed silent. I worked my clenched jaw. My anger had mounted with every word the elder had spoken. Seren cared for her clan. She put Blaidd above all else. It galled me to hear such vitriol spewed at her.

"I will remain here with my warriors for a few days to further investigate what all has happened here," Seren said. "I am glad to hear that the people are well, though if anyone else falls ill, I encourage you to remember that I have brought healers with me who can help share the load, one of whom is one of the gifted. And my warriors will help in whatever way necessary to make certain the people of Glas have a safe supply of water."

"If that is what you wish, Ri Seren," Gwendolen replied even as she bristled, fidgeting with her hands.

"This healer who passed through," I said, turning to Felim. "Could you describe him? Was there anything unique about him?"

"As I said," Felim answered, noticeably not meeting my gaze. "He's a friend. I've known him a long time and I can assure you he's no threat. But if you must know, he's an average looking man, light-colored hair. He's known to travel these parts and aid people with his gift."

"He had a bird," the boy, Ellis, blurted out, half-stumbling over his words. "A hawk that was a pet. It went everywhere with him."

Alannah. Aengus *had* been here, then, going by a different name this time, for Spirits knew what purposes.

"Thank you," Seren told Ellis, giving the boy a kind smile. "Any information you have to share is helpful. Pennathe Lewella and I will see to getting the warriors settled, then we will have you show us the doe's body, Dilwyn. Domhnall, I would like you to make certain that Elder Gwendolen has everything she needs as far as seeing to the people's needs for fresh water."

Domhnall nodded stiffly, not looking any more thrilled about the arrangement than Gwendolen. Still, he remained at the house at Seren's instructions while the rest of us returned to the square.

"I'm going with you to check the carcass," Seren said to Lewella as we stopped a few feet away from the tall standing stones. "If this is Fianna's work, there could be some of its darkness lingering on what is left of the creature that I might be able to sense with my gift."

"A wise idea," Lewella replied.

"I'll have the warriors set up camp outside the village," Lewella said. "I also think it would be worth taking a look down at the river ourselves to see if we find anything."

"I agree," Seren replied. "And we need to know more about this healer. I suspect it is Aengus, and that Alannah is with him, but we need to gather as much information as we can."

"Felim is hiding something," I said, setting my jaw and crossing my arms.

"I don't disagree," Lewella replied. "I intend on questioning him as well. And I want you to see what you can glean of Alannah. Aengus poses a threat, but we cannot forget the danger she brings as well. Odds are high they've moved on, as Gwendolen suggested, but if not..."

"I'd prefer to get started now," I said. "I'd rather not wait if there's any chance they might be nearby."

Lewella agreed and I gave them both respectful nods before turning and walking away. I'd go to the edge of the village and shift. Hopefully that would prevent me from causing too much alarm among Glas' people. Seren had outlawed the hunting and killing of shapeshifters, but most folk still didn't trust us.

"Bran, wait."

Seren's voice made me start and I abruptly stopped on the other side of the standing stones, turning to face her.

I slightly raised a brow. "Yes?"

She'd come striding over with such purpose, but the second she stopped and looked me in the eye, all of that faltered.

"I just..." She dipped her chin for a split second. "Be careful."

She wasn't so indifferent, after all, then. Perhaps that moment we'd shared in the stables *had* meant something to her too.

"I will be," I told her. "I'll be back by nightfall. I promise."

"I fear we cannot trust Aengus. Not if he's thrown his lot in with Alannah. I never thought that—"

She stopped herself abruptly, biting her lip as a sheen of moisture built in her eyes. I had long admired her strength, but I never wanted her to think she couldn't feel. To try and shove all her pain inside until it had no choice but to leech out as anger and bitterness. That had been what had destroyed Cadfael in the end. I didn't want that for her.

Gently, I placed my hands on her upper arms. "You never thought what, Ren?"

She averted her gaze and silence fell between us, but she didn't move away. I was close enough I could feel the warmth of her, close enough that only mere inches separated us and yet somehow, it felt like there was a chasm between us. I forced myself to wait, to not push her. *Let me in, Ren,* I thought, as if I could silently will it to be so. *Like you used to. Before all of this. Please.* Tense moments passed before finally, she let out a shaky breath.

"I never thought I would be hunting my own kin," she said, her voice barely above a whisper.

As much as it hurt me to think of the end that must come for Aengus, a man who I'd called friend and owed my life, how hard must it be for her? To find your blood and then be forced to end it? I wrapped my arms around her in an embrace, reacting almost on instinct as I sought to give what comfort I could, all the while knowing it wouldn't be enough. At first, she stiffened, and I worried I'd ruined what progress had been made between us with my impulsive actions, but then she sagged against me, pressing the side of her face into my chest.

I had waited so long for this moment, to have her in my arms again, and I soaked up every fleeting second of it. She felt right here, like a missing piece of myself I'd lost that had finally slipped back into place. It was over far too soon and I let my arms fall away as she stepped back.

Taking a deep breath, she squared her shoulders. "Come back to me."

I couldn't stop myself from cupping the side of her face as I held her gaze. "I will always come back to you, Ren. No matter what happens."

Her chest hitched and it took everything in me not to lean forward and touch my lips to hers. *She* would be the one to decide when we would take that step. After what I had done, the least I could do was let her be the one to make that choice. She would be the one to guide this thing between us. I would not take that from her, even if everything inside me screamed that all I wanted to do was kiss her. I let my hand fall, still burning from the touch of her skin, and made myself turn away. I had quarry to hunt. For there would be no future, not for us or for Blaidd, if I did not bring Fianna and its servants to heel.

CHAPTER 31

THE STAG'S GAME

Aengus

I WISHED MORE THAN anything that we had left this place. Instead, I was safely tucked away behind a large cluster of boulders, twisting my hands in my nervousness as I awaited Alannah's return. Fianna had sworn we could trust him, this advisor who Alannah had gone to fetch, but it wouldn't take much for him to betray us. Not with Seren in Glas.

A low hiss caused me to glance over my shoulder. One of the shadow creatures had woken from its slumber. Alannah had left them under my control while she had snuck into Glas, insisting it would be too much for her to try and control them while she was luring out the advisor. It had taxed her, keeping control of the creatures from afar the last few days. I wanted to help her shoulder that burden, but I feared the creatures would decide to get into mischief while she was away. They were capricious beings, always looking to sow some manner of chaos whenever they could.

The creature cocked its head, focusing on something in the distance, its eyes blazing. I followed its gaze, only to see nothing, but then again, the thick trees surrounding me obscured much of my vision. The creature remained on alert and I tensed, grabbing the hilt of the dagger that hung at my waist. The shadow creatures had far better hearing and eyesight than I did.

Moments later, the creature let out an almost gleeful little growl as Alannah appeared from among the trees. A man trailed slightly behind her, one I almost immediately recognized. He looked much the same as when I'd last seen him, with his finely embroidered clothes and slicked-back dark hair. Alannah had failed to share the name of the advisor she was fetching but this man was no stranger to me. Domhnall had come to my home in Beag a few months ago, searching for Seren after she had been kidnapped by Lorcan. His quick temper and surly disposition had made sure I remembered him, and I doubted his temperament had improved with time.

But Fianna had given its command and I would have to follow it. If it said Domhnall was ripe to be twisted to our side, I would have to believe it. Really, I didn't doubt that the man was mercenary. I straightened as they drew nearer, squaring my shoulders and absently rubbing Fianna's mark on my wrist. I was its chosen Ri. My father's blood, the blood of Ris, ran through my veins. I wouldn't let Domhnall intimidate me.

"Aengus," Alannah said, "this is Domhnall, Ri Seren's chief advisor."

Chief advisor, I thought as I surveyed him. His attire did look a good bit finer than when I had last laid eyes on him. Someone had moved up within the walls of Clogwyn, it seemed.

"Domhnall," Alannah continued, "this is the last of Fionn's blood kin, Aengus."

"We've met," I said, holding Domhnall's gaze. "In Beag."

There was a flicker of recognition from him, his eyes widening before he quickly schooled his expression. "So we have." He paused, looking behind me at the creatures, his face losing a bit of its color. "Though I must ask what sort of game it is you're playing with those monsters present."

"The creatures will not harm you," Alannah said. "They are under our control."

He scoffed. "You expect me to believe you can promise such a thing?"

She flashed him a cold smile, arching one brow. "Shall we test them then?"

The creature closest to me let out a low snarl, its eyes blazing as sparks flew from its nostrils.

Domhnall visibly swallowed, shifting where he stood. "I don't believe that is necessary. You say you have some sort of deal you wish to strike? One that will bring new order and leadership to the Clan of Blaidd?"

"Tell me, Domhnall," I replied, widening my stance before clasping my hands behind me and lifting my chin. It would do no good to show him any weakness, even if my stomach was quivering. "How am I to know that you would be even willing to agree to such a deal? Much less not betray me behind my back. For the last I saw you, you were quite loyal to Seren."

His gaze shuttered and his shoulders stiffened. "Circumstances change," he said, his tone flat. "I had hopes for Seren, but it is clear to me that she will not turn away from her foolish, misguided ways."

"Then you see the heart of Blaidd's troubles."

"I see that Seren does not have the strength to rule this clan. But what, exactly, is it that you want from me?"

"I do not wish to bring more bloodshed upon the people of Blaidd. Seren must be removed, but to do so without costing the clan greatly, it will be up to the council to act."

Domhnall held up a hand, shaking his head. "I cannot go to the council without proof. I can tell them that there is another who could claim the title of Ri, but on what basis do you expect them to believe you? Much less rule in your favor?"

"Ask Esyllt," I replied, a pain igniting in my chest as I spoke her name. "Ask my mother about the child she willingly abandoned. She will tell you the truth."

"You seem to be quite confident in that."

"I have every reason to be," I replied, my tone hard. I *was* her son and I would not forget that injustice she had dealt me. "I have heard of you and your exploits and how you have captured such a powerful position at such a young age. Who better to convince the council that a new Ri is what is best for Blaidd than you?"

A smug smile crept across Domhnall's face as he practically preened at the flattery. "And if I do this for you, what do I get in return? For it *is* a risk you are asking me to take."

I had expected this from him. He struck me as the sort who only did things that ultimately served him in the end. But Fianna had prepared me for that.

"You will remain as my chief advisor," I said. "A title that, I swear to you, I will let you keep until your dying breath. You will be given a place of honor for helping restore Blaidd to its rightful Ri. Land, coin... I can make it well worth your while once I am seated in Castle Clogwyn."

"And Seren and her mongrel of a Tiarna?" he asked, jealousy lacing his voice and making his cheeks flush.

"Will meet the end that all traitors must meet," I answered, managing not to flinch. They could not live—Fianna would not allow it—but the thought of what I must do one day, that I must one day destroy them both, still unsettled me. Bran's death, in particular, would be a wrenching one to bring about. Not so long ago, I had called him friend.

Get your mind where it needs to be, Fianna snapped, a tingling pain making me rub my wrist and bite the inside of my cheek to suppress a grimace. *He is a traitor and if you spare him again, it will be your own life you forfeit.*

I gave a slight shake of my head, fighting to bring myself back to my senses as Domhnall rubbed his jaw, tension filling the air.

"If Esyllt confirms your claim," he finally said, "then I will make it clear to the council that you must take Seren's place as Ri of Blaidd. I do not suspect it will be difficult to convince them if you are indeed telling the truth. They have no love for Seren; they never have."

"And I will hold you to that." The shadow creatures hissed behind me, sparks flying from their nostrils, and Domhnall took a small step back before he gave a stiff nod.

"I trust you can find your way back to the village?" Alannah said. "I'm afraid we aren't so foolish as to linger and risk the possibility that you betray us."

Domhnall let out a rough laugh, giving the two of us a twisted smile. "I'll manage."

He turned and strode back off into the trees. As I watched his retreating back, a wave of envy washed over me. To be as bold and as sure of myself as he was.

"Bran is supposed to be dead."

The cold fury in Alannah's tone made my stomach twist.

"I made a mistake," I said. "One that I regret bitterly."

"You are going to pay for sparing him."

"I already have," I retorted. If only she knew just how deeply and painfully I had paid for my folly.

Annoyance contorted her features for a few moments longer before she tossed her hair, focusing on the creatures.

"Come," she said. "We need to get out of here and the creatures are restless. They will need to hunt soon."

"Another fire?" I asked, shoving aside the guilt that tried to well within me. A little suffering for the greater good was necessary at times. Wasn't it?

"A little excitement for Seren on her return journey," she said with a twisted smile. "And if we remove a few more obstacles in our way in the process, all the better."

The creatures let out eldritch yips of excitement, getting to their feet and trotting along after her as she strode off deeper into the forest. With a quiet sigh, I followed along behind them. The greater good; that was what I had to remember.

CHAPTER 32

NOT LIKE THIS

Seren

IN THE END, THE two days we spent in Glas were fruitless. Lewella had gotten nothing out of Felim, the healer stubbornly tight-lipped about his mysterious friend. And while Bran had found remnants of Alannah and Aengus' scents outside the village, they'd disappeared into the wilderness before warriors could apprehend them.

We had at least been able to ensure fresh, untainted water for the village, in a manner that would keep them supplied until Cian was able to return and confirm that the river was once again flowing clean. I'd hoped my actions would have gained me more trust from my people, but there'd been no such luck.

And the deer doesn't make sense, I thought as I navigated Ceol around a grouping of stones that jutted out onto the narrow road we were following south. The creature had been young and the butcher had been correct in his assessment of it; there had been no signs of sickness, injury, or drowning as far as the carcass was concerned. Cian had voiced a possibility that I hadn't wanted to consider; that Aengus had used his gift to kill the creature. But the more I'd thought on it, the more I had begun to fear that it was indeed the truth. What would have driven Aengus to such ends? He would have known the price he'd pay for those actions. He'd forever become dependent on the life force of others, forced to kill to survive.

The thoughts left a sick feeling in the pit of my stomach as I urged Ceol back into a steady trot once we left the rocks behind. With the good weather, we should be back at Clogwyn before nightfall tomorrow. The thick trees on either side of the road made a dense canopy above us, blocking out much of the late afternoon sun with their lush green leaves. Just beyond the trees to my right, the Weindio roared, the river swollen from torrential storms a few days ago. Bran rode just behind me on Copar, with Lewella and another warrior having taken the lead of our small party after we had stopped for a brief midday meal a few miles back.

Ceol spooked and I lost one of my stirrups. I chastised myself for getting so lost in my thoughts, turning the stallion in a small circle before sliding my foot back in place. Ceol snorted, his body rigid as stone beneath me. Behind us, Copar skidded to an abrupt halt, his nostrils flaring as he planted his feet, refusing to go forward. Lewella called back a warning, the other horses beginning to balk and spook as well, picking up on something only they could hear and smell.

Lewella shouted for the warriors to ready their weapons and I readied Rhonwen's bow. I glanced over my shoulder, looking for Bran just as he swung off Copar, hastily handing the gelding off to another warrior before shifting. He'd be a fierce foe in his wolf form against whoever, or whatever, was lurking nearby.

I felt the darkness before I saw it. Fianna's presence rolled over me in a wave that tightened my chest and made my stomach roil. The scent of smoke came next, the air thick with Fianna's power as a shadow creature slunk out of the trees. Its ember eyes blazed and it snarled, sparks flying from its mouth and setting the grass and twigs beneath its feet alight.

The fire engulfed the greenery surrounding us, spreading rapidly as it closed us in, trapping us on the road. I steadied Ceol, the stallion ready to bolt, wanting nothing more than to get away from the otherworldly creatures. Lewella had rallied the warriors, but these were no mortal foes we were fighting. The creature sprang from its haunches and I nocked the bow, loosing an arrow.

My arrow dug into the creature's shoulder, causing it to falter, but the air was now filled with eldritch yips and screeches. Damn it all, there were more of the wretched things. I loosed my arrow at a creature just as it swiped at Bran with its long talons. The arrow found its mark, embedding itself into the creature's chest, but my relief was short-lived. Unfortunately, the creature fell, only for another to take its place. Bran whirled around, snapping at the creature's jugular.

I whipped another arrow from my quiver, Ceol nervously dancing beneath me. I'd just gone to draw when my stallion spooked, jerking hard to the right. Before I could regain control of him, something slammed into me, knocking me off his back and onto the ground.

The force of the impact left me gasping, the wind knocked out of me. As precious air filled my lungs again, I scrambled onto my hands and knees, searching frantically for the bow. It had landed a few feet away, but I wasn't the only one seeking it. A shadow creature was racing toward it, oddly more intent on the weapon than it was on me. I forced myself to move despite a sharp pain in my ribs, scrambling over rocks and sticks to the bow. That was our only defense against the creatures, the only thing that could destroy them.

My heart thumped loudly in my chest as I flung myself at the bow, barely managing to grab it before the shadow creature could. It let out a shriek of rage, wheeling around toward me as sparks of flames shot from its mouth, a few of them singeing my clothing. I fumbled for an arrow from the quiver I'd miraculously managed to keep hold of, but the creature was closing in, mere inches from me.

The tremble in my hands made me fumble with the bowstring, but suddenly, the creature was knocked to the ground. It hissed and shrieked as Bran latched onto its neck, flinging itself against a rock in an attempt to lose him. I winced as his body slammed into the stone, but he clung fast to the creature. *Focus*, I told myself, taking a firmer grip on the arrow in my hand. Taking a deep breath, I nocked the bow, trying to ignore the quiver in my stomach. The last thing I wanted to do was accidentally hit Bran, but if I did nothing, the creature would kill him instead.

Bran and the creature were a blur of blood, smoke, and gnashing of teeth, neither of them ready to give up their fight. Releasing a long breath, I loosed the arrow. It grazed the creature's shoulder but then sailed harmlessly into the dirt. The creature screeched before darting away, Bran still stubbornly holding fast.

I raced after the two of them, my only thought killing the damn thing before it killed Bran. The creature's movements were becoming more erratic and I readied another arrow. It was weakening, its breathing more labored and its efforts to remove Bran not as strong as they'd been moments ago.

The riverbank came into view, the dirt of the forest floor replaced with smooth stone. The creature faltered over the rocks and I readied my arrow, looking for a clear moment to loose it. The creature had gone dangerously close to the rushing water.

For a split second, it paused, its gaze locking with mine as its ember eyes flared and caused a chill to course through me.

Before I could even blink, it reared up and flung itself into the rapid waters of the Weindio, taking Bran with it. I couldn't stop the scream that tore from my lips as I raced for the edge of the river. The creature resurfaced and I didn't hesitate, loosing my arrow, which embedded itself right between its eyes. It let out one last screech of rage before it dissipated into a ball of ash and soot, its charred remains floating on top of the water.

I screamed Bran's name, searching for any sign of him, but there was nothing, only the steady roaring of the water. Fear gripped me, leaving my body numb and my throat tight. He couldn't have drowned. I couldn't have lost him. I still loved him, damn it. And even after as coldly as I'd treated him, he'd still risked his life for mine. Blinking back the tears that stung my eyes, I bolted off down the riverbank, calling his name. I'd find him. He wasn't dead. He couldn't be.

Chapter 33

Never Stopped

Bran

I'D MANAGED TO SHIFT back into my human form moments after I was plunged into the icy waters of the Weindio, but the current was strong. It swept me downstream, forcing me to fight against it to keep my head above water as it tried to pull me under over and over again. I choked and gasped, desperately seeking some way to get to dry land. I had to get back to Seren and the others. My life wasn't going to end in a drowning by a shadow creature.

I slammed into something hard, the blow to my back leaving me gasping in pain. It took me a second too long to realize what I'd hit had been a boulder, but I was able to spy another rock jutting out less than a foot away. I sent up a prayer to the Spirits to allow the water to push me toward it, my gaze fixed on what would hopefully be my salvation.

As soon as I got near the jagged rock, I latched onto it, but the numbness in my fingers left me grappling to hold onto the smooth, slick stone. I cursed, fighting for a better handhold. When I finally got one, I heaved myself up onto the rock, slipping and sliding so badly that I almost plunged back into the river. Groaning, I flung myself onto the riverbank, my chest heaving as I began to cough and retch up the water that had gotten into my lungs.

Once my body had purged every last drop of water, I was left on my hands and knees, gasping and altogether too aware of how close I'd come to death once again. The few small swipes on my skin from the shadow creature's claws and teeth were already beginning to burn. I'd just pulled myself onto my knees when I heard Seren yelling my name.

I hoarsely called back to her, relief flooding me. She was alive. Moments later, she burst out of the trees, her face almost completely white. When she reached me, she flung down the bow, wrapping her arms around me and pressing her face into the side of my neck.

"I'm alright, Ren," I murmured, clinging to her in return. "I'm alright."

She released a shuddering breath before putting space between us, wiping at the tears that stained her cheeks.

"I thought...." She choked, biting down hard on her lower lip before continuing. "That creature could have killed you."

"But it didn't." I cupped the side of her face and brushed a few of her lingering tears away with my thumb. "Not this time at least."

"Not ever," she said fiercely. "Not if I have anything to say about it."

My chest hitched, my gaze dropping to her lips. I'd been so worried the love we'd once shared had been broken, but now... had we begun to find our way back to it after all? We were close enough that our breath mingled and I wanted nothing more than to close the fraction of space between us and press my lips to hers, but I forced myself to wait, to let her tell me that she wanted this as much as I did.

And then, in one blissful moment, she leaned forward, her lips covering mine. It was everything I had longed for, everything I had missed. That connection I'd feared severed was forged once again as my mouth moved over hers, unearthing all the desire and love I'd held so close to my heart since Fianna's darkness had ripped us apart. I worked a hand into her hair while she gripped the front of my soaking wet shirt. I pulled her closer with a barely restrained groan, but too soon we were forced to part for air. Seren still held my shirt as we both took in ragged breaths and I rested my forehead against hers.

"I was a fool," I softly told her, "but I never stopped loving you."

She blinked rapidly, moisture building in her eyes again. "I love you. I want us back."

"Then let's try and find our way back to what we once were."

She leaned in again, lightly brushing her lips over mine. "I want that."

I was moments away from wrapping my arms around her and kissing her again when nearby shouts made us both start. Lewella called Seren's name a third time and a few moments later, the warrior chief emerged from the tree line with a few warriors in tow. Seren helped me get to my feet and I grimaced when I swayed slightly, the burning sensation in my wounds growing stronger and hotter.

"He needs Cian," Seren called to Lewella, keeping a firm hold of my arm.

"He's back with the others," Lewella replied. "We've gotten around the fire and seem to have lost the creatures. For now, at least."

Seren stayed on one side of me while Lewella instructed one of the other warriors to come on the other side. As I began to shuffle along between them, the slightest cold sweat began to break out over my skin. I needed Cian, and sooner rather than later. The shadow creature's claws and fangs were poisonous. I had borne witness to the agonizing deaths such poison could cause during my time in Lorcan's command. Cian would need to draw it out with his gift as soon as possible. Every step I took felt labored, my skin becoming slicker with each passing moment, but I pushed myself on over the rocks and roots. I hadn't lost Seren and I hadn't finally gotten her back just to perish at Fianna's hands.

CHAPTER 34

BLOOD KIN

Seren

BY THE TIME WE returned to Clogwyn the following night, Bran was fully healed from his injuries, largely thanks to Cian's gift. A few of the other warriors bore injuries as well from our ambush on the road, but no one had lost their life at the hands of Fianna's creatures, something I was immensely grateful for. The shadow creatures had killed more than enough of my people.

But despite my relief at our safe return, trouble had greeted me upon our return to the castle. It had only taken a few hours to discover that Laoise had gone behind my back in my absence, reaching out to King Evander in Darnic and telling him that Blaidd was not entirely saying no to his proposal of marriage. I'd spent the last half hour in my study, staring across the table at Laoise, barely able to contain my fury, the audacity of what she had done leaving a pounding in my ears and my muscles twitching.

"You had no right to undermine me in such a way," I said. "You will send word to the Darnian ambassadors and tell them that you were mistaken and make it clear that Blaidd has no interest in entering an agreement with King Evander that requires a contract of marriage."

"It is almost time for the harvest and what then, Seren?" Laoise retorted, her arms tightly folded across her chest. "If the land yields nothing and the people are unable to prepare their herds for the lean months ahead, how do you expect them to survive? Most of this clan lies in ruin and the last I saw, you are no closer to ridding this land of Fianna than your father ever was. It's nothing short of folly to turn down King Evander's proposal. If you could put aside your pride for one second, you would see that. Evander can supply the people of Blaidd with what they need to survive with little cost to himself. Darnic has prospered greatly in recent years. You would be a queen, for Spirit's sake. Think of that, if nothing else."

"I am already wed," I said through gritted teeth. "Signing such a marriage contract signs away Blaidd's independence. I will not put my people at Darnic's mercy. Young I might be, but I know they were not always our ally. And I *will* rid this land of Fianna. I only need more time."

Laoise scoffed, curling her lip. "How like your father you sound."

My cheeks flushed, my nails biting into my palms as I clenched my hands. "You will watch your tongue, Laoise. I am not above throwing you off of this council if you continue to go behind my back and cause trouble."

"You and I both know that you cannot do that." Laoise smirked. "And even if you could, who would replace me? It's been almost four months and you still don't even have a replacement for Mair. You would be wise to remember that even *you* can be replaced, if the people call for it."

Laoise got to her feet, striding out of the room before I could even dismiss her. How in the blazes had I ever been so foolish as to think I could trust her? I rubbed my forehead as the door slammed shut, stifling a groan before getting to my feet and pacing over to the window, the speed of my pulse doubling. The rumors of Aengus had been growing with every passing day, but surely even Laoise wouldn't put the clan in the hands of a servant of Fianna. Would she?

I didn't like the way my stomach hardened at that thought. If one thing had been made clear to me these last few months, I'd clearly never known her as well as I'd thought I had. Still, no one knew the truth of Aengus' ties to me and our family. Well, no one save for Bran and Lewella, but I trusted them to keep such a secret until I was ready to reveal it. A heavy sigh escaped my lips as I massaged my temples, dreading the headache that was forming. Tonight, I needed to carve out time to seek the guidance of the Spirits and hope they would show me more than hints and shadows. If there were answers to be found in the Spirit Realm, I needed to find them, and quickly.

A knock at the door made me start and I called for whoever was outside to enter. A few moments later, Domhnall slipped in, his expression grave as he joined me near the window, looking out over the forest. Not so long ago, his presence would have soothed me, but now it only put me more on edge. Things between us had been tense since I'd last rebuffed him. I feared I was losing his support, but my heart belonged to Bran. I couldn't change that.

"Arwel and Laoise are going to be pressing for an emergency council meeting soon," he said, clasping his hands behind his back as he, too, turned his gaze to the distant trees, their limbs swaying in the light late summer breeze.

"If this is about the marriage contract, I have already spoken with Laoise. That problem should be solved and she should not be going behind my back in such a way again."

"This isn't about Darnic," he replied with a shake of his head. "The rumors are growing, Seren. The people are restless. This Aengus is not letting go of his supposed claim as Ri. More incidences like the one in Glas and you're going to have a problem on your hands that you cannot ignore. He's earning their trust, servant of Fianna or not. No one can deny that."

A cold feeling settled in the center of my chest. "The rumors of his heritage are just that. Rumors."

"Rumors that are growing. You cannot ignore this. The people are not going to allow that, and neither is this Aengus."

"He has no proof."

"He has no proof yet." He glanced over at me, his jaw tight. "As your chief advisor, I must know. Is this man your kin or is he nothing more than an opportunistic liar?"

A tense silence passed between us and I worried my lower lip, my stomach clenching. The truth would out itself, one way or another. How long could I keep up this lie?

"If he is not your kin, then the answer is simple," Domhnall said. "The man is nothing more than delusional and that is the end of it. But if he is not..."

I didn't answer, gripping the edge of the windowsill so tightly, my knuckles turned white.

"It is better to tell people the truth than to make them feel lied to." He softened his tone, lightly covering one of my hands with his own. I released a shuddering breath. He was right, even if I was loathe to admit it.

"Aengus is Fionn's son," I said quietly, "and we share the same mother."

Domhnall took in a sharp breath before his mouth pulled down into a frown.

"The people must be told," he said. "It would be better for them to hear it from you. I would advise the same with the council. Tell them the truth of the matter and be done with it."

"I do not want my mother on the receiving end of any sort of backlash from this. Her child was conceived before she made promises to my father."

"I cannot make any promises that people will not cast their own judgments, but that particular truth can be emphasized to the rest of the clan."

I nodded, a quiver settling in my belly. I fidgeted with the clan ring, the cool metal seeming to bear down on me with a new, crushing weight. I'd vowed to the Wolf Spirit that I would fight for my place as Ri, but I'd never imagined my challenger would be Aengus, much less that he would be my own blood kin. "And if Aengus is who the people of Blaidd want leading them once they hear his claim is true?"

Domhnall gave a strained smile. "We will deal with that when we must. If this man is truly a servant of Fianna, the people will not want to be led into further darkness. Spirits know they have been forced to contend with enough of it these last few years."

"I will tell the council the truth in the morning," I said, swallowing hard. "Then a statement will be put forth to the people."

"A wise plan." He took a step back before respectfully inclining his head. "I will see to the arrangements for the council meeting."

I stayed where I was as he left and once the door had closed behind him, I rested my forehead on the cool glass pane. *I am trying,* I thought, my chest tight, *but you never told me it would be like this.*

A vow to the Spirits is never a thing that is easily fulfilled, Daughter of Blaidd, the Wolf Spirit whispered. *But to not fulfil it will condemn your people to darkness. Will you leave the people of Blaidd to such an end?*

I squeezed my eyes shut. I couldn't do such a thing. If I did not fight this, Blaidd would pass into ruin. There would be no future for the land or my people. I could not give up now, even if I feared this fight would test me in ways I'd never imagined.

It was after the evening meal by the time I made it to see Mother. I wanted to warn her of what was to come and promise to shield her from it however I could. But my fears and anxieties over what was to come with the light of dawn had worn on me. I'd barely had an appetite for my meal, only picking at my food, and the unsettled feeling that had kept me from eating remained in my middle as I strode down the shadowy halls in the castle, headed for Mother's chambers. *And I still haven't seen Bran,* I thought, my shoulders tight with frustration. All my intentions of finding him and speaking to him of the kiss that was seared in my memory had been for nothing. I'd been delayed at every turn and tomorrow, I would be caught up dealing with the inevitable fallout my confession would bring.

When I reached the door to Mother's chambers, I took a deep breath and knocked. Olwen answered, the older woman greeting me with a smile as she ushered me inside.

"Mistress Esyllt was just getting ready for bed," Olwen said as she closed the door behind us. "But I'm sure she'll be glad to see you."

The title she used to refer to Mother was still jarring to me, even after months of hearing it. For my entire life, Mother had been Blaidd's Banrion—but no longer. Not now that I was Ri. She still had a place here. I would make sure she always had a place here, but the responsibilities of the clan no longer fell on her shoulders. Now, they fell on mine.

Mother was seated in a chair near the window that looked out over her beloved gardens and she angled herself toward me as I walked over to join her, Olwen disappearing into the bedchamber. The smile Mother greeted me with did little to abate the churning in my stomach. I dreaded what I had to tell her, dreaded the truth I would have confess to the council the next morning.

"I wasn't expecting to see you tonight," Mother said when I took a seat on the bench across from her. "You've been kept busy since you returned from Glas, from the sounds of it."

"I have been, more than I intended to be." I twisted my hands in my lap. "Mother, I... there is something I must do tomorrow. Something that involves Aengus."

She went suddenly still. "What is it, Seren?"

"The people have begun to suspect who he is, that he is Fionn's kin. And he has been calling for what is owed to him by his birthright. It's created unrest. Many are wondering if it is true and if so, why our family hid it. I do not wish to do so, but... Mother, I must confess the truth. Tomorrow morning, I will tell the council that Aengus is indeed my half-brother. But I swear to you that I will not let anyone lay blame at your feet."

"I will bear whatever gossip spreads," she replied, pulling back her shoulders despite the paleness of her features. "Have you reached out to him? To Aengus?"

"Mother, I..." A lump settled in my throat as I fought for the words I knew I must say. The words I knew would break her heart. "There is reason to believe that Aengus is servant of Fianna. At the very least, there is reason to believe he is keeping company with someone who is such."

Mother covered her mouth with her palm, moisture pricking her eyes. "You are certain this is more than just rumor?"

I nodded, releasing an unsteady breath. "I do not wish to believe it any more than you do. I know Aengus, or at least I knew the man he was. He saved my life when Bran and I fled Lorcan and he helped us safely get away, at great cost to himself."

"Perhaps..." Mother's voice caught and she cleared her throat. "Perhaps there is a way for you to speak with him. Fionn was a good man, a kind one. Far kinder than his brother ever was. Aengus bears that blood."

"Believe me, Mother, if there is any choice before me other than striking against my own kin, I will take it."

She nodded, a perceptible tremble in her chin. My heart ached for her, for all of us. For the darkness Fianna had sown and Father had encouraged and for the tragic ending I saw before me. There was not even a chance that the path to defeating Fianna wouldn't end in heartbreak. A few moments later, Olwen returned to the common room and Mother expressed that she was ready to retire for the night.

I left her chambers feeling more defeated than when I'd entered them. How had this all gotten so tangled? And yet even as I silently asked myself the question, I could see the intricate web that the years of lies and secrets had woven. With a weary heart, I made my way back down the empty castle hallways. I should have been headed for bed myself with the late hour, but there was one thing, one person, I wanted more than anything else. One person I would trust with my shattered soul, even after the mistakes that had torn us apart. I only had to find him.

CHAPTER 35

A LIGHT AMIDST THE DARKNESS

Bran

MY HOPES OF SEEKING out Seren after the evening meal had been dashed when she had retreated to the Ri's wing of the castle. I hadn't thought that she'd been avoiding me since we'd returned from Glas, but tonight, I wasn't so sure, despite the kiss and confessions of love we'd shared days ago by the river. Instead of allowing myself to sit in my room and stew over my insecurities, I'd retreated to Father's cottage. I hadn't made time to see him nearly as much as I should have because of the hunt for Alannah. Tonight, I could make up for some of that.

A storm had started on my walk down to the cottage and by the time I arrived, I was soaked to the bone. Father had started a small fire in his hearth to help me dry off and we sat at a table in his kitchen, sharing a drink. The rain pounded on the thatched roof, and wicked flashes of lightning continually lit up the room through the thin hide windows. As was typical in the late summer, the storm had come up quickly and fiercely.

"I'm glad to hear they've been treating you better in the war band," Father said as he took a sip of his ale.

"So am I," I replied with a wry smile.

That was one thing that had improved in the last week. Whether it was from Lewella's command or Seren's, quite possibly even both, I was grateful for it. I still didn't have much in the way of friends within the war band or the castle at large, but no longer was I forced to suffer the rampant disrespect and insults as when Cadfael had been Ri.

"And still no word of an annulment?" Father asked.

"Not that I've heard." Just the thought of such a thing made my chest tighten and I swirled my ale in my mug. "I think... I think we can fix things between us."

"Then I'm happy for you. If that's what the both of you want."

"It is."

Seren had said as much at the river and the kiss we'd shared had told me all on its own that she still felt the spark between us.

"Lewella still plans to send you out again?" Father asked.

I nodded. Those plans had already been made. Two days from now, I'd be headed north again to hunt for my ever-elusive prey.

"We didn't glean nearly as much in Glas as she'd hoped," I replied. "We need to find Alannah, and sooner rather than later."

"I just hope that—"

A knocking at the door cut Father off and he frowned, getting to his feet.

"Can't think of who would be out in this weather," he said, shaking his head. "I'll be right back."

I couldn't think of who would be venturing out in this mess either. The rain was still coming down in sheets, the thunder and lightning constant interruptions in the otherwise quiet cottage. I stayed where I was as Father left the room, though I couldn't seem to shake the slight tension that crept into my muscles. It was late and the weather outside hardly made it a pleasant night to be wandering around out of doors. Was yet more trouble headed my way? I listened to the steady noise of Father's footfalls, followed by the creak of the front door. I rubbed at my lips, able to discern that he was letting someone in. At first, I told myself I would wait where I was, but when Seren's low tones drifted into the kitchen, I bolted to my feet.

In seconds, I was in the great room. She stood just inside the doorway with Father, her gaze downcast as she fidgeted with her clan ring. The torrential storm had left her drenched, water dripping from the bottom of her cloak and the end of her long braid. When she looked up at me, the haunted look in her eyes left a sharp pain in my chest.

"I didn't mean to intrude," she said, her gaze shifting from me back to Father. "I was just... looking for Bran."

Father glanced over at me and I gave him an almost imperceptible nod. She had sought me out for a reason and I certainly wasn't going to turn her away.

"I'll just be in the kitchen, if you need me," Father said and granted us our privacy.

Seren bit down hard on her lower lip, not fully meeting my gaze. "I'm sorry. I just... I needed to... I needed someone would understand. Tomorrow, I—"

She cut herself off, staring in the direction of the kitchen for an overlong moment.

"Would you rather discuss this somewhere more private?" I asked.

She hesitated before giving a brief nod. "It's not that I don't trust him."

"I know." I motioned for her to follow me. "This way."

The cottage wasn't large by any means, but Father had still left my old room empty. It would give us the privacy Seren wanted—privacy that I didn't hold against her. Father wasn't a gossip, but things still had a way of traveling in a place like Clogwyn. Of course, I suspected that wasn't the only reason she wanted her privacy. I knew her well enough to know that she preferred to nurse her wounds and hurts in private. And one look at her face tonight told me that those hurts, whatever they were, were particularly raw.

I ushered her into the small bedroom ahead of me, closing the door behind us before lighting a few half-burned candles that were still in the room. As the room became faintly illuminated, I was able to see that Seren had come to linger by the window, a few feet away from the narrow bed. I couldn't stop the memories that came to me as I looked at her, bathed in shadows. Memories of our childhood growing up at Clogwyn together and memories of the countless hours she'd spent in this room with me when I'd been recovering from the attack on the road that had almost cost us both our lives. The history between us ran deep and the trust we'd shared had too—once. *She sought you out,* I reminded myself as I leaned against the wall.

"In the morning," she said, letting out a shaky breath, "I'll have to go before the council. I'll have to admit that Aengus is my half-brother, my mother's son, and that by the laws of this land, he has as much of a right to the title of Ri as I do."

She hugged her arms around herself. Her shoulders drooped and her chest caved in as she stared hard at the floor. Just looking at her left my chest aching. I moved slowly, giving her every opportunity to move away, but she stayed where she was.

"*You* were chosen as Ri," I told her, gently placing my hands on her upper arms. "The people will remember that."

"I was chosen because there was no other choice."

"There was another choice. They rejected Domhnall for you."

"Because of how it would look. Because he is his mother's son. Because of my mother's sway as Banrion." Her breath hitched and she averted her gaze again, swallowing hard. "They've made it clear I am not the one they want to lead them."

I didn't know how to fix this, how to make her believe in herself again. It was startling, seeing her this way. I'd always seen her as confident, as knowing what she wanted, and now she was floundering. She'd been the one to bring me back from the abyss; now it seemed I was the one who needed to do that for her. Only I'd never felt so woefully inept.

"The Wolf Spirit chose *you*," I said.

"And now I fear I will not be able to keep the promise I made to it. I'm so tired of fighting." The last words came out as little more than a hoarse whisper, as if it pained her to admit them.

I pulled her into my arms, relieved when she immediately relaxed into my embrace. "You have every right to be tired. We've all been fighting this for far too long."

"I fear what they'll say of Mother," she said, her words slightly muffled by my chest. "That they'll hold things against her that they shouldn't. And I have seen firsthand the sway Aengus has with the people. What if they do choose him over me?"

"You're forgetting one very important thing," I replied, stroking her hair. "As much as I still hate to say it, Aengus very likely is a servant of Fianna. Or at the very least, keeping company with one. The people of Blaidd have seen what Fianna has done to them and their land. They will want no part of that."

"But if he's a servant of Fianna, why is he still healing them? When healers give themselves over to a dark spirit, that isn't what happens. They're forced to kill to survive. Why isn't Aengus doing that?"

"I don't know. Maybe he hasn't given himself fully to it yet. Maybe Alannah is still trying to convince him."

She sighed heavily. "Sometimes I want so badly for things to go back to the way they were. Before all of this. Before the Purge."

"I know," I murmured.

Silence fell between us, though not an uncomfortable one, and I found myself holding my breath, waiting for her to pull away from my embrace, but to my surprise and pleasure, she didn't.

"What are you doing tomorrow?" I asked softly. "After the council meeting."

"Dealing with the inevitable fallout, I suppose."

"Could you get away at some point, do you think? At least for a little while?"

She pulled back slightly, though she still kept her arms around me, her brows slightly wrinkling. "Possibly. Why?"

"I'm to head north the day after tomorrow. I thought..." I paused, clearing my throat before plunging forward, silently praying to the Spirits I wouldn't find myself on the receiving end of her rejection. "I thought we could go down to the river. Just the two of us, like we used to."

She tilted her head to the side, studying me for what felt like an excruciatingly long moment. We had plenty of memories of happier times on the banks of the Bywyd river that flowed just a mile south of Clogwyn. We'd retreated there often—first as children, then as lovers not so very long ago. Perhaps it was foolish to want to recapture some of that with her before I left. I wanted to help ease her impossible burdens and I wanted a hint of light amidst all the darkness, for the both of us.

"I just have one question," she said, her lips curling up in the slightest of smiles. "Can the wolves come?"

I let out a quiet chuckle. "The wolves can always come."

"The midday meal. That will be the easiest time for us to get away. I'll get Rhodri to throw something together from the kitchens."

"I'll find you then."

She leaned up, brushing a kiss across my cheek before releasing her hold on me and taking a few steps back. My gaze was locked on her, my blood heating just at the touch of her lips on her skin. I wanted more, so much more, but not now. Not until she was ready. This was a step and I'd take as many of them as I had to in order to win her complete trust again.

"Thank you," she said, her expression softening. "Until tomorrow."

I saw her out, following quietly behind her as we crossed the great room to the front door. Father remained in the kitchen, but Seren called a farewell to him, smiling at his return wishes. The storm outside had finally started to let up, now down to a light drizzle and a few distant rumblings of thunder. I lingered at the door, watching Seren disappear into the darkness down the crushed shell path that led back to the castle. I didn't envy her with what she had to confess come morning, but I would be there to offer support to her in the aftermath. *And surely no one would wish for a man with ties to Fianna as their Ri,* I thought as I closed the door behind me. For all their hatred of Seren, they could not hate her that much.

CHAPTER 36

THE WAY THINGS WERE
Seren

AS I STEPPED OUT of the council chambers, it felt as if the very weight of what I had just transpired would crush me. My confession had not been well-received. Arwel and Mair had been stunned by the news, while Domhnall had met it with a grim, determined air and Laoise had gleefully gloated. I supposed I should have at least been thankful that they hadn't attempted to strip me of my title on the spot.

The truth would spread with the ferocity of one of Fianna's fires; no doubt the gossip was already starting to flood its way through the castle. And while it may have been cowardly, I found I was more than happy to be leaving the Ri's study behind to retreat into the forest with Bran.

I hurried through the castle, doing my best to ignore the muttered words from servants and warriors as I went. When I finally stepped through one of the servants' doors, I let out a sigh of relief. The sun shone brightly in the blue sky and the world around me was painted in brilliant shades of green; summer's one last gasp before autumn staked its claim on the land. It was a beautiful day to escape.

Striking out across the courtyard, I made my way to the stables where Bran awaited me. I craved his company this morning, almost as desperately as I had craved it last night. Now that I'd opened my heart to him, there was no holding back the torrential waves of longing.

The stables themselves were mostly quiet, the horses already tended to and most of them out in the pastures beyond the castle walls for the day. I found Bran easily, outside Ceol's stall. He had both my stallion and Copar tacked, and a few feet away, Awyr and Cryfder were lying on the dirt aisleway, attentively watching Bran. He smiled when I walked up, the brilliance of it causing my heart to stutter for a few beats. Even after all of this, he still had the power to take my breath away.

"Ready to go?" he asked, passing me Ceol's reins.

I nodded, tossing the reins over my stallion's head. "Thank you. For getting the wolves and tacking up the horses."

"I was happy to. I have our food in my saddlebags. I think Rhodri even slipped in a pastry or two."

My mouth watered a little at the last bit. The castle's head cook had long been known for his excellent baking skills.

We led the horses out of the stable before mounting up. I called Awyr and Cryfder to Ceol's side, both wolves well trained to stay with the horses without getting underfoot. I let Bran lead the way across the courtyard and soon, we'd passed through a side gate, following the well-maintained trail into the forest.

The trail would lead us to the river, the path wide enough for us to ride side by side. The comforting scent of pine filled the air and the sun dappled the forest floor as it broke through the trees. I listened to the steady footfalls of the horses' hooves, the quiet creak of leather, and the occasional birdsong echoing in the air and I could feel my fear receding. Bran had been right; this had been exactly what I had needed today.

There was a comfortable silence between us as we wound our way through the trees down to the riverbank and I was glad that Bran seemed to sense that I didn't need the space between us filled with words right now. Eventually, the trees thinned and the bramble-covered forest floor was replaced by smooth rocks.

We dismounted, tying our horses to trees, and Bran pulled our food out of his saddlebags. After trekking across the uneven ground, we settled on a large flat boulder near the water's edge. It had been a favorite place of both of ours from the time we were children, and memories of happier, simpler times filled me as I clambered up onto the boulder, the stone now warmed by the sun.

Bran split up the food and I was especially pleased to see that Rhodri had indeed slipped us each a pastry; apple, from the smell of it. Resisting the urge to dive into the sweet treat first, I helped myself to the small feast of bread, cheese, nuts, fruit, and roasted meat, Bran following suit.

"How did it all go?" he asked, leaning back on one hand as he stretched out his legs.

I sighed, breaking the chunk of bread in my hands in two. "They were shocked, as I expected. Laoise practically gloated, but I wouldn't expect anything less of her these days. And of course, they're worried about how it's all going to look. Not to mention how much more difficult it makes this situation with Aengus."

"He seems to have disappeared in the last week. People still speak of him, but there have been no reports of anyone seeing him."

"He's done this before, though." I frowned as I took a bite of cheese. "Disappearing and then showing up again at the site of disaster."

"Alannah learned that trick well from Lorcan," Bran said with a grimace.

"And it seems she's taught it to Aengus."

"Lewella has a few leads for me at least. I'll hope their trail hasn't gone completely cold."

My chest tightened at the reminder that he was leaving this place once more come morning, once again putting himself in the thick of the danger for me and for our people. But I couldn't hold him back even if I tried. He was as determined as I was to defeat Fianna and we needed his skill.

We were almost done with our meal when Cryfder trotted down to the riverbank, coming back with a large stick held awkwardly in his mouth. He brought it over to the rock and leapt up beside Bran, though the stick threw him just enough off-balance that he had to scramble to make it all the way up. He dropped the stick mere inches from Bran's legs, looking expectant and wagging his tail. Bran cast me a sidelong glance and I was quick to give him a wave of encouragement.

"Go on," I said, unable to hide my smile. "I know I'm not nearly as good of a playmate as you and he's been missing that."

Bran grinned, grabbing the stick before getting to his feet. He and Cryfder jumped off the rock, striding down to the shoreline. Seconds later, Awyr took off after them, my older wolf apparently eager to get in on the fun as well. I stayed where I was, content to watch the three of them.

Light glimmered on the water, making it sparkle and gleam as Bran and the wolves ran along the river's bank. The branches of the trees hanging over the water gently swayed in the light breeze along with the reeds that popped up here and there at the river's edge. To the north, the Dail made a dark outline against the sky line, but to the south, the land sloped more gently as it slowly made its way to the shores of the Niwl Channel. I let my eyes drift closed, basking in the warmth of the sun, the feel of the breeze, and the fresh woodsy scent in the air.

The splash of water and loud laughter caused my eyes to flutter back open. Awyr and Cryfder had plunged into the river, taking off after the large stick that now bobbed in the gently rolling water. Bran stood at the shore, grinning as he called encouragement to them. At some point, he had discarded his boots and rolled up the bottoms of his pants so that he could wade into the water up to his ankles. His black hair was even more tousled than usual with the breeze and his face lit up as Cryfder snatched the bobbing branch and began swimming back to Bran, Awyr in hot pursuit.

For a moment, there was an ache in my chest as I watched them. I could almost pretend there wasn't a battle waging for the clan's very existence and that I was free of the heavy burdens that weighed me down so hard, they threatened to drown me. I wanted to take this little bit of happiness and cling to it.

Cryfder reached Bran, dropping the stick at Bran's command. He picked it up, throwing it back into the water and the wolves were off again, diving back in with a loud splash. A smile crept over my face as I continued to watch their revelry. What I would give for life to be simply this again.

After a while, both Cryfder and Awyr tired of Bran's game and the trio wandered back to the rock. The wolves were soaked, their tongues lolling out of their mouths, but there was a bright, contented look in their golden eyes. Bran was wet as well, though it was mostly limited to his lower half. He climbed up onto the rock with the panting wolves, indicating they should lie down. My heart twisted a little as he poured a bit of water from the waterskin into his cupped hands and let each of the wolves drink. At his core, he was a good man, and a kind one; he had always been.

"Thank you," I said as he straightened, wiping his hands on his pant leg. "For today."

His eyes softened. "You're welcome. I'm glad you were able to get away."

"As am I." I inclined my head toward the wolves, both of whom had stretched out and started to doze. "You are cleaning them up, though, when we get back."

He gave a soft chuckle. "Happily."

My gaze flitted to the tree line on the other side of the river, catching a glimpse of a doe near the water's edge before the creature took notice of us and darted deeper into the forest. "You leave in the morning."

He nodded. "At first light."

I twisted the clan ring with my thumb, taking a deep breath before allowing my gaze to return to him. "I'll miss you. When you go."

"And I'll miss you," he said, holding my gaze. "Every second I'm away from you."

He moved slowly, his motions tentative as one of his hands came to rest on the side of my face. I didn't move away from him, leaning into his touch. I was finished with pretending that I didn't want him or need him.

His lips covered mine, gently at first, and then more insistently as we let ourselves get carried away by our desire. This part was easy with him; it always had been. I wrapped an arm around his neck, pulling him closer to me as I felt a piece of my heart slipping back into place. How I had missed this: his kisses, his touch, his love, and this fire he ignited within me. Too soon, he pulled away, both of us breathing hard as we rested our foreheads against each other.

"I love you, Ren," he said softly.

"And I love you," I whispered.

He gently tucked back a few strands of my hair that had come loose from my braids during our passionate kissing, then wrapped an arm around me. I scooted closer to him, closing my eyes again and soaking in the warmth of the sun beating down on us, along with the sparks of desire and delight that coursed through me at the feeling of him holding me close. If only our lives could forever be like these few moments of bliss.

"We should get back," I eventually sighed.

I didn't want to go back to the castle. I wanted to stay here, where I could almost pretend that things were the way they'd once been, but we couldn't. Not with Bran leaving in the morning and not with the storm that had erupted at Clogwyn with the news of Aengus' true parentage.

Bran let out a sigh of his own and then nodded. He brushed a light kiss over my forehead before getting to his feet. The wolves woke at our movements and Bran gathered up what remained of our lunch before we abandoned our rocky perch. I released a long, low breath as we crossed the uneven bank, squaring my shoulders as I inwardly steeled myself for what I had to return to. Bran stepped a little closer to me, slipping his hand in mine and giving a gentle squeeze. I laced my fingers with his, soothed by the feel of his skin on mine and his nearness. This time, we would face Fianna's darkness together, and this time we *would* win.

CHAPTER 37

POWER AND PROMISES

Aengus

FIANNA WAS CLOSING IN on Seren, and as such, it had driven us south to Castle Clogwyn. We were miles out from the castle itself, secluded in the dense and largely untouched forest. Thus far, our little hideout had gone undetected. Whether that was sheer luck or Fianna's power, I wasn't certain. I turned the wooden spit I had created over the fire, making sure the roasting rabbit cooked evenly. I'd killed the creature hours ago with my gift and I was determined not to waste its sacrifice. Not only had its life force sustained my growing needs, it would feed Alannah and me tonight. Tomorrow, I would need to venture out and bring down something bigger. A deer, perhaps. The smaller animals like the rabbit weren't enough to completely sustain me.

What my soul longed for more than anything else was the life of a human, but I could not stomach such a thing. The excuse I had used with Alannah was that taking the life of a human would draw far more attention than taking the lives of wild animals, but I knew I would not be able to hide my secret loathing forever.

Behind me, a shadow creature stirred, lifting its head, its glowing eyes fixed on the trees just in front of us. I followed its gaze, spying two shadowy figures emerging through the trees. Despite knowing who they were and the creature's lack of aggression, I still latched onto the hilt of my dagger. If I had learned nothing else these last few months, it was that caution was never unwise.

The creature let out a low rumble, releasing a few puffs of smoke from its nostrils before laying its head back down. The figures drew nearer, soon illuminated by the light of the fire. Alannah greeted me with a sly, triumphant smile while Domhnall trailed behind her, not looking nearly as comfortable or as pleased, judging by his bunched shoulders and the way his eyes darted around our small camp. Alannah had left a little more than an hour ago to fetch him, a potentially treacherous task that I'd worried over. All it would take was one mistake or one careless word to bring the entire war band of Blaidd down on us. But Alannah had been flying to Clogwyn for days, watching Domhnall's comings and goings and waiting for the perfect opportunity to lure him away from the keep.

I straightened when they reached the edge of the fire. All five of the creatures got up from where they had been dozing to greet Alannah, rubbing against her as she petted them. I felt a slight twinge as I watched her. Despite being Fianna's servant, I still couldn't muster the affection she had for the strange creatures. Another failure to add to my growing tally. One of the creatures strode over to Domhnall, smoke billowing from its nostrils as it sniffed at him. Domhnall grimaced, wrinkling his nose and taking a few steps back. The creature let out a disgruntled hiss before returning to Alannah.

Domhnall cleared his throat. "It seems you indeed spoke the truth. Seren went to the council this morning and has admitted that you are her half-brother."

A wave of relief washed over me; another small piece of Fianna's plan falling into place.

"And," Alannah said with a smirk, "it seems that news has not been well received."

"How much support does she have?" I asked Domhnall as a slight, sharp tingle settled in my wrist. This was my moment to take control. I could not fail Fianna in this.

"Not as much as she thinks," Domhnall replied. "I doubt that her intermediary advisor, Mair, will be swayed to stand against her, but she has fallen greatly out of favor with the other two council members, Laoise and Arwel. The two of them carry more power and weight than Mair ever will. And while Lewella may support Seren wholeheartedly as warrior chief, there are plenty in the war band itself who do not."

The last bit was particularly good news. Having the war band's support would do much in helping ensure I was able to take control of Castle Clogwyn, and then the clan, with little to no bloodshed.

"Just how much power does the council wield when it comes to fully stripping Seren of her title?" I asked.

"Enough," Domhnall answered. "Three-fourths of the council is needed for a vote of no confidence. I believe I can get you that easily. The council would state no confidence in Seren's abilities to lead and then name you as the successor."

It could not be more perfect, both in its simplicity and in the way it eased my conscience. There would be no uprising, no upheaval, and no further loss of life. Thank the Spirits Seren had led so ineptly.

"You will get the agreement for a vote of no confidence," I told Domhnall, lifting my chin as I drew my shoulders back. "And then you will report back to me here. Alannah will be able to find you."

"And you will keep your promises to me?" Domhnall raised his brows.

"So long as you keep your end of this bargain."

He nodded stiffly. "I'll need a few days."

"You'll have them," I said. "I assume you can find your way back? Or do you need Alannah to escort you?"

Domhnall cast Alannah a sidelong glance, wrinkling his nose again. "I need no escort."

With one last dark look at the creatures, he inclined his head to Alannah and me before turning and striding back off into the forest.

"Do you trust him?" I asked Alannah as soon as he was gone. It would be disturbingly easy for him to simply turn us in to Seren.

"I trust him enough, as does Fianna," she answered, pursing her lips and staring intently in the direction he'd gone. "He has no love for Seren, I can tell you that. Not anymore."

"I hope you're right," I said with a heavy sigh.

"You worry too much, Aengus." She waved a finger at me, narrowing her eyes. "It's time you broke yourself of that—before you become Ri of Blaidd."

I gritted my teeth, turning my attention back to the roasting rabbit. Both she and Fianna had become far less patient with my shortcomings since we'd traveled south. By the time I pulled the rabbit off the fire, Alannah had settled down on the ground in front of the blaze, the shadow creatures coming to lie at her feet. I placed the cooked meat on a small piece of hide and began dividing it up between the two of us.

"I'm ready to see them all burn," Alannah said as I worked, her cheeks lightly flushing as she took on a more sullen look.

"I'm tired of watching them all up there, living their lavish lives while we have to scrounge a living from nothing."

"Hopefully it won't be long," I replied, passing her her portion of the meat, trying to adopt a soothing tone. She had a temper, one I admittedly didn't like to see on display or be on the receiving end of.

It had been grating on her more and more these last few days, our desolate conditions. The more time she spent at Clogwyn, the more irate about the matter she became. Even a night in each other's arms wasn't enough to fully distract her from her growing bitterness. Not that I could entirely blame her. I, too, was weary of this desperate way of living. I certainly wouldn't complain about the comforts of the castle when they finally became ours. We were close, so close. All we needed to do was stay the course.

CHAPTER 38

THE WOLF'S WARNING
Bran

I LEAPT EASILY OVER the fallen log, my nose to the wind as I traversed the pitch-black forest. There was no strange smell in the air tonight, nothing other than the earthy smell of the forest, and I felt none of Fianna's distinctive darkness, but still, I didn't let my guard down. My trip to the other side of the Dail mountains had unfortunately been for nothing. There had been nothing out of sorts, no signs of new fires, and no new rumors or whispers of Aengus. Things had been quiet, too quiet, and I found that made me even more alert for trouble.

The trees thinned around me, the ground leveling out, and I broke into a lope. I wasn't far from the castle, only a mile or so out by now. It would be late by the time I reached it. I supposed I could have stopped when night had fallen and slept in the woods before continuing on in the morning, but I was eager to get home. Eager to return to Seren.

She'd been constantly in my thoughts since I'd left. That afternoon by the river was one I'd be remembering for a long time. What had been broken between us was mending and I had hope that soon, I'd be her husband again in every way. But I could be patient until then; patience had certainly served me well thus far.

The scent of smoke startled me out of my introspection, causing me to trip over a fallen branch. Scrambling to my feet, my gaze darted around the forest, my ears swiveling as I searched for any noise. An overwhelming darkness engulfed me, making me shudder. Fianna was here, though in what form, Spirits only knew.

There was a piercing screech and a shadow creature lunged at me, springing from between two trees. I darted away, my heart pounding. I couldn't kill the damned thing, but I could injure it enough to safely get away. Flames shot from the creature's mouth as it closed in on me and I just barely managed to keep myself from getting singed.

I crouched low, the creature and I circling one another. I lunged before it could, getting in a bite to its shoulder before I sprang away again, but not before it swiped at me with its claws. My side burned where it had struck me, the creature's claws having broken the skin, but I couldn't afford to be distracted.

Our little dance continued, neither one of us making a marked gain at defeating the other and soon, I could feel myself tiring. The glowing ember gaze of the creature told me it still had plenty of energy to spare, imbued by Fianna's power. It lunged again and I skittered away, only to realize too late that I'd gotten myself cornered between three large boulders. I bared my teeth, my hackles raised, determined to make some sort of stand.

The creature's hindquarters bunched and I braced myself to feel the burn of its claws and teeth, but instead, there was an ear-splitting screech as a massive white blur barreled into it. At first, I thought I was imagining things, but as the massive white wolf tumbled to the earth with the creature, I knew what I was seeing was real. The wolf's body was made of snow and its fangs were made of ice. The ground trembled as it pinned the creature down.

Go, Son of Blaidd, the Wolf Spirit said. *Warn them that Fianna is near.*

I raced off into the darkness, the creature's wails ringing in my ears. Ignoring my shaking muscles, I pushed myself as hard as I could. I had to reach the castle before my body failed me. There would be no warning the others if I was dead or trapped in my wolf form. Gritting my teeth, I lowered my head and plunged on despite the growing burning in my side as the creature's poison began to take root. *Get to Clogwyn and get to Cian,* I repeated to myself. The healer would able to reverse the effects of the poison if I made it in time.

It was a hard run, through thick underbrush, rocky ground, and dense trees, but eventually I reached the main road. With the massive grey walls of Clogwyn looming ahead of me, I let myself slow my pace. My breath was coming fast and a cold sweat had broken out over my skin, dampening my coat. The burning in my side was growing harder to ignore and I barely had the energy to shift as I closed in on the portcullis. I almost fell flat on my face as I transformed, feeling slightly lightheaded. My side throbbed and when I touched it, my hand came away coated in blood. Warriors rushed over as I staggered through the gate, my head feeling like it was in a fog. Someone gripped my shoulder and I started, throwing myself off-balance again.

"Easy," Tudwal said, his eyes widening as his gaze darted to my side. "Let's get you to the infirmary."

I managed a nod, grateful when the other man slipped an arm around my shoulders to help steady me. In hindsight, I don't know how I made the long walk, but I was determined. Seren and Lewella needed to know there were shadow creatures this close to the castle. With the late hour, the infirmary was largely empty, but the healer's assistant overseeing things for the night took one look at me and ushered me into a room before sending for Cian.

Once in the room, the assistant helped me to a chair, instructing me to remove my shirt while he fetched what he needed to clean my injuries. Tudwal hung back at the door while I discarded my ripped and bloodstained shirt. Another piece of clothing ruined; the castle tailors were going to be exhausted from having to mend and make me so much clothing.

"Send for Ri Seren and Pennathe Lewella," I told Tudwal. "There was a shadow creature a little less than a mile outside the castle."

Tudwal grimaced and gave a quick nod before striding off. I leaned against the wall behind me, closing my eyes and letting my shoulders slump. My side pained me fiercely. The assistant eventually returned and I was fighting to stay conscious as he began to clean my wounds. I barely registered the door being shoved open again, the noise making the assistant start. I hissed at the pain that erupted in my side from his jerky motion and Cian shooed him out of the way as he strode into the room.

"What happened?" Cian asked as he crouched down beside my chair and began gently probing my wound.

"Shadow creature," I said through gritted teeth.

"You do have a penchant for tangling with those monsters, don't you?" Cian's attempt at levity distracted me long enough for him to do something that made the entire right side of my body erupt in burning pain.

"We'll need a yarrow paste," Cian said to his assistant. "See to that while I tend to him with my gift. You'll likely have to go digging in the stores to find more of the dried leaves; we used the last of what was made yesterday."

The assistant scurried out of the room.

"Alright," Cian said, rolling up the sleeves of his shirt, "let's get you stable. I have a feeling Seren and Lewella are going to be here any moment."

He covered my wounds with his hands, blood still oozing out of the gashes, and I released a deep breath. The pain slowly dissipated, a peculiar warmth coursing through my body as Cian worked to draw out the poison before beginning to knit the muscles and skin back together. By the time he was done, the excruciating burning had receded to a dull ache. I opened my eyes just as Cian got to his feet, stumbling slightly, his features a touch pale. It always took much from him, using his gifting to heal, especially on a wound such as this one.

"I'll treat it again in the morning," he said, wiping a bit of sweat off his brow. "It should be fully healed after that. You were lucky; it wasn't as deep as I first thought."

"Thank you," I told him, feeling a little less muddle-headed now that he'd seen to the worst of it.

The door banged open again, Seren bursting into the room with Lewella on her heels. To my surprise, Domhnall strode in as well, but I didn't have much time to ponder his presence before Cian jumped out of Seren's way and she wrapped her around me. There was a twinge in my side but I ignored it, embracing her in return. For a brief moment tonight, I'd worried I wouldn't return to her at all.

"You're alright," she murmured, pressing her face into the hollow of my neck.

"I'm alright," I replied, brushing my lips over the top of her head. "Cian's seen to the worst of it."

Out of the corner of my eye, I noticed Domhnall flush, his mouth pinching, but I was more concerned with Seren than his petulance right now. She released a shuddering breath and eased away from me. As she did so, her arm bumped against my tender side and I hissed, unable to hold back a grimace.

"Don't undo all my hard work," Cian said with a slight frown.

Lewella cleared her throat, stepping forward and focusing on me. "A creature did this?"

"A little less than a mile outside the castle," I replied. "There was only one, as far as I could tell, but where there's one, there are others."

Lewella's mouth turned down, a wrinkle settling in her brow. "I'll send warriors out. I don't like them resurfacing so close to the castle after their little disappearing act."

"Is that necessary?" Domhnall asked. "It's only one, after all, and clearly it didn't pursue the shifter all the way back to Clogwyn."

Both Lewella and Seren narrowed their eyes at him while I scowled.

"The only reason it didn't chase me all the way back here is because the Wolf Spirit intervened," I snapped, my jaw tight. "There's nothing to say it and the rest of its kind won't be at the gates sooner rather than later."

"Last I checked," Domhnall retorted, "you are not the warrior chief of Blaidd, now, are you?"

"But *I* am," Lewella said, fixing him with a withering gaze. "And I say that warriors will be sent out to hunt for the creatures."

Domhnall mumbled something under his breath and tightly folded his arms.

"Ri Seren," Lewella said, giving Seren a low nod of respect, "I'll be certain to report to you the moment I have news regarding the creatures."

"Thank you," Seren replied. "I wish the warriors good hunting. Domhnall, the council must meet in the morning to discuss this newest development."

"If that is what you wish." His face was still twisted into a sour expression but he left the room behind Lewella.

Spirits only knew what his tantrum was about this time. At least Lewella had put him in his place. Seren needed a new chief advisor; if there only there was someone she trusted who was up for the task.

"I'd feel a bit better if Bran stayed here tonight," Cian said, "just to be safe. I've pulled the poison out, but a wound from a shadow creature is nothing to take lightly."

Letting out a quiet sigh, I nodded. I'd rather have been in my own bed, but I trusted Cian's judgment. "If that's what you think is best."

"I'm staying as well then," Seren said, lifting her chin a just a fraction, as if she dared Cian to argue against it.

"I'm assuming you aren't opposed to that arrangement, Bran?" Cian glanced over at me, slightly raising his brows.

"Absolutely not," I answered him, even as I focused on Seren. I only wished the next few hours I was going to spend with her didn't involve me being injured.

"I'll have someone bring in an extra sleeping pallet," Cian said. "And as soon as that yarrow paste is ready, I'll be back to finish treating the wounds."

He left us on our own and with some effort, I got to my feet, swaying slightly as I walked toward the small bed tucked in a corner. Despite Cian's gift, I still very much felt like I'd fought for my life tonight.

"Easy," Seren said, placing a hand on my arm as she helped me over to the bed. "I feared the worst when I heard you'd returned here wounded."

"Not going to get rid of me that easily." I sank down onto the mattress and stretched out my legs, leaning back against the pillows.

Slowly, with the slightest hint of hesitance, she sat down on the edge of the bed, mere inches from me. "Maybe I don't want to get rid of you ever."

My pulse quickened. Why did I have to be injured now, of all times?

"That's good. Considering I don't want to leave your side ever again." I managed a strained smile, even with my aching side. "Well, not without telling you first."

She laughed softly, leaning forward and brushing a light kiss over my lips. "You need to rest or Cian is going to have my hide. And I think I might need to consider venturing into the Spirit Realm to thank the Wolf Spirit for saving you tonight, as well as try and discern Fianna's next move."

The door creaked open and the assistant stepped in, handing a rolled-up sleeping pallet to Seren before departing once more. She placed in on the floor, looking at it with a slight frown as she resumed her place on the edge of the bed.

I lightly covered her hand with my own. "If a sleeping pallet is what you want, I won't argue against it, but... I wouldn't mind if you joined me here."

She pressed her lips together, her gaze downcast as a brief silence stretched between us. I inwardly scolded myself. Hadn't I learned my lesson about pushing her too fast? But just as I was about to descend into a spiral of self-loathing, she looked back up with a tentative smile.

"I think I would like that. Just for tonight."

My own smile broadened and I settled back into the pillows as she stretched out beside me. Another step toward what we'd once had. Another little bit of hope that one day she'd trust me again like she used to. I covered a yawn, my fatigue staring to get the better of me.

"Rest," she murmured, brushing my hair off my brow. "Spirits know you need it. I'll wake you when Cian comes back with the yarrow mixture."

Despite longing to keep myself awake just to marvel at the feeling of having her lying beside me once more, another yawn, one big enough to crack my jaw, had me giving up that idea. The fight and the agonizing flight back to the castle had taken much out of me. I drifted into a doze, Seren lacing her fingers with mine, the warmth of her nearness soothing the deepest parts of me. There was a storm of darkness coming—I could feel it in my bones—but we would face it together.

CHAPTER 39

CAST ASIDE
Aengus

ALANNAH WAS FURIOUS. I didn't think I had ever seen her so angry before. She paced in front of the fire, glowering at me each time she looked at me. She'd stopped her screaming and cursing for now, but somehow, the silence was worse. I knew I'd failed, and failed miserably. Fianna still punished me even now, a burning pain radiating up my arm and into my shoulder, leaving me clutching it. Why was I always such a continual disappointment?

"You were supposed to watch them!" Alannah snapped, her nostrils flaring. "You weren't supposed to let them out of your sight. How can you expect to control a whole clan if you can't even manage to control the creatures for less than two days?"

I winced, dropping my chin. She'd left early yesterday, to hunt. We'd depleted this part of the forest of game, forcing us to go farther and farther out as the days had dragged on. Last night, she had been the one to hunt and I had been left to watch over our camp and the creatures. Not that I'd managed to do so successfully.

"They were anxious to hunt," I said. "It's been too long since they've been able to do so. You know how intractable and belligerent they get. I tried to keep them under control, I swear."

I regretted the excuse almost as soon as I said it, the pain in my shoulder leaving me gasping. *You did not try hard enough,* Fianna growled. The creatures hissed behind me, the four of them curled up in front of the fire, as if offended at having the blame laid on them.

"If you continue to indulge in this weakness, you will *never* keep control of Blaidd!" Alannah huffed loudly. "I expected better of you, Aengus. Fianna expects better."

"I know," I mumbled, my chest caving in. I'd expected better of myself. There was no doubt now that Clogwyn was on high alert, possibly even aware of our presence. The creatures had told Fianna they had tangled with a wolf that was a man before the Wolf Spirit had driven them off. It could have been none other than Bran. He had multiple lives, it seemed, with his continual brushes with death. *Or the Wolf Spirit is protecting him,* I thought, rubbing at my sore shoulder. Its presence had unnerved me and it had infuriated Fianna.

"I suppose we will see what news is brought from Clogwyn to see if this situation can be salvaged." Alannah sighed, toying with the end of her braid. "He should be here any moment now."

I nodded, my thoughts racing ahead to our visitor as the morning sun continued to rise higher in the sky. In the early morning hours, Fianna had commanded Alannah to seek out Domhnall on her way back to our encampment and the advisor was supposed to have come to us shortly after dawn. Alannah had sworn she hadn't been seen, but every second we'd waited, I'd grown more and more afraid that Seren was on to us.

The creature closest to me let out a high-pitched hiss, swiveling its head as it focused on the trees to our left. Alannah and I turned, following its gaze just as Domhnall emerged from the trees and I allowed myself a quiet sigh of relief. He was alone, with no warriors in sight; we weren't thwarted yet, at least. Domhnall skirted the fire, giving the creatures a large berth as he approached us.

"You have good news, I take it?" Alannah asked.

"News that I suspect will please you," Domhnall answered. "Though I do come with a warning as well."

"What warning?" I asked, my chest clenching. Had I already ruined our scheme with my inability to make the creatures obey?

"It seems one of your creatures," Domhnall replied, his mouth down turning in thinly veiled disgust as he spoke of them, "got themselves into a tangle with Seren's little shifter. The castle is on full alert and warriors have been sent out to scour the forest for you."

"They will not find us." Alannah gave a wave of her hand. "Fianna will ensure that. What of news that will please us?"

Domhnall openly stared at her before shaking his head. "I have swayed the council to make a vote of no confidence against Seren. They will do so tomorrow morning. With pressure from me and supportive words from a few of the more prominent village elders, they will be willing to name Aengus as Ri of Blaidd. *If* he can assure them that he is not a servant of Fianna."

My stomach clenched but Alannah dismissively waved her hand.

"That is an easy enough lie," she said. "Especially once the castle is free of the gifted rabble that inhabit it. Though I feel bound to remind you that if you do subvert us and raise suspicion against Aengus, you will have Fianna's wrath to fear."

"Aengus' business regarding the Spirits is his own," Domhnall replied as he swallowed hard.

A lightness settled in my chest as elation coursed through me. Could it be this easy? Could it truly be done with no bloodshed?

Do not think keeping your place will be this easy, Fianna said, a shooting pain coursing through my wrist before it quickly disappeared. *I do not have the patience to deal with complacency and you have much work to do if you wish to keep Blaidd in your control.* I swallowed hard. Spirits helped me if I failed it, for it was Fianna that held my soul in its hands.

"There still might need to be some convincing tomorrow on your part," Domhnall continued, focusing on me. "Seren has spread alarm and concern about your ties to Fianna. Though your little... acts of late seem to have endeared you to the villagers. Many of the elders have made it clear they see you as some savior. But do not be surprised if my fellow advisors show you more skepticism."

"That will be dealt with," I replied, pulling my shoulders back. I needed to project confidence now, even if I didn't entirely feel it. "I will make certain there is no doubt in their minds that I am the right choice for the next Ri of Blaidd."

"Be sure that you do," Domhnall said. "The council will meet at the tenth hour tomorrow morning. I will make certain that the gate guards will accept you and I will handpick warriors to see you to the council chambers."

"Good," I replied. "We will see you in the morning."

"And do not forget the price that comes with betrayal," Alannah said, her tone taking on an icy edge.

Domhnall's gaze flitted to the creatures. "I swear that you will have no such betrayal from me."

He took his leave and a smug smile crept across Alannah's face.

THE SEER

"It seems this part of the plan will be easy enough after all," she said. "They must hate Seren greatly to be so easily convinced to cast her aside."

"What about them?" I motioned to the shadow creatures. "I don't think it wise to bring them with us, not now at least, and they can't be left unattended."

"I will stay behind and watch them. Besides, my presence will arouse too much suspicion at Clogwyn." She closed the distance between us, her voice taking on a soothing tone as if all her earlier fury was completely erased. When she reached me, she wrapped her arms around my waist, running her fingers up and down my back, causing goose bumps to rise on my skin. "You will go to the castle and the moment the clan ring is on your finger, you will send for me. They will have no choice but to accept me and the creatures once you are Ri."

"I wish you were to be there beside me," I said, dropping my chin. Her volatile temper aside, she had seen me through every step of this treacherous plan.

"I will be. As your Banrion, remember? Once Blaidd is yours for the taking, it will be exactly as we have wished."

She leaned up, covering my lips with her own, and snaked her arm around my neck before pulling me down to her. I closed my eyes, opening my mouth to hers, letting her chase my foolish fears away. This was a moment to celebrate. One more day and Blaidd would be ours.

CHAPTER 40

BLOOD AND BETRAYAL
Seren

I'D SEEN THE GOLDEN wolf and once again, it had tried to kill me, this time by shoving me off the ledge of a tall mountain peak. The memories of what I had seen in the Spirit Realm haunted me as I strode down the hallway to the Ri's study, leaving a jittery feeling in my chest.

And it wasn't just my vision that had me unnerved. The warriors had found no trace of the creature that had tried, and thankfully failed, to kill Bran. It and its companions had vanished, like the smoke they were made of. Fianna's power was growing stronger and I was at a loss for how to stop it. All I saw in the Spirit Realm was my death and I had begun to fear that would either spell the end to the clan or perhaps be the only thing that would end the Stag Spirit's reign of terror.

I gave myself a brief shake as I rounded a corner, releasing a long breath. I didn't need to show the council my doubts and fears, not when they were ready to spring on me at a moment's notice. When I reached the study, the warriors outside gave me a respectful nod before opening the door.

To my surprise, Domhnall, Arwel, and Laoise were already seated and waiting for me. We were still missing Mair, but I knew for a fact that I wasn't late and neither was she. What had drawn the others here so early? *Don't jump to conclusions,* I reminded myself as I took a seat at the table next to Domhnall. He murmured a greeting before returning to his hushed conversation with Laoise.

I strained to hear what he was saying, not entirely trusting the two of them, but I could only pick up bits and pieces. It seemed innocuous enough, something to do with the village elder in Gefell, Tesni. The elder wasn't someone who regarded me in any sort of high standing, but she had never outright tried to undermine me—yet. The door opened again and Mair walked in, greeting me with a quick smile as she sat next to Arwel. I cleared my throat to gain Domhnall and Laoise's attention, the two of them quieting.

"Though it grieves me to have to do this," I said, "I must begin this session with a report from Pennathe Lewella regarding the shadow creature that attacked Bran. Unfortunately, the warriors have found no trace of it, or any of its potential companions. The search will continue, but I believe it wise if the castle continues taking extra precautions for the time being."

"I don't think anyone here can argue with that," Domhnall replied. "But I'm afraid that there is another, much more pressing, issue that I must bring to attention this morning."

My stomach dropped and I clenched my hands in my lap. What new destruction had Fianna wrought now? "And that is?"

"Last night," he replied, "a decision was made among council. One that it grieves me to bring forth, but alas, there is no other choice. The council has decreed a lack of confidence in your abilities to lead the Clan of Blaidd. You are to be stripped of your title henceforth, immediately."

My mouth fell open, a strange ringing filling my ears. I had feared many things, but not this. And from Domhnall, no less. Our relationship had been strained, that was true, but this?

"I did not agree to such a decision," Mair said, glowering at Domhnall. "No one consulted me on this matter."

"No one needed to," he replied. "As a temporary member of this council, your opinion does not count in this matter. The *permanent* advisory has every right to unseat the standing Ri, if they deem it so necessary."

He'd said it all with such a lack of remorse, as if dealing me such a devastating blow was of no consequence to him. And regrettably, every last damn word he spoke was true. *Not that they had the courage to do so to Father when he was Ri,* I thought, my face heating as my rage simmered. *No matter how many misguided, deplorable choices he made.*

"And who will lead in Ri Seren's absence?" Mair asked with a scoff. "Certainly not you; the council has already denied you once."

Domhnall bristled, his cheeks flushing. "Ri Seren's successor has been already been chosen. Someone I believe the people will be most gratified to have leading them."

The door to the study opened. At first, there were only two warriors, but then, Aengus strode in behind them. Seeing him again left a visceral shock coursing through me. Now when I looked at him, the similarities between us, between him and my deceased older brother, Eamon, seemed so clear. He was my blood kin, my half-brother, and he was here to take my clan from me. *And they're going to let him do it,* I thought, clenching my jaw and glowering at Domhnall, Arwel, and Laoise. They would hand Blaidd over to Fianna and seal Blaidd's doom, the damn traitors. Aengus stopped a few feet away from the table, the warriors, *my* warriors flanking him as if they were his own personal guard.

"Seren," Domhnall said, motioning to me, "I must ask that you hand over the ring of Blaidd and stand down. There is no need for unnecessary bloodshed."

"You give the title of Ri to him and you hand this clan right over to Fianna," I retorted, bolting to my feet as I stared them all down with rage. "Have you all lost your minds as well as your good sense?"

Their betrayal hurt so deeply, it left my chest tight and my body shaking, but it had also fueled a rage inside me beyond anything I had ever felt before. They could not do this. They could not destroy our people and our land this way.

"I assure you," Aengus said, flashing me a cold smile, "the last thing I wish to do is to destroy Blaidd. I only wish to bring about the peace the people, and the land, have longed for. A peace that has been absent for far too long, despite your failing efforts."

"My efforts have been thwarted by Fianna," I snapped. "They are hardly for lack of trying. And can you swear to this council that you are no servant of the Stag Spirit's darkness?"

"I do think it prudent that the council be assured that this man does not seek this clan's destruction, considering the rumors of late," Mair said, narrowing her eyes at Aengus.

"Again," Domhnall said, rapping his knuckles on the table, "as a temporary member of this council, one who should have been well replaced by now, your opinion on this matter carries no weight." His turned back to me. "Hand over the clan ring, Seren."

"I have not fought to save this clan from Fianna to simply hand it over to its servant!" I unsheathed the dagger at my waist, silently thanking Lewella's insistence that I always carry it with me since the incident in Traeth.

The warriors moved quickly, surrounding me on all sides. Though it pained me to strike against those who had sworn to protect me, many of whom I had grown up with inside these walls, I wouldn't go quietly. I clearly felt the darkness rolling off Aengus, even if the others in the room were blind to it. He was Fianna's servant. There was no doubt of it.

Two warriors grabbed me by the upper arms. I fought them, striking one of them in the shoulder with my blade, but I was outnumbered. The dagger was ripped from me and a punch to the gut sent me doubling over, gasping for breath. My arms were wrenched behind me, my wrists swiftly bound, before I was yanked back up. Despite the burning pain that had settled in my middle, I resisted those who held me.

Aengus stepped forward and Domhnall got up to join him. Laoise and Arwel watched in stone cold silence. Laoise stared at me with a smug expression and I wanted nothing more than to free myself and wipe it off her face. Aengus and Domhnall strode over to me as I continued to strain against those who held me, breathing hard.

To my surprise, Aengus ignored me, instead going to the warrior I'd wounded. Blood soaked through the warrior's shirt and Aengus covered it with his hand. He closed his eyes, the power of his gift healing the injury as if it had never happened. Yet even as he healed, I could feel Fianna's darkness.

When he released the warrior's shoulder, she smiled tentatively at him. It unnerved me, the glimpses of the man I'd once known, the compassionate healer who had once saved my life, somehow mixed with the usurper who had given himself to darkness. Leaving the warrior, he came to stand before me.

"The ring," he said, motioning to the warriors.

I flinched as a warrior grabbed my hand. I tried to clench it into a fist, but the warrior pried it open, ripping the ring from my finger. Everything within me screamed, a pain in my throat as I stared at the man in front of me, the kin who had betrayed me in the worst of ways. My vision blurred, moisture filling my eyes as Aengus slipped the ring onto his finger. There was a gut-wrenching, crushing wrongness to seeing the gold ring with its glimmering blue gemstone on his right hand.

"I'm afraid that with Seren's aggression," Aengus said, speaking to the warriors holding me, "we cannot risk letting her roam free. I'm afraid the only place for her right now is the dungeons. And though I regret to say it, I think it wise if her loyalist companions join her there as well for the time being."

"You can't do this! You are fools, all of you, if you think for a moment that what you have not done is handed this clan to Fianna with welcoming arms!" I dug my heels in, fighting every step of the way as the warriors dragged me toward the door. But my protests were ignored, Aengus and Domhnall both putting their backs to me as they began to address Laoise and Arwel. Mair was seized by warriors as well, loudly protesting. My head was shoved forward and I was forced out into the hallway, my heart beating so hard, it throbbed in my neck. I still fought my captors, fear coursing through me with every step I took: fear for Bran, for my mother, for my people, for the very land I had sworn to protect. All of it was now in the Stag Spirit's hands.

CHAPTER 41

BLINDED

Bran

I WISHED I COULD have been with Seren at the council meeting to offer her support, but my presence wouldn't have been welcome there. Not yet. Eventually, I would resume my full role of Tiarna, but that was another battle to fight, and Fianna's most recent threat was more pressing. I'd consoled myself that at least I'd had last night with her and I would seek her out at the midday meal once the meeting was over. In the meantime, despite slight protest from Cian, I'd ventured from the infirmary back to the warriors' wing of the castle.

While Lewella had told me it would be another day before she let me go out with warriors to hunt for the creatures, she didn't completely prevent me from contributing to the matter at hand. A map of the castle and the surrounding areas was laid out on the table in Lewella's study, the two of us poring over it as we looked for any and all possible hideouts for Alannah, the creatures, and quite possibly Aengus. Having grown up at

Clogwyn, I knew the tract of wilderness surrounding the castle better than most, and I appreciated that Lewella was willing to consider my input.

I was just mulling over an area by the river that had a few small, narrow caves when the door behind us burst open. Lewella and I both started, turning around as five warriors stormed into the room, Seachnall leading them. Everything from the warrior's stances and the way they gripped the hilt of their blades screamed aggression and my heart immediately began to race, my stomach growing hard.

"What exactly is going on?" Lewella asked, frowning at the warriors as they marched toward us.

"I'm afraid that your days as warrior chief are over. You are under arrest," Seachnall said. "You and the shifter."

I jerked my head back. That couldn't be. Only Seren would be able to order such a thing, and she would never.

Lewella blinked rapidly before she shook her head. "By whose orders?"

"By the orders of Ri Aengus," Seachnall replied.

"*Seren* is Ri of Blaidd," Lewella retorted. "You will stand down. All of you!"

The warriors didn't heed her, surrounding us instead. The clang of blades rang out as Lewella struck against the warriors who had so utterly turned against us. I went to shift, but three warriors wrestled me to the ground, binding me with a thin cord that would hobble me even in my wolf form. I was yanked back to my feet, only to find that Lewella had been restrained as well, blood dripping from the side of her mouth and bruises already starting to form on her face and neck.

"What has become of Seren?" I snapped.

"I'm afraid the council has stripped Ri Seren of her title," Seachnall answered. "You will find there is a new Ri of Blaidd now. And he is not foolish enough to take chances with those who have shown Seren such blind loyalty."

We had missed something, something important. Because how in the blazes had Aengus stolen Seren's title? And with no great attack or battle or bloodshed, catching us all unawares. My stomach clenched as Lewella's hands were bound before we were forced out of the room. Fianna had gotten the upper hand on us all.

Lewella and I were brusquely shoved out into the hallway and before too long, I was able to discern exactly where we were going: the dungeons. Fear engulfed me, my heart hammering and my mouth dry. If Aengus had become Ri, what had become of Seren?

CHAPTER 42

NO WAY OUT

Aengus

IT WASN'T SUPPOSED TO feel like this. I rubbed my chest as I stared at my reflection in the mirror. I had done it. I had become Ri of Blaidd and taken control of the clan from Seren. Fianna was pleased—I could sense its elation—and yet I felt hollow, uncertain about the future that lay before me. As if there were some weight that refused to be lifted from my shoulders.

It had taken everything in me to show the bravery I had the day the council had named me Ri, and now I felt like I was drowning. Everything here haunted me, made me feel like an intruder in this place. The castle with its reminders of the Wolf Spirit everywhere I turned. This very room in the Ri's chambers that had hints of Seren everywhere I looked, despite all of my attempts at purging the space.

The new warrior chief I had appointed at the Stag Spirit's instructions had proven adept at making it clear to those inside and outside Clogwyn that any lingering loyalty to Seren would not be tolerated. The council seemed amenable enough to my new role. I had no reason for this continued unease. Three days had passed and no one had challenged me.

Is it because of her? The thought brought with it a sharp ache in my chest, one that had me rubbing it again. My mother was within these walls—now in a dungeon cell below me. I hadn't wanted to face her. Hadn't wanted to relive her rejection all over again. If she had wanted to, she could have kept me. At the very least, she could have searched for me after Cadfael died. She could have told Seren that she had a half-brother and let her reach out to me. But Esyllt had done none of those things. No, I didn't want to see her. I didn't owe her that.

The door opened and I started, half-turning to see Alannah glide into our new bedroom in the Ri's chamber. In just three days, it was like she had transformed. She was as breathtaking and grand as this opulent room and the castle we now called home, dressed in a flowing green gown with an air of happiness about her that I'd never seen before. She'd thrived inside these walls, even if the shadow of her ruthlessness still lingered. *You would have never gotten this far without her,* I reminded myself as she came to a stop in front of me. She pulled me down for a kiss, the flowery scent she now wore every day tickling my nostrils.

"You're sure you don't want to me to go with you?" she asked. "I'm not needed anywhere else today. I've made the arrangements I needed to make for the handfasting."

We were to be wed in a week, Alannah getting the extravagant ceremony she had dreamed of. At Fianna's command, we hadn't announced our union to the clan, not with the suspicion still surrounding Alannah and her former ties with Lorcan. But Alannah had been more than happy to throw herself into the planning, even if most of it was done in relative secrecy.

"No," I told her with a slight shake of my head. "I'll manage. I need to show them that I'm strong."

She kissed me again, giving me a sultry smile as she eased away. "I'll be waiting, then. And when you get back..."

The not-so-subtle suggestion should have had desire streaking through me. It would have even just days ago. But something had changed. Something I didn't want to admit even to myself. Almost as if the spell she'd woven around me was starting to fade. I made myself lean down and kiss her cheek, murmuring to her that I'd be back as soon as I could before leaving the room, trying not to seem in too much of a hurry.

Once out in the hallway, I rolled my shoulders, letting out a few low breaths as I sought to brace myself for what was ahead. I was to meet with the council again this afternoon, to decide what was to be done with Seren, though I already had the answer, even if it made me sick to my stomach. But Fianna had made its command clear: Seren was to be executed, publicly, her death at the hands of Fianna's creatures. It would be a show of strength for me and one of humiliation and suffering for her. And Bran, Esyllt, and the rest of Seren's loyalists would follow her to their deaths.

It had to be done this way, I knew that, but I couldn't stomach it. My wrist tingled and I gritted my teeth. I had no choice. There was no other path before me. But it had brought doubt after doubt, keeping me awake until dawn had broken over the mountains, taunting me with questions and fears that I was doing the wrong thing, following the wrong path away from the healer I'd been to the murderer I'd become.

I furiously rubbed my burning wrist, setting my jaw. There was no way out of this. I'd seen to that the moment I'd sworn my soul to Fianna. I would have to see this through, even if it broke me. By the time I reached the study, I'd quelled some of my persistent fear. Drawing my shoulders back, I pushed past the warriors standing guard, grasping the cold steel door handle and letting myself in.

I'd arrived a touch early and only Domhnall was present, mulling over some piece of parchment laying in front of him on the table. He looked up when I entered, greeting me with a respectful nod. He'd been true to his word thus far, even if I still didn't entirely trust him.

"Ri Aengus," he said as I took a seat. "I expect Laoise and Arwel to be along shortly."

I nodded in acknowledgement. The place that Mair had occupied on the council would need to be filled soon. Though at least with a little persuasive coercing, Mair had sworn her loyalty to me. I couldn't say the same for the rest of Seren's supporters, all of whom I had locked away in the dungeons to keep them from retaliating against me. I'd kept Mair out of a cell for now, but I was still having her watched.

"There have been some concerns," Domhnall said, rolling the parchment up before setting it aside. "About the creatures... and about your choice of Banrion."

My spine stiffened. I was aware of the concerns he spoke of; there were no secrets in a place like this one. But I would not be swayed in my choice of Banrion. I couldn't be, really. Alannah fulfilling that role was part of Fianna's plan. And as far as the creatures went, the people of Blaidd would have to learn to accept them. They were doing Fianna's work, cleansing the land of Blaidd.

"I will address such concerns with the council," I replied with a wave of my hand.

Domhnall made a noise in the back of his throat but didn't press me further. Moments later, Laoise and Arwel strode in. Arwel looked particularly troubled, judging by his stiff strides and pinched brow. Did I already have division starting to set in?

It does not matter, Fianna said. *Today they will learn who controls the Clan of Blaidd. And they will learn not to challenge you as my servant.*

I swallowed hard, not entirely certain what the Stag Spirit had in mind. I supposed I would find out soon enough. Domhnall called the meeting to order, but before he could speak further, Laoise interrupted him.

"Three fires have ravaged the villages of Gefell, Cnoc, and Traeth. Fires that were started by shadow creatures. What, exactly, do you plan to do about that, Ri Aengus?" she said, narrowing her eyes at me.

"I'm afraid there is nothing to be done," I replied.

"Nothing to be done?" Laoise's face reddened and she slammed her palm down on the table. "People are losing their homes, their livelihoods, even their very lives! Not to mention your choice to wed a shifter who is said to be one of Fianna's own. You promised us peace! And all you bring is destruction."

I sat taller in my chair, feeling Fianna's darkness swirling in the air as the Spirit's anger deepened, matching my own. "I would not expect one such as you to understand a being such as Fianna. As far as my Banrion is concerned, that is my choice, not the council's. There will be no actions taken against the shadow creatures. This land must be cleansed before it can be rebuilt."

Laoise sputtered, striking the table a second time.

"So," Arwel said, his lips curling into a sneer, "you have lied to us. You *are* its servant, just like the woman you brought into this castle and intend to wed. You've stolen the title of Ri only to bring us all to ruin."

Laoise's gaze darted to Domhnall, the pitch of her voice rising. "Did you know of this, Domhnall? Were you in on this elaborate scheme?"

He cleared his throat, his chin dipping as his face flushed.

"Enough of your wicked tongues!" I snapped. "I stole nothing. What I have taken was rightfully mine by blood. And I *will* bring peace to this clan. Even if you do not agree with the means by which I obtain it."

"Peace?" Laoise snorted in disgust. "What peace will there be when this land lays in ruin? I will not stand for this! Not for one moment longer!"

She shoved back her chair and a fiery pain erupted in my wrist.

Kill her, Fianna yelled. *Kill her now!*

My chest tightened and my stomach lurched. The act it wanted me to commit was the very one I had sworn I would never do.

I own your soul, Fianna growled, pain traveling up my arm and inching toward my chest. *Refuse me and I will destroy you and everything you hold dear. Kill her now!*

I made myself bolt to my feet, not allowing myself to think about what would come next. If I did, I would never follow through. Darting around the table, I grabbed onto Laoise's wrist, yanking her to me before she could flee. It took no more than seconds to connect to Laoise's life force and only a few seconds more to pull it from her body into mine. A euphoria, one I'd never felt with the animals that I'd killed, filled me, and for a brief few moments it almost outweighed my self-loathing. But then Laoise's body went limp and she dropped to the ground with a loud thud, crumpling at my feet.

Bile rose in my throat but I pushed it down, slowly turning. Arwel wore a look of horror, his mouth dropped open and his eyes wide as he stared at Laoise's dead body, while Domhnall had sprung to his feet, his face deathly pale as he gripped the back of his chair.

"The shadow creatures are to be left unharmed," I said. "I *will* wed Alannah and Seren will be executed in three days' time."

I didn't wait for their response, turning on my heel and stalking out of the study. My stomach churned, my hands shaking as I brushed past the warriors and continued down the hallway, headed back to the Rí's chambers. I needed Alannah right now, needed her to remind me why we were doing this. I'd done the one thing I had sworn I'd never do. I'd killed someone.

CHAPTER 43

FLIGHT OF THE WOLF
Bran

I SLAMMED MY FIST against the wall hard enough that my hand stung. I had no clue where Seren was and I needed to find her. How in the blazes had I managed to land myself in the damn dungeons again? Whatever had happened to Aengus, he was no longer the man I'd once called friend. Alannah and Fianna had both twisted him into some sort of monster. Spirits only knew what he'd done to Seren since usurping her. Releasing a frustrated growl, I got up from the old pile of straw I'd been sitting on and began pacing my narrow cell again.

I didn't know how long I'd been here. Neither did I know where any of the others were. Seachnall had separated me from Lewella the moment we'd reached the dungeons and I hadn't seen her since. One of my hands balled into a fist, frustration rushing through me. I'd been heavily guarded from the moment I'd been thrown in here, making my odds of escape dismally poor. The cords that had been wrapped around my wrists and ankles had been removed after they'd begun to dig into my skin, but even if I shifted, I was woefully outnumbered.

Muttering under my breath, I came to a stop near the door, the set of bars along the top letting in scant light. For what felt like the hundredth time, I made a study of the door, searching for any weakness in it, but I found nothing. *And even if you did, how are you going to get past six warriors?* I leaned a hand against it, pressing my forehead to the bottom of the cool bars in frustration. There had to be a way out of this damn place.

A faint scraping noise on the other side of the door made me start and I almost slammed my chin on the metal bars as I jumped back. My muscles tensed at the turning of the lock but as three figures stepped inside and my eyes adjusted to the glow of a torch, I was suddenly filled with relief. Lewella stood before me, with Mair and Emer at her side.

"Come; we don't have much time," Lewella said, motioning for me to follow them. "Tudwal is seeing to the others."

"Seren?" I asked, my chest clenching painfully.

"Tudwal is retrieving her," Emer replied, grabbing me by the arm and tugging me along. "Along with Esyllt, Cian, Sioned, and Gruffudd." She paused, her next words laced with undeniable disgust. "It seems our new Ri wanted to leave nothing to chance in regards to Seren's supporters."

Anger and fear rose within me at the mention of my father, my pulse quickening. For Aengus' sake, Father and Seren both had best be unharmed.

"We'll discuss it all later," Lewella said. "We need to move. Tudwal has bought us time, but not much."

I was full of more questions, but I understood Lewella's urgency. Whatever plan had been concocted, I trusted her. We hurried down the rows of cells, racing up the stairs to the tower. When we reached it, we burst through the door, relief coursing through me at the sight of Tudwal and the others. I hurried over to Seren, pulling her into my arms and holding her tight. She was here, alive and back at my side once more.

"You're alright?" I asked her, stepping back and searching her face, my anger rising again when I noticed bruising along her left cheek.

She nodded before dropping her chin, but not before I saw the haunted look in her eyes. Aengus, it seemed, had felled a blow to her spirit as well as her body. He would pay for what he had done, not only to her, but to our people. I searched our party for Father, letting out a sigh of relief when I spotted him standing next to Tudwal. Father looked as rough as the rest of us after our time in the dungeon, his clothes rumpled and dirty, but he appeared mostly unharmed. Seren stepped away from me with a quiet word that she wished to check on Esyllt and I followed after her. Esyllt, too, had clearly received rough treatment at Aengus' command, dirt staining her skin and clothes and her joints more swollen that I had ever seen them. She leaned heavily on Cian and Sioned, her face pale. I worried that our flight from Clogwyn might prove too much for her.

"If we follow the path I've laid out," Tudwal said, turning my attention back to him, "I've made certain there will be no gate guards or warriors posted to detain us, but that won't last indefinitely."

"There is a passageway in the Ri's study that leads out into the courtyard, close to a gate that lets out into the forest," Lewella said. "I doubt Aengus knows of it, as it has long been kept secret for the Ris and warrior chiefs alone. Aengus and Alannah won't be in the Ri's chambers tonight; they'll be taking dinner in the hall. Mair has made certain of that."

I raised my brows, glancing down at Seren, but she kept her gaze averted. I hadn't been aware of such a passageway, even after a little over a month of sharing those chambers with her.

"We need to get moving before it's too late," Lewella said, ushering us on once more.

As our party filed out of the tower, I briefly stepped away from Seren to come up behind my father, clasping his shoulder.

"I'm glad you're alright," I told him.

He covered my hand with his own, giving it a quick squeeze. "And I'm glad you are as well."

There was no more time for more conversation. The moment we entered the castle hallway, Lewella and Tudwal picked up the pace. Seren had joined Sioned in helping support Esyllt, who was struggling to keep up. I jogged up next to Seren, ready to lend a hand if needed. The hallways were eerily empty and while I trusted Lewella, I worried how long it would be before Aengus was on to us. *And Spirits help us if Alannah and the creatures are here,* I thought as we ducked through a servants' door to take a set of stairs that led up to the castle's second level. Moments later, we darted down the empty hallways again but Seren suddenly faltered, favoring one leg.

"Here," I said, taking hold of her arm and inclining my head toward Esyllt. "I've got her."

Seren hesitated for a brief moment before stepping away. I slipped an arm under Esyllt's shoulder to help support her weight.

"Thank you, Bran," Esyllt said, slightly out of breath. "I know I'm slowing everyone down."

"We'll get you out of here," I replied. "I promise."

Esyllt managed a weak smile before we continued on. Seren's limp was growing more noticeable with every step and I used my free hand to take hold of one of hers. She needed Cian to tend to her, but there was no time.

"Lean on me if you have to," I told her.

She nodded, clutching my hand and pressing on despite her obvious pain. Finally, we reached the Ri's chambers. We were almost to freedom. Tudwal thrust open the door, motioning for us to enter. Lewella led the way inside, making her way over to a corner of the common room. It was difficult to see in the dark, but there were no signs of Alannah, Aengus, or the creatures. Lewella fiddled with something on the wall and then there came a loud crack, followed by the creak of hinges. I winced, glancing over my shoulder. Hopefully no one had heard us.

"Come," Lewella called. "This way."

A short and narrow door had opened in the wall. Cobwebs hung from the doorway and there was nothing but inky blackness on the other side, but Tudwal hurried over with his torch, lighting the entrance so that we could safely enter.

The doorway itself was narrow and short enough that only one of us could go through with Esyllt. Cian stepped forward, offering to go down the passageway with her, and Sioned and I stepped back to let him. Seren followed right behind Cian and her mother, and I scurried after her. We all had to duck low to get through the door, and the passageway on the other side also had a narrow ceiling. I had to hunch to keep from hitting my head, and we were all forced to walk practically pressed on top of one another. Moments later, the trapdoor clanged closed and we were plunged until almost total darkness, left to follow the faint light of Tudwal's torch.

There was no way to move through the passageway with any real speed, certainly not with the numbers we had, but knowing that didn't ease my fears. Aengus had the entire war band at his disposal, not to mention the creatures. I worried it wouldn't be long before they found us.

When we eventually reached the end of the winding passageway, I muttered a quiet thanks to the Spirits as we stepped out into the cool night. The way we came up a small flight of rickety steps through another trapdoor, hidden by strategically placed bushes, left me assuming we'd traveled underground. We were now on the western side of the castle, on the opposite side of the wing containing the Ri's chambers.

Only a few feet away from the bushes was a narrow side gate, one that was thankfully unguarded. Tudwal's work, I assumed. I hurried over to join Cian in supporting Esyllt again as we broke into a run, headed for the gate. The older woman was struggling, her breathing heavy and labored, but she doggedly pressed on. I half expected someone to stop us at the gate, but we passed through unimpeded and soon, we were hidden by the thick trees that made up the forest on the back side of the castle. Our pace slowed and Seren and Sioned came up on my left, both of them casting worried gazes at Esyllt.

"Do you know where we're headed?" Seren asked.

"A cave of some sort, I think," Cian answered. "Down near the river."

"If it's the one I'm thinking of," I said, "it's a bit far from here, but the path to get there should be easy."

I hoped it was the one I was thinking of. The cave that came to mind was one that I had told Lewella about days ago. I'd found it as a child when exploring the woods in my wolf form, as any young, precocious shifter would do. The cave was well hidden from any passersby and large enough to fit our party.

Esyllt stumbled over a large tree root, but Cian and I steadied her. Still, I worried she wouldn't be able to make the long trek through the pitch-black forest. Esyllt stumbled again and as Cian and I caught her, a familiar darkness swirled in the air.

"Fianna." Seren let loose a curse in Old Pernish and the unmistakable eldritch screech of a shadow creature pierced our ears.

The screech of the shadow creatures grew louder and I smelled smoke in the air.

"I've got her," Cian said. "You're our only hope of holding those things off. Especially since Tudwal was unable to get his hands on Rhonwen's bow."

I didn't waste a moment, shifting into my wolf form. Without the bow, I was our only hope, but even I couldn't hope to fend off the creatures indefinitely. I fell back as the others broke into a run and my heightened hearing allowed me to discern that our attackers were coming from behind. The creature's screams of rage made my skin crawl, but perhaps we could outrun them.

No sooner had I had that thought than flames burst forth mere inches away from me, making me start as they danced across the forest floor before racing up a tree. The others had gotten ahead of me, but before they could flee to safety, the flames boxed them in. We were trapped.

A creature leapt out of a blazing tree, almost barreling into me. I barely managed to dodge it, scrambling out of the way before whirling back around with my teeth bared. The beast and I circled each other, locked in a strange sort of dance. Out of the corner of my eye, I spied two more creatures in the fray, attacking Seren and Emer.

I struck at the creature in front of me, managing to dig my teeth into its neck. If I could wound the three monsters enough so they couldn't pursue us, perhaps there was hope of us getting out of here alive. I dug my claws into the creature's smoky hide, but the whiz of an arrow flying by my ear broke my focus and the beast threw me off.

Six warriors walked through the flames as if they weren't even there, armed with bows and swords. But it wasn't the warriors who filled me with dread. It was the woman behind them. Alannah shouted at the warriors, a murderous gleam in her eyes, before she shifted into her hawk form.

I lunged at the shadow creature again, the monster swiping me with its claws before I could latch onto its jugular. It screamed, fighting to rid itself of me, but in the end, I brought it down, black blood gushing from its neck. It wasn't dead, but it wouldn't be killing anyone else anytime soon. I whirled around, intent on going after the next creature, only to discover that Seren had been separated from the rest of our party, embroiled in a fight with two warriors and Alannah. I desperately wanted to spring to Seren's aid, but no one else could stop the remaining creatures but me.

The creature, then Seren, I told myself, racing across the forest floor, dodging flames as I went. I barreled into a creature that was attacking Lewella, knocking it to the ground. It got up fighting, its teeth grazing my side. Behind me, I heard a cry of pain from Seren. The noise made my heart hammer and my chest twisted, but I couldn't reach her now. Not while I was stuck tangling with this shadow creature.

We were a flurry of smoke and fangs, both of us determined to kill. The creature slammed me into a tree and a searing pain left me favoring one foot. Flames had burned my paw, giving the creature the upper hand. It bit into my shoulder and I howled in agony.

For a moment, I saw no way out, the creature rearing its head back, its ember gaze intent on my jugular, but then came Lewella's war cry. She swung at the creature with her sword, the weapon only going straight through its smoky hide, but it was enough to distract it.

The pressure against me loosened and I ripped away from the creature's hold. I almost fell in the process, forced to balance on three legs. I started to stumble toward the creature again, but Lewella grabbed me by the scruff of my neck. I let out a pained yelp and she grimaced.

"We have to go!" she yelled. "Now, while we still can!"

I followed her gaze to a small break in the circles of flames and suddenly, I could sense the Wolf Spirit's presence in the air. It was giving us a way out. Worriedly, I searched for Seren among the smoke and flames, a coldness washing over me when I saw her in the hands of warriors, her arms pinned behind her back and blood dripping from her face. I yanked against Lewella's hold, but she held fast and my injured limbs wouldn't cooperate.

"There isn't time," Lewella said, pain lacing her voice. "We have to go *now!*"

I didn't care. I couldn't leave her. Alannah and Aengus would kill her. I attempted to yank away again, but this time my burned and bleeding leg gave out, causing me to crumple to the ground. Lewella scooped me up, grunting as she did so; even in my wolf form, I wasn't light. I made a weak effort at jumping out of her arms, but it did me no good. My skin was growing clammy and the world around me spun as nausea built in my belly. The shadow creature's poison was coursing through my blood, leaving me feeling as if I was on fire, but all I could think of as I fell into the inky blackness was Seren. I would do anything, sacrifice anything, to save her.

CHAPTER 44

MOMENTS WASTED
Bran

"For Spirit's sake, Bran hold still!"

I'd woken in the cave, now stuck in my wolf form due to my injuries. I wouldn't be able to shift back until Cian had my wounds mostly healed. And still, despite the searing pain, all I could think of was finding Seren. I made an attempt at wiggling toward the mouth of the cave again and Cian let out an exasperated sigh, his hold my burned foot tightening. I yelped and pain shot up my leg.

"If you would *hold still,* this would go a lot less painfully," Cian grumbled before calling over his shoulder to Emer.

I could count on one hand the number of times I'd seen Cian lose his temper, and tonight was one of them. Not that he was the only one. The tension in the cave was thick. We'd barely gotten away with our lives and had lost Seren in the process. Alannah, the warriors, and the creatures could still be out there hunting us for all we knew. But unlike the others, I wasn't content to follow Lewella's decision to lay low. Every moment that passed, Seren's life was in danger. I refused to think that Alannah had already killed her, couldn't let myself fall into that dark despair. If only my damned body would work so I could get out of this place and track her down.

I tried to wriggle free of Cian's hold again, only to have Emer suddenly looming over me. She took a strong hold of my neck, wrestling me back down. I bared my teeth, giving a rumbling growl, but she was unphased, still holding me tight. Didn't they understand? I had to get back out there. Every moment we wasted could cost Seren her life.

"Almost done," Cian said, the pain in my foot easing some, but not enough to give me the strength to break free of his and Emer's holds. "Then I think we're going to have to give him something to calm him. Thank the Spirits Mair was able to get into the infirmary."

Oh, blazes, no. I released another growl, thrashing and fighting to get away.

Emer cursed, holding me fast. "Whatever you're going to do, let's do it quickly."

Cian rummaged through a canvas bag before coming around in front of me.

"You'll thank me later when you still have that foot," he said, his tone stern as he crouched down in front of me, holding a small amber vial. "Do *not* bite me."

Well, that I couldn't promise. Not when Seren's life was in danger. He went to open my mouth and I snapped at him, growling fiercely. They needed to let me go find her. I wouldn't let them sedate me. Soon, however, the two of them had pried my mouth open, both of them cursing profusely. I tried to spit the liquid back out, but Cian clamped my muzzle shut, forcing me to swallow the bitter concoction.

"There," Cian said with a sigh. "That should set in fairly quickly."

I grumbled, shaking my head at the taste and the fuzziness I was starting to feel in my head. Curse it; Cian's sedative *was* acting quickly. Cian was saying something to Emer, but their words were becoming muffled. It wasn't much longer before my head dropped to my paws and I drifted off into a dreamless sleep.

When I eventually woke, I wasn't certain how long I'd slept, but apparently it was long enough that dawn was starting to make its presence known outside the cave, letting in a dim grey light. A quick assessment of my body told me that my rest and Cian's treatment had done me some good. My strength was back.

In mere seconds, I was standing on two feet once more, but damn it all if I didn't soon discover that I still had a limp, along with a moderate pain in my foot. It was impossible to see what state the appendage was in, as Cian had apparently bandaged it after treating me. My shoulder where the creature had bitten me was still sore and wrapped in bandages as well. Thankfully Cian had done the bandages tight enough that they were snug against my skin, under my clothes and boots now that I was back in my human form.

"Cian is liable to murder us both if he catches you up on that foot."

Lewella's voice made me start and I whirled around, almost toppling over in the process. I reached out a hand, leaning heavily on the stone wall. Lewella was standing at the mouth of the cave, on watch, I assumed. A quick glance behind me showed me that the others were all asleep, laid out in a small huddle on the ground.

"What Cian doesn't know won't kill him," I said, only making it a few halting steps before I was forced to lean against the wall again.

"You're not in any condition to be going anywhere."

I gritted my teeth, one of my hands bunching so tightly into a fist that my nails dug into my palm. "She's out there, Lewella. They have her. And they won't hesitate to kill her."

"I know." Lewella's voice caught on the last word and she cleared her throat before continuing. "Believe me, Bran, I know. I am well aware that I failed at my most important task, keeping my Ri safe."

"I can find my way back to where the attack was. Track her scent back to Clogwyn. I might even be able to slip in as just another one of the wolves."

"When you're fully healed, I will be happy for you to do so. Cian said it shouldn't be more than a day or two."

I shook my head with a scowl. "She might not have that long."

"And *you* might not even make it to the castle in your current state. As soon as you're not hobbling around here on one good leg and Cian says you're healed, I'll gladly send you out."

"I'm not hobbling," I grumbled.

She raised a brow. "Let go of that wall, then."

The back of my neck flushed and I ducked my chin. I couldn't, not without losing my balance, and we both damn well knew it.

"Go rest, Bran," she said, her tone softening. "And pray to the Spirits that they'll spare her."

I didn't want to rest. I wanted to act, but Lewella had made her point. With a heavy sigh, I turned, my movements slow and stiff as I shuffled back to where I'd been laying, using the wall to support myself. The twinge in my injured foot had grown to a throbbing ache by the time I lay back down and my shoulder was starting to pain me as well. I released a heavy sigh, making a useless effort at trying to get comfortable on the cold, hard ground. As soon as I could walk on my own two feet, I would hunt down Seren, and Spirits help Aengus and Alannah if they had further harmed her.

CHAPTER 45

DOOM THEM ALL
Aengus

I HALF STUMBLED OUT of the dungeons, bile rising in the back of my throat over what I had just been forced to do. Fianna had been furious over our prisoners' unexpected escape last night and it had taken out its rage on the people of Clogwyn, using me to do it—something that inevitably became my own unbearable punishment.

As I stepped out of the tower, I made a vain attempt at straightening my shoulders, avoiding the gazes of the warriors as I passed them. There was no visible blood on my hands after my time spent in the bowels of the dungeons this morning, but blood stained my soul. Four lives, gone in an instant with a touch of my hand. My victims had been warriors who had been accused of collaborating with Seren and lost their lives for it.

At least we have her, I thought, forcing myself to release a long breath, trying to rid myself of the tension that wracked my body. Bran and the others had gotten away, but Alannah had fetched Seren back. She would meet her end tonight. Fianna had planned a particularly gruesome death for her. She would be burned alive by its creatures for all the castle to see.

I wasn't a fool. I knew she could not remain alive if I was to keep my place as Ri, but the more death I wrought, the more it sickened me. Even worse was knowing that Fianna was tired of my weakness; it had no patience for it. I greatly feared that at some point, I might push the Stag Spirit too far and it would take my life in return.

Despite my best efforts, I hadn't managed to push off all of my doubts and fears by the time I reached the Great Hall. Fianna had directed me here. I had no choice but to obey, even if all I wanted to do was retreat to my chambers in solitude for the rest of the afternoon. I stepped into the expansive hall to find it almost completely empty.

But my steps faltered when my gaze fell on Seren. She was held between two warriors, her hands bound behind her back, the three of them standing at the far end of the hall. Her clothes were tattered, her face bruised with stains of dried blood. Alannah stood across from her, two shadow creatures on either side of her and a wicked smile on her face as she absently twirled a longbow in her hands. My heart jolted at the sight of the weapon. It was time then. Fianna had every intention of destroying Rhonwen's legendary bow, and today appeared to be the day it sought its vengeance.

"So good of you to join us, Ri Aengus," Alannah said smugly as I came up beside her. "We wouldn't want you to miss such an important moment, after all. I'm afraid we must purge more of the Wolf Spirit's hold on this place."

"The people of Blaidd will never accept you," Seren said, lifting her chin as she glowered at me. "Not when you destroy their homes and everything they hold dear."

Alannah let out a mocking laugh while I shifted uncomfortably where I stood. There *were* already signs of unrest, though Fianna insisted we would keep the people in line through fear. Alannah had no qualms with such an arrangement, but I didn't share her feelings. The brief bit of bliss she'd shown when we first entered the castle had vanished and now, it seemed Alannah's soul grew darker and more twisted by the day. Or perhaps she had always been that way and I had been too blinded by my lust and my desire to save everything and everyone to see it.

"They already accept us," Alannah retorted, "and they will accept us more once Aengus does for them what you could not."

"Does Ri Aengus not speak?" Seren asked. "Or does he let you do all the speaking for him?"

"Enough!" Alannah snapped. "You're here to see the end of what you hold most dear before you meet your own end tonight. If you cannot do so without holding your tongue, then someone will have to ensure that for you. Gag her."

The warriors looked over at me with questioning expressions and despite the churning in my stomach, I nodded. Seren fixed her stony gaze on me as they forced the gag into her mouth, tying it behind her head. Alannah threw the bow on the floor, calling out a command in Old Pernish.

The shadow creatures sprang from where they'd been sitting, fire bursting forth from their mouths and engulfing the bow. Seren struggled against the warriors, her words muffled and left unintelligible by the gag, but her horror was clear, her head recoiling and her eyes wide as she stared at the burning weapon.

I tried to take deep, steadying breaths as I was forced to watch, tried to hold myself tall and confident, but deep down, I could not shake the wrongness of it. Could not seem to stop myself from questioning how it had come to this. I had wanted to save Blaidd and its people, but now it was difficult not to feel like I had become nothing more than a purveyor of death and destruction.

You will know more death and destruction than you can even imagine if you do not cease this foolishness, Fianna hissed, a fiery pain erupting in my arm.

I swallowed hard and clenched my jaw, resisting the urge to rub my aching arm. The bow was only barely visible through the flames and once they ceased, I could not imagine how there could be anything left. Alannah called the creatures off with a triumphant smile and they scurried back to her side, but her face soon contorted in rage when the flames disappeared.

The bow was still intact. Blackened and charred, its once beautiful carvings now not even visible, but its shape had remained, along with its string, which had taken on an odd golden glow. Alannah let out a screech, her cheeks flushing as she turned to the warrior closest to her.

"Give me your damn blade!" she shouted.

He obliged, fumbling some with the weapon as Alannah screamed at him to hurry. She unsheathed the blade with a growl and raised it over her head before slamming it down. The bow shattered into a million slivers but somehow, the string still gleamed brightly. Alannah commanded the creatures again and flames shot out of their mouths once more, but still the weapon would not be destroyed.

Alannah stiffly held up her chin, a vein in her neck throbbing as she addressed Seren. "The Wolf Spirit's line *will* end with you and its precious weapon will never strike against the Stag Spirit again. Do not think you will win this. Take her away!"

The warriors hauled Seren out of the room despite her protests, and Alannah continued to hold her chin high, her back ramrod straight, until the hall doors slammed shut.

Alannah's gaze frantically shot to the bow and she shook her head, a slight tremor in her hands. "I don't understand. It should have been destroyed."

"It is. No one can use it in the state it's in. Who could even piece it back together?" I said, coming over and placing my hands on her shoulders, only to have her roughly shrug me off.

She clutched at her right wrist, where her own mark from Fianna marred her skin, her face paling. "That's not good enough," she said through gritted teeth. "There can be no possibility that it is ever again used against us." She paused, her eyes growing wild. "You must take it. Take it out to the forest and bury it, as deep as you can. Let the earth decompose what is left of it."

I eyed the bow dubiously, but a tingling in my own wrist kept me from arguing against her plan, no matter how foolish it seemed. The bow was nothing more than a pile of rubble now, but refusing would only earn me Fianna's wrath. One of the creatures let out another puff of flame and I watched in odd fascination as a small canvas bag materialized. Cautiously, I picked the still warm bag up off the granite floor before turning my attention to what remained of the bow. The silvers of wood were oddly cool for having just been burned by Fianna's flames, as was the glimmering string. I gathered it all into the bag, making sure nothing remained, and then straightened.

"I will leave you to it," Alannah said.

She brushed past me, rubbing her wrist, the shadow creatures on her heels while I remained where I was. Her words had been brusque and it was difficult to ignore how the affection that had once flowed so freely between us was fading, as if the woman I'd fallen in love with was becoming nothing more than a mere shadow of her former self.

As if you are not? Murderer. The sinister words of my conscience left my stomach twisting and I hurried out of the room, ducking out into the courtyard, as if I could somehow flee my mounting guilt. I had a job to do, a ruined weapon to bury, if I did indeed value my life. It didn't matter if I had changed, if I had truly become nothing more than a murderer. I was in this too deep, was I not? What hope was there for me?

You cannot destroy me. Not when I was made with power older than this land itself.

The strange voice made me start. I looked around, seeking the source of it, only to realize that I was alone in the courtyard, not a single other soul in sight.

What will your choice be, Son of Blaidd? The voice asked. *Will you doom them all to darkness? For your choices can still be your own.*

I swallowed hard, shaking my head. That voice I had known, but surely, I had to be hearing things. I hadn't heard the Wolf Spirit's voice in months, not since I had given my soul to Fianna. Seren's face flashed through my thoughts, beaten and bruised. And even though we had taken everything from her, broken her completely, she had still met Alannah and me with defiance. How could I be anything more than a weak wretch in comparison? I had forsaken any ties to the Wolf Spirit, but hearing its voice... would it accept me again? The thought was almost too impossible to believe. I knew the stories. Once a soul was given to a Dark Spirit, there was no going back.

You are mine, Fianna growled, a jolt of pain traveling up my arm.

But did I have to be?

CHAPTER 46

A REASON TO TRUST

Seren

I NEEDED A HEALER. My ribs hurt with each breath I took and there had been no way to keep the open wounds on my body clean. At this rate, it wouldn't be long before infection set in. Readjusting how I leaned against the wall, I let out a hiss as the movement brought sharp pain to my ribcage. I couldn't get the images of what I'd seen in the hall out of my thoughts: the bow burning, then shattering into a million pieces. Aengus was nothing like the man I'd known, the one who had saved my life at great risk to himself. Fianna had twisted him—with a little aid from Alannah, it seemed—and a coward had taken that man's place.

I had gone in circles in my thoughts, trying to think of some way to get out of here before they killed me, to stop Aengus and Alannah from destroying everything I loved, but I'd gotten nowhere. My throat tightened painfully and I gritted my teeth. I didn't even know if the others had made it out alive or if they'd perished in the forest at the hands of Alannah and the creatures.

Bran's fate, in particular, haunted me. I would give anything now to let myself love him in every way, like I once had. But it was too late for that. Was this truly how it was all going to end? Like my visions in the Spirit Realm where the golden wolf devoured me? I couldn't hold back a shudder.

The cell door clanged open and I made myself lift my chin as the warriors entered, wretched traitors that they were. They had no loyalty to me; they never had. A lone figure lingered in the cell's doorway, half-hidden by shadow, but my chest clenched all the same. It was Aengus. The warriors hauled me to my feet with little care for my injuries. I fully expected them to gag me, but to my surprise, they didn't.

"Come to watch the spectacle?" I asked Aengus as I was roughly forced over to the door, trying to ignore my quivering stomach. For all I knew, they were taking me to my execution.

Aengus didn't answer, his jaw tight as I was shoved past him.

"It will destroy you as soon as it finds no more use for you!" I shouted over my shoulder, the warriors pushing me down the narrow hallway while Aengus trailed behind us. "You can't be that much of a fool that you don't realize that!"

"Gag her." His statement was short and clipped and in moments, the warriors had silenced me.

I inwardly seethed as I was marched up the steps into the tower. A few moments later, the warriors dragged me out into the hallway.

"Ri Aengus!"

A warrior rounded the corner, racing toward us.

"What is it?" Aengus asked with an impatient huff.

"There's villagers trying to breech the gate," the warrior answered. "Pennathe Seachnall fears that they're trying to stop the execution."

Hope lit within me. Had my people come to my aid? Was it possible Bran and the others had survived the carnage in the forest?

"You two," Aengus said, motioning to the warriors who held me. "Go help stop whatever is going on at the gate. I'll stay with the prisoner for now."

The two warriors exchanged nervous glances with one another before Aengus barked at them to be on their way. They released me and Aengus latched onto my upper arm. I took in a few deep breaths to steady myself, waiting for the warriors to round the corner and disappear from view. This was my chance, and I was going to take it. I kicked out with my right leg but Aengus was onto me, throwing me slightly off balance before yanking me back to him.

"I'm getting you out of here," he hissed. "But you're going to have to play along."

I jerked my head away from him. Was this a trick? Or had he truly had some miraculous change of heart? He took off in the opposite direction of the warriors, pulling me along with him, his grip on my arm tight enough to prevent me from yanking free. I'd go along with him for now—I didn't really have much of a choice—but if he proved to be a liar or I saw another opportunity to escape, I wouldn't continue to acquiesce.

We wound our way through Clogwyn, Aengus' path entirely convoluted. I hated that I was put in a position of being forced to trust him. Not so long ago, I would have done it gladly, but knowing what he was now, knowing the oath he had sworn, that trust no longer came easily. My ankle had begun to ache fiercely as we continued our mad dash, but stopping now wasn't an option. Not if I wanted to stay alive.

Aengus came to an abrupt halt, tugging me through a servants' door with him. I half-stumbled out into the courtyard, my limp growing as my ankle burned, but Aengus gave me barely a moment to catch my breath before we were off again. In the distance, I could hear shouts and yells, from the gate, I assumed. My stomach twisted as part of me yearned to run to the upheaval, to ensure that Alannah didn't do something as deadly as turning the creatures loose on my people, but Aengus put an end to those thoughts, making me continue on with him through a suspiciously unguarded side gate.

We were both breathing heavily by the time we crossed the narrow strip of grass and raced into the trees. On the one hand, I felt a bit safer, hidden away under the boughs of the ancient oaks, beeches, and poplars, but on the other hand, I felt more exposed. It would be easy enough for Aengus to slit my throat out here and be done with it.

He skidded to a stop again and I almost slammed right into him. My eyes widened at the sight of Copar and my two wolves, all three of them tied to the trunk of a tall, sturdy oak. Awyr and Cryfder whined and pulled against the rope leads that held them in place, fighting to get to me. I cursed the damn gag covering my mouth, wanting to soothe them. What game was Aengus playing?

He unsheathed a blade and I tensed, my shoulders bunching as I readied myself to bolt, but he came around behind me instead and second later, my gag was gone. I coughed, trying to moisten my dry mouth as he sliced through the rope that bound my wrists.

The moment I was free, I whirled around, putting space between us and narrowing my eyes at him. "What is the meaning of all of this?"

He ignored me, walking over to my wolves instead and slicing them free of their tethers. "Your wolves can track, yes? They can find Bran?"

My chest hitched ever so slightly. Bran was alive then. I hadn't lost him. Awyr and Cryfder bounded over to me, rubbing against me and licking my hands. I murmured softly to them, trying to assure them that I was well.

"Tell me why you're doing this and I'll answer your question," I said, turning my attention back to Aengus.

He sighed and straightened, though he kept his back to me. "Seren, there isn't much time."

"And you've hardly given me any reason to trust you. May I remind you that just hours ago, you were planning my execution."

Again, he stayed silent and I cursed under my breath as he walked off. At first, I was too wrapped up in my anger to notice where he was going, but then, in the moonlight, I noticed a hole in the ground. He crouched down, pulling something out of it before walking back over to me. A wrinkle settled in my brow as I gazed at the canvas bag in his hand.

"I believe this belongs with you," he said, passing it to me, swallowing hard before continuing. "I still have questions that need answering, but I am beginning to see that I have gotten myself all too deep into a situation where there can be no victor other than death."

A sliver of hope ignited in my chest, but my suspicions overcrowded it. An oath to Fianna was an oath until death; I'd do best to remember that. Cautiously, I opened the bag. When I saw what was inside, I was left covering my mouth in shock. It was Rhonwen's bow. Now burned beyond recognition and in a thousand small pieces, but not completely destroyed.

"If anyone can get us out of this mess," Aengus said, holding my gaze, "I have faith that you can."

My throat thickened and I clutched the bag tightly in my hands as he fished something out of his pocket.

"This is Bran's," he said, passing me a balled-up shirt. "I stole it from his room. I had a feeling your wolves might require a fresh scent." He paused, glancing back behind us in the direction of the castle. "But you must hurry. There's not much time."

I had a million questions, ones that I was desperate for answers for, but he was right: We didn't have time. I took the shirt and turned my attention to the wolves, bending down to let them catch the scent. Once they had it, I spoke to them in Old Pernish, giving them the command to track Bran down. They darted off into the woods, though they were careful not to get out of sight, pausing a few feet away and waiting for me to join them.

"Ah," Aengus said with a wry grin. "That's how you get them to listen."

I could only imagine the trouble the wolves would have given him, being taken away by a stranger who didn't even know how to communicate with them.

"Old Pernish, it's... so rarely spoken." He paused, clearing his throat. "I assumed that only a being such as Fianna still used such language."

"It is still spoken in Clogwyn. The Ris have long kept such traditions of honoring the Spirits."

I almost caught myself telling him that perhaps one day I could teach him the language of our ancestors and teach him how to handle the wolves before I was abruptly reminded of the opposite sides we were on. There would likely be no *one day* for us. Especially considering how dearly he would pay for aiding me. A Spirit like Fianna did not suffer betrayal lightly.

"Come with me," I said. I didn't want him to be my enemy. I never had.

He slowly shook his head, giving me a strained, sad smile. "It is too late for me, Seren. I have already set my destiny in stone. There will be no changing it."

My throat tightened and moisture welled in my eyes. He was Fianna's servant. There was no going back on a vow such as that.

"Thank you," I told him, my voice choked with emotion.

He gave a solemn nod, stepping back as I went and untied Copar. I used the lead rope to make a set of reins before pulling myself up onto the gelding's back. There was a sharp pain in my ribs and my ankle screamed as I did so, but I gritted my teeth and fought to ignore it. I had to get out of here and find the others. I called to Awyr and Cryfder in Old Pernish again, telling them to continue their hunt.

They took off into the trees and I urged Copar into a gallop to follow after them, clutching the gelding's mane to keep my balance. I stole one last look at Aengus and he raised his hand in a somber acknowledgement. I was free, and just maybe Aengus was not the enemy I'd thought him to be.

CHAPTER 47

ONCE AGAIN WHOLE
Bran

IT HAD TAKEN TOO long to heal my injuries. I should have set out from this place at the first light of dawn, but I'd been forced to wait until nightfall. When I reached the mouth of the cave, I rolled my shoulders, my gaze on the pitch-black forest before me. I was going to find Seren and nothing was going to stop me.

"Be careful on that leg," Cian said from behind me. "That foot could really use for you to wait until morning before you go running for miles on it."

"Seren might not have that long," I said, my tone sharp. I winced, immediately regretting my temper.

Cian was exhausted; his shoulders drooped and he had heavy bags under his eyes. He'd spent himself trying to heal me as quickly as he could, all while trying to tend to the wounds of the others. He didn't deserve my short temper, but it was difficult to keep it in check. Seren was out there, somewhere, in the hands of Fianna.

"I know," Cian replied. "Be careful."

"I will be. And I swear to you that I won't return here without her."

I was moments away from transforming into my wolf form when the pounding of hoofbeats reached my ears. Cian took in a sharp breath.

"I'll alert Lewella," he said, ducking back into the cave.

Before I could shift, a horse burst out of the wall of trees, its neck lathered in sweat and a shadowy rider slumped on its back. That alone would have been enough to startle me, but I barely had time to brace myself before Awyr and Cryfder came barreling into me, tails wagging and eyes bright. I briefly greeted the two of them before rushing over to the horse, a ray of moonlight illuminating the rider on its back. It was Seren.

I grabbed one of Copar's reins, taking control of the horse with one hand while resting the other on Seren's knee. Her face was pale, her jaw clenched, and she clutched her side with her one arm.

"Cian!" I yelled, hoping he hadn't gone so deep into the cave that he wouldn't hear me. "It's Seren! She's hurt."

"The bow," she mumbled, fumbling with the canvas bag that haphazardly hung from her shoulder. "Keep it safe."

I didn't entirely know what she was talking about as she thrust me the bag, but I took it from her. "Were you followed?"

She shook her head. "No. Aengus... Aengus helped me. Helped me escape."

I couldn't stop my jaw from dropping at her rasping words. Aengus? Aengus, who had sworn his soul to Fianna and tried to kill us all? I didn't have long to dwell on the shocking news, however, as she slumped forward and almost fell off Copar.

I caught her and eased her off the horse's back. She swayed when her feet hit the ground and I slipped an arm around her shoulders to steady her, my pulse racing as I searched the cave's entrance for any sign of Cian. She limped along next to me for a few steps before I lifted her into my arms, carrying her the rest of the way. She was in no state to be walking on her own. Awyr and Cryfder stayed right on my heels and Cian and Lewella met us just inside the cave.

"I have no idea what this is," I said, awkwardly passing Lewella the bag while trying not to drop Seren. "But can you hang on to it for safekeeping?"

Lewella nodded, taking it from me. "Did you see anyone else? Any sign of the creatures?"

"Just her and the wolves," I answered. "And Copar."

"Tudwal and I will take a look around," Lewella said. "Perhaps Gruffudd can see to the horse and the wolves."

I nodded, knowing my father was more than capable of the task. Cian ushered us over to an empty part of the cave and I eased Seren down to the ground. She groaned and my stomach hardened. Even I could see how badly she was hurt. I backed away so that Cian could examine her, but I didn't stray far. I wasn't going to be separated from her again.

Her eyes fluttered shut as he worked, her breathing labored. Bruises marred her face and neck and there was a cut along her right cheek. I hadn't expected that Alannah and Aengus would be kind to her, but seeing the evidence of the torment she'd gone through still left me hot with fury.

"Her ribs are broken," Cian finally said. "I feared the ankle was as well, but it's just a bad sprain. Everything else is superficial in comparison. Send Mair, over, will you? Between the two of us, I think we can have her in good shape come morning."

I hesitated for a brief moment, my gaze still fixed on Seren.

"She'll be alright, Bran," Cian gently said. "I promise."

I managed a nod before striding off to track down Mair. I found her with Esyllt, the two of them seated in front of a small fire that had been carefully lit at the cave's center. I saw no sign of my father, leaving me to assume he was tending to the animals, and Lewella and Tudwal were already gone. Sioned, from the looks of it, had already gone to bed, laid out on a blanket on the other side of the fire. While Mair went to help Cian, I stayed behind with Esyllt. I knew the two healers would work more easily without me underfoot, but it didn't make my worries any less.

"Thank the Spirits she's alive," Esyllt said as I sank down onto the cold ground beside her. "How badly is she hurt?"

"Cian said broken ribs and a bad sprain to her ankle, as well as other more minor wounds," I answered, fidgeting with my hands as my gaze continued to drift beyond the fire to where Seren was being treated. "They weren't kind to her."

Esyllt let out a deep sigh. "In many ways, I never wanted this for her. I knew she would have the strength to become Ri, but I have always feared what the cost would be."

"It's a cost she would bear a million times over, though. For her people." Because that was who Seren was: a fighter. How many times had I seen her defy those around her for what she felt was right?

"She would," Esyllt said with a sad smile. "She certainly didn't get that from her father."

Silence fell between us, only broken by the occasional crackle and pop of the fire. The more time passed, the more my stomach churned. When Cryfder and Awyr eventually wandered over, I was glad for the distraction they offered. The wolves curled up at my feet, Cryfder laying his head in my lap.

"I've tied the horse up outside," Father said, joining us at the fire. "He's not far."

"Thank you," I replied, "for seeing to them."

"How is Seren?" he asked.

"Injured. But Cian and Mair are tending to her."

Father placed a hand on my shoulder, giving it a squeeze. I appreciated the quiet assurance, stroking Cryfder behind the ears in an attempt to work out my nervous energy. Father and Esyllt seemed content to hold vigil with me, and thankfully neither of them wanted to fill the space with words. I appreciated the silence, tense as it was, my thoughts racing.

It was possible Seren had misspoken when I had helped her off Copar—she was wounded, after all—but I knew what I'd heard. And deep down, part of me hoped my former friend had perhaps seen the error of his ways. Surely there could be no reason for him helping Seren escape other than a change of heart. Lewella and Tudwal had yet to return, but there'd been no sign of a trap. I absently stroked Cryfder behind the ears again, letting my thoughts wander until Mair returned.

"She's stable," she said. "Her ribs, ankle, and what's left of her minor wounds should be fully healed by morning."

I let out an audible sigh of relief.

"Cian thought you would want to see her, Bran," Mair added.

I was immediately on my feet, Cryfder grumbling as my sudden movement disturbed his dozing. For a moment, laying eyes on Seren was the only thing I could think of, but as I went to step away, my gaze dropped to Esyllt. Things between her and Seren had changed in recent months. I would have never thought it before when we were younger, but Esyllt too might want to see her daughter.

"Go," Esyllt said, motioning me on with a kind smile. "I'll see her in the morning."

"Thank you," I told her before looking over at Father. "Could you keep the wolves with you? Until Seren is up to seeing them?"

He nodded, letting out a quiet chuckle as Cryfder curled up next to him, seeking to use Father's lap as a pillow now that I'd abandoned him. "I suppose they're my grand-pups now, after all."

I gave a quiet laugh of my own before following Mair to a small alcove in the back part of the cave. A makeshift bed had been created for Seren out of a small assortment of blankets and she appeared to be resting peacefully.

"I expect she'll sleep until morning," Cian said. He stood a few feet away, wiping his hands off with a cloth and water. "The last little bit of healing she requires, her body should be able to do on its own with a little rest."

I nodded, Mair gathering up what remained of the healing supplies.

"You know where to find me if she needs anything," Cian said and a few moments later, he and Mair had retreated back to the fire.

There wasn't much space on Seren's blankets, but I managed to curl up behind her, slipping an arm around her. My heartbeat slowed as I listened to her soft, steady breathing. Whatever had caused the change in Aengus, I was grateful for it; he had brought her back to me.

"Bran."

My eyes fluttered open at Seren's hushed whisper. It was still dark, the fire that had been blazing in the cave before now burned out. Seren was cast in shadow as she lay next to me, though we were close enough to the mouth of the cave that the moon offered some light.

She rested a hand on the side of my face, running her thumb across my cheek, over the short stubble I'd garnered over the last long few days. I couldn't stop myself. I kissed her. It was not a tentative thing. No, this was the kiss of a desperate man. My hands were in her hair, her arms wrapped around my neck, and there was only her and the press of my lips to hers. When we were finally forced to part for air, she released a shuddering breath, clinging to me still and pressing her face into my chest. I held her close, rubbing her back as I let out a deep breath of my own.

"Spirits, Ren," I murmured. "I thought I'd lost you. How are you feeling?"

"Not nearly as bad as I would have expected. A little sore in my side; nothing more. Cian's work, I presume?"

"His and Mair's."

"The others? Everyone else survived the attack?"

"They did," I replied, smoothing back a few wild strands of her hair.

"The bow. The bag I'd brought with me—where is it?"

She tried to get up, only to wince and half-fall back down.

"Easy," I told her. "I gave it to Lewella for safekeeping."

"She destroyed it." Her voice was hoarse, barely above a whisper, and she bit down hard on her bottom lip.

"Who destroyed what, Ren?" I asked, rubbing her back and wishing I could take away the pain that was etched across her face.

"Alannah. She destroyed the bow, with the creatures. And I... I fear there will be no repairing it. It was all we had, the only thing that could stand against Fianna's power."

My stomach lurched. That was indeed horrifying news, but I smoothed my expression. Fianna had dealt us a devastating blow, but we could still defeat it. We had to.

"We'll find a way to destroy Fianna, bow or no bow. I promise you that." I paused, my voice catching slightly when I spoke again. "I'm sorry I left you behind. I swore I wouldn't do that again, if it hadn't been for those damn—"

She gently pressed a finger to my lips, silencing me.

"We were outnumbered. You didn't leave me by choice," she said. "I know that. And..." She paused, taking a deep breath before letting it out slowly. "I've been holding you at arm's length, convincing myself that it was necessary, telling myself I needed more proof I could fully trust you."

I shook my head. "You had every right to feel that you couldn't trust me. After what I—"

"Let me finish." She silenced me with a kiss and I forced myself not to take things further as she eased away. She was still healing, after all.

"It wasn't fair. Especially not after all the ways you've begged for my forgiveness and all the times you've put yourself in harm's way to spare my life these last few weeks. I was afraid, but I love you. I will always love you. And I don't want to be afraid anymore."

My breath hitched as she pulled me back in for another kiss, one I gladly gave into. One of her hands slipped under my shirt and I froze.

"Ren," I groaned. "We can't. Your injuries..."

"I feel perfectly fine."

"Cian is going to kill me."

"I'll handle Cian."

She kissed me again and this time, I didn't stop her, more than happy to follow down whatever path she led. As we kissed, touched, tasted, and basked in one another's nearness, there were no walls between us, no chasm that couldn't be crossed. We didn't need words to express how deep our love for one another ran. We'd been broken, but we were once again whole.

CHAPTER 48

A Ri's Gamble

Seren

As I lay in Bran's arms in the early morning hours, it was as if a broken part of me healed. Dawn had broken outside the cave and though we were in the secluded little alcove away from the others, I could still see and hear them as they all began to rouse for the day.

Hopefully they hadn't heard Bran and me last night. I stretched where I lay, pressing my back into Bran's bare chest, taking a moment to relish the fact that he was here, with his arms around me. I was a little sorer than I perhaps would have been if I hadn't made love with Bran last night, but I'd needed that. *We'd* needed that. Another broken piece of us had been mended in those moments.

"Good morning," he murmured in my ear and I couldn't help but smile as he kissed the top of my shoulder. If only I could capture this moment and keep the two of us right here forever, but I knew it couldn't last. Fianna had to be defeated.

Still, I let Bran lull me away for a moment as he trailed kisses up my neck before gently nipping at the bottom of my ear. A clang from over the fire broke the magic of the moment, however, and Cian cleared his throat.

"I've almost got breakfast ready," he called. "If the two of you can tear yourselves away from one another long enough to eat."'

I couldn't stop the light flush that crept over my cheeks and Bran grumbled something about nosy healers. So maybe they *had* heard us last night. Not that I regretted what Bran and I had shared. We got up and got dressed before joining the others around the fire. The burdens I had momentarily discarded last night when I was in Bran's arms returned as I took in the haggard faces around me. I was their Ri. I was the one who was supposed to protect them and bring them hope, but how much hope could I muster when our one weapon against Fianna had been destroyed?

There was an empty feeling in my chest as Bran and I sat down on the ground near Mair, my stomach grumbling loudly. Cian had managed to pull together a porridge of sorts, which didn't taste nearly as bad as it looked. Before long, Mother joined me, settling down on the ground with a slight wince.

"How are you feeling?" she asked after Sioned brought a bowl of porridge over to her.

"Better," I answered. "My ribs barely ache this morning."

"Good. I'm relieved to hear it." She paused, resting a hand on my knee and giving it a gentle squeeze. "I'm so glad you're still with us."

I covered her hand with my own, my throat thick. "As am I."

I was tempted to tell her of how Aengus had helped me get away, but I still felt confused about what all had happened last night, uncertain of where exactly his loyalties lay in all of this. I didn't want to give her false hope. I'd just taken the last bite of my porridge when Lewella came up behind me, placing a hand on my shoulder.

"We need to talk," she said, keeping her voice low.

The canvas bag with the bow was in her right hand and my chest tightened. "Now is as good a time as any."

I passed my empty bowl to Bran and he brushed a light kiss over my cheek before I got up and followed Lewella. We went just outside the cave, the bright sunshine and clear blue sky feeling at odds with the weighty burdens bearing down on me. And yet, as I looked around at the vibrant forest, just beginning to shed the green of summer for the golden tinges of autumn, I knew what I must do. This land would be a barren, desolate place if Fianna kept its control over the clan.

"Bran gave this to me last night," Lewella said, handing me the bag. "For safekeeping. Though I'm afraid I must ask why."

I couldn't hold back a sigh as I took it, my shoulders slumping. "It's Rhonwen's bow. Or at least what's left of it."

Lewella's eyes widened. "It was destroyed? How?"

"The shadow creatures," I answered with a grimace. "And Alannah sealed its fate."

"You fixed it before. Do you suppose it could be fixed again?"

I massaged my temple with one hand. "I don't know. It was only the bow string before that needed fixing. This, though... the whole weapon is in shambles. I'm not a bowyer; no one here is. I'll try, but I think it would be wise if we prepare ourselves to not have it at our disposal. Of course, even with the bow, there's the matter of even getting back inside the castle."

"As far as getting inside the castle goes, leave that to me. I doubt Aengus is aware of the passage we took to escape; with any luck, we'll be able to use it a second time. But I fear there will be no way to stop the creatures without the bow."

"As do I. But... perhaps we don't need it. I didn't escape on my own. Aengus aided me."

"He aided you?" Lewella jerked her head back. "Why?"

"Truthfully, I don't entirely know. But I think that it's possible he might regret what he has done. The decisions he's made."

"But there's no way to know that for certain." Lewella shook her head. "And trusting him is quite the gamble, especially when there's no destroying Fianna without destroying him and Alannah."

"I know, but he might be our only chance."

Lewella let out a long breath, pursing her lips as she looked beyond me to the forest. "That's not a chance I like."

"Let me see if I can mend the bow. But I don't want to wait too long to act. Every moment gives Fianna more time to entrench itself."

"Agreed. And every moment we stay in this place gives its lackeys more time to find us here. If you need anything to aid you in bringing that bow back to life, you know where to find me."

I gave her a tentative smile and the two of us walked back into the cave. The weight of the shattered remains of the bow seemed even heavier in my hands. She was right. It was a gamble, not only in hoping the bow could be re-made, but also in trusting Aengus. A gamble that could cost us our very lives, not to mention Blaidd's future.

CHAPTER 49

THE STAG'S JUDGMENT

Aengus

"YOU BROUGHT THIS UPON yourself, you know."

Alannah's voice dripped with resentment and disdain as she watched the healer tying off the bandage on my right hand, her arms folded and her eyes narrowed. I didn't respond, clenching my jaw to hold back my grunts of pain. At least the bleeding had finally stopped.

It had happened moments after I'd stepped back inside the castle walls after helping Seren escape. An excruciating pain had erupted in my hands and I'd looked down to see them covered in burns, smoke rising from my skin. The burns had come from seemingly out of nowhere, but I knew what was responsible. This was Fianna's punishment for my disobedience, a punishment that should have gotten me back in line, reminded me of the vow I had made, but that was not what the pain had done.

I was becoming increasingly aware that I had made an irreversible mistake. I had let Alannah twist me with her words and nights in her bed, believed I could do what Seren could not. I had been a fool, believing Fianna that the end would justify the means. I had let it turn me into a monster. Seren should have loathed me. She should have seen me as her enemy. She should never have offered to let me escape with her. She clearly had the strength of character to be the Ri of Blaidd. I was the one who was lacking.

The healer finished with my hands, giving me a respectful nod before scurrying out of the room. I hated being feared, hated the way the rest of the castle cowered and tiptoed around me, worried they would be the next ones I would kill. Even more than that, I hated this compulsion to keep taking life in order to sustain my own. The life force of animals wasn't enough anymore; I was drawn to human lives, even as it left me sick inside.

"There truly are no bounds to your foolishness," Alannah said with a snort of disgust, slowly shaking her head. "What I cannot understand is how you can be so ungrateful. Fianna has given you everything! What has Seren *ever* done for you?"

I didn't answer, clenching my jaw as I stared down at my bandaged hands. I didn't love her anymore, not like I once had, and every hateful word she spoke further transformed what had once been a potent mixture of love and lust into loathing.

"Every second she's alive, you risk her trying to take your title from you. Surely you do not expect her to fade into obscurity? You're so wretchedly weak—and mark my words: It will be your undoing."

"It is not weak to wish to spare a life," I said through gritted teeth.

"It is weak when that life is an unquestionable threat!"

I held up my hands, unable to stop myself from glowering at her. "Has Fianna not done enough? Must you punish me as well?"

"If that is what it will take to make you see sense. You cannot keep doing this, Aengus. You're going to push it too far one day and when you do, you stand to lose everything. *I* stand to lose everything. You swore an oath to it in blood. You cannot go back on that."

"I know that!" The shout ripped from me before I could stop it, my face flushing and my body hot. "You think I do not know the oath I made?"

I expected her to show her temper in response. I'd never before raised my voice to her and I knew she did not suffer such things lightly, but instead, a slow smirk crept across her face.

"Finally, some anger," she said. "I was beginning to wonder if you had it in you. If you have any sense, you'll hold onto that and let it feed you. Anger is something Fianna can use."

The fight immediately drained from me, my chest caving in. I didn't want to let Fianna use anything. Not anymore.

"I have to speak with Rhodri about the feast after the handfasting," Alannah said airily with a flick of her hair before heading for the door. "Don't be a fool, Aengus. And don't forget that if you test its patience too many times, it *will* kill you."

She left the room, slamming the door behind her, and as soon as she was gone, I allowed my shoulders to slump. Spirits, what I would give for a way out of this. A way to go back and stop myself from making my blood oath to Fianna. But it was too late for all of that now. *But is it too late for Blaidd?* That question gnawed at me, leaving my thoughts racing and my face twisting into a grimace. And if it wasn't too late for Blaidd, was I willing to risk my very life for its future?

CHAPTER 50

FORGED IN BLOOD

Seren

At midday, I retreated to the river. Bran came with me with me in his wolf form to stand guard. Understanding that the last thing I needed right now was any sort of distraction, he'd taken up a perch on a grouping of rocks a few feet away, his gaze fixed on the forest. The bag with what remained of Rhonwen's bow was in my lap and I'd settled cross-legged by the banks of the river.

I was here in front of the rolling waters of the Bywyd on a hunch. A hope, really. It had been at the banks of a river that I'd repaired the bow's string months ago, and it was Blaidd, the Wolf Spirit, who had dug the rivers and lakes when the island had been formed. I hoped the water would call it as it had once done before.

The forest was quiet here, the only noise the murmuring of the water, the soft breeze brushing through the trees and the occasional call of birds, but quiet was what I needed to separate my soul from my body to send it into the Spirit Realm. I would be vulnerable when I traveled from one realm to the next, but that was why I had Bran. He would not let any harm come to me. I slowed my breathing, intentionally tuning out the noises around me, connecting with that deeper part of myself. As always, it was a sudden shift, my body going rigid as my vision blurred—

The river water shone so brightly, it made me shield my eyes and turn my gaze away from it. Even in the darkness of night, it was like glittering glass. A low mist clung to the ground, snaking through the trees. To my surprise, the canvas bag was in my hands and quick peek inside confirmed that what was left of the bow was still there.

The piercing hoot of an owl drew my attention to the sky above me. Though my view was obscured by the trees, I still was able to make out the shadowy form of a massive bird swooping down, the creature skillfully dodging through the maze of branches.

The lumbering huff of a bear came next and I whirled around, my heart pounding at the sight of the three beings emerging from the darkness. The bear, wolf, and horse were abnormally large and their translucent forms gave off an otherworldly glow. I let out a shaky breath, my eyes so wide they were practically bulging as I took in Blaidd, Arth, and Ceffyl. The few occasions I had seen Blaidd had been rare enough, but to see three Spirits at once? That was unheard of, even for a seer.

A shriek came from my right and I started as two more beings joined me, the massive owl along with an enormous hawk perching on the low hanging branches of a nearby tree: Tyll and Seabhac. They were all here then, all five of them. Blaidd, Ceffyl, and Arth surrounded me in a semicircle and every single one of the Spirits' gazes were focused on the bag in my hand, but none of them uttered a sound.

The heavy silence stretched out and I cleared my throat. "Please," I said. "You must help. The bow has been destroyed by Fianna and its servants."

Arth let out a low, rumbling laugh and Blaidd cocked its head.

"You assume Fianna's power can destroy a weapon such as that?" Blaidd asked.

I bit the inside of my cheek to hold back a sharp retort. Instead, I opened the bag, dumping the charred and splintered remains onto the forest floor. "It has been destroyed and I must know if there is a way to fix it."

"You still intend to fulfil your vow then?" Seabhac asked, lightly flapping its wings. "Despite the people of Blaidd turning against you."

The reminder of my unjust removal from Clogwyn stung, but I pushed it down. "They have been misled."

"It was Rhonwen's blood that made that bow, Daughter of Blaidd," Blaidd said. "And it is her blood that will remake it."

"I bear her blood," I said, lifting my chin, "and I will willingly give it."

"Then let it be so." Blaidd threw back its head, letting out a howl that made the earth rumble.

I fought to steady myself, the shuddering ground threatening to throw me off balance, but it was thankfully short-lived. For a moment, there was nothing and then, another bright, translucent figure emerged from the trees, this one bearing a more human form.

It was a woman, I realized as she drew closer and my breath caught when she glided past Blaidd. She paused, placing a hand on its shoulder, and the Spirit respectfully inclined its head to her. Her clothing was in an older style, one that had not been seen in hundreds of years, and her dark brown hair was half plaited in intricate braids, the likes of which I had never seen. But I had seen her portraits in the halls of Clogwyn and though they were not an exact likeness, I still knew that it was Rhonwen of Blaidd who stood before me.

She held my gaze, unsheathing a shimmering dagger that hung from her waist. Wordlessly, she held out her hand so that it was above what remained of the bow, slicing her palm. Blood dripped from the wound, hitting the shards of the bow and causing it to take on a golden glow. She motioned to my right hand and despite the tightness in my chest, I held it out to her. She took hold of it, pulling me to her.

"Tell Fianna I sent you," she said before raising the dagger and slicing it across my palm.

I wasn't able to hold back my hiss as the blade cut my skin, blood welling up to the surface. Rhonwen turned my hand, letting the blood from my palm dribble down onto the shards of the bow. The golden glow grew, engulfing the entire remains and obscuring them from view. Suddenly, Rhonwen was surrounded by a ball of mist, disappearing into it moments later. The glow covering the bow receded and as it faded, my breath hitched. The weapon was whole, as if it had never even been touched by Fianna's fire. A sense of reverence filled me as I knelt down and carefully picked it up, once more feeling a hum of energy bursting forth from it.

"Fulfil your vow, Daughter of Blaidd," the Wolf Spirit said. "Destroy Fianna's hold on the land and send it back to the shadows."

"But be cautious," Arth said. "Do not let your compassion for the Son of Blaidd, noble though it may be, blind you."

"Is there no hope for him?" I asked, my grip on the bow tightening at the mention of Aengus.

"His choices will be his own," Blaidd answered. "He must decide what he will do with the web of darkness he has let himself be ensnared in."

It was hardly an answer and a hint of frustration rose in me again, but now wasn't the time to provoke the Spirits. Not when they'd just handed me the one thing that could be our salvation.

"Thank you for your aid," I told them, looking at each one in turn and giving them a nod of respect. "I will fulfil my vow. I swear it."

Blaidd threw back its head, letting out another howl and causing the ground to shake again—

"Easy, Ren." Bran had his arms around me and was rubbing my back as I came to, my whole body shaking and my breathing ragged.

I took a moment, pressing my back into his chest as I waited for the shakes to cease, but even in my current unsteady state, elation filled me. For in my lap, with my hands clutching it, was Rhonwen's bow, as whole and as real as it had been in the Spirit Realm. My palm still stung where Rhonwen had sliced it with her dagger, but I bore no mark and the skin showed no evidence of what had taken place. Still, my connection with the bow felt somehow stronger than it ever had before.

After a few moments, Bran eased back from me, his gaze dropping to the bow. "They did it, then? They remade it?"

I nodded, taking a deep breath before getting to my feet. I still felt drained and a bit weak, but there was no time to waste. We had our weapon. It was time to use it against Fianna.

"We must tell the others," I said. "Make our plan to strike against Fianna and take back the castle."

Bran nodded, his jaw tightening at the mention of the Stag Spirit. My legs still felt a bit weak and I pulled a glass vial out of my pocket, putting a few drops on my tongue; Cian had given me one of the restorative tinctures before we'd left the cave. Bran came alongside me as we strode back into the trees, slipping his hand in mine and giving it a squeeze. I cast him a sideling glance, giving him a soft smile and squeezing back. We would do this together, as we had once promised one another not so long ago. Darkness would not tear us apart again.

CHAPTER 51

WILLING SACRIFICE
Aengus

THE CLACK OF NAILS on the floor woke me. I rolled over in bed, silently cursing when it took my sight a few moments to adjust in the dark, but when it did, the glowing eyes that stared back at me were unmistakable. They were not the eyes of a shadow creature. The golden orbs belonged to something, someone, else entirely. The moon gave the scantest of light to the bed-chamber, enough that I could make out Bran's raised hackles. He was here for one thing and one thing only: to kill.

Before I could even sit up, Alannah had awoken, leaping out of bed and grabbing the dagger she always kept at our bedside. The two shadow creatures lying at the foot of the bed stirred as well, hissing and shrieking at Bran as they leapt to their feet. A growl rumbled from Bran's throat and he lowered himself into a crouch, preparing to pounce.

"Call for Seachnall," Alannah said before unsheathing her blade and turning her attention to Bran. "Come to die, have you? I'm more than happy to oblige you in that. You don't have the faintest idea how long I've been waiting for this particular moment."

One of the creatures went to lunge at Bran but Alannah stopped it, yelling at it in Old Pernish. I'd finally gleaned enough of the commands to be able to make out what she was saying. She wanted the creatures to stand down so that she could take the kill for herself. I half fell out of bed, the sheets tangling around my legs as Alannah lunged at Bran. My heart pounded, pulsing so rapidly I could feel it in my neck as I ran to the door. Bran had latched himself onto Alannah's thigh, throwing her off balance and trying to yank her down to the ground as she wildly stabbed at him with her blade.

The door to the common room opened a bit too easily, as if it hadn't been fully closed all the way, which was strange, considering I had known for a fact that I had shut it firmly before coming to bed. Shaking my head, I barreled through it, but what awaited me on the other side made me stop dead in my tracks. Seren stood in the center of the room, the light of the moon illuminating her and Rhonwen's bow. She gripped an arrow in one hand, ready to nock it on the bow.

"Take one more step and I loose this," she said.

I swallowed hard, the noises from the ongoing fight in the bedchamber reaching my ears. Alannah was cursing, her voice tinged with pain, Bran's snarls were deep with fury, and the ear-splitting shrieks could only mean the creatures had entered into the fight. My arm burned, pain shooting up into my shoulder and neck, but I could not tear my gaze away from Seren's. I didn't want what I had become and yet I knew I could not be the one to end it all. I could not kill Alannah and send Fianna's creatures back to the darkness, but she could.

Holding up my hands, I slowly stepped out of her way, hoping I was making it clear to her that I would not impede her. Her eyes widened but her hesitation lasted for no more than a split second. She bolted, racing past me to burst into the bedchamber and nock her bow. I remained rooted where I stood, clutching my arm to my chest as the fiery pain erupted throughout my whole body. I gasped, clutching the doorframe to try and hold myself upright.

Alannah was screaming, and through my pain-filled haze, I could make out one of the creatures laying prone on the floor, an arrow protruding from its side. Alannah and Bran were both covered in blood, Alannah lunging for Seren. Bran stopped her, latching onto her leg and yanking her back. Alannah fell to the ground cursing and screaming, but Bran held fast. A few moments later, however, she got the upper hand, kicking out with her free leg, connecting with his ribs and sending him slamming into a wardrobe. He hit it with a loud thud and did not rise.

My breath was coming in short bursts and I clutched at my heart, the pain so immense I almost wished Fianna would be done with me. Seren had wounded the remaining creature with an arrow, but still it attacked her, forcing her to dodge around the room as she tried to evade it. Somehow, despite the blood that drenched her body, Alannah was up again, crawling toward her dagger.

Seren's back was to her. She was too occupied with the last remaining creatures to notice Alannah's movements. I didn't know how I did it, with the pain so intense it left tears streaming down my face, but I half stumbled, half crawled into the room. Somehow, I reached the dagger before Alannah, slamming my foot down onto the hilt to stop her from grabbing it.

"You idiot," she shrieked, blood dripping from the side of her mouth. "What in the blazes do you think you're doing?"

I didn't answer her, instead focusing on keeping her from the blade, even as she clawed at me. A deafening screech made me want to cover my ears as Seren's arrow felled the last shadow creature. Alannah's clawing at my leg intensified, her nails scraping at my skin through the fabric of my pants. A fresh wave of pain coursed through my body, this one so intense it brought me almost flat on the ground. Seren whirled around to face us, nocking another arrow, but my crumpling fall had given Alannah the chance she needed to snatch up the blade. With a feral snarl, Alannah plunged it into my chest.

I fell back onto the granite floor and Alannah retracted the blade with a sickening squelch. I was a healer; I knew what future lay before me as blood began to soak my shirt. I heard the dull thud of an arrow, and even as the edges of my vision blackened, I saw Alannah fall to the ground mere feet from me, an arrow in her chest. The blade clattered from her hand, coated in my bright red blood. This was it then. This was death. My pulse was slowing, each breath becoming more labored with each passing second.

"Aengus!"

I managed to barely turn my head at Seren's voice. She had come to kneel beside me, trying to stop the blood with her hands as silent tears tracked down her cheeks.

"Too... late," I said, half choking on my own blood.

"No!" She furiously shook her head. "No, it's not too late. Cian is here; he'll heal you. I only need to get you to him."

I did my best to muster up what I hoped was a smile. "It's... done. It's... gone."

My eyes fluttered closed, my breathing so shallow I was certain my chest was barely rising and falling. Just as I was ready to slip away and let my life in this Realm come to its merciful end, something changed. There was a blinding flash of light from one corner of the room. Seren let out a gasp and I cracked my eyes open just in time to see an odd white mist engulf me.

The pain was gone, vanished in a matter of seconds. The hole in my chest was somehow knitting itself back together and my heart beat strongly once again. The mist vanished, soaking into my skin as a jolt passed through my body. *Use your second chance wisely, Son of Blaidd. For we will not be so forgiving a second time.* The Wolf Spirit's voice left me gasping in disbelief. Clutching my chest, I sat up, staring wide-eyed at the stark absence of blood. Seren gave a half sob before pulling me into an embrace. At first, it shocked me, but then I embraced her in return.

"Thank you," she murmured.

As she eased back from me, her face paled as her gaze fell on Bran's limp form.

"Bran," she whispered, the word coming out half-strangled.

She was on her feet in seconds and I scrambled up after her as she raced to the wardrobe on the other side of the room. She fell to her knees next to him, her tears flowing freely and a sob tearing from her throat. He was as marred as Alannah had been, covered in gashes and his fur matted in blood. I dropped to the ground, placing my hands on his side, feeling for the rise and fall of his breath, as well as his life force. It was there, faint and almost gone, but there.

Closing my eyes, I pulled my power from deep within me, whatever magic the Wolf Spirit had worked on me leaving me feeling as strong as ever. I started with the worst of his wounds, healing as much as I could before moving on to the minor ones. When I took my hands away, I was drained, but the worst of his injuries had been tended.

He shifted, transforming from wolf to man. He scrambled to his knees, immediately crawling over to Seren and wrapping an arm around her before fixing me with a threatening gaze. His free hand darted around the floor, no doubt looking for a weapon.

"It's alright," Seren said, placing a soothing hand on his thigh. "It's alright, Bran. He's alright."

Bran still eyed me warily. "Alannah?"

"Dead," I answered, a brief pang in my chest. Whatever we'd shared had never been real. I'd known that the moment she'd stabbed a dagger into my chest.

"The Wolf Spirit saw Aengus' willingness to sacrifice his own life to try and stop her," Seren said, holding my gaze as she spoke. "It honored that."

Bran gave a slow nod, despite the tightness in his jaw. I had a feeling it would take a bit more convincing before he trusted me again. Not that I blamed him.

"The others," Bran said, more to Seren than me, climbing to his feet. "And I doubt that was the last of the creatures."

"It wasn't," I replied. "There are five more. I suspect they're likely dead now with Alannah gone. The two of us were their anchor to this world, but I can help you find the rest. If Seren will wield that bow." I inclined my head toward the weapon she still held in her one hand.

"Rest assured," she said, "I will gladly do that."

I walked over and gathered up weapons, a sword Alannah had kept stashed in a wardrobe and another dagger that had been hidden away in a drawer. I couldn't bring myself to pick up the dagger Alannah had used to kill me, and no one else made a move for it. I tossed the sword to Bran, fairly confident he would wield it better than me, hanging onto the dagger for myself.

"Let's get hunting," Bran said, unsheathing the blade and leading the way into the common room.

Seren and I followed behind him and I squared my shoulders when we stepped out into the hallway. Fianna's hold on this land was over and I would see this through to whatever bitter end awaited me.

CHAPTER 52

DESTINED TO PREVAIL
Bran

AENGUS, IT TURNED OUT, had been right. The shadow creatures had died with Alannah. We found their ashes throughout the castle, along with dead bodies of warriors and the occasional servant, on our race to the warriors' wing. Our plan had been twofold. We had used the tunnels to gain entry to the Ri's chambers, Seren and I remaining there to contend with Alannah and Aengus while Lewella, Emer, and Tudwal had set out to get hold of Seachnall and hopefully gain more warriors to their cause.

Tudwal had been strongly convinced that many of those serving Aengus were only doing so out of fear. I only hoped he was right and that some ill hadn't already befallen them. I had already seen far too much death. Whatever had happened while we had been battling Fianna and Aengus had left its scars on Clogwyn everywhere I looked, even if now the castle was eerily silent and empty. As we rounded a corner, Seren came to an abrupt stop. I almost barreled right into her, Aengus muttering a curse as he bumped into my back.

"Seren, what—" I cut myself short as I peered around her, my gaze falling on the body on the floor and the pile of ash a few feet away.

Though he was burned and mauled almost beyond recognition, I still was able to identify him. Whether Domhnall had died trying to defend from himself from the creature, from trying to flee, or from trying to attack it, I supposed we'd never know. Regardless, he was dead, and his death looked as if it had been an excruciating one. *Dabble with treachery and darkness and you'll find you meet your ending sooner or later,* I thought, tearing my gaze away from his body, uncomfortably aware that I had come close to my own dark end with Lorcan not so very long ago.

"Let us finish this," Seren said, setting her jaw before taking off at a run again.

Aengus and I raced on behind her, through the maze of hallways that would lead us to the west side of the castle. A small part of me still hesitated to trust Aengus, but I believed Seren's account of what had happened, and there was no denying that he had healed me from the brink of death. He'd been a good man once, a friend. More than anything, I wanted him to be that man again.

We soon reached what had once been Lewella's study, our agreed meeting place, and I caught myself holding my breath as Seren pushed open the door. I sent up a quick silent prayer to the Spirits that what awaited us would be what we had hoped for, then followed her inside.

To my relief, we had not been the only victorious ones. Lewella had Seachnall, her sword at his throat as she held him in place. Emer, Tudwal, and Cian also had brandished their blades, keeping a handful of warriors at bay and crowded into a corner. Most of the warriors had their hands on the hilts of their swords and daggers, but they looked uneasy as they glanced between Lewella and Seachnall. *Hopefully regretting their decisions to follow that bastard,* I thought. Cian's eyes widened when he looked at Aengus while Tudwal and Emer let loose a couple of curses.

"Aengus will do us no harm," Seren said. "I can promise you that."

"I'd feel a lot better if he wasn't holding a blade," Lewella said, narrowing her eyes at him.

Aengus bent down and placed his dagger on the floor, holding up his hands as he straightened. "I understand your hesitance to trust me, but I swear to you, I mean you no harm. I am here to recant the error of my ways and acknowledge that my sister is the leader the Clan of Blaidd needs."

He looked at Seren as he said the last words and something passed between them, something unspoken but still strong. A sheen of moisture shone in both of their eyes.

"Her?" Seachnall spat, struggling against Lewella's hold. "What kind of an idiot are you? You're going to hand over this clan to that weak-willed bitch?"

Lewella yanked him hard, her sword just nicking the soft skin of his neck. "May I remind you who is holding a blade to your throat."

He grunted but then fell silent.

"I can see I was gravely mistaken in ever naming you warrior chief," Aengus said, his expression hard. "Your fate will be up to Seren to decide, as I do not wish for such power any longer. Though I will not blame her if she chooses to withhold mercy."

That, at least, made Seachnall pale.

Seren lifted her chin, her gaze going from Seachnall to the huddle of warriors on the opposite side of the room.

"I understand that there has been much upheaval in this castle these last few weeks. I will be willing to let you retain your places as warriors of Blaidd, but only if you swear an oath that you will not turn against your Ri ever again. If you do so, you will be punished and banished from these walls. If you are willing, lay down your weapons and come forward. If not, you will be escorted from these walls, never to return. As for you"—she paused, looking back at Seachnall—"I find it hard to believe you're the same man my brother once called friend. I will let Pennathe Lewella determine your punishment, but until then, you will be finding yourself getting well-acquainted with the dungeons."

A tense silence filled the room before the first warrior came forward, laying her sword and daggers at Seren's feet. The rest followed, one by one relinquishing their weapons before returning to stand with Tudwal and Emer.

"I will let Pennathe Lewella resume her duties and guide you in what she expects from you next," Seren said, giving Lewella a respectful nod.

"For now," Lewella said, addressing the warriors, "you will return to your quarters under the knowledge that if a single one of you steps out of line, the consequences will be swift." She paused, addressing Emer and Tudwal. "I will leave this one with you two. I want him bound and sent to a cell. Make certain to have him watched, and only by those you explicitly trust. I won't stand for him causing any more trouble."

Emer and Tudwal came forward and took Seachnall from her, binding his hands behind his back before forcing him out of the room. He glowered at Seren as he was hauled past her, but she didn't acknowledge him.

"I'll have Emer and Tudwal help me make certain the castle is secured as soon as they're done with him," Lewella said to Seren, "and send for the others."

We had left Father, Esyllt, and Sioned back at the cave with Mair, not wanting to put them in the middle of any sort of fight.

"I'll go back for them," Cian said, coming over to join us.

"I would greatly appreciate it," Seren replied. "I will breathe a bit easier when I know they're safe inside the castle."

"We passed dead bodies," I said, "and the remains of shadow creatures. It seems they perished when Alannah died, but they must have taken out half the castle before they did."

Lewella grimaced. "They were in some sort of crazed frenzy when we left the Ri's chambers. I fear they caused many deaths before they vanished into soot and ash."

Seren brought a hand to her chest, dropping her gaze for a brief moment before letting out a heavy sigh. "There will be much for Clogwyn, and Blaidd, to heal from after all of this."

"I suspect you are right," Lewella said with a grim nod.

The topic of conversation shifted to securing the castle, as well as formulating a plan to return to the cave. Aengus took a few steps back, fidgeting with his sleeve and uncomfortably shifting his weight, clearly feeling out of place in this moment. I took a few steps back as well to join him. Seren and the others had the next few steps ahead of us well in hand.

"I didn't want to kill you, you know," I said quietly. "Neither did she."

"I know," Aengus replied. "I let Alannah and Fianna twist me, let them build her up into something she was not. And I let my own hurt fuel my anger. I'm not proud of what I have done, and do not think for a moment that I do not recognize the mercy the Spirits have shown me."

"Thank you. For saving her life. And mine."

He let out a quiet sigh before looking over at me. "That is all I have ever wanted to do."

Seren called my name, beckoning me over. I placed a hand on Aengus' shoulder, giving it a reassuring squeeze before striding over to join my wife. His repentance was sincere, I believed that, and even though there would be much to untangle as Seren and I worked to repair our damaged relationship with him, and he with us, I had faith we would sort it out in the end. It was time to put this darkness behind us, once and for all.

CHAPTER 53

MOTHER'S LOVE

Aengus

A LESSER PERSON WOULD have banished me from the walls of Clogwyn, never allowing me to step foot inside them again after what I had done. But Seren was no lesser person. There was still trust to be mended between us, but she'd allowed me a place here.

It had been almost three days since Fianna's darkness had been driven out and Seren was confident in her victory, expressing that finally, her visions were neither clouded nor full of lingering darkness. It still felt a bit like we were collectively holding our breaths, for we had certainly thought to have defeated Fianna before, only for that not to be true, but there was hope that this newfound peace would last. For myself, such darkness had not been so easily banished. I still carried deep regret and guilt over what I had done, the role I had played in all of this, but the Spirits had given me a second chance and I would not waste it.

I had been eager to throw myself into helping Cian in the infirmary. The shadow creatures had left a trail of destruction throughout the castle before their demise. Many people had died long before anyone had reached them, including, I learned, Domhnall and Arwel, but others had survived. Most of them were skeptical of me treating them after seeing me use that very same gift to kill, something that I could not blame them for. So I'd made myself useful in other ways, fetching water to clean wounds, rolling and folding bandages, making salves, and other small tasks. I saw it as part of my repentance, in a way.

With care to not waste a drop of it, I transferred the yarrow poultice I had created out of the large basin and into a jar. Cian and the other healers would need it to help treat those wounded by the creatures. A knock at the door almost made me knock over the basin and I let out a sigh of relief when I managed to catch it before it tipped over.

"Come in," I called, up to my wrists in sticky poultice.

The door creaked open as I grabbed a nearby cloth, wiping off my hands as I turned. My breath caught when I saw who entered and I dropped the cloth on the floor. Bending down, I snatched it up, my face flushing. Even after Alannah's death, I had still avoided Esyllt. How could I be anything more than a disappointment to her after all that had happened and what I had done? She had rejected me once, had given me away to strangers, and I feared her rejection again.

"Mistress Esyllt," I said, respectfully inclining my head and looking anywhere but at her.

She walked over to a row of shelves on the opposite side of the room, quietly perusing them, angled slightly away from me. She moved with a slight limp, steadied by a carved wooden walking stick, but even from here, I could see that the fingers she had wrapped around it were swollen. Seren had told me of the illness that affected her joints and caused her much difficulty, something that had only furthered the guilt I felt over having thrown her in the dungeons with the others.

"Seren said I would find you here," she said, her gaze still on the glass jars littering the shelves.

I allowed myself a quiet, relieved sigh, my shoulders slightly unhunching. I appreciated her subtle way of taking off some of the mounting pressure I felt in this moment. When she reached the end of the shelves, she fully faced me, her eyes wet.

"I can only imagine what you must think," she said, her voice wavering slightly. "I blame myself for going along with it. For not fighting him harder than I did." She paused, her voice cracking. Taking a deep breath, she began again, each word feeling like it was as piercing as an arrow. "I didn't want to send you away. I never should have allowed it. It is no excuse, but Cadfael was a cruel, jealous man. When he discovered that you were Fionn's son... he made me feel as if I had no other choice."

"You didn't want to send me away?" I asked, my own voice unsteady.

One of the tears brimming in her eyes began to make a track down her cheek and she shook her head. "Never. I swear that to you."

I unsuccessfully tried to blink back my own tears, but they blurred my vision and rolled down my cheeks. How quick I had been to believe the words Fianna and Alannah had whispered to me—that my mother had never wanted me, that she *would* never want me. I wasn't certain which one of us moved first, but suddenly I was embracing her, both of us continuing to shed tears. She hugged me with a fierceness that I imagined only a mother could and, in that moment, one tiny piece of my broken heart felt as if it mended.

"They were good people," I told her after a few moments passed and my tears had slowed. "I cannot say they didn't care for me or that they did not love me."

"I am glad for that," she replied, easing back from me and wiping at her face. "But I have regretted every single moment that has passed since I let Cadfael rip you from my arms not even an hour after you were born. If I could go back and change that moment, I would." She let out a deep breath before placing her hands on my upper arms, mustering up the faintest of smiles. "But you are here now. And Seren says you perhaps plan to stay here. For a little while, at least."

"For the time being, yes. I... I would like to get to know her better. And you."

"That is something I am very happy to hear," Esyllt replied, her smile becoming less strained. "But I do not wish you to feel forced. I understand that this will not be easy between us, not after all that has happened. But I would like to try."

I covered one of her hands with my own. "So would I."

"Aengus, do you have any of that poultice ready?"

We both jumped slightly when Cian poked his head in the door and he winced.

"Sorry," he said. "Was I interrupting something?"

"I know you have work to do," Esyllt told me, giving my upper arms a gentle pat. "I'll let you get back to it. But perhaps I will be able to find you again at dinner tonight? At the Ri's table?"

I bit my lip, hesitating for a moment before giving a nod. Seren had invited me to dine with the family yesterday. I'd declined, feeling unworthy of the seat and also wishing to avoid Esyllt, but perhaps tonight, I could try.

Esyllt's smile broadened and she backed away from me and shuffled out of the room, though she paused at the door to briefly greet Cian before continuing on her way.

"I assume you do need the poultice?" I asked Cian once she was gone.

He chuckled softly. "I do. Whenever you're finished with it."

"I have two jars ready." I picked them up, walking them over.

"Thank you," he said, taking them from me. "You've been a lot of help these last two days."

"I've been happy to do it."

"We can always use a good healer around here," he said. "Just so you know."

A slight thickness settled in my throat. "I'll remember that."

Cian went on his way, poultice in hand, and I returned to the basin to finish filling the last few jars, my heart a little lighter than it had been moments ago. Perhaps there was a future here for me after all.

Epilogue: From Now Until Death

Seren

THE LAST TIME BRAN and I had stepped foot in these woods, we had almost lost one another. That memory was still with us, and I suspected it would be for some time. Like the land, we had not come through our trial unscarred, but as I crouched down on the burned forest floor and stared at the tiniest sprig of green shooting up from the charred earth, I was reminded that beauty and healing could still come from even the ashes.

"There's more of it sprouting a little farther to the north."

I looked up as Bran approached, leading Copar behind him, unable to keep the smile off my face. Spirits, I loved him so. We had ridden out early this morning, wanting to take a look at the land closest to Clogwyn that had been burned, both of us almost afraid to hope that the rumors from the people of Gefell were true: that the land was finally showing signs of growth. How long it would last, I wasn't certain, as the change of seasons was upon us, with cooler nights and shorter days, but the reversal of the decay was another sign that Fianna was truly gone. Our people, shifters and others alike, would live in peace, their land and their lives no longer threatened by darkness.

I straightened as Bran tied Copar to a tree a few feet away from Ceol, my stallion standing patiently where I'd left him. Bran came up behind me a moment later, wrapping an arm around my waist and gently pulling me to him. I happily nestled into his embrace, resting my head back against his shoulder as he lightly kissed the top of my head. A breeze brushed the back of my neck, ruffling the ends of both of our hair and I felt a familiar presence in the air.

Your vow is fulfilled, Daughter of Blaidd, the Wolf Spirit said. *Lead your people well.*

"It's truly gone, isn't it?" Bran said, his gaze drifting to the sprig of young grass.

"It is," I answered. "And may it never return."

He gently turned me toward him, looking down and holding my gaze. "I love you. And I swear to you, Ren. I will never leave you doubting that again."

"I know," I told him, resting a hand on the side of his face. He covered it with his own, leaning into my touch. "Not once have you doubted me, not even when I have doubted you. We'll always be stronger together. I love you. I always have. I swear to you that I always will."

He captured my lips with his, pulling me even closer as every ounce of the passion we felt for one another was poured into our kisses. The breeze came again, swirling around us. It lifted a few of the dead leaves that still littered the forest floor and out of the corner of my eye, I saw them flash gold for the briefest of moments before they drifted back to the ground.

"Together," Bran whispered when we were forced to part for air, resting his forehead against my own.

"Together," I echoed. "From now until death."
There was no other future for us than that.

Read More

Ready for more stories in the world of Pern Coen?

Tales of Pern Coen

The Hunter (Rhiannon & Conor's Story)

The Huntress (Rhiannon & Conor's Story)

The Successor (Briallen & Torin's Story)

The Betrayer (Ciara & Niall's Story)

The Ascendant (Ciara & Niall's Story)

Tales of Kelnore

The Duchess (Faustina & Idris' Story)

You can also connect with Hannah E. Carey on her website
www.hannahecarey.com.

About The Author

Hannah E. Carey began telling stories as soon as she was old enough to talk and she hasn't stopped since. As a Dysautonomia warrior, writing and her love of stories allow her to explore new places & worlds, no matter what her body throws at her. She loves all things romance and writes romantic fantasy with fierce heroines that is inspired by her love of mythology, along with romantic women's fiction that stars loveable four-legged companions and is inspired by her years of being a horse & dog mom, her background in equine rescue, and her years of working as a certified Centered Riding Instructor. When she's not writing, you'll find her reading romance novels and spending time with her husband, horses, and dog on her small hobby farm.

www.ingramcontent.com/pod-product-compliance
Lightning Source LLC
Chambersburg PA
CBHW030628020726
47493CB00006B/1614